Margaret Maliphant

by

Alice Vansittart Strettel Carr

Double9
BOOKS

Margaret Maliphant
by Alice Vansittart Strettel Carr

ISBN: 978-93-63058-21-7

Published by

DOUBLE 9 BOOKS
2/13-B, Ansari Road
Daryaganj, New Delhi – 110002
info@double9books.com
www.double9books.com
Tel. 011-40042856

ABOUT THE AUTHOR

Alice Vansittart Strettel Carr was a British costume designer whose work is linked to the Aesthetic clothing movement. Alice Vansittart Strettell was the daughter of Laura Vansittart Neale and the Reverend Alfred Baker Strettell, a British consular chaplain in Genoa, Italy, and later the rector of St. Martin's Church in Canterbury. Her sister Alma was a writer and translator. In 1873, Alice married J. Comyns Carr, a drama and art critic, novelist, writer, and director of the Grosvenor Gallery. They had three children: Philip, Dorothy, and Arthur, who later became a member of parliament. As a costume designer, Carr was linked with the Aesthetic dress movement, which championed looser, more flowing gowns with theatrical embellishments like lace and embroidery. It was said that she was the inspiration for the comic persona "Mrs Cimabue Brown" created by cartoonist George du Maurier to lampoon the Aestheticists in several of his Punch magazine illustrations. Carr, who succeeded Patience Harris as Ellen Terry's chief costume designer, worked for two decades. Carr authored a fashion analysis for The Woman's World magazine in 1850, following Oscar Wilde's appointment as editor. Carr published a collection of memories in 1926.

CONTENTS

PROLOGUE

It is twilight upon the marsh: the land at the foot of the hill lies a level of dim monotony, and even the sea beyond is lost in mystery. In the middle of the plain one solitary homestead, with its clump of trees, stands out just a little darker than anything else, and from afar there comes to me the sound of the sea, sweetly lulling, as it has come to me ever since I was a little child. A chill breeze creeps up among the aspens on the cliff, and for a moment there steals over me the sense of loneliness of ten years ago, and I seem to see once more a tall, dark figure thread his way down among the trees, and disappear forever onto the wide plain. But this is only for a moment; for as I look, the past lies stretched, as the plain is stretched, before me—vivid, yet distant as a dream. The white mill detaches itself upon the dark hill-side, the cattle rest upon the quiet marsh; and still the sound of the sea comes to me, tenderly murmuring, as it did when I was a happy child, and tells me of a present that is wide and fair as, above the lonely land, the coming night is blue and vast.

CHAPTER I

My sister Joyce is older than I am. At the time of which I am thinking she was twenty-one, and I was barely nineteen. We were the only children of Farmer Maliphant of Knellestone Grange, in the county of Sussex. The Maliphants were an old family. Their names were on the oldest tombstones in the graveyard of the abbey, whose choir and ruined transepts were all that was left standing of a splendid church that had been the mother of a great monastery, and of many other churches in the popish days, when our town was a feature in English history. I am not sure that our family dated as far back as that. I had read of knights in helmets and coats of mail skirmishing beneath the city wall, of which there were still fragments standing, and of gallant captains bringing the King's galleys to port in the bay that had become marsh-land, and I hoped that there might have been Maliphants too, riding up and down the hill under the gate-ways that were now ivy-grown; but I am afraid that, even if the family had been in existence at the time, they would only have been archers, shooting their arrows from behind the turrets on the hill.

At all events—to leave romancing alone—Maliphants had owned or rented land upon the Udimore hills and the downs of Brede for more than three hundred years, and it must have been nearly as long as that that they had lived in the old stone house overlooking the Romney Marsh. For almost all our land had been a manor of the old abbey, and had been granted to my father's family at the dissolution of the monasteries in 1540, and it was not much more than a century since the Maliphants had been obliged to sell most of it to the ancestors of him who was now squire at the big house. But they had never left the old home, renting the land that they had once owned, and tilling the soil that they had once been lords of. Our house was the oldest house in the place, antiquaries testifying to the fact that it was built of the same foreign stone that fashioned the walls of the old abbey; and our name was the oldest name, a fact which my father, democrat as he was, never really forgot. But we were not so well-to-do as we had once been, even in the memory of living folk.

Family portraits of ladies in scanty gowns and high waists, and of gallants in ruffled shirts, made pleasant pictures in my fancy, and there were whispered stories of kegs of spirits stored at dead of night in the old cellars beneath the house in my grandfather's time, and of mother's old Mechlin lace having been brought, at the risk of bold lives, in the merry little fishing-smacks that defied the revenue-cutters. But smuggling was a dead art in our time, and respectable folk would have been ashamed to buy smuggled goods. We lived the uneventful life of our neighbors, and were no longer the great people that we had been even in my grandfather's time; for farming was not now so lucrative.

My sister Joyce was very handsome. I have not seen much of the world, but I am sure that any one would have said so. She was tall, taller than I am, and I am not short, and she was slight, and fair as a rose. There was a sort of gentle Quaker-like dignity about Joyce which I have never seen in one so young. She had it of our mother. Both women were very tall, and both bore their height bravely. Sometimes, it is true, when Joyce walked along the dark passages of the old Grange, her arms full of sweet-scented linen, and bending her little head to pass under the low door-ways, or when she made the jam in the kitchen, or pats of butter in the dairy, she stooped just a little over her work; but when—of a June eve+ning—she would come across the lawn with her hands full of guelder-roses and peonies for the parlor, no one could have said that she was too tall, so erect and gracefully did she seem to flit across the earth.

Of course I did not consciously notice these things when I was nineteen; but as I think of her again now, I can see that it was not at all to be wondered at that the country-folk used to talk of Joyce Maliphant as a poor slip of a thing, not fit to be a countryman's wife. There was an over-sensitiveness about her—a sort of tremulous reserve—that marked her as belonging to a different order of beings. It was not that she was weak either in mind or in body. Joyce would often surprise one by her sudden purposes; and as for fatigue, that slender figure could work all day without being tired, and though the cheek was as dainty as the petal of a flower, it had nothing frail about it: it told of health, just as did the clearness of the blue eye and the wealth of the rippling auburn hair.

Joyce kept her complexion, partly because she was less out-of-doors than I was; but if I had known that I could have had her lovely skin instead of my own freckled face, I do not believe that I would have changed with her. No doubt mother was right, and I might have kept that—my one good point—if I had cared to. Red-haired people generally do have fresh skins, and my hair is just about the color of Virginia-creeper leaves in autumn, or of the copper kettle in the sunlight. I was very much ashamed of it in those days.

Luckily, I gave little heed to my appearance. I was quite content to leave the monopoly of the family beauty to my sister, if I might have freedom to scour the marsh-land with Taff, the big St. Bernard; and so long as my father treated me like a boy, and let me help him superintend the farm, he might banter as much as he liked about "Margaret's gray eyes that looked a different color every day," and even rail at me for heavy eyelids that didn't look a bit as if I led a healthy out-door life. But I did: when there was neither washing nor baking nor butter-making to help with, I was out-of-doors from morning to night. When I was a child it was with Reuben Ruck the shepherd, and his black collie Luck, who was the best sheep-dog in the country.

Reuben taught me many things—where to find the forms of the hares upon the marsh-land, the nests of the butcher-birds and yellow-hammers and wheat-ears that were all peculiar to our home; he taught me to surprise the purple herons upon the sands or by the dikes at eventide, to find the pewits' eggs upon the shingle, to tame the squirrels in the Manor woods, to catch gray mullet in the Channel, to spear eels in the dikes, to know when every bird's brood came forth, to welcome the various arrivals of the swifts and martins and swallows.

At the time of which I write, Reuben had had to give up his shepherd's duties, owing to ill health, and used to do odd jobs about the house and garden; but he had bred the love of the country in me, and now it was useless for mother to bemoan my wandering habits, or even for our old nurse, Deborah, to take me to task for not caring more about the home pursuits in which my sister so brilliantly excelled. Whatever related to a bird or a beast I would attend to with alacrity; but as for household duties, I only got them over as quickly as I could, that I might the sooner be out in the air. I knew every hill's crest inland, every headland out to sea, every shepherd's track across the marsh, every plank across the channels. The shepherds and the coast-guards were all my friends alike, and I think there was not one of them who would not have braved danger rather than I should come to harm, although I do not suppose that I ever exchanged more than six words' conversation with any of them in all my life. Words were not necessary between us.

"Farmer Maliphant's little miss" had always been a favorite, and "Farmer Maliphant's little miss" was always his youngest daughter. I like to remember the title now; I like to remember that if Joyce was mother's right hand in the house, I was father's companion in the fields. I was very fond of father; I was very fond of any praise of his. I did not get on so well with mother. I suppose daughters often do not get on so well with their mothers. For though Joyce was a fresh, neat, deft girl, just after mother's own heart, and I know that she thought there was none to equal her, they never got on well together. I was always fighting her battles. She was too gentle, or too proud—I was never sure which—to fight them for herself. A cross word, only spoken in the excitement of a domestic crisis—which meant worlds to a woman to whom house-keeping was an art—would shut Joyce up in an armor of reserve for days, and I often laughed at her even while I fought for her.

As for me, I used to think I could manage mother. I wish I had the dear old days back again! It's little managing I would care to do. It came to very little good. I believe that every quarrel I had for Joyce only did her harm with mother; I was such a headstrong girl that it took a deal to set me down, and I am afraid that she got some of the thrusts that were meant for me in consequence.

One of the special, though tacit, subjects of difference between mother and myself was upon the choice of a husband for my sister. I quite agreed with the country-folk, that she was not suited to be a countryman's wife, but I did not agree with mother's idea of a suitable husband for her.

Mother was a very ambitious woman. She wanted us to rise in the world; she wanted us to hold once more something of the position she knew the family had once held. She was not a highly educated woman herself, but she was a shrewd woman. She had had us educated to the best of her abilities, a little better than other farmers' daughters; if she had had her way, she would have sent me, as the cleverer, to school in London. But father would have none of it. He never denied her a whim for herself, but he did not hold with boarding-school learning.

I was left to finish my education by living my life. But mother was none the less ambitious for us, and being an old-fashioned woman, her ambition aspired to good marriages for us. And I—foolish girl that I was—chose to think that the particular man whom she hoped that Joyce's beauty would secure was a very commonplace lover, and not at all worthy of her. In the first place, he occupied a better position in the world than she did, and would probably consider that he was raising her by the marriage, which my pride resented. For, after all, it was only what the world considered a better position; he owned the land that we worked. But the land had only been bought by his ancestors; whereas our forefathers had owned it for more than two hundred years before that, so that we considered that we were of the finer stock.

As I set this down now in black and white I smile to myself; it represents so very badly the real relations that existed between our two families, for the man of whom I speak has always been to us the best and stanchest of friends, and even at that time there was hearty simple intercourse between us that was quite uninfluenced by difference of rank or party-spirit. But the words express a certain side of our feelings, especially a certain side of my own particular feelings, and therefore they shall stand.

The man whom mother hoped Joyce might marry was Squire Broderick. Ever since we girls could remember, he had been squire at the big house, for his father had died when he was scarcely twenty-one, and from that time he had been master of the thousand rooks that used to fly across the marsh at even, to their homes in the beeches and elms that sheltered the Manor from the sea-gales.

I remember thinking when I was a child that it was very strange the rooks should always fly to Squire Broderick's trees rather than to ours. For we had trees too, although not so many nor so big, and our house only stood at the other end of the hill, that sloped down on both sides into the marsh. His house was large and square and regular—a red brick Elizabethan house—and had a great many more windows and chimneys than ours had, and a great many more flower-beds on the lawn that looked out across the marsh to the sea.

But although the Grange had been often added to in the course of its history, and was therefore irregular in shape and varied in color, according to the time that the stone had stood the weather, or to the mosses and ivy that clung to its gray walls, I am sure that it was just as fine an old structure in its way, with its high-pitched tiled roof and the lattice-windows, that only looked like eyes in the empty spaces of solid stone.

We certainly had a better view than the squire. From the low windows of the front parlor we could see the red-roofed town rise, like a sentry-tower out of the plain, some three miles away; and, beyond the ruin of the round stone fortress, lying like a giant asleep in the tawny marsh-land, we looked across the wide stretch of flat pasture-land to the storms and the blue of the sea in the distance.

I do not suppose that I was conscious of the strange beauty of this marsh-land as I am conscious of it now; but I know that I loved it—though people do say that country-folk have no admiration of nature—and I know that I was glad that we saw more of it than they did from the Manor, where a belt of trees had been allowed to grow up and shut out the view. But the rooks loved that lordly belt of trees, and I think that, as a child, I envied the squire the rooks. If I did, it was the only thing I ever did envy him.

As the child of the squire's tenant, and proud of my family pride, it was born in me rather to dislike him than otherwise for his fine old house and his many acres. But this was only when something occurred to remind me of these sentiments—to wit, mother's desire for a marriage between my sister and the village big-wig. Otherwise I did not think of him in this light at all, but rather as the provider of the only treats that ever came our way in that quiet life; for it was he who would make up a party to take us to the travelling shows in the little town when they came by, or even sometimes to the larger seaport ten miles off. I can still remember the school feasts at the Manor when we were little girls, and the squire had but just come into his own; and how, when the village tea and cake had been handed round, he would take us two all over the grounds alone, and give us lovely posies of hot-house flowers to take back to the Grange parlor.

I can even recollect a ride on his back round the field when I tried to catch the pony, and how wildly I laughed all the time, making the meadows ring with my merriment; but that must have been when I was scarcely more than five years old. Since then he had been a husband and a father, and now he was a widower, and in my eyes quite an old man; although, I suppose, he can have been little more than five-and-thirty.

I do not remember Mrs. Broderick. I asked mother about her once, and she told me that she had died when I was scarcely ten years old. And from our old servant, Deborah, I had further gleaned that it was in giving birth to a little son, who had died a year after her, and that mother could not bear to speak of it, because it was just at the same time that we lost our little brother John. Both children had died of scarlet-fever, and mother had nursed the squire's motherless boy before her own. I suppose that was why the squire was always so tender and reverential to her.

I know I was sorry for the squire; for it seemed hard he should have no heir to all his acres, and should have to live in that big house all alone. But he did not seem to mind it much: he was always cheery; his fair, fresh face always with a smile on it; his frank, blue eyes always bright. It did one good to see him; it was like a breath of fresh air. I think everybody felt the same thing about him. It was not only that he was generous, a just landlord, "always as good as his word"—there was something more in it than that; there was something that made everybody love him, apart from anything that he did. And as I look back now to the past, I can see that the squire can have had no easy time of it among the people. He had a thorn in the flesh, and that thorn was my father.

The squire was an ardent Conservative, and father was—well, whatever he was, he was opposed to the squire; and as he was one of those people who have the rare gift of imparting their convictions and their enthusiasms to others, he had great influence among the working-classes, and his influence was not favorable to the squire's party. And yet father was no politician. I knew nothing about shades in these matters at that time, and because father was not a Tory I imagined that he must be a Liberal. But he was not a Liberal, still less was he a Radical, in the party sense of the word. As I have said, he belonged to no party. The reforms that he wanted were social reforms, and they could only be won by the patient struggles of the people who required them. That was what he used to say, and I suppose that was why he devoted all his strength to encouraging the working-classes, and cared so little for their existing rulers. But I did not understand this at the time; it was not till long afterwards that I appreciated all that my father was. Then it occurred to me to wonder how he had come by such advanced ideas living in a quiet country village, and I remembered of a sudden some words that he had said to me one day when I had asked him about a little crayon sketch that always hung above the writing-table in his business-room. It was the portrait of a young man with a firm square chin, a sensitive mouth, liquid, fiery eyes. He wore his hair brushed back off his broad forehead, and had altogether a foreign air. It was a fascinating face.

"That, Meg," he had said, "was a great man—a man who made war against the strong, who helped the poor and down-trodden, and fought for the laws of justice and liberty. He gave his affections, his goods, his brains, and his life to the service of others. He died poor, but was rich. He was a real Christian. His name was Camille Lambert."

He said no more, and I never liked to broach the subject again; for mother had told me afterwards that he had had a romantic friendship for the young Frenchman shortly after her engagement to him, and that he could never bear to speak of him after the time when he laid him to rest under the shadows of the old abbey church.

Mother could tell me little about him beyond the fact that he was some years older than father, and that his parents had belonged to the remnants of that colony of French refugees who had inhabited our town during the last century, and still left their names to many existing houses. Indeed, I thought no more of it at the time; but when long afterwards I remembered the matter, I hunted up a little manuscript pamphlet in father's handwriting, telling the story of his friend's life.

Camille Lambert was a disciple of St. Simon, who had died when my father was yet but a lad. Of an eager and romantic temperament, his enthusiasm had been early fired by those exalted doctrines, and he had given all his substance to the great "school," which had just opened its branch houses in the provinces.

In all the works connected with it, Camille Lambert had taken an active part; and when financial troubles and dissensions between the leaders led popular ardor to cool and the scheme to be declared unpractical, he broke his heart over the failure of his hopes, and came home to the little English village to die.

As I read those pages in after years, I felt that it was no wonder that such an enthusiasm should have kindled a kindred flame in the heart of a man so just and so tender as I knew my dear father to be. I love to think of that friendship now; it explains a great deal to me which has sometimes been a puzzle, when I have looked at my father's character with the more mature eyes of my present years. But in those days I did not think deeply enough for anything to be a puzzle. I was proud of my father's influence among the country-folk; I liked to hear the shouts of applause with which he was greeted when he stood up to speak at winter evening assemblies in the old town-hall. I knew that the crusade he preached was that of the poor against the rich; and a confusion had arisen in my mind as to our attitude towards the squire. I fancied I noticed a restive feeling in father towards the man to whom he paid the rent of his land; and when I guessed at that secret hope in mother's heart, I began to class the squire with "the rich" against whom he waged war in theory, and forgot the many occasions in which they were one at heart in the performance of kindly and generous actions.

My mood did not last long, for the old habit of a lifetime was stronger than a mood, and the squire was our friend, but for the moment that was my mood. The squire belonged to an antagonistic class; perhaps, even worse than that in my eyes, he was a middle-aged man, and Joyce must not marry him. Mother never spoke of her hopes to me. It was old Deborah who sometimes discussed them; she always did discuss the family concerns far more freely than any one else in the house. She was with us when Joyce was born, and it was natural she should talk most of what mattered to those whom she loved most in the world. But Deborah could not be expected to enter into the delicacy of such a situation, and I felt sure that on me fell the duty of fighting to the death before my beautiful sister should be sacrificed to commonplace affluence, instead of shining in the world of romance that I loved to fancy for her.

CHAPTER II

Captain Forrester was the hero of the romance that I had fashioned in my head for Joyce. One bright, frosty winter's day I had driven her into town to market. The sky was blue, the air was sharp, the little icicles hung glittering from the trees and hedge-rows as we drove down the hill; the sea lay steely and calm beyond the waste of white marsh-land that looked so wide in its monotony. The day was invigorating to the spirits, and it had the same effect on father's new mare as it had on us; the road, besides, was as hard as iron and very slippery.

Joyce was nervous in a dog-cart, and she had her doubts of the new purchase. For the matter of that, so had I. The mare pulled very hard. However, we got into town well enough, and in the excitement of her purchases Joyce forgot her uneasiness. It was a long time before she was quite suited to her mind in the matter of soap, and ham, and kitchen utensils; and just as we were leaving I remembered that mother had told me to bring her some tapes and needles.

"I've forgotten something, Joyce," said I. "Get in a minute and take the reins. I'll call a boy to hold the horse's head."

She got in, and I beckoned a lad hard by, who went to the animal's head. But before I had been in the shop a moment a cry from Joyce called me back. The mare was rearing. Whether the lad had teased her or not I do not know, but the mare was rearing, and at her head, instead of the lad I had called, was Captain Forrester. We did not know what his name was then; we merely saw a tall, good-looking man in smarter clothes than were usually worn by the dandies of the neighborhood, soothing the restless animal, who soon showed that she recognized a friend. Joyce was as white as a sheet; but when the young man turned to me and said, raising his hat, "Miss Joyce Maliphant, I believe," she blushed as red as a poppy.

It was strange that he should know her name so well.

"No," said I, "I am not Joyce; I am Margaret Maliphant. My sister's name is Joyce."

I waved towards her as I spoke. Perhaps I was a little off-hand; folk say I always am. I suppose I must have been, for he muttered a half-apology.

"I should not have ventured to intrude," said he, "but that I know the nature of this animal. Strangely enough, she belonged to me once. She is not suitable for a lady's driving."

"Why," said I, puzzled and half doubtful, "father bought her only last week from Squire Broderick."

"Exactly," smiled he, and I noticed what a pleasant, genial smile he had. "I sold the mare to Squire Broderick myself. I know him very well."

"Oh!" ejaculated I, I am afraid still far from graciously.

He was still standing by the horse, stroking its neck.

"Yes," he repeated, and his tone was not a jot less pleasant because I had spoken so very ungraciously. "She used to belong to me. She has a bit of a temper."

"I like a horse with a little temper," answered I. "A horse that has a hard mouth is dull driving."

I said it out of pure intent to brag, for I had been offended at its being supposed I could not drive any horse. As I spoke, I put my foot on the step to mount the dog-cart. As soon as the mare felt the movement behind her she reared again slightly. Captain Forrester quieted her afresh, but still there was no doubt about it, she had reared.

"Oh, Margaret," sighed Joyce, "I'm sure we shall never get home safely!"

"Nonsense!" cried I, impatiently.

I hated to have Joyce seem as though she mistrusted my power of managing a restive horse, and I hated equally to have her show herself off as a woman with nerves. I had already got up into my place, and I now took the reins from her hands and prepared to give the mare her head.

"I think I shall walk, Margaret," said Joyce, in a voice which I knew meant that there would be no persuading her from her purpose. She was not generally obstinate, but when she was frightened she would not listen to any reason.

Rather than have a scene, I knew it would be best to give in.

"Very well; then we will both walk," said I. "You had better get down, and I will drive on and put the cart up at the inn. Reuben will have to walk out this evening and take it home."

I know I spoke crossly; it was wrong, but I was annoyed. However, before Joyce had had time to get down I saw that our new friend had gone round to the other side of the dog-cart and was talking to her.

"Miss Maliphant," said he—and I could not help remarking what a charming manner he had, and what a fascinating way of fixing his wide-open light-brown eyes full in the face of the person to whom he was speaking, and yet that without anything bold in the doing of it—"Miss Maliphant, will you let me drive you and your sister home? I know how uncomfortable it is to be nervous, and I don't think you would be frightened if I were driving, for, you see, I understand the mare quite well."

Joyce blushed, and I bit my lip. It certainly was very mortifying to have a perfect stranger setting himself up as a better whip than I was.

Joyce answered, "Oh, thank you, I don't think we could trouble you to do that," she said, with a bend of her pretty head.

"It would be no trouble," replied he, looking at her. "I am going in your direction." He did not say it eagerly, only with a pleasant smile as though his offer were made out of pure politeness.

I looked at him. He was young and handsome, and he was most certainly a gentleman, for he had the most perfect and easy manners that I had ever met with in any man; and he was looking at Joyce as I fancied a man might look at the woman whom he could love. Suddenly all my offence at his want of respect to my powers of driving evaporated; for a thought flashed across my mind. Might this be the lover of whom I had dreamed for my beautiful sister? He had learned her name beforehand; therefore he must have seen her, and also have been sufficiently attracted by her to wish to find out who she was.

Why was it not possible that he had fallen in love with her at first sight, and that he had sought this opportunity of knowing her? Such things had been known to happen, and Joyce was certainly beautiful enough to account for any ardor in an admirer. I stood a moment undecided myself. A young man from the shop where I had made my little purchase came out and put the parcel in the dog-cart. He held another in his hand.

"This is for the Manor, captain," said he. "Shall I put it in the carriage?"

"No, no, thank you," answered our new friend. "The squire will be driving over one of these days and will fetch it."

This settled the question for me.

"Captain!"

There was something so much more romantic about a captain than about a plain mister. And such a captain! I had met captains before at the Volunteer ball, but not like this one. It did not occur to me for a moment that if the gentleman was a friend of the squire's he must needs belong to the class which I thought I abhorred, and therefore should not be a suitable lover for my sister. I was too much fascinated by the individual to remember the class. Joyce looked at me for help.

"I don't know what to say, I'm sure," murmured she.

The horse began to fidget again at being kept so long standing. There could be no possible objection to a friend of the squire's driving us over.

"Thank you," said I, trying to be cool and dignified and not at all eager. "If you would be so kind as to drive us, I shall be very much obliged to you." And turning to the shop-boy I added, "Put the parcel into the carriage."

I do not know what the captain must have thought of my sudden change of manner; I did not stop to consider. I jumped to the ground before he had time to help me, and began to let down the back seat of the cart.

"No, no; don't leave the horse," cried I, as he came round to the back to help me. "I know how to do this perfectly well. Do get up. Joyce is so very nervous."

"As you like," said he, still smiling; and he got up beside Joyce.

In a moment I had fixed the seat and jumped into it, and we started off at a smart trot down the village street. Joyce was not entirely reassured, although vanity prevented her from openly expressing her alarm, as she would have done if I had been at her side. She sat holding on to the cart, with lips parted and eyes fixed on the horse's ears. I had turned round a little on the seat so that I could see her, and I thought that she looked very lovely. I thought Captain Forrester must be of the same mind; but I think he had not much time to look at her just then—the mare kept his hands full. We rattled down the hill over the cobble-stones and out of the town. Soon its red roofs, crowned by the square tower of the ancient church at its summit, were only a feature in the landscape, which I watched gradually mellowing into the white background as I sat with my back to the others. Before long I was lost in one of what father would have called my brown studies, and quite forgot to notice whether the two in front of me were getting on well together or not. The vague dream that I had always had about my sister's future was beginning to take shape—it unrolled itself slowly before me in a sweet and delightful picture, to which the fair scene before me imparted life and brilliancy as the sense of it mingled imperceptibly with my thoughts. I had never known what it really was that I desired for my sister's lot. To be the wife of a country bumpkin she was far too beautiful; and yet I thought that nothing should have induced me to help towards mating her with one of the gentry who crushed the people's honest rights. Sir Walter Scott's "Fair Maid of Perth," which I had just finished reading, had lent wings to my youthful imagination; but there were no burghers in these days who held the honorable positions of those smiths and glovers, although no doubt at that time there had been many such living in the very town where we had just been to market, and which was in days of old one of the strongholds of his Majesty's realm. If there had been any such suitors, I think I would have given our "Fair Maid" to one of them; but there was all the difference between the man who owned the linen-draper's shop—even if he did not measure off yards of stuff behind the counter—and the man who fashioned the goods with his own hand and took a pride in making them beautiful. And nowadays there were no men who made armor—there were no men who needed it. War had become a very brutal thing compared to what it was then, when it really was a trial of individual strength; nevertheless, of the professions of which I knew anything, it was still to my mind the finest, and it seemed to me that a fine profession was the only thing between a countryman and a landed proprietor such as Squire Broderick. I wonder if I should have thought all this out so neatly if the fine, handsome, and gentlemanly young man who had come across our path had not borne the title of "Captain?" Anyway, it had struck my fancy, as he had struck my fancy—for Joyce.

There was something fresh and brave and bright about him, with those wide-open brown eyes, that he fixed so intently upon one's own. I felt sure that he was full of enthusiasm, full of courage and of loyalty—every inch a soldier. He was the first man I had ever seen who impressed me by his personality; and yet with all that, he was so simple, so light and easy.

As I look back now upon my first impression of Captain Forrester, I do not think it was an unnatural one; I think that he really had a rare gift of fascination, and it was not to be wondered at that I said to myself that this was the noble hero of whom I had dreamed that he should carry off the lily nurtured in the woodland shade. He was just the kind of man to fit in with my notion of a gallant and a hero—a notion derived solely from those old-fashioned novels of father's library which I devoured in the secrecy of my bedchamber when I could snatch a moment from household darning, and mother was not by to pass her scathing remarks upon even such profitable romance-reading as the works of Sir Walter Scott and Jane Austen.

As I sat there in the midst of the snow-plain, with the ocean beyond it, and the weather-worn old town the only human thing in the wide landscape, I fixed my thoughts upon that one little spot with all the concentration of my nature, and fell to weaving a romance far more brilliant than anything I had read, or than anything that had yet suggested itself to me in my quiet every-day life. The days of gay tournaments, and fierce hand-to-hand combats, and warriors clad in suits of mail, were no longer; but still, to fight for one's country's fame, to win one's bread by adventure and glory, to kill one's country's foes and save the lives of her sons, was the grandest thing that could be, I thought; and this Captain Forrester did.

As I dreamed, my eyes grew dim thinking of the wife who must send her lover from her, perhaps forever—even though it be to glorious deeds; and as I dreamed, the dog-cart gave a jolt over a stone, and I awoke from my foolish fancies to see that Captain Forrester's hard driving had taken all the mischief out of the mare, and that she was trotting along quite peaceably, while he let the reins hang loose upon her neck, and turned round to talk to my sister Joyce. And as we passed the clump of tall elms at the foot of the cliff, and began slowly to climb the hill towards the village, I looked out across the cold expanse of white marsh-land to the calm sea beyond, and wondered whether it were true what the books said that the peace of a perfect love could only be won through trouble and heartache. Anyway, the trouble must be worth the reward, since we all admired those who fought for it, and most of us entered the lists ourselves. But no doubt the trouble and the fighting was always on the man's side, and as I caught a glimpse of Joyce's blushing profile and of the Captain's eager gaze, I said to myself that Joyce was beautiful, and that Joyce was sweet, and that Joyce would have a lover to whom no trouble in the whole world would be too much for the sake of one kiss from her lips.

CHAPTER III

I had jumped down as we ascended the hill, and had walked by the side of the cart. Captain Forrester had turned round now and then to say a word to me, making pleasant general remarks upon the beauty of the country and the healthiness of the situation. But he did it out of mere politeness, I knew. When we reached the top of the hill, he gave the reins to Joyce and got down.

"You'll be all right now, won't you?" said he, helping me in. "I won't come to the door, for I'm due at home;" and he nodded in the direction of the Manor.

Then he must be staying in our village.

I said aloud, laughing, "Well, we could hardly get into trouble between this and our house, could we?"

"Hardly," laughed he back again, looking down the road to the right, which led to the ivied porch of our house.

How well he seemed to know all about us! Was he the squire's guest as well as his friend? If so, Joyce would see him again.

"Won't you come in and see my father and mother?" said I.

I was not sure whether it was the thing to do in good society, such as that to which I felt instinctively that he belonged, but I knew that it was the hospitable thing to do, and I did it. Joyce seconded my invitation in an inarticulate murmur.

I think we were both of us considerably relieved when he said with that same gay smile, and speaking with his clear, well-bred accent: "Not now, thank you. But I will come and call very soon, if I may."

He added the last words turning round to Joyce. She blushed and looked uncomfortable. We were both thinking that mother might possibly not welcome this stranger so cordially as we had done. However, I was not going to have this good beginning spoiled by any mistake on my part, and I hastened to say: "Oh yes, pray do come. I am sure mother will be delighted to welcome any friend of Squire Broderick's."

He gave a little bow at that, but he did not say anything. He held out his hand to me, and then turned to Joyce. I fancied that hers rested in his just a moment longer than was necessary; but then I was in the mood to build up any romance at the moment, and no doubt I was mistaken. But anyhow, I turned the dog-cart down rather sharply towards the house, and Captain Forrester had to stand aside. I was not going to have the villagers gossiping; and such a thing had not been seen before, as Farmer Maliphant's two daughters talking with a stranger at the corner of the village street.

"I wonder whether he is staying at the Manor," said I, as we drove up the gravel.

And Joyce echoed, "I wonder."

But she had plenty to do when she got in, showing her new purchases to mother, and telling her the market prices of household commodities, and I do not suppose that she gave a thought to her new admirer for some time. At all events, she did not speak of him. Neither did I. I did not go in-doors.

I always was an unnatural sort of a girl in some ways, and shopping and talk about shopping never interested me. I preferred to remain in the yard, and discuss the points of the new mare with Reuben. But all the time, I was thinking of the man whom we had met in town, and wondering whether or not he would turn out to be Joyce's lover. As I have said before, Reuben and I were great friends. He was a gaunt, loose-limbed old fellow, with a refined although by no means a handsome face, thin features, a fair pale skin, with white whiskers upon it. In character he was simple, obstinate, and taciturn, and had a queer habit of applying the same tests to human beings as he did to dumb animals. In the household—although every one respected his knowledge of his own business—I think that he was regarded merely as an honest, loyal nobody. It was only I who used sometimes to think that it was not all obtuseness, but also a laudable desire for a quiet life, which led Reuben to be such an easy mark for Deborah's wit, and apparently so impervious to its arrows.

"She pulled, did she?" said he, with a smile that showed a very good set of teeth for an old man. "Ah, it takes a man to hold a mare, leastways if she's got any spirit in her."

"She didn't pull any too much for me," answered I, half vexed. "What makes you fancy so?"

"I seed the young dandy a-driving ye along the road," said he. "I can see a long way. She pulled at first, but he took it out of her."

If there was any secret in our having driven out of town with Captain Forrester, Reuben had it.

"Joyce was frightened, and he had driven the mare at the squire's," said I. "She reared a bit in town, but I don't think he drove any better than I could have done."

Reuben took no notice of this remark. "She's a handsome mare," said he. "The handsomer they be, the worse they be to drive. Women are the same—so I've heard tell; though, to be sure, the ugly ones are bad enough."

Deborah was not handsome; but then, had Reuben ever tried to drive her? Oh, if she could have heard that speech! She came up the garden cliff in front of us as I spoke, with some herbs in her arms—a tall, strong woman, with a wide waist and shoulders, planting her foot firmly on the ground at every step, and swaying slightly on her hips with the bulk of her person. When she was young she must have had a fine figure, but now she was not graceful.

"Yes, she's a beauty," said I, stroking the mare's sleek sides, and alluding to her and not to Deborah. "When we are alone together we'll have fine fun." The mare stretched out her pretty neck to take the sugar that I held in my hand. She was beginning to know me already.

"Yes, Miss Joyce is nervous," said Reuben, meditatively. "Most like she *would* have more confidence in a beau. Them pretty maids are that way, and the beaux buzz about them like flies to the honey. But the beasts be fond of you, miss," he added, admiringly, watching me fondling the horse.

It was the higher compliment from Reuben, and it was true that every animal liked me. I could catch the pony in the field when it would let no one else get near it. I could milk the cow who kicked over the pail for any one but Deborah. I could coax the rabbits to me, and almost make friends with the hares in the woods. The cat slept upon my bed, and Taff watched outside my door.

I laughed at Reuben's compliment; but Deborah strode out of the back door just then, to hang linen out to dry, and Reuben never laughed when she was by. She gave me a sharp glance.

"You've got your frock out at the gathers again," said she. She did not often trouble to give us our titles of "miss."

"Have I?" replied I, carelessly.

"Yes, you have; and how you manage it is more than I can tell," continued she, tartly. "Now you're grown up, I should think you might have done with jumping dikes, and riding horses without saddles, and such-like."

"Why, Deb," cried I, laughing, "I haven't jumped a dike since I was fourteen. At least, not when any one was by," added I, remembering a private exploit of two days ago.

"Yes; I suppose you don't expect me not to know where that black mud came from on your petticoat last night," remarked she, sententiously. "Anyhow, I'd advise you to mend your frock, for the squire's in the parlor, and your mother won't be pleased."

"The squire!" cried I. "Is he going to stay to dinner?"

"Not as I know of," answered the old woman. "But you had better go and see. Joyce let him in, for I hadn't a clean apron, and I heard him say that he had come to see the master on business."

"Well, so I suppose he did," answered I.

Deborah smiled, a superior sort of smile. She did not say anything, but I knew very well what she meant. She was the only person in the house who openly insisted that the squire came to the Grange after Joyce. Mother may have thought it; I guessed from many little signs that she did think it, but she never directly spoke of it. But Deborah spoke of it, and spoke of it frankly.

It irritated me. I pushed past her roughly to reach the front parlor windows. I wanted to see the squire to-day, for I wanted to find out whether our new friend was staying at the Manor.

"You're never going in like that?" cried she.

"Certainly," replied I. "What's good enough for other folk is good enough for the squire. The squire is nothing to me, nothing at all."

"That's true enough," laughed Deborah. "I don't know as he is anything to you. But he may be something to other folk all the same. And look here, Miss Spitfire, there may come a day, for all your silly airs, when you may be glad enough that the squire is something to some of you, and when you'd be very sorry if you'd done anything to prevent it. You go and think that over."

I curled my lip in scorn. "You know I refuse to listen to any insinuations, Deborah," said I. "The squire comes here to visit my father, and we have no reason to suppose that he comes for anything else."

This was quite true. The squire had certainly never said a word that should lead us to imagine that he meant anything more by his visits to the Grange than friendship for an old man laid by from his active life by frequent attacks of gout; but if I had been quite honest, I should have acknowledged that I, too, entertained the same suspicion as Deborah did.

"The women must always needs be thinking the men be coming after them," muttered Reuben, emerging from the darkness of a shed to the left with an axe over his shoulder.

If I had been less preoccupied I should have laughed at the audacity of this remark, which he would certainly not have dared to make unless it had been for the support of my presence.

"It don't stand to reason," went on Deborah, scorning Reuben's remark, "that a gentleman like the squire would come here and sit hours long for naught but to hear the gentry-folk abused by the master. It is a wonder he stands it as he do, for master is over-unreasonable at times. But, Lord! you can't look in the squire's eyes and not know he's got a good heart, and it's Miss Joyce's pretty face that'll get it to do what she likes with, you may take my word for it. The men they don't look to the mind so much as they look to the face, and the temper—and Joyce, why, her temper's as smooth as her skin; you can't say better than that."

This was true, and Deborah was right to say it in praise, although I do believe in her heart she had even a softer spot for me and my bad temper than for Joyce and her gentle ways.

"Birds of a feather, I suppose."

"You seem to think that it's quite an unnatural thing for two men to talk politics together, Deborah," said I, with a superior air of wisdom. "But perhaps the squire is wiser than you fancy, and thinks that at his time of life politics should be more in his way than pretty faces."

Deborah laughed, quite good-humoredly this time.

"Hark at the lass!" cried she. "The time may come when you won't think a man of five-and-thirty too old to look at a woman, my dear."

"Oh, I don't mind how old a man is!" laughed I, merrily, recovering my good-humor at the remembrance of that second string I had to my bow for my sister. "The men don't matter much to me—they never look twice at me, you know well enough. But Joyce is too handsome to marry an old widower, and I dare say if she waits a bit there'll come somebody by who'll be better suited to her."

"Well, all I can say is, I hope she may have another chance as good," insisted the obstinate old thing, shaking out the last stocking viciously and hanging it onto the line. "But she hasn't got it yet, you know; and if folk all behave so queer and snappish, maybe she won't have it at all. But you must all please yourselves," added she, as though she washed her hands of us now. And then giving me another of her sharp glances, she said, in conclusion, "And you know whether your mother will like to see you with a torn frock or not."

I went in with my head in the air. I thought it was very impertinent of Deb to talk of "good chances" in connection with my sister. I have learned to know her better since then.

Her desire for that marriage was not all ambition for Joyce. But at that time I little guessed what she already scented in the air.

CHAPTER IV

It was a quarter of an hour before I reached the parlor, for I did mend my frock in spite of my bit of temper. The cloth was laid for dinner—a spotless cloth, for mother was very particular about her table-linen—and the bright glass and the dinner-ware shone in the sunlight. I can see the room now: a long, low room, with four lattice-windows abreast, and a seat running the length of the windows; opposite the windows a huge fireplace, across which ran one heavy oaken beam bearing the date and the name of the Maliphants, and supported by two stout masonry pillars, fashioned, tradition said, out of that same soft stone of which a great part of the abbey was built. Two high-backed wooden chairs, with delicate spindle-rails, highly polished, and very elegant, stood close to the blaze. There was also a pretty inlaid satinwood table in the far corner that had belonged to mother's grandfather, and had been left to her; but the rest of the furniture was plain dark oak, and had been in the house ever since the Maliphants had owned it. It was a sweet, cosey room, and if the windows, being old-fashioned and somewhat small, did not admit all the sunlight they might, they also did not let in the wind, of which there was plenty, for the parlor faced towards the sea, and the gales in winter were sometimes terrific.

We had another best-parlor, looking on the road, where were the piano and the upholstered furniture, covered in brown holland on common days; but though the pale yellow tabaret chairs and curtains looked very pretty when they were all uncovered, we none of us ever felt quite comfortable excepting in the big dwelling-room that looked over the marsh. How well I remember it that day when we were all there together! Father sat by the fire with his boots and gaiters still on. He had been out for the first time after a severe attack of his complaint, and he was very irritable. I thought Joyce might have helped him off with the heavy things, but no doubt he had refused; any offer of help was almost an insult to him. They used to say I took after father in that. He was bending over the fire that day, stretching out his fingers to the blaze—a powerful figure still, though somewhat worn with hard work and the sufferings which he never allowed to gain the upper-hand. But his back was not bent—an out-door life, whatever other marks it may leave, spares that one; his head was erect still—a remarkable head—the gray hair, thick and strong, sticking up in obstinate little tufts without any attempt at order or smoothness. It was not beautiful hair, for the tufts were quite straight, but at least it was very characteristic; I have never seen any quite like it. It was in keeping with the bushy eyebrows that had just the same defiant expression as the tufts of hair. The brow was high and prominent, the eyes keen and quick to change, the jaw heavy and somewhat sullen. At first sight it might not have been called a lovable face; it might rather have been called a stern, even an unbending one; but that it was really lovable is proved by the sure love and confidence with which it always inspired little children. They came to father naturally as they would have gone to the tenderest woman, and smiled in his face as though certain beforehand of the smile that would answer theirs in return. But father's face was sullen sometimes to a grown-up person. It looked very sullen as he sat by the fire that day. I knew in a moment that something had ruffled him.

Mother seemed to be doing her best, however, to make up for the ill reception which her husband was giving his guest; and mother's best was a very pretty thing. She was a very pretty woman, and she looked her prettiest that day. She was tall—we were a tall family, I was the shortest of us all—and her height looked even greater than it was in the straight folds of the soft gray dress that suited so well with her fair skin. She had a fresh white cap on; the soft fluted frills came down in straight lines just below her ears, framing her face; and the bands of snow-white hair, that looked so pretty beside the fresh skin, were tucked away smoothly beneath it. Mother's face was a young face still—as dainty in color as a little child's. Joyce took her beauty from her.

Mother was standing up in the middle of the room talking to the squire, who apparently was about to take his leave. Joyce was putting the last touches to the dinner-table. She looked up at me in an appealing kind of way as I came in, and I felt sure that there had been some sort of difference between father and the squire. They often did have little differences, though they were the best of friends in reality; but I always secretly took father's side in every argument, and I never liked to see mother, as it were, making amends for what father had said. Yet it was what she was doing now. "I'm sure, Squire Broderick," she was saying, "we take it very kindly of you to interest yourself in our affairs. Laban is a little tetchy just now, but it's because he ain't well. He feels just as I do really."

Father made an impatient sound with his lips at this, but mother went on just the same.

"I'm quite of your mind," she declared, shaking her head. "I've often said so to Laban myself. We can't go against Providence, and we must learn to take help where we can get it, though I know ofttimes it's just the hardest thing we have to do."

What could this speech mean? I was puzzled. I glanced at father. He sat quite silent, tapping his foot. I glanced at Joyce. There was nothing in her manner to show that the subject under discussion had anything whatever to do with her. The squire had turned round as I came into the room, but mother kept him so to herself that he could do no more than give me a smile as I walked across and sat down in the window-seat.

"I know it would be the best in the end," mother went on, with a distressed look on her sweet old face.

It rather annoyed me at the time, simply because I saw that she was siding with the squire against father; but I have often remembered that, and many kindred looks since, and have wondered how it was that I never guessed at the anxiety of that tender spirit that labored so devotedly to cope with problems that were beyond its grasp.

"However," added mother, with the pretty smile that, after all, I remember more often than the knitted brow, "he'll come round himself in time. He always does see things the way you put them after a bit."

She said these words in a whisper, although they were really quite loud enough for any one to hear. I saw father smile. He was so fond of mother, and the words were so far from accurate, that he could afford to smile; for there were very few instances in which he came round to the squire's way of seeing things at that time, although he was very fond of the squire. The squire himself laughed aloud. He had a rich, rippling laugh; it did one good to hear it.

"No, no, ma'am," he said, "I can't agree to that; and no reason why it should be so either." He held out his hand to mother as he spoke.

"I must be off now," he added. "I ought to have gone long ago. We'll talk it over again another time."

"Oh, won't you stay and have a bit of dinner with us, squire?" cried mother, in a disappointed voice. "It's just coming in. I know it's not what you have at home, but it is a fine piece of roast beef to-day."

"Fie, fie, Mrs. Maliphant! don't you be so modest," said the squire, with his genial smile, buttoning up his overcoat as he spoke.

He always had a gay, easy manner towards the mother—something, I used to fancy, like what her own younger brother might have had towards her, or even her own son, although at that time I should have thought it impossible for a man as old to be mother's son at all. I suppose it was in consequence of that sad time in the past that he had grown to love her as I know he did.

"I don't often get a dinner such as I get at your table," added he; "but I can't stay to-day, for I'm due at home."

Just the words that young man had used at the foot of the village street. I was determined to find out before the squire left whether that young man was staying at the Manor or not.

"Perhaps Mr. Broderick has visitors, mother," I suggested.

I glanced at Joyce as I spoke. Her cheeks were poppies.

"What makes you think so?" asked the squire, turning to me and frowning a little.

"We met a gentleman in town," said I, boldly, although my heart beat a little; "he helped us with the mare when she reared, and he said he was a friend of yours."

Mother looked at me, and Joyce blushed redder than ever. Certainly, for a straightforward and simple young woman who had no more than her legitimate share of vanity, Joyce had a most unfortunate trick of blushing. I know it was admired, but I never could see that folk must needs be more delicate of mind because they blushed, or more sensitive of heart because they cried. The squire frowned a little more and bit his lip.

"Ah, it must have been Frank," said he. "He did say he was going to walk into town this morning. My nephew," added he, in explanation, turning to mother. "Captain Forrester."

"Your nephew!" exclaimed mother, quite reassured. "He must be but a lad."

"Oh, not at all; he's a very well-grown man, and of an age to take care of himself," answered the squire, and it did not strike me then that he said it a little bitterly. "My sister is a great deal older than I am."

"Of course I have seen Mrs. Forrester," said mother, "and I know she's a deal older than you are, but I never should have thought she had a grown-up son—and a captain, too!"

"Oh yes, he's a captain," repeated the squire, and he took up his hat and stick from the corner of the room and put his hand on the door-knob. "Good-bye, Mr. Maliphant," cried he, cheerily, without touching any more on the sore subject.

Father did not reply, and he turned to me and held out his hand. "Good-bye," he said, more seriously than it seemed to me the subject required. "I'm sorry the mare reared."

"See the squire to the door, Joyce," said the mother. And Joyce, blushing again, glided out into the hall and lifted the big latch.

CHAPTER V

I was dying to hear what had been the subject of the difference between Squire Broderick and father, for that it was somehow related to something more closely allied to our own life than mere politics, I was inwardly convinced. I came up to the fireplace and began toasting my feet before the bars. I hoped father would say something. But he did not even turn to me, and Deborah coming in with the dinner at that moment, mother took her place at the head of the table, and father asked a blessing. Mother did not look sad; she looked very bright and pretty, with the sunshine falling on her silvery hair, and on her white dimpled hands, lovely hands, that were wielding the carvers so skilfully. I thought at the time that she did not notice father's gloomy face, but I think it is far more likely that she did notice it, but that she thought it wiser to leave him alone; those were always her tactics.

"Father," began she, as soon as she had served us all and had sat down, "the girls mustn't drive that mare any more if she rears; it isn't safe."

"No, no, of course not," assented father, absently. Then turning to me, "What made her rear, Meg?"

"I don't know, father," answered I. "I was in a shop when she did, and a boy was holding her. I suppose he teased her. But it's not worth talking about; it would have been nothing if Joyce hadn't been so easily frightened."

"I couldn't help it," murmured Joyce. "I know I'm silly."

"Well, to be sure, any old cart-horse would be better for you than a beast with any spirit, wouldn't it?" laughed I.

"Well, Margaret, the animal must have looked dangerous, you know," said mother, "for no strange gentleman would have thought of accosting two girls unless he saw they were really in need of help."

I laughed—I am afraid I laughed. I thought mother was so very innocent.

"I hope you thanked him for his trouble," added she. "Being the squire's nephew, as it seems he was, I shouldn't be pleased to think you treated him as short as you sometimes treat strangers. You, Margaret, I mean," added mother, looking at me.

"Oh yes, we were very polite to him," said I. And then I grew very hot. Of course I knew I was bound to say that Captain Forrester had driven us home. I hoped mother would take it kindly, as she seemed well disposed towards him, but I did not feel perfectly sure.

"We asked him to come in, didn't we, Joyce?" added I, looking at her.

"Yes, we did," murmured my sister, bending very low over her plate.

"Asked him to come where?" asked mother.

"Why, here, to be sure," cried I, growing bolder. "He drove us home, you know."

Mother said nothing, for Deborah had just brought in the pudding, and she was always very discreet before servants at meal-times. But she closed her lips in a way that I knew, and her face assumed an aggrieved kind of expression that she only put on to me; when Joyce was in the wrong, she always scolded her quite frankly. There was silence until Deborah had left the room. She went out with a smile on her face which always drove me into a frenzy, for it meant to say, "You are in for it, and serve you right;" and I thought it was taking advantage of her position in the family to notice any differences that occurred between mother and the rest of us.

When Deborah had gone out, shutting the door rather noisily, mother laid down her knife and fork. She did not look at me at all, she looked at Joyce. That was generally the way she punished me.

"You don't mean to say, Joyce, that you allowed a strange gentleman to get into the trap before all the townsfolk!" said she. "You're the eldest—you ought to have known better."

I could not stand this. "It isn't Joyce's fault," said I, boldly; "I thought we were in luck's way when the gentleman offered to drive us. He knew the mare, and of course I felt that we were safe."

"It will be all over the place to-morrow," said mother, pathetically.

"Well, the gentleman is the squire's nephew, and everybody knows what friends you are with the squire," answered I, provokingly.

"You might see that makes it all the worse," answered mother. "I don't know how ever I shall meet the squire again. I'm ashamed to think my daughters should have behaved so unseemly. But the ideas of young women in these days pass me. Such notions wouldn't have gone down in my day. Young women were forced to mind themselves if they were to have a chance of a husband. Your father would never have looked at me if I had been one of that sort."

Father was in a brown-study. I do not think he had paid much attention to the affair at all, but now he smiled as mother glanced across at him, seeming to expect some recognition. She repeated her last remark and then he said, bowing to her with old-fashioned gallantry, "I think I should have looked at you, Mary, whatever your shortcomings had been. You were too pretty to be passed over."

And he smiled again, as he never smiled at any one but mother; the smile that, when it did come, lit up his face like a dash of broad sunshine upon a rugged moor.

"But mother's quite right, lassies," added he; "a woman must be modest and gentle, not self-seeking, nor eager for homage, or she'll never have all the patience she need have to put up with a man's tempers."

He sighed, and the tears rose to my eyes. A word of disapproval from my father always hurt me to the quick, and I felt that in this case it was not wholly deserved, as, however mistaken I might have been, I had certainly not been self-seeking or eager for homage.

"I'm very sorry," said I, but I am afraid not at all humbly; "I didn't know I was doing anything so very dreadful. Anyhow, it wasn't I who was afraid of the horse, and it wasn't for me that Captain Forrester took the reins."

This was quite true, but I had no business to have said it. I wished the words back as soon as they were spoken. Joyce blushed scarlet again, and mother looked at me for the first time. I felt that she was going to ask what I meant, but father interrupted her.

"There, there," said he, not testily, but as though to put an end to the discussion. "You should not have done it, because mother says so, and mother always knows best, but I dare say there's little harm done. A civil word hurts nobody; and as for the mare, you needn't drive her again."

So that was all that I had got for my pains. I opened my mouth to explain and to remonstrate, but father rose from the table and said grace, and I dared not pursue the subject further. For the matter of that, the look of pain in his face, as he moved across the room and sat down heavily in the chair, was quite enough to chase away my vexation against him. "Meg, just take these heavy things off for me, I'm weary," said he. I knelt down and unfastened the gaiters, and unlaced the heavy boots, and brought him his slippers. He lay back with a sigh of relief.

"The walk round the farm has been too much for you, Laban," said mother, sitting down in the other high-backed chair near him.

"Let be, let be," muttered he.

"Nay, I can't let be, Laban," insisted mother. "I must look after your health, you know. I can see very well that it is too much for you seeing after the farm as it should be seen after. And that's why I don't think the squire's notion is half a bad one."

I stopped with the spoons and forks in my hand that I was taking off the table. Father made that noise between his teeth again. I always knew it meant a storm brewing.

"Anyhow, I hope you won't bear him a grudge for what he thought fit to advise," mother went on. "He did it out of friendship, I'm sure. And the squire's a wise man."

Father did not answer at first. He had risen and stood with his back to the fire. His jaw was set, his eyes looked like black beads under the overhanging brows.

"Of course I know you'll say he just wants to get a job for his friend's son," continued mother. "And no doubt he mightn't have thought of it but for this turning up. But he wouldn't advise it if he didn't think it was for our good. The squire has our interests at heart, I'm sure."

"D—n the squire," said father at last, slowly and below his breath. Mother laid her hand on his arm.

"Hush, Laban, hush; not before the girls," said she, in her gentle tones.

"Well, well, there," said he, "the squire's a good man and an honest man, but I say neither he nor any one else has a right to come and teach a man what to do with his own."

"He doesn't do it because of any right," persisted mother. "He does it because he's afraid things don't work as well as they used to do, and because he's your friend."

"And what business has he to be afraid?" retorted father. "I say the land's my own, though I do pay him rent for it, and it's my business to be afraid. Does he think I shall be behind-hand with the rent? I've been punctual to a day these last twenty years. What more does he want, I should like to know?"

"Now, Laban, you know that isn't it," expostulated mother. "He knows he is safe enough for the rent, but he's afraid you ain't making money so fast as you might. And of course if you aren't, it's clear it's because you're not so strong to work as you were, and you haven't got a son of your own to look after things for you."

Mother sighed as she said this, but I am afraid I looked at her with angry not sympathetic eyes.

"The squire takes a true interest in us all," repeated she for the third time, her voice trembling a little.

"Well, then, let him take his interest elsewhere this time, ma'am, that's all I've got to say," retorted father, in no way appeased. "If things were as they should be, there'd be no paying of rent to eat up a man's profits on the land, but what he made by the sweat of his brow would be his own for his old age, and for his children after him. And if we can only get what ought to belong to the nation by paying for it, then all I bargain for is—let those who get the money from me leave alone prying into how I get it together."

I had stood perfectly still all this time, with the spoons and forks in my hand, listening and wondering. Father's last speech I had scarcely given heed to. I had heard those opinions before, and they had become mere words in my ears. I was entirely engrossed with wondering what was the exact nature of the squire's suggestion, and with horror at what I feared. I was not long left in doubt.

"Well, you make a great mistake in being angry with Squire Broderick, Laban, indeed you do," reiterated mother, shaking her head, and without paying any attention to his fiery speech. She never did pay any attention to such speeches. She always frankly said that she did not understand them. "If the squire recommends this young Mr. Trayton Harrod to you, it is because he knows him and thinks he would work with you, and not be at all like any common paid bailiff, I'm sure of that."

"Well, then, mother, all I can say is—it's nonsense—that is what it is. It is nonsense. If a man is a paid bailiff, the more like one he is the better. And I don't think it is at all likely I shall ever take a paid bailiff to help me to manage Knellestone."

With that he strode to the door and opened it.

"Meg, will you please come to me in my study in a quarter of an hour?" said he, turning to me as he went out. "There are a few things in the farm accounts that I think you might help me with."

CHAPTER VI

I went into the sunlight and stood leaning upon the garden-hedge looking out over the glittering plain of snow to the glittering blue of the sea beyond. The whole scene was set with jewels of light, and even the gray fortress in the marsh seemed to awaken for once out of its sleep; but I was in no mood to laugh with the sunbeams, for my heart was beating with angry thoughts. A bailiff, a manager for Knellestone—and Knellestone that had been managed by nobody but its own masters for three hundred years! It was impossible! Why, the very earth would rise up and rebel! From where I stood I could see our meadows down on the marsh, our fields away on the hills towards the sunset, the pastures where our shepherds spent cold nights in huts at the lambing-time, the land where our oxen drew the plough and our laborers tilled the soil and harvested the ingatherings. Would the men and the beasts work for the manager as they worked for us? Would the land prosper for a stranger and a hireling, who would not care whether the cattle lived or died, whether the seasons were kind or cruel, whether the trees and the flowers flourished or pined away, who would get his salary just the same, though the frost nipped the new crops, though the wheat dried up for want of rain or rotted in the ear for lack of sun, though the cows cast their calves and the lambs died at the birth? How absurd, how ridiculous it was! Did it not show that it had been suggested by one who took no interest in the land, but who let it all out to others to care for? Of course this was some spendthrift younger son of a ruined gentleman's family, or some idiot who had failed at every other profession, and was to be sent here to ruin other people without having any responsibility of his own—somebody to whom the squire owed a duty or a favor. Perhaps a man who had never been on a farm in his life, maybe had not even lived in the country at all. In my childish anger I became utterly unreasonable, and gave vent in my solitude to any absurd expressions that occurred to me. I smile to myself as I remember the impotent rage of that afternoon. Indeed, I think I hated the squire most thoroughly that day. It was the idea, too, that I was being set at naught that added to my anger. Hitherto it was I who had transmitted father's orders to the men whenever he was laid by or busy; and, as I have said before, he often trusted me to ride to the bank with money, and even to take stock of the goods before sales and fairs came on. Of course I know

now that I was worse than useless to him. I was a clever girl enough, and dauntless in the matter of fatigue or trouble, but I was entirely ignorant of the hundred little details that make all the difference in matters of that kind, and pluck and coolness stood me in poor stead of experience. But at that time I was confident, and as I stood there looking at the brightness that I did not see, tears came into my eyes—tears of mortification, that even the squire should have considered me so perfectly useless that I could be set aside as though I did not exist. How often I had wished to be a boy! How heartily I wished it that afternoon! If I had been a boy there would never even have been a question of getting a paid manager to help father. I should have been a man by this time, nearly of age, and no one would have doubted that I was clever enough and strong enough to see after my own.

Father called from the window, and I went in. He was sitting by the table, surrounded by papers, his foot supported on a chair.

"Sit down, Meg," said he. "I want you to help me remember one or two things in the books that I don't quite understand—I think you can."

He spoke quite cheerfully. I had been setting down things in the book while he had been ill, and paying the wages to the men, and it was quite natural he should want to see me about it. I sat down, and we went over the books item by item. We had had a very sound education, though simple, quite as good as most girls have, and I had been considered more than usually smart at figures. But that day I think I was dazed. I could not remember things; I could not tell why the books were not square; my wits were muddled on every point. Father was most patient, most kind. I think he must have seen that I was over-anxious, but his kindness only made me more disgusted with myself; for I knew that that dreadful question was in his mind the whole time, as it was in mine.

Whenever I told him anything that was not satisfactory in the conduct of affairs, or anything that had failed to turn out as he expected, I knew that it was in his mind, although he did not think I saw it.

"We can't expect old heads to grow on young shoulders," said he at last, patting mine gently, a thing most rare for him to do. "It takes many a long day to learn experience, my dear. And sometimes we don't do so much better with it than we did without it." He put the books away as he spoke, and leaned back in his chair. "That'll do now, child," he added; "to-morrow I shall be able to see the men myself. I am well and hearty again now—thank the Lord—and a good bit of work will do me good."

"You mustn't begin too soon, father," said I, timidly; "you know the weather is very cold and treacherous yet."

"Oh, you women would keep a man in-doors forever for fear the wind should blow in his face," cried he, testily. "But there's an end to everything. When I'm ill you shall all do what you like with me, but when I'm well I mean to be my own master."

"But I shall still be able to help you, father, as I have done before, sha'n't I?" added I, still, singularly, without my accustomed self-confidence.

"Why, yes, child, of course," he replied. "And you and I will be able to get on yet awhile without a stranger's help, I'll warrant." It was the only allusion he had made to the horrible subject during the whole of our interview. It was the only allusion he made to it in my presence for many a long day. He rose from his chair as he spoke the last words, and walked across to the window.

The afternoon was beginning to sink, and the sun had paled in its splendor. The lights were gray now over the whiteness of the marsh, and the snow looked cold and cruel. Something made my heart sink, too, as I noticed how gray was father's face in the scrutinizing light of the afternoon. I had not noticed before that he had really been ill. I left the room quickly, and went out again. The stinging March air struck a chill into my bones, and yet it was scarcely more than four o'clock. Two hours of daylight yet! How was it possible that any man but the strongest should work as a man must work whose farm should prosper? And was father really a strong man? I was sick with misgivings. What if, after all, the squire were right? But I would not believe it. Father had had the gout; it was always the strongest men who had the gout.

I turned to go in-doors. A laugh greeted my ears from the library. I passed before the window. Yes; it was father who was laughing as he shook hands with a man who had just entered the room. I looked. The man was a tall, blond, spare fellow, with a sanguine complexion, very marked features, small gray eyes, and a bald head. I knew him to be a Mr. Hoad, father's solicitor in town. He was well dressed in a black suit and gray trousers. He was a very successful man for his time of life, people said. I knew that father liked him, and I was glad that father should have a visitor who cheered him to-day. But for my own part, I knew no one who filled me with such a peculiar antipathy. I could not bear the sight of the man. Yet he was a harmless kind of fellow, and very polite to ladies. Joyce often used to take me to task for my excessive dislike to him. If it was because I did not consider him on equal terms with us, from a social point of view — for I must confess I was ridiculously prejudiced on this score, and where I had learned such nonsense I do not know — then the ship-owners and other people of that class to whom I could give "good-day" in town were much less so. But

I could not have told why I disliked him so particularly; I could not have told why I wondered that father could have any dealings with him—why I was always on the watch for something that should prove that I was in the right in my instinct. And somehow his appearance on this particular evening affected me even more uncomfortably than usual, and I felt that I could not go in and see him—perhaps even have to discuss the very subject that was weighing on my mind, when I wanted to be alone to nurse my own mortification, and lull my fears to rest by myself. I crept into the hall quietly and fetched a cloak and hood, and then, running round to the yard, I called the St. Bernard. He came, leaping and jumping upon me, this friend with whom I was always in tune. I opened the gate gently, and together we went out upon the road.

I think Taff and I must have walked three miles. The roads were stiff and slippery, the air was like a knife; but I did not care. The quick movement and the solitude and the quiet of the coming night soothed me. We got up upon the downs where lonely homesteads stud the country here and there, and came back again along the cliffs that crown the marsh-land. There I stood a long while face to face with the quiet world upon which the moon had now risen in the deep blue of a twilight sky. It looked down upon the wide, white marsh upon whose frozen bosom gray vapors floated lightly; it looked down upon the dark town that rose yonder so sombre and distinct out of the mystery of the landscape; the channel that flows to the sea lay cold and blue and motionless at the foot of the hill like a sheet of steel. It made me shudder. There was not a ripple upon its deathly breast. The snow around was far more tender. For the first time in my life I felt the sadness of the world; I realized that there was something in it which I could not understand; I remembered that there was such a thing as death.

CHAPTER VII

I did not escape Mr. Hoad by my walk. He had stayed to tea. I do not think that he was a favorite of mother's, but she always made a great point of welcoming all father's friends to the house, and I saw that she had welcomed him to-night. He sat in the place of honor beside her, and there were sundry alterations on the tea-table, and a pot of special marmalade in the middle.

It was very late when I came in. I took off my things in the hall and went in without smoothing my hair. I thought I should have been in disgrace for coming in late, and for having my hair in disorder when a guest was present; but mother had forgotten her displeasure, and smiled as she pushed my cup towards me. She never made any allusion to by-gone differences—her anger never lasted long.

The mood that I had brought with me from without was still upon me, and when I saw that father's face had lost its gray pallor, that his eyes shone with their usual fire, and that his voice was strong and healthy, I sighed a sigh of relief and told myself that I was a fool, and that Mr. Hoad must really be a good fellow if he could so soon chase away the gloom from my parent's brow.

"Your husband looks wonderfully well again, Mrs. Maliphant," he was saying; "it's quite surprising how soon he has pulled round. When I met the doctor the other day driving from town, and stopped to ask after him, he said it would be weeks before he could be about again. But he has got a splendid constitution—must have. Not that I would wish to detract from your powers of nursing. We all have heard how wonderful they are."

Mr. Hoad smiled at mother, but she did not smile back again. There were people whom she kept at arm's-length, even though carefully civil to them. I don't suppose she knew this, for she was a shy woman, but I recollect it well.

"We can all nurse those we are fond of," she said. "I'm sure I'm very pleased to think you should find Mr. Maliphant looking better."

"Better! Nonsense!" exclaimed father. "I'm as well as I ever was in my life. Don't let's hear any more about that, wife, there's a dear soul."

"Nay, you shall hear no more about it than need be from me, Laban, I can promise you that," smiled mother, pouring out the tea, while Joyce, from the opposite side of the table, where she was cutting up the seed-cake that she had made with her own hands the day before, asked the guest after his two daughters.

"They are very busy," answered Mr. Hoad. "A large acquaintance, you know—it involves a great deal of calling. I'm afraid they have been remiss here."

"Oh, I pray, don't mention such a thing, Mr. Hoad," exclaimed mother, hastily. "We don't pay calls ourselves. We are plain folk, and don't hold with fashionable ways."

Mr. Hoad smiled rather uncomfortably.

"And we have not much to amuse them with," I put in. "We do nothing that young ladies do."

I saw mother purse up her lips at this, and I was vexed that I had said it, but father laughed and said: "No, Hoad, my girls are simple farmer's daughters, and have learned more about gardening and house-keeping than they have about French and piano-playing, though Meg can sing a ballad when she chooses as well as I want to hear it."

I declared my voice was nothing to Miss Hoad's; and Joyce, always gracious, looked across to Mr. Hoad and said: "I wonder whether Miss Jessie would sing something for us at our village concert?"

"I'll ask her," said Mr. Hoad, a little diffidently. "I'm never sure about my daughters' engagements. They have so many engagements."

"We shall be very pleased to see them here any afternoon for a practice, sha'n't we, mother?" added Joyce.

"The young ladies will always be welcome," replied mother, a little stiffly; and I hastened to add, I fear less graciously:

"But pray don't let them break any engagements for us."

Mr. Hoad smiled again, and then father turned to him and they took up the thread of their own talk where they had left it.

"You certainly ought to know that young fellow I was speaking of," Mr. Hoad began. "I was struck with him at once. A wonderful gift of expressing himself, and just that kind of way with him that always wins people—one can't explain it. Handsome, too, and full of enthusiasm."

"Enthusiasm don't always carry weight," objected father. "It's rather apt to fly too high."

"Bound to fly high when you have got to get over the heads of other folks," laughed Mr. Hoad.

Father looked annoyed. "I wasn't joking, I wasn't joking," said he. "If men want to go in for great work, they can't afford to take it lightly." And then he added with one of his quick looks, "But don't misunderstand me, Hoad. Enthusiasm of the right kind never takes things lightly. It's the only sort of stuff that wins great battles, because it has plenty of courage and don't know the meaning of failure. Only there's such lots of stuff that's called enthusiasm and is nothing but gas. I should like to see this young man and judge for myself. God forbid I should think youth a stumbling-block. Youth is the time for doing as well as for dreaming."

Father sighed, and though I could not tell why at the time, I can guess now that it was from the recollection of that friend of his who must have been the type of youthful enthusiasm thus to have left his memory and the strength of his convictions so many years in the heart of another.

"Well, you can see him easily enough," said Mr. Hoad. "He's staying in your village, I believe. He's a nephew of Squire Broderick's."

"What! Captain Forrester?" cried I.

"Ah, you know him of course, Miss Maliphant. Trust the young ladies for finding out the handsome men," said Mr. Hoad, turning to me with his most irritating expression of gallantry. I bit my lips with annoyance at having opened my mouth to the man, especially as he glanced across at Joyce with a horribly knowing look, at which of course she blushed, making me very angry.

"I fancy the squire and he don't get on so extra well together," said Mr. Hoad. "Squire don't like the look of the lad that'll step into his shoes, if he don't make haste and marry and have a son of his own, I suppose."

"I should think this smart captain had best not reckon too much on the property," said mother, stiffly, up in arms at once for her favorite. "The squire's young enough yet to marry and have a dozen sons."

"Yes, yes, ma'am, only joking, only joking," declared Mr. Hoad. "I shouldn't think the lad gave the property a thought."

"If he's the kind of man you say, he can't possibly care about property," said I, glibly, talking of what I could not understand. Father smiled, but smiled kindly, at me. Mr. Hoad laughed outright and made me furious.

"I see you're up in all the party phrases, young lady," said he.

"How did you come to know the young man, Hoad?" asked father, without giving me time to reply. "You seem to have become friends in a very short time."

"He came to me on a matter of business," repeated Hoad, evasively. "I fancy he's pretty hard up. Only got his captain's pay and a little private property, on his father's side, I suppose, and no doubt gives more than he can spare to these societies and things."

Father was silent. Probably he knew, what I had no notion of, that there was another branch to Mr. Hoad's profession besides that of a solicitor. Evidently he did not like to be reminded of the fact, for he knitted his brow and let his jaw fall, as he always did when annoyed.

"I don't know how we came to talk politics," Hoad went on, "but we did, and I thought to myself, 'Why, here's just the man for Maliphant.' I never knew any one else go as far as you do; but this young fellow—why, he nearly beat you, 'pon my soul he did!"

"Politics!" echoed father, frowning more unmistakably than ever; "what have they got to do with the matter?"

"Come, now, Maliphant, you're not going to keep that farce up forever," cried Mr. Hoad, in his most intimate and good-natured fashion. Oh, how I resented it when he would treat father as though he were on perfect equality with him! For my father's daughter I was intolerant; but then Mr. Hoad patronized, and patronizing was not necessary in order to be consistent.

"What do you mean?" asked father.

"It was all very well for you to swear you would have nothing to do with us before," continued Mr. Hoad. "You did not think we should ever get hold of a man who looked at things as you do. But now we have. And if you really have the Radical cause at heart, as you say, you will be able to get him in for the county. He has got everything in his favor—good name, good presence, good-breeding. Those are the men to run your notions; not your measly, workaday fellows—they have no influence with the masses."

Father rose from the table. His eyebrows nearly met in their overhanging shagginess, and his eyes were small and brilliant.

"I don't think I understand you, Hoad," said he. "We seem to be at cross-purposes. Do you mean to say that this young man wants to get into Parliament?"

"Oh, no plans, no plans whatever, I should say," said Hoad. "He merely asked me who was going to contest the Tory seat; and when I asked him if he was a Radical, he aired a few sentiments which, as I tell you, are quite in your line. But I should think we might easily persuade him—he seemed so very eager. If you would back our man, Maliphant, we should be safe whoever he was, I do believe," added the solicitor, emphatically. "He has a really wonderful influence with the working-classes, that husband of yours, ma'am," he finished up, turning to mother.

"Yes," said she, proudly; "Laban's a fine orator. When I heard him speak at the meeting the other day he fairly took my breath away, that he did."

Mother looked up at father with a pleased smile, for she loved to hear him praised, but for my own part I knew very well that he was in no mood for pleasant speeches.

"I have always told you, Hoad, that it's no part of my scheme to go in for politics," said he, in a low voice, but very decisively. "I see no reason to change my mind."

"Well, my dear fellow, but that's absurd," answered Mr. Hoad, still in that provokingly friendly fashion. "However do you expect to get what you want?"

"Not through Parliament, anyhow," said father, laconically. "I never heard of any Act of Parliament that gave bread to the poor out of the waste of the rich. I'll wait to support Parliament till I see one of the law-makers there lift up a finger to right the poor miserable children who swarm and starve in the London streets, and whose little faces grow mean and sharp with the learning to cheat those who cheat them of their daily bread."

I can see him now, his lip trembling, his eye bright, his hands clinched. It was the cry with which he ended every discourse; this tender pity for the many children who must needs hunger while others waste, who must needs learn sin while others are shielded from even knowing that there is such a thing; those innocent sinners, outcasts from good, patient because hopeless, yet often enough incurably happy even in the very centre of evil—they were always in his heart. It was his most cherished hope in some way to succor them, by some means to bring the horror of their helplessness home to the hearts of those who had happy children of their own.

I held my face down that no one should see my tears, and I knew that father took out his big colored pocket-handkerchief and blew his nose very hard. Mr. Hoad, however, was not so easily affected.

"Ah, you were right, Mrs. Maliphant," said he, in a loud, emphatic voice. "Your husband would make a very fine orator. All the more reason it's a sin and a shame he should hide his talents under a bushel. Now, don't you agree with me?"

"Oh, Laban knows best what he has got to do," answered mother. "I think it's a great pity for women to mix themselves up in these matters. They have plenty to do attending to the practical affairs of life."

Mr. Hoad burst into a loud fit of laughter. "Ah, you've got a clever wife, Maliphant," cried he. "She's put her finger upon the weak joint in your armor! Yes, that's it, my boy. They're fine sentiments, but they aren't practical; they won't wash. But you would soon see, when you really got into the thing, that the best way to make the first step towards what you want is not to ask for the whole lot at once. The thin edge of the wedge— that's the art. And I should be inclined to think this young fellow was not wanting in tact."

"Anyhow," answered father, quietly, "if Squire Broderick's nephew were minded to oppose the Tory candidate for this county, I should certainly not wish—as Squire Broderick's old friend—to support him in his venture."

"Ah, you're very scrupulous, Maliphant," laughed Mr. Hoad. But then, seeing his mistake, he added, quickly, "Quite right, perfectly right of course, and I don't suppose the young man has any intention of doing anything of the kind."

"No doubt it was rather that the wish was father to the thought in you, Hoad," answered father, frankly.

"Ah, well, you may be as obstinate as you like, Maliphant," said the solicitor, trying to take father's good-tempered effort as a cue for jocoseness, "but we can get on very well without you if the young ladies will only give us their kind support. I hope you won't be such an old curmudgeon as to forbid that; and I hope," added he, turning to Joyce with that sugary smile of his, "that the young ladies will not withdraw their patronage if, after all, a less handsome man than Captain Forrester should be our Radical candidate."

"Oh, thank you," said Joyce, blushing furiously, and looking up with distressed blue eyes; "indeed, we scarcely know Captain Forrester at all. We couldn't possibly be of any use to you."

"Of course not," cried I. "Whoever were the candidate we should not canvass. We never canvass. We are not politicians."

I wonder that nobody smiled, but nobody did. Father was too busy with his thoughts, and perhaps Mr. Hoad was too much astonished. But as though to cover my priggishness, Joyce said, sweetly, when Mr. Hoad rose to go: "You won't forget the concert, will you? And, please, will you tell Miss Bessie that I shall be very glad to do what I can to help her with her bazaar work?"

He promised to remember both messages, and shook hands with her in a kind of lingering way, which I remember was a manner he always had towards a pretty girl. I thought mother took leave of him a little shortly. Father alone accompanied him out into the hall, and saw him into the smart little gig that came round from the stable to pick him up. I went to the pantry for the tray to clear the tea-things. When I came back again into the parlor Joyce had gone up-stairs, and father and mother were alone. I do not know why it was, but as soon as I came in I felt sure that the discussion with Hoad, eager as it had been at the time, was not occupying father's mind. I felt sure that mother had alluded to that more important matter hotly spoken of after the squire's visit. She was standing by the fire, and father held her hand in his. He asked me to bring a lamp into his study, and went out. I glanced at mother.

"What does father want to go to work for so late?" said I. "Why don't he sit and smoke his pipe as usual?"

Mother did not answer; her back was turned towards me, but there was something in its expression which made me feel sure that she was crying.

"But he seems much better to-night, mother," I added, coming up behind her; "he was quite himself over that argument."

"Yes, dear, yes; he can always wake up over those things," answered she, and sure enough there was a tremble in her voice, and every trace of the dignity that she had used towards me since the scene at the dinner-table had entirely disappeared.

"Dear mother, why do you fret?" said I, softly. "I'm sure there's no need."

"No, no, of course there's no need," she repeated. "But, Margaret," added she, hurriedly, as though she were half ashamed of what she were saying, "if he could be brought to see that plan of the squire's in a better light, I'm sure it would be a good thing. I don't think his heart has ever been in farm-work, and I can't a-bear to see him working so hard now he is old. It would have been different, you see, if—if little John had lived."

I kissed her silently. The innocent slight to my own capacities, which had so occupied my mind an hour ago, passed unnoticed by me. And as father that night at family prayers rolled forth in his sonorous voice the beautiful language of the Psalms, the words, "He hath respect unto the lowly, but the proud he knoweth afar off," sank into my heart, and I thought that I should never again want to set myself up above my betters.

CHAPTER VIII

I lay awake quite half an hour that night, and I made up my mind—just as seriously as though my feelings were likely to prove an important influence—that I would in no way try to bias my father in his decision about taking a bailiff. But real as was my trouble about this matter that to me was so mighty, it was all put to flight the next morning by an occurrence of more personal and immediate interest. Such is the blessed elasticity of youth. The occurrence was one which not only brought the remembrance of Captain Forrester, and my romantic dreams for Joyce, once more vividly to my mind, but it also gave no small promise of enjoyment to myself. It consisted in the sudden appearance of a groom from the Manor, who delivered into my hands a note for mother.

It was morning when he came; mother was still in the kitchen with Deborah, and Joyce and I had not finished making our beds and dusting our room. But I do not think there was any delay in the answering of that door-bell. I remember how cross I was when mother would insist on finishing all her business before she opened the note; she went into the poultry-yard and decided what chickens and what ducks should be killed for the week's dinners, she went into the dairy to look at the cream, she even went up herself into the loft to get apples before she would go and find her spectacles in the parlor. And yet any one could have imagined that a note from the squire meant something very important. And so, indeed, it did. It contained a formal invitation to a grand ball to be given at the Manor-house. The card did not say a "grand" ball, but of course we knew that it would be a grand ball. We were fairly dazed with excitement. Actually a ball in our quiet little village. Such a thing had not been known since I had been grown up, and I had not even heard of its having occurred since the days when young Mrs. Broderick had come to the Manor as a bride. Of course we had been to dances in town once or twice—once to the Hoads', and once to a county ball, got up at the White Hart Inn, but I think these were really the only two occasions on which I had danced anywhere out of the dancing academy. Joyce, being a little older, could count about three more such exciting moments in her life. The card was passed round from hand to hand, and then stuck up on the mantle-shelf in front of the clock, as though there were any danger that any of the family would be likely to forget on what day and at what hour Squire Broderick had invited us to "dancing" at the Manor.

"I wonder what has made the squire give a ball now," said mother. "I suppose it's the prospect of the elections. He thinks he owes it to the county."

"Why on earth should he owe the county a ball because of the elections?" cried I. "He is not going to stand, and I don't think he can suppose that a ball would be likely to do the Farnham interests much good, if that's the only man they have got to put forward on the Conservative side."

"I don't think it's a young girl's business to talk in that flippant way, Margaret," said the mother. Father was not present just then. "I don't think it's becoming in young folk to talk about matters they can't possibly understand."

I was nettled at this, but I did not dare to answer mother back.

"You never heard your father talk like that of Mr. Farnham, I'm sure," added mother. "He likes him a great deal better than he does Mr. Thorne, although Mr. Thorne is a Radical."

"Well, I should think so! Mr. Thorne is a capitalist, and father doesn't think that men who have made such large fortunes in business ought to exist," cried I, boldly, applying a theory to an individual as I thought I had been taught. "It is no use his being a Radical, nor giving money to the poor, because he oughtn't to have the money. It's dreadful to think of his having bought a beautiful old place like the Priory with money that he has ground out of his workpeople. No, nobody will ever like Mr. Thorne in the neighborhood."

"I know squire and he don't hold together at all," answered mother. "Though they do say Mr. Thorne bought the property through that handsome young spark of a nephew of the squire's. The families were acquainted up North."

"Who told you that, mother?" asked I, quickly.

"Miss Farnham said so when she called yesterday," replied mother. "And she said it was Mr. Thorne was going to contest the seat with her brother, so I don't know how Mr. Hoad could have come suggesting that young captain to your father as he did yesterday. A rich man like the manufacturer would be sure to have much more chance."

I was silent. I was a little out of my depth. "I don't believe Mr. Hoad knew anything at all about it," I said. "How could a man be going to contest a seat against the candidate that his own uncle was backing? It's ridiculous. Mr. Hoad has always got something to say."

"Margaret, you really shouldn't allow yourself to pass so many opinions on folk," repeated mother. "First Mr. Farnham, and then Mr. Thorne, and now Mr. Hoad. It's not pretty in young women."

"Very well, mother, I won't do it again," said I, merrily. "At all events Parliament doesn't matter much, father says so; and anyhow, squire's going to give us a ball, and nothing can matter so much as that."

Nothing did matter half so much to us three just then, it is true. Mother was just as much excited as we were, and we all fell to discussing the fashions with just as much eagerness, if not as much knowledge, as if we had been London born and bred.

"You must look over your clothes and see you have got everything neat. Joyce, I suppose you will wear your white embroidered 'India'?" said the mother. And from that it was a very natural step to go and look at the white muslin, and at the other clothes that our simple wardrobes boasted, so that we spent every bit of that morning that was not taken up with urgent household duties in turning over frocks and laces and ribbons, and determining what we should wear, and what wanted washing before we did wear it. Yes, I think I thought of my dress that day for the first time in my life. There was no need to think of Joyce's, because she was sure to be admired, but if there was any chance of my looking well it could only be because of some happy thought with regard to my costume; and so when mother suggested that she should give me her lovely old sea-green shot silk to be made up for the occasion, my heart leaped for joy. I was very much excited. For Joyce, because I had quite made up my mind that it was Captain Forrester who had persuaded the squire to give this ball; and for myself, because it was really a great event in the life of any girl, and I was passionately fond of dancing. I spent the afternoon washing my old lace ruffles, and pulling them out tenderly before the fire, and all the time I was humming waltz tunes, and wondering who would dance with me, and picturing Joyce to myself whirling round in the arms of Captain Forrester. I thought of Joyce and her lover so much that it was scarcely a surprise to me when, just as the light was beginning to fade and tea-time was near, I heard a sharp ring at the front door, and running to the back passage window with my lace in my hand, I saw that Squire Broderick was standing in the porch, and with him his nephew Captain Forrester. I heard Joyce fly through the hall to the kitchen. I think she must have seen the two gentlemen pass down the road, and then she ran back again into the parlor, and Deborah went to the door.

"Mrs. Maliphant at home?" said the squire's cheery voice; and scarcely waiting for a reply, he strode through to the front room.

I threw down my lace, turned down my sleeves, and without any more attention to my toilet I ran down-stairs. Mother had gone to do some little errands in the village and had not come in; Joyce stood alone with the visitors. She had her plain dark-blue every-day gown on, but the soft little frills at her throat and wrists were clean. I remember thinking how fortunate it was that they were clean. She was standing in the window with Captain Forrester, who was admiring our view over the marsh.

"It's a most beautiful country," said he. And his eyes wandered from the plain without that the shades of evening were slowly darkening to the face at his side that shone so fair against the little frilled muslin curtain which she held aside with her hand.

The squire sat at the table; he had taken up the morning paper, and I supposed that the frown on his face was summoned there by something that he read in the columns of this the Liberal journal. Captain Forrester left Joyce and came towards me as soon as I entered the room.

"Miss Maliphant, I am delighted to meet you again," said he, with his pleasant polished manner that had the art of never making one feel that he was saying a thing merely to be agreeable. "After our little adventure of the other day, I felt that it was impossible for me to leave the neighborhood without trying to make our acquaintance fast."

"Oh, are you leaving the neighborhood?" said I—I am afraid a little too anxiously.

"Well, not just yet," smiled Captain Forrester. "I think I shall stay till over the ball."

"Nonsense, Frank," said the squire, rising and pushing the paper away from him. "Of course you will stay over the ball." Then turning to me, he said, merrily, "No difficulty about you young ladies coming, I hope?"

"I don't know, Mr. Broderick," answered I. "You must wait and ask mother. It's a very grand affair for two such simple girls as Joyce and me."

"Oh, Margaret, I think we shall be allowed to go," put in Joyce, in her gentle, matter-of-fact voice. "You know we went to a very late ball last Christmas in town."

Considering that we had been sitting over frocks all the morning, this would have been nonsense, excepting that Joyce never could see a joke.

"I think I shall have to take Mrs. Maliphant in hand myself if she makes any objection," said the squire, "for we certainly can't spare you and your sister."

Joyce blushed, and Captain Forrester turned to her and was going to say something which I think would have been complimentary, when father entered the room. He had his rough, brown, ill-cut suit on, and his blue handkerchief twisted twice round his neck and tied loosely in front, and did not look at all the same kind of man as the two in front of him. I noticed it for the first time that evening. I was not at all ashamed of it. If I had been questioned, I should have said that I was very proud of it, but I just noticed it, and I wondered if Captain Forrester noticed it too. It certainly was very odd that it never should have occurred to me before, that this lover whom I had picked out for Joyce belonged to the very same class as the squire, whom I thought so unsuitable to her. I suppose it was because Captain Forrester was not a landed proprietor, and that any man who belonged to the noble career of soldiering atoned for his birth by his profession.

"How are you, Maliphant?" said the squire, grasping him by the hand as though there had been no such thing as any uncomfortable parting between them. "I'm glad to see you are none the worse for this cursed east wind. It's enough to upset many a younger and stronger man."

Father had taken the proffered hand, but not very cordially. I am not sure that he ever shook hands very cordially with people; perhaps it was partly owing to the stiffness in his fingers, but I believe that he regarded it as a useless formality. I imagine this because I, too, have always had a dislike to kissings and hand-shakings, when a simple "good-day" seemed to me to serve the purpose well enough.

"Pooh!" said father, in answer to the squire's remark. "A man who has his work out-doors all the year round, Squire Broderick, needs must take little account whether the wind be in the east or the south, except as how it'll affect his crops and his flock."

The squire took no notice of this speech. It was so very evident that it was spoken with a view to the vexed question.

"I've brought my nephew round," said he, and Captain Forrester left Joyce's side as he said it, and came forward with his pleasant smile and just the proper amount of deference added to his usual charming manner. "He wanted to see the Grange," added the squire, again with that frown upon his brow that I could not understand, but which no doubt proceeded, as he had affirmed, from the effect of the east wind upon his temper.

"I'm very glad to see you, sir," said father, shortly. "I hear you rendered my daughters some assistance the other day."

Captain Forrester smiled. "It could scarcely be called assistance," he said. "Your daughter"—and he looked at me to distinguish me from Joyce—"would have been capable of driving the horse, I am sure."

"Oh, I understood the mare reared," answered father.

"Well, she is not a good horse for a lady to drive," allowed Captain Forrester, as though the confession were wrung from him; and I wondered how he guessed that it annoyed me to be thought incapable of managing the mare. "But some women drive as well as any man."

The squire took up the paper again. I did not think it was good-manners of him.

"What a splendid view you have from this house," continued Captain Forrester. "I think it's much finer than from our place."

The squire's shoulders moved with an impatient movement. The article he was reading must decidedly have annoyed him.

"Yes," answered Joyce; "but you should come and see it in summer or in autumn. It's very bleak now. The spring is so late this year."

"Ay; I don't remember a snowfall in March these five years," said father.

"But it has a beautiful effect on this plain," continued the young man, moving away into the window again. And then turning round to Joyce, he added, "Do you sketch, Miss Maliphant?"

"No, no," answered father for her. "We have no time for such things. We have all of us plenty to do without any accomplishments."

"Miss Margaret can sing 'Robin Adair,'" put in the squire, "as well as I want to hear it, accomplishments or not."

"Indeed," said Captain Forrester, with a show of interest. "I hope she will sing it to me some day."

He said it with a certain air of patronage, which I found afterwards came from his own excellent knowledge of music.

"Are you fond of singing?" said I, simply. I was too much of a country girl to think of denying the charge. I was very fond of good music; it was second nature to me, inherited, I suppose, from some forgotten ancestor, and picking out tunes on the old piano was the only thing that ever kept me willingly in-doors. Father delighted in my simple singing of simple ditties, and so did the squire; I had grown used to thinking it was a talent in me, my only one, and I was not ashamed of owning up to it. "I'll sing it to you now if you like."

"That's very kind of you," said the young man, with a little smile. And I sat down and sang the old tune through. I remember that, for the first time in my life, I was really nervous. Captain Forrester stood by the piano. He was very kind; I don't know that any one had ever said so much to me about my voice before, but in spite of it all I knew for the first time that I knew nothing. I felt angrily ashamed when Joyce, in reply to pressing questions about her musical capacity, answered that I had all the talent, and began telling of the village concerts that I was wont to get up for the poor people, and of how there was one next week, when he must go and hear me sing.

"Certainly I will," he answered, pleasantly, "and do anything I can to help you. I have had some practice at that kind of thing."

"Why don't you say you are a regular professional at it, Frank?" put in the squire, I fancied a little crossly. "He's always getting up village concerts—a regular godsend at that kind of thing."

Frank laughed, and said he hoped we would employ him after such a character, and then he asked what was our programme. Joyce told him. I was going to sing, and Miss Hoad was going to sing—and she sang beautifully, for she had learned in London—and then I would sing with the blacksmith, and Miss Thorne would play with the grocer on the cornet, and glees and comic songs would fill up the remainder. The smile upon Captain Forrester's face clouded just a little at the mention of Miss Thorne.

"Miss Thorne is not very proficient on the piano," said he. "Have you already asked her to perform?"

"Do you know Miss Thorne?" asked Joyce, surprised.

"Yes," answered the captain; "she lived in the village where I was brought up as a boy—not far from Manchester. Her father was a great manufacturer, you know."

"Yes; we know that well enough." And I glanced uneasily at father; for if he knew that this young fellow was a friend of the Thornes, I was afraid it would set him against him. Luckily, he was busy talking to the squire.

"She's a very nice girl," said Joyce, kindly, wanting to be agreeable, although indeed we knew no more of Mary Thorne than shaking hands with her coming out of church on a Sunday afternoon.

"Charming," acquiesced the captain; "but she's not a good musician, and I shouldn't ask her to perform unless you're obliged to."

We said we were not obliged to; but Joyce said she wouldn't like to do anything unkind, and she was afraid Mary Thorne wanted to be asked to perform. And then they two retired into the window again, discussing the concert and the view, and I soon saw proudly that they were talking as though they had known one another for years. It generally took a long while for any one to get through the first ice with Joyce, but this man had an easy way with him; he was so sympathetic in his personality—so kind and frank and natural.

"That's a most ridiculous article in the *Herald*," said the squire to father. "I wonder Blair can put in such stuff. He's a sensible man."

"I wonder you'll admit even that, squire," answered father, with a little laugh. The paper, I need not say, was the Liberal organ.

"Oh, well," smiled the other, "I can see the good in a man though I don't agree with him. But I think *that*"—pointing to the print—"is beneath contempt."

"I don't hold with it myself," answered father; "the man has got no pluck."

"Oh no, of course—doesn't go far enough for you, Maliphant," laughed the squire; and at that moment mother came in or I do not know what father would have answered. She came in slowly, and stood a moment in the doorway looking round upon us all. Joyce blushed scarlet, and came forward out of the recess. The squire rose and hastened towards her.

"We have been invading your house while you have been away, Mrs. Maliphant," said he. "That wasn't polite, was it? But you'll forgive me, I know."

Mother's eyes scarcely rested on him; they travelled past him to Captain Forrester, who stood in the window.

"My nephew, Frank Forrester," said the squire, hastily following her look. The captain advanced and bowed to mother. He could do nothing more, for she did not hold out her hand.

"I am very glad to see any friend of yours, squire," said she. And then she turned away from him, and unfastened her cloak, which I took from her and hung up in the hall.

"Joyce, lay the cloth," said she. "We'll have tea at once." I left the room with sister.

"Never mind," whispered I, outside, as we fetched the pretty white egg-shell cups that always came out when we had any company; "mother doesn't mean to be queer. She is just a little cold now, because she wants

Captain Forrester to understand it wasn't with her leave we let him drive us home. But she isn't really cross."

"Cross! Oh, Margaret, no—of course not," echoed Joyce. She was taking down a plate from under a pile of cups, and said no more at the moment. I was ashamed and half vexed. That was the worst of Joyce. Sometimes she would reprove one when one was actually fighting her battles.

"Of course we ought not to have done it," continued she, setting the cups in order on the tray. "I felt it at the time."

"Then, why in the world didn't you say so?" cried I.

"I didn't know how to say so; you scarcely gave me a chance," answered she. "Of course, I know you did it because I was so stupidly frightened, but it makes me rather uncomfortable now."

"Oh, I thought you seemed to get on very well with Captain Forrester, just now," said I, huffily, kneeling down to reach the cake on the bottom shelf. "You seemed quite civil to him, and you didn't look uncomfortable."

"Didn't I? I'm glad," answered Joyce, simply. "Of course one wants to be civil to the squire's friends in father's house. And I do think he is a very polite gentleman."

She took up the tray and moved on into the parlor, and I went across into the kitchen to fetch the urn. I had never been envious of Joyce's beauty up to the present time. Nothing had happened to make me so, and I was fully occupied in being proud of it. But if her beauty was of such little account to her that she had not even been pleased by this handsome man's admiration of it—well, I thought I could have made better use of it.

When I went into the parlor again the groups were all changed. Father stood by the fire and the squire had risen. Father had his hands crossed behind his back and his sarcastic expression on, and the squire was talking loudly. Joyce was laying the cloth, and mother stood by the window where sister had stood before; Captain Forrester was talking to her as if he had never cared to do anything else. I could not hear what they were saying, the squire's voice was too loud; but I could see that mother was quite civil.

"I never liked that man Hoad," the squire was saying, and I felt a throb of satisfaction as I heard him. "I don't believe he's straightforward. Do anything for money, that's my feeling."

"He's a friend of mine," said father, stiffly.

"Oh, well, of course, if he's a friend of yours, well and good," answered Mr. Broderick, shortly. "You probably know him better than I do. But I don't like him. I should never be able to trust him."

"Perhaps that is because you do not know him," suggested father.

"No doubt, no doubt," answered the squire.

"I hear he has turned Radical now," added he, coming to the real core of the grievance. "He used to call himself a Liberal, but now I hear he calls himself a Radical, and is going to put up some Radical candidate to oppose us."

"Yes, I know," answered father, too honest to deny the charge.

"Oh, do you know who it is?" asked the squire, sharply.

"No, I don't," answered father, in the same way.

The squire paused a moment, then he said, unable to keep it in, "Are you going to support him too?"

The color went out of father's face; I knew he was angry.

"Well, Mr. Broderick, I don't know what sort of a candidate it'll be," said he, in a provoking manner. "There's Radicals and Radicals."

The squire smacked his boot with his walking-stick and did not answer. Captain Forrester came forward, for mother had gone to the table to make the tea.

"Did I hear you say that you were a Radical, Mr. Maliphant?" asked the young man, looking at father.

"I am not a Tory," answered father, without looking up. I thought his tone was cruelly curt.

"Well, I am a Socialist," answered Frank Forrester, with an air that would have been defiant had it not been too pleasant-spoken. Father smiled. The words must have provoked that—would have provoked more if the speaker had not been so good-tempered.

"Ah, I know what you young fellows mean by a Socialist," he murmured.

"I should say I went about as far as most men in England," said Frank, looking at him in that open-eyed fixed way that he used towards men as well as towards women.

"I should say that you went farther than you can see," said the Squire, laconically.

Frank laughed, good-humoredly. "Ah, I refuse to quarrel with you, uncle," said he, taking hold of the squire's arm in a friendly fashion. It was said as though he would imply that he could quarrel with other people when he liked, but his look belied his words.

"If you will let me, I'll come in and have a chat one of these days, Mr. Maliphant," continued he. "When uncle is not by, you know." He said the words as though he felt sure that his request would be granted, and yet with his confidence there was a graceful deference to the elder man which was very fascinating. Why did father look at him as he did? Did he feel something that I felt? And what was it that I felt? I do not know.

"I am a busy man and haven't much time for talk, sir, but you're welcome when you like to call," answered father, civilly, not warmly.

The squire had sat down again while his nephew and father were exchanging these few words. He crossed one knee over the other and sat there striking his foot with his hand—a provoking habit that he had when he was trying to control his temper.

"There'll be a nice pair of you," said he, trying to turn the matter off into a joke. "It's a pity, Frank, that you have no vote to help Mr. Maliphant's candidate with."

"I don't know that any so-called Radical candidate would or could do much in Parliament to help the questions that I have at heart," said Captain Forrester. "As Mr. Maliphant justly observed, there are Radicals and Radicals, and the political Radical has very little in common with those who consider merely social problems."

Father did look up now, and his eyes shone as I had seen them shine when he was talking to the working-men, for though I had not often heard him—the chief of his discourses being given in the village club—I had once been to a large meeting in town where he had been the chief speaker.

"One never knows where to have any of you fellows," laughed the squire, rather uncomfortably. "You always led me to believe, Maliphant, that you would have nothing to do with political party spirit. You always said that no party yet invented would advance the interests of the people in a genuine fashion, and now, as soon as a Radical candidate appears, you talk of supporting him."

"I am not aware that I talked of supporting him," said father.

"But you won't return a Radical," continued the squire, not hearing the remark. "The country isn't ripe for that sort of thing yet, whatever you may think it will be. You're very influential, I know. And if you're not with us, as I once hoped you might be, you'll be a big weight against us. But with all your influence you won't return a Radical. The Tories are too strong; they're much stronger than they were last election, and then Sethurst was an old-fashioned Liberal and a well-known man in the county besides. You won't return a Radical. I don't believe there's a county in England would return what you would call a Radical, and certainly not ours."

"I don't believe there is," said father, quietly.

"Then why do you want to support this candidate?"

"I don't," answered father. "I'm a man of my word, Squire Broderick. I told you long ago I'd have nothing to do with politics, and no more I will. If I am to be of any use, I must do it in another way—I must work from another level. The county may return what it likes for all I shall trouble about it."

"Well, 'pon my soul," began the squire, but at that moment mother's voice came from the tea-table. She saw that a hot argument was imminent, and she never could abide an argument. I think that father, too, must have been disinclined for one, for when she said, "Father, your tea is poured out," he took the hint at once. The squire looked disappointed for a moment, but I think he was so glad that father's influence was not going to take political shape against his candidate that he forgave all else.

Mother was just making Captain Forrester welcome beside her as the newest guest, when Deborah opened the door and ushered in Mr. Hoad. I had quite forgotten that father had invited him. He stood a moment as it were appraising the company. His eyes rested for less than an instant on Squire Broderick, on Captain Forrester, and then shifted immediately to mother.

"Oh, I am afraid that I intrude, Mrs. Maliphant," said he.

"Not at all, not at all, Hoad," declared father. "Come in; we expected you."

Mother rose and offered him her hand. Then Captain Forrester, who had been looking at him, came forward and offered his too in his most genial manner. It was not till long afterwards that I found out that he made a special point of always being most genial to those people whom he considered ever so little beneath him.

"Oh, how are you, Hoad?" said he. "I thought I recognized you, but I wasn't quite sure. I didn't expect to meet you here."

"No; nor I you!" exclaimed Hoad, gliding with ready adaptability into the position offered him—a quality which I think was perhaps his chief characteristic. "Delighted to see you."

Forrester gave up his place next mother, and sat down beside Joyce. The squire just nodded to Mr. Hoad, and then the conversation became general till the squire and his nephew left, very shortly afterwards.

CHAPTER IX

Three weeks had passed since the day when Captain Forrester drove us out from town. Winter was gliding slowly into spring. The winds were still cold and piercing, and the bright sun and keen air sadly treacherous to sensitive folk, but the snow had all melted and the grass sprung green upon the marsh, throwing the blue of the sea beyond into sharp contrast; the cattle came out once more to feed; yellow-hammers and butcher-birds began to appear on the meadows; and over earth and sea, soft gray clouds broke into strange shapes upon the blue.

I remember all this now; then I was only conscious of one thing—that, in spite of the east wind, I was happy.

Father was well again; he rode over the farm on his cob just as he used to do, and mother had forgotten the very name of a poultice. Joyce and the captain showed every sign of playing in the romance that I had planned for them; no one had mentioned the subject of a bailiff for Knellestone from that day to this; and the squire's ball was close at hand.

How was it possible that I should be otherwise than happy?

It was the very night before the dance. Jessie Hoad, who had consented to sing for our village concert, had been over and we had been having a practice under Captain Forrester's directions. She was a fashionably dressed, fashionably mannered, fashionably minded young woman, and quite content with herself; she generally resented directions, but she had submitted with a pretty good grace to his.

Miss Thorne had also been in. Joyce in this had shown one of those strange instances of obstinacy that were in her. Mary Thorne had asked to come, and she should not be refused. I remember noticing that Captain Forrester and that particularly gay-tempered young lady seemed to be very intimate together; just, in fact, as people who had known one another from childhood would be. They took the liberty of telling one another home-truths—at least Mary Thorne did (I fancied Frank responded less promptly), and did it in a blunt fashion that was peculiar to her. But I liked blunt people. I liked Mary Thorne very much.

Although she was an heiress to money that had been "sucked from the blood of the people"—to money made from a factory where girls and little children worked long hours out of the sunlight and the fresh air—although she lived in a great house that overlooked acres of land that belonged to her—and although my father could scarcely be got to speak to hers—I liked Mary Thorne. She was so frank and jolly, and took it so as a matter-of-course that we were to be friends, that I always forgot that she rode in a carriage when I walked, and that she and I ought, by rights, not to be so much at ease.

That day she was particularly jolly, and she and I and Captain Forrester laughed together till I was quite ashamed to see that I had left Joyce all the entertaining of Miss Hoad to do in the mean time. For the captain had not paid so much attention to Joyce on that day as on most others; I suppose he thought it was more discreet not to do so before strangers.

Both our lady visitors had left, however, by half-past five o'clock, and Captain Forrester stood on the garden terrace now with Joyce alone, while I had returned to the darning of the family socks. It was close upon sunset, and they were looking at the lilacs that were beginning to swell in the bud. Joyce wore a lilac gown herself, I remember. The captain had once admired it, and I had noticed that she had put it on very often since then.

I watched them from the parlor window where I sat with my work. For the first time I was half frightened at what I had done. I wondered what this romance was like that I had woven for Joyce. I felt that she was gliding away out of my ken, into an unknown world where I had driven her, and where I could not now follow her. Was it all happiness in that world?

Although the light was fading, and I wanted it all for my work, I moved away from the window-seat farther into the room. It seemed indelicate to watch them; although, indeed, they were only standing there side by side quietly, and what they were saying to one another I could not have heard if I had wished to do so. But it was my doing that they were alone at all. Joyce had stockings to darn too, but I had suggested that the parlor posy wanted freshening, and that there were some primroses out on the cliff.

Mother was out; she had gone to assist at the arrival of a new member of the population, and such an event always interested her so profoundly that she forgot other things for the moment. Such an opportunity might not occur again for a long time, and I was not going to miss it—otherwise those two had not been alone together before. At least not to my knowledge.

Once Joyce had gone out into the village marketing by herself, and when she had come home she had run straight up into her room instead of coming into the parlor. I had gone up to her after a little while, as she did not come down, and had found her sitting by the window with her things still on, looking out to the sea with a half-troubled expression on her face. I had asked her what was the matter, and she had smiled and said, "Nothing at all," and I had believed her.

However, even in the most open way in the world, Captain Forrester had managed to get pretty well acquainted with Joyce by this time, for he had come to the Grange almost every day since the squire had brought him to pay that first call. He came on the plea of interest in father's views; and though mother, I could see, had taken a dislike to him, simply because he was a rival to the squire, and took every opportunity of saying disparaging things about him to us girls when he was not present, even she felt the influence of the friendly manner that insisted on everything being pleasant and friendly in return, and did not seem somehow to be able to deny him the freedom which he claimed so naturally, of coming to the house whenever the fancy seized him. Certainly it would have been very difficult to turn Captain Forrester out.

Although it was evident enough to every one but father, in his dreamy self-absorption, that the young man came to see my beautiful sister, and was quickly falling hopelessly in love with her, still he was far too courteous to neglect others for her—he was always doing something for mother, procuring her something that she wanted, or in some way helping her; and as for me, he not only took all the burden of the village concert off my shoulders, the musical part of which always fell to my lot, but he also taught me how to sing my songs as I had no idea of how to sing them before, and took so much interest in my voice and in my performance that he really made me quite ambitious for the time as to what I might possibly do. And however much mother might have wished to turn the captain out, there were difficulties attending this course of action.

In the first place, he was the squire's nephew, and she could not very well be rude to the squire's nephew, however much she may have fancied that the squire would, in his heart, condone it; and then father had taken such an unusually strong fancy to the young man, that it would have been more than mother had ever been known to do to gainsay it. This friendship between an old and a young man was really a remarkable thing.

Father was not at all given to marked preferences for people; he was a reserved man, and his own society was generally sufficient for him. Even in the class whose interests he had so dearly at heart—his own class he would have called it, although in force and culture he was very far above the typical representatives of it—he was a god to the many, rather than a friend to the individual. And apart from his friendship with the squire, which was a friendship rather of custom than of choice, I do not remember his having a single intimate acquaintance. For I do not choose to consider that Hoad ever really was a friend in any sense of the word.

I have always fancied that father's capacity for friendship was swallowed up in that one romantic episode of his youth, that stood side by side with his love for our mother, and was not less beautiful though so different.

At first I think Forrester's aristocratic appearance, his knowledge of hunting and horse-flesh, and music and dancing, and all the pleasures of the rich and idle, his polished manners, and even his good coat, rather stood in his light in the eyes of the "working-man;" but it was only at first. Forrester's genuine enthusiasm for the interests that he affected, and his admiring deference for the mind that had thought the problem out, were enough to win the friendship of any man; for I suppose even at father's age one is not impervious to this refined sort of flattery.

Those were happy days in the dear old home, when we were all together, and none but the most trivial cloud of trouble or doubt had come to mar the harmony of our life.

I never remember father merrier than he was at that time. He and Frank would sit there smoking their pipes, and laughing and talking as it does one's heart good to remember. There was never any quarrelling over these discussions, as there used to be over the arguments with the squire. Not that the young man always agreed at once about things. He required to be convinced, but then he always was convinced in the end. And his wild schemes for the development of the people and the prevention of crime, and the alleviation of distress, all sounded so practical and pleasant, as set forth in his pleasant, brilliant language, full of fire and enthusiasm, and not at all like the same theories that father had been wont to quarrel over with the squire in his sullen, serious fashion.

Everything that the captain proposed was to be won from the top, by discussions and meetings among the great of the land. He could shake hands on terms of equality with the poorest laborer over his pot of beer, but it was not from the laborer that the reform would ever be obtained; and he quite refused to see the matter in the sombre light in which father held it, who believed in no reform—if reform there could be—that did not come from the class that needed it, and that should come without bitter struggles and patient, dogged perseverance. And in the end he convinced—or seemed to convince—Frank that this was so.

I noticed how, imperceptibly, under the influence of father's earnest, powerful nature, the young man slowly became more earnest and more serious too. He talked less and he listened more; and truly there was no lack of food.

The great subjects under discussion were the nationalization of land and the formation of trade corporations for the protection of the artisan class. These corporations were to be formed as far as possible on the model of the old guilds of the Middle Ages; they were to have compulsory provident funds for widows, orphans, and disabled workmen; they were to prevent labor on Sundays, and the employment of children and married women in factories; they were to determine the hours of labor and the rate of wages, and to inquire into the sanitary condition of workplaces.

There were many other principles belonging to them besides these that I have quoted, but I cannot remember any more, though I remember clearly how father and Frank disagreed upon the question of whether the corporations were to enjoy a monopoly or not. I suppose they agreed finally upon the point, for I know that Frank undertook to air the matter at public meetings in London, and seemed to be quite sure that he would be able to start a trial society before long. I recollect how absolutely he refused to be damped by father's less sanguine mood; and best of all, I remember the smile that he brought to father's face, and the light that he called back to his drooping eye.

There was only one blot: the squire did not come to see us. No doubt I should not have allowed at this time that it was any blot, and when mother remarked upon it, I held my tongue; but I know very well that I was sorry the squire kept away.

On this evening of which I am thinking, however, the squire did not keep away. I am afraid I had hurried a little over the darning of father's socks, that I might get to the making up of my own lace ruffles for the great event of the next night, and as I was sitting there in the window, making the most of the fading daylight, he came in. I heard him ask Deborah for father in the hall, and when she answered that she thought he was still out, he said he would wait, and walked on into the parlor. He was free to come and go in our house. I fancied that he started a little when he saw me there alone; I suppose he expected to find the whole party as usual.

"Oh, how are you?" said he, abruptly, holding out his hand without looking at me. "Is your mother out?"

I explained that mother had gone to the village to see a neighbor.

"I'll just wait a few minutes for your father," said he. "I want particularly to see him to-night."

"Is it about that young man?" asked I.

I do not know what possessed me to ask it. It was not becoming behavior on my part, but at his words the recollection of that Mr. Trayton Harrod, whom he had recommended to father as a bailiff, had suddenly returned to me. No mention having been made of him again, I had really scarcely remembered the matter till now, the excitement of the past three weeks had been so great.

He knit his brows in annoyance, and I was sorry I had spoken.

"What young man?" asked he.

"That gentleman whom you recommended to father for the farm," said I, half ashamed of myself.

"Oh, Trayton Harrod!" exclaimed the squire, with a relieved expression. "Oh no, no, I shall not trouble your father again about that unless he speaks to me. I thought it might be an advantageous thing, for I have known the young man since he was a lad, and he has been well brought up—a clever fellow all round. But your father knows his own business best. It might not work."

It was on my lips to say that of course it would not work, but I restrained myself, and the squire went on:

"I'm so delighted to see your father himself again," he said. "There's no need for any one to help him so long as he can do it all himself; and of course you, I know, do a great deal for him," added he, as though struck by an after-thought. "I saw you walking round the mill farm this morning."

"Did you?" answered I. "I only went up about the flour. I didn't see you."

"No," he said. "I was riding the other way."

He walked up to the window as he spoke, and looked out over the lawn.

Somehow I was glad that I had just seen Joyce and Captain Forrester go down the cliff out of sight a few minutes before the squire arrived.

"Everybody out?" asked he.

"Yes," answered I. "Everybody."

He did not ask whether his nephew had been there. He drew a chair up to the table and began playing with the reels and tapes in my work-basket. Mother and Joyce would have been in an agony at seeing their sacred precincts invaded by the cruel hand of man, but it rather amused me to see the hopeless mess into which he was getting the hooks and silks and needles. My basket never was a miracle of orderliness at any time.

"Is Miss Joyce quite well?" said he at last, trying to get the scissors free of a train of cotton in which he had entangled them.

I felt almost inclined to laugh. Even to me, who am awkward enough, this seemed such an awkward way of introducing the subject, for of course I had guessed that he had missed her directly he had come into the room.

"Yes, quite well, thank you," answered I. And then I added, laughing, and seeing that he had got hold of a bit of my lace, "Oh, take care, please, that's a bit of my finery for to-morrow night."

He dropped it as if it had burned him. "Oh dear, dear, yes, how clumsy I am!" cried he, pushing the work-basket far from him. "I hope I have spoiled nothing."

"Why, no, of course not," laughed I. "I oughtn't to have spoken. But you see I have only got that one bit of lace, and I want it for to-morrow night."

"Oh yes; I suppose you young ladies are going to be very grand indeed," smiled he.

"Oh no, not grand," insisted I, "but very jolly. We mean to enjoy ourselves, I can tell you."

"That's right," said he; "so do I."

But he could not get away from the subject of Joyce.

"Has your sister gone far?" asked he, in a minute.

"I don't know," I answered, quite determined to throw no light upon the subject of where she was and with whom.

A direct question made it difficult now to keep to this determination.

"Do you know if my nephew has been here this afternoon?" was the question.

I looked down intently at my work.

"Yes, he came," answered I. "He sat some while with father, till father went out."

I did not add any mention of where he had been since. It was a prevarication of course, but I thought I did it out of a desire to spare the squire's feelings. He asked no more questions. He sat silent for a while.

"Your father and Frank seem to be great friends," observed he, presently, and I fancied a little bitterly.

"Yes," I replied, "Captain Forrester has quite picked father's spirits up. He has been a different man since he had him to sympathize with over his pet schemes."

I felt directly I had said the words that they were inconsiderate words, and I regretted them, but I could not take them back.

Squire Broderick flushed over his fair, white brow.

"Yes; my nephew professes to be as keen after all these democratic dodges as your father himself," he said, curtly.

"Oh, it's not that," cried I, anxious to mend matters. "Father doesn't need to have everybody agree with him for him to be friends with them."

"No, I quite understand," answered the squire, beginning again on the unlucky basket. And after a pause he added, as though with an effort, "Frank is a very delightful companion, I know, and when he brings his enthusiasm to bear upon subjects that are after one's own heart, it is naturally very pleasant."

"Yes," I agreed. "That's just it, he is so very enthusiastic. He would make such a splendid speaker, such a splendid leader of some great Democratic movement."

The squire left my work-basket in the muddle in which he had finally put it, and stuck his hands into his pockets.

"Do you think so?" he said.

"Oh yes, I'm sure of it," continued I, blindly. "And I am sure father thinks so too."

"Indeed!" answered the squire, I thought a little scornfully. "And, pray, how is my nephew going to be a great Democratic leader? Is he going into Parliament? Is he going to contest the county at the next election?"

"Why, how can you think he would do such a thing, Mr. Broderick," exclaimed I, "when he knows that you are supporting the opposite side?"

"Oh, that would be no objection," said the squire, still in the same tone of voice. "The objection would be that a Radical stands such a small chance of getting in."

"Besides," added I, collecting myself, "I am sure he has no wish to go into Parliament. Father and he both agree that a man can do a great deal more good out of Parliament than in it. They say that the finest leaders that there have been in all nations have been those who have got at the people straight—without any humbug between them."

"Pooh!" said the squire. Then controlling himself, he added, "Well, and does Frank think that he is going to get at the people that way? Does he suppose it will cost him nothing?"

"Oh no; I suppose it will cost money," assented I.

"Ah!" said the squire, in the tone of a man who has got to the bottom of the question at last. "Well, then, I think it's only fair that your father should know that there is very little chance of Frank's being of any use to him. If he is pinning his faith on Frank as a possible representative of his convictions, he is making a mistake, and it is only right that he should be warned. Frank has no money of his own, no money at all. He has nothing but his captain's pay, and that isn't enough for him to keep himself upon."

The squire spoke bitterly. Even I, girl as I was, could see that something had annoyed him to the point of making him lose control over himself.

"I don't think father has pinned his faith on Captain Forrester," said I, half vexed. "I don't think there has been any question between them such as you fancy. I think they are merely fond of discussing matters upon which they agree. At all events, I am sure it has never entered father's head to consider whether Captain Forrester had money or not."

"Well, I think, for several reasons, it is just as well there should be no mistake about the thing," repeated the squire, vehemently, walking up and down the room in his excitement. "Frank has no money and no prospects, excepting those which he may make for himself. I sincerely hope that he may do something better than marry an heiress, which is his mother's aim for him, but meanwhile he certainly has very little property excepting his debts."

A light suddenly broke upon me. The words "marry an heiress," had suddenly flashed a meaning on Squire Broderick's strange attitude. He was afraid that Captain Forrester was winning Joyce's affections. He was jealous. I would not have believed it of him; but perhaps, of course, it was natural. I was sorry for him. The remembrance of the sad bereavements of his youth made me sorry for him.

After all, though I did not then consider him a young man, it was sad to have done with life so early, to have no chance of another little heir to the acres that he owned, instead of that poor little baby of whom mother had told us. For, of course, there was no chance of that, and Captain Forrester would finally inherit them. I had not thought of that before. No wonder he was bitter, and I was sorry for him. He spoke no more after that last speech. He came and stood over me where I was working.

"But after all," said he, presently, in his natural genial tones, "I don't know why I troubled you with all that. You are scarcely the person whom it should interest. I beg your pardon."

I did not know what to say, so I said nothing.

Margaret Maliphant | 69

The squire moved to the window, and I put down my work and followed him. The daylight had gone; there was no more sewing to be done that evening without a lamp. As I came up I saw the tall, slight figure of Captain Forrester standing up against the dim blue of the twilight sky, and holding out his hand to help my sister up the last, steepest bit of the ascent to our lawn. I glanced at the squire. His face was not sad nor sorry, but it was angry. He turned away from the window, and so did I, and as we faced round we saw mother standing in the door-way. She had her bonnet and cloak still on; she must have come in quietly by the back door, as she had a habit of doing, while we were talking. How much had she heard of what the squire had said?

He went up to her and bade her good-day and good-bye in one breath. He said he would not wait longer to see father. He went out and away without meeting his nephew. I was very glad that he did, for thus mother went up-stairs at once to take off her things, and being in a garrulous frame of mind, from her experiences of the afternoon with the new-born baby, she stayed up-stairs some time talking to Deborah, and did not come down to the parlor again till after Captain Forrester had taken his leave. So she never knew anything of that long half-hour spent upon the garden cliff at the sun-setting.

CHAPTER X

I think I saw the dawn that day on which the ball was to be. Whether I did or not, the morning was still very gray and cold when I crept out of my bed and stole to the wardrobe to look at our two dresses. There they hung, carefully displayed upon shifting pegs such as were used in old-fashioned presses: one soft white muslin; the other of that pale apple-green shot silk which had belonged to mother in the days of her youth, and which I had been allowed to make up for the occasion. We had worked at them for days.

Joyce was clever at dress-making: she was clever at all things that needed deftness of fingers. She had fitted me with my frock, and we had both worked together. But now the dresses were finished, the last ruffle had been tacked in; there was nothing more to do, and the day wore away very slowly till evening.

At last the hour came when it was time to dress, and such a washing of faces and brushing of hair as went on in that little attic chamber for half an hour no one would believe.

Joyce insisted on "finishing" me first. She coiled up my hair at the back of my head, brushing it as neatly as she could, and laying it in two thick bands on either side of my temples. It never will look very neat, it is such vigorous unruly hair, this red hair of mine, and to this day always has tendrils escaping here and there over forehead and neck. But she did her best for it, and I was pleased with myself. I was still more pleased with myself when I got on the green shot silk with the lace ruffles. Joyce said she was surprised to see what a change it made in me. So was I.

My skin was very pink and white wherever it was not spoiled by freckles, and the green of the frock seemed to show it up and make the red lips look redder than ever. It is true that my neck and arms were frail still with the frailness of youth, but then my figure was slim too, and my eyes were black with excitement, and shone till they were twice their usual size. I thought, as I looked in the glass, that I was not so very plain. Yes, I was right when I had begged the shot silk. Joyce could wear anything, but I, who was no "fine bird" by nature, needed the "fine feathers."

I was pleased with myself, and I smiled with satisfaction when Joyce declared again that she was quite surprised to see what a good appearance I had. "If you would only keep yourself tidy, Margaret, you have no idea how much better you would look," said she.

It was what Deborah was always saying, but I did not resent it from Joyce—she was gentle in her way of saying it; and I remember that I promised I would brush my hair smooth in future, and wear my collars more daintily. I do not believe that I kept to my resolution, but that evening I was not at all the Margaret of every-day life as I surveyed myself in the glass.

"But come," said I, hurriedly—half ashamed of myself, I do believe—"we shall be late if we don't make haste. Do get on, Joyce."

Joyce began brushing out her long golden hair—real gold hair, not faint flaxen—and coiled the smooth, shining bands of it round her little head. It was a little head, such as I have seen in the pictures of the Virgins painted by Italian painters of long ago.

"I sha'n't be long," said she.

I sat down and watched her. She would not have let me help her if I had wanted to do so. She would have said that I should only disarrange myself, and that I should be of no use. Certainly nothing was wanted but what she did for herself, and she did it quickly enough. When she stood up before the mirror—tipped back to show the most of her person, for we had no pier-glasses at the Grange—I do not believe that any one could have found a thing to improve in her. Her figure looked taller and slenderer than ever in the long white dress, and the soft little folds of the muslin clung tenderly around her delicate shape, just leaving bare her neck and arms, that were firm and white as alabaster. Her face was flushed as a May rose; her lips were parted in her anxiety to hasten, and showed the little even white teeth within. Her blue eyes were clear and soft under the black lashes.

She moved before the glass to see that her dress was not too long, and bent back her slender throat, upon which she had just clasped mother's delicate little old-fashioned gold necklace with the drops of yellow beryl-stone. It was the only bit of good jewellery in the family, and Joyce always wore it, it became her so well.

"Come now, Meg," said she, "I am quite ready. Let's go and see if we can do anything to help mother."

We went down-stairs. Deborah was there in mother's room waiting to survey us all. She had just fastened mother's dove-colored satin gown that had served her for every party she had been at since she was married.

Mother had just the same shaped cap on that she always wore; she never would alter it for any fashion, but that night the frill of it was made of beautiful old lace that she kept in blue paper and lavender all the rest of the year. I thought she looked splendid, but Joyce was not so easily pleased.

"Dear mother, you really must have another gown before you go anywhere again," said she, shaking out the skirt with a dissatisfied air. "This satin has lost all its stiffness."

Mother looked at it a little anxiously herself, I remember, when Joyce said this. We considered Joyce a judge of dress and the fashions, and of course the squire's ball was a great occasion. But she said she thought it did very well for an old lady, and indeed so did I, although that may perhaps have been because I was very anxious to be off.

Dear mother! I do not think she gave much thought to herself; she was taken up with pride in us. Yes, I do believe that night she was proud even of me.

She smiled when Deborah, with her hand on the door-knob, said, patronizingly, that although she did not hold with bare arms and necks for modest females, she never would have thought that I should have "dressed up" so well. Mother bade her begone, but I think she was pleased.

"Dear me!" said she, looking at me. "I recollect buying that silk. It must have been in '52, when father took me up to town to see the Exhibition. It was cheap for the good silk it is. It has made up very well."

She turned me all round. Then she went to her jewel-case, unlocked it, and took out a row of red coral beads.

"That's what you want with that dress," said she, fastening them round my throat. "And you shall have them for your own. Red-haired women ought to wear coral, folk say. Though for my part, I always thought it was putting on too many colors."

How well I remember my pleasure at that gift! Joyce wanted to persuade me not to wear them; she said the pale green of the frock was prettier without the red beads. But I wouldn't listen to her; I was too pleased with them, and I do not believe that it was entirely owing to gratified vanity; I think a little of it was pleasure that mother thought my appearance worth caring for.

I should not have thought it worth caring for myself two days ago, and I should not have cared whether mother did or not. But something had happened to me. Was it the sight of Joyce and her lover that had made me think of myself as a woman? I cannot tell. All I know is that when we walked into the squire's ball-room a quarter of an hour afterwards, I felt my face flame as I saw his gaze rest upon me for a moment, and I longed most heartily to be back again in my high-necked homespun frock, with no corals round my throat at all. So inconsistent are we at nineteen!

Fortunately my awakening self-consciousness was soon put to flight by other more engrossing emotions. There was a fair sprinkling of people already when we got into the room, and more were arriving every moment. Mr. Farnham and the maiden sister with whom he lived were going busily about welcoming the squire's guests almost as though they were the host and hostess themselves: he was the Conservative member. A quiet, inoffensive old gentleman himself, who would have been nothing and nobody without the squire; but blessed with a most officious lady for relative, who took the whole neighborhood under her wing.

She rather annoyed me by the way she had of trading on the squire's support of her brother. He supported her brother because he was a Conservative, not at all because he was Mr. Farnham, or even Miss Farnham's brother.

Poor Mr. Broderick, I dare say, if the truth had been known, he must often heartily have longed to get rid of them. But the old thing was a good soul in her way, if it *was* a dictatorial, loud-voiced way, and was very active among the poor, although it was not always in the manner which they liked.

She and mother invariably quarrelled over the advantages of soup-kitchens and clothing clubs; for mother was every bit as obstinate as Miss Farnham, and being an old-fashioned woman, liked to do her charity in a more personal fashion.

I looked with mingled awe and amusement upon their meeting to-night. Miss Farnham had an aggressive sort of head-dress, with nodding artificial flowers that seemed to look down scornfully upon mother's old lace and soft frills. She had not seen me for some time, and when mother introduced me as her youngest daughter, she took my hand firmly in hers, and held it a while in her uncompromising grip while she looked at me through and through.

"Well, I never saw such a thing in my life!" exclaimed she presently, in a loud voice that attracted every one's attention.

I blushed. I was not given to blushing, but it was enough to make any one blush. I thought, of course, that she was alluding to my attire, in which I had felt so shy and awkward from the moment that I had entered the ball-room, from the moment that I had felt the squire's glance rest upon my neck and arms.

She dropped my hand.

"The very image of him," said she, turning to my mother.

"Yes, she is very like her father," agreed the mother.

"Why, my dear, the very image of him," repeated the aggravating creature. "Got his temper too?" asked she, turning to me again.

"I don't know, ma'am, I'm sure," answered I, half amused, but still more annoyed. "I dare say."

"Oh, I'll be bound you have, and proud of it too," declared she, shaking her head emphatically. "Girls are always proud to be like their fathers."

"I don't suppose it'll make any very particular difference who I'm like," said I. "Things will happen just the same, I expect."

Miss Farnham laughed and patted me boisterously on the back.

I do not think she was an ill-natured woman, although she certainly had the talent of making one feel very uncomfortable.

"Well, you're not so handsome as your sister," added she. "But I don't know that you hadn't better thank your stars for that."

With that she turned away from me and sat down beside mother, arranging her dress comfortably over her knees as though she meant to stay there the whole evening.

The people kept coming fast now. The squire stood at the door shaking hands as hard as he could. There was the old village doctor with his pretty granddaughter, and the young village doctor who had inherited the practice, and had just married a spry little wife in the hope of making it more important.

And then there was the widow of an officer, who lived in a solid brick house that stood at the corner of the village street, and had two sons in the ship business in town. And there was the mild-eyed clergyman with his delicate young wife, who had more than enough babies of her own, and was only too thankful to leave the babies of the parish to Miss Farnham or any one else who would mother them.

She was a sweet little woman, with a transparently white face and soft silky hair, and she wore her wedding-dress to-night, without the slightest regard to the fact that it was made in a somewhat elaborate fashion of six years back, and was not exactly suited to her figure at that particular moment. She sat down between mother and Miss Farnham, and must have been considerably cheered by that lady's remark to the effect that she looked as if she ought to be in her bed, and that if she did not retire to it she would most likely soon be in her grave.

I left mother and went up to greet Mary Thorne, who had just come in with her father. He was a great, strong, florid man, rather shaky about his *h's*, but very much the reverse of shaky in any other way; shrewd and keen as a sharp knife or an east wind.

I don't know that I ever spoke to him but this once in my life. Father had such an overpowering aversion to him that we were not allowed to keep even the daughter's acquaintance long after this, but he made that impression on me: that there was only one soft spot in him, and that for the motherless girl, who was the only person allowed to contradict him.

She contradicted him now.

The squire had gone up to receive them bluntly enough, even I could see; but the squire might be allowed to have an aversion to the man who was going in as a Radical to contest his Conservative's long-occupied seat, though indeed I believe his dislike to the manufacturer was quite as much, because he had bought up one of the old places in the neighborhood with money earned in business. I fancy the Thornes were only invited that night as old friends of Frank Forrester's, and I don't think Frank was thanked for the necessity.

"You must have had a rare job, Broderick, lighting this old place up," he was saying as I came up; "all this dark oak, so gloomy looking!"

"Oh, papa, how can you!" laughed his daughter. "Why, it's what everybody admires; it's the great sight of the whole neighborhood."

"Yes, yes; I know, my dear," answered Mr. Thorne; "you mean to say that we should like to live here ourselves. Well, yes, I should have bought the place if it had been in the market, but—"

"But you would have done it up," broke in the squire, bristling all over; "whereas there's been nothing new in the Manor since—"

He stopped.

I fancied that he was going to say, "Since I brought my bride home;" but he said, after a pause, "since my father died."

"Well, to be sure, I do like a bit of brightness and color," acknowledged Thorne, whose fine house, although in excellent taste, was decidedly ornate and splendid; "and it is more suited to festal occasions."

"There, papa, you know nothing about it," declared Mary, emphatically. "I declare I never saw the Manor look better. Those flags and garlands are beautiful."

"Oh, my nephew Frank did all that," answered the squire, carelessly; "he likes that sort of thing."

"Captain Forrester?" repeated the girl, with just a little smile on her frank, fresh face. "Well, it does him credit then. It isn't every one would take so much trouble."

"He likes taking trouble," said I. "Just look at the trouble that he has taken over our concert."

"He likes playing first-fiddle," laughed Miss Thorne, gayly, her rosy face—that was too rosy for prettiness, although not too rosy for the perfection of health—flushing rosier than ever as she said it; "I always tell him so."

I did not answer. Mr. Thorne and his daughter moved on, and I looked round the room in search of the captain. The place did look very beautiful, although I do not think that I should like now to see its severe proportions and splendid wood wainscoting disfigured by flags and garlands. We were dancing in what used long ago to be the monks' refectory. The house had been built on the site of a part of the monastic buildings belonging to the abbey, and this portion of the old edifice had been retained, while the remainder of the house was in Tudor style. I heard the squire explaining it to the new parson, who had lately come to the next parish. I had heard him explain it before, or I do not suppose that I should have known anything at all about it.

"I suppose you consider it shocking to be dancing in any part of the monastery?" I could hear him say, laughing; "but it isn't so bad as a friend of mine who gives balls in what used to be the chapel."

The parson was a young man, with a sallow, shaven face and very refined features; the expression of his mouth was gentle, almost tremulous, but his eyes were dark and penetrating.

"I'm not quite so prejudiced as that," he said, laughing also, "although I do wear the cloth."

"That's right," said the squire, heartily. "We have the remains of a thirteenth-century chapel of the purest period in the grounds, and we don't desecrate that even by a school-feast. You must come and see it in the day-time."

Father came up at that moment. He was dreadfully like a fish out of water, poor father, in this assembly, and looked it. The squire, in a hasty fashion, introduced him to the Rev. Cyril Morgan, and passed on to shake hands with a portly wine-merchant, who had lately retired from business in the neighboring town, and had taken one of the solid red-brick houses that were the remnants of our own town's affluence.

This gentleman introduced his wife, and she had to be introduced to the company, and the host's hands were full. Father moved away with the parson. He looked rather disgusted at first, but the young man looked at him with a smile upon his gentle mouth and in his dark eyes, and said, diffidently, "I have heard a great deal of you, Mr. Maliphant—the whole neighborhood rings with your name. I am proud to meet you."

Of course, I liked that young man at once, and as I went to sit down again beside the mother and Joyce, I was pleased to see across the room that father and the Rev. Cyril Morgan had entered upon a conversation. But, to tell the truth, I soon forgot him; I was too busy looking about me.

I could not help wondering where Captain Forrester could be, and I was quite angry with Joyce for being so dignified and seeming to care so little. She seemed to be quite engrossed with the Hoad girls, who sailed in, followed by their father, just late enough to be fashionable, and to secure a good effect for their smart new frocks.

I am afraid I was not gracious to the Hoads. I could not be so gracious as Joyce, who took all their patronizing over the concert in the utmost good faith. I turned away from them, and continued my search for Joyce's admirer. I disliked them, and I am afraid that I showed it.

But they passed on, Bella, who was the better-looking of the two, pursued by two town-bred youths asking for a place on her card; Jessie, the elder, talking with an old lady of title from the seaport town, who wished her to sing at a charity concert.

They seemed to be very much engrossed; nevertheless, when presently the band struck up the first waltz, they, as well as many other people in the room, turned round to look who was dancing it. They put up their long-handled eye-glasses and fairly stared; for, as soon as the music began, the squire had walked up to my sister and had asked her to open the ball with him.

Mother blushed with pleasure and triumph; her dear blue eyes positively shone. She did not say a word, but I know that if she had spoken she would have said that she was not surprised.

I was not surprised either, but I was very much annoyed, and I was not at all in a good temper with Captain Forrester when, two minutes afterwards, he appeared coming out of the conservatory with Mary Thorne upon his arm. What had he been about? No wonder that his face clouded when he saw that he was too late. But it was his own fault; I was not a bit sorry for him. Mary Thorne was laughing and looking up half-defiantly in his face. She looked as if she were saying one of those rough blunt things of which she was so fond; and she might well say one at this moment to Captain Forrester, although I scarcely supposed it could be on the topic on which he deserved it.

Could she possibly be chaffing him on having missed the first dance with my sister? No; for she had had no opportunity of noticing his devotion to her. She dropped his arm and nodded to him merrily, as much as to bid him leave her—as much as to say that she knew there might be better sport elsewhere. And after a word in reply to what she had said, he did leave her and came across to me.

There was a troubled, preoccupied look on his bright face, which was scarcely accounted for by the fact that he had missed a dance with Joyce. He greeted me and sat down beside me without even asking after father. We sat and watched Joyce float round in the strong grasp of the squire, but I do not think that we were either of us quite so pleased at the sight as was mother, upon whose face was joy unalloyed.

She was simply genuinely proud that the squire should have opened the ball with her daughter. I think she would have been proud of it had there been no deeper hopes at the bottom of her heart. But there were deeper hopes, and as I watched Joyce that night I remembered them.

In the excitement of watching the romance that I had fancied developing itself more quickly and more decisively than I had even hoped, I had at first quite forgotten my fears about the squire wanting to marry Joyce. They had not occurred to my mind at all until that afternoon two days ago, when he had talked so vehemently about Frank's position. But now, as I watched him with her, the notion which I had rather refused to entertain at all before took firmer shape.

I was afraid that the squire really did mean something by this very marked attention to his tenant's daughter. It must needs excite a great deal of comment even among those who knew our rather particular position in the village, and the unusual intimacy between two families of different social standing. Would he have courted that comment merely for the sake of gratifying his old friend? What if he should propose to Joyce—if he should ask our parents' consent to the marriage at once? Would Captain Forrester, the unknown stranger, have any chance beside the friend of years? Would the soldier, who had nothing but what he earned by his brave calling, have a chance against the man who could give her as fine a home as any in the county?

Not with mother; no, I felt not for an instant with mother. But with father?

I knew very well that father, whatever his respect for the man, would never see a marriage between the squire and his daughter with pleasure, and I even thought it likely that he would downright forbid it. But what would be his feelings with regard to the captain? Would they be any different because, belonging by birth to another class, he yet desired to work for the interest of the class that was ours? I could not tell.

I was roused from my dream by the voice of Captain Forrester at my side. He was asking me for a dance—this very next one. There was something in the tone of his voice that puzzled me—a harsh sound, as though something hurt him. Of course I gave him the dance. I was only too delighted.

My feet had begun to itch as soon as I had heard the music, and when I had seen Joyce sailing round, and no one had come to ask me, I had felt very lonely. We stood up, even before the squire had brought Joyce back to mother—we stood up, and with the first bars of the new waltz we set forth. I soon forgot all thought of Joyce, or any one else, in the pure joy of my own pleasure.

I did love dancing. I did not remember that it was Captain Forrester with whom I was dancing, I only knew that it was a man who held me firmly, and whose limbs moved with mine in an even and dreamy rhythm as we glided across something that scarcely seemed to be a floor, to the slow lilt of magic music. I was very fond of dancing. I suppose Captain Forrester guessed it, for he never paused once the whole dance through.

When we stopped, just pleasantly out of breath, as the last chords died slowly away, he said, with his eyes on my face in that way that I have described, "Why, Miss Maliphant, you are a heavenly dancer. Where did you learn it?"

"I had six lessons at the academy in the town," answered I, gravely; and I wondered why he burst out laughing, "but Joyce gets out of breath sooner than I do, although she had twelve lessons."

The laughter faded out of his face as I mentioned Joyce's name.

"I don't mean to say that Joyce doesn't dance beautifully," I added, hastily, "she dances better than I do, because she is so tall and slight, but she does get out of breath before the end of a waltz."

He did not make any remark upon this. He only said, "Shall we go back to your mother?"

We got up and walked across the room. Miss Thorne was talking to mother, and a clean-shaven, fresh-colored young officer was inscribing his name on Joyce's programme.

Captain Forrester just shook hands with Joyce, and then he came and sat down beside mother and began talking away to her in his most excited fashion, telling her all about the waxing of the floor and the hanging of the banners and the trimming of the evergreen garlands, and how the gardener would put the Union Jack upside down, until she was forced to be more gracious with him than was her wont.

Joyce's sweet mouth had the look upon it that I knew well when mother and she had had an uncomfortable passage, but I could not imagine why she should wear it to-night. I could look across upon her programme, and I could see that there were names written nearly all the way down it, although I could not read whose names they were, and especially after my one taste of the joy of waltzing, I was beginning to think that no girl could have cause for sadness who had a partner for every dance. Alas! I had but one, and my spirits were beginning to sink very low. I had forgotten love affairs; I wanted to waltz.

"There is a dreadful lack of gentlemen," said Jessie Hoad, who had come up beside us, putting up her eye-glass and looking round the room. "That unfortunate man must have his hands full."

"Do you mean Squire Broderick?" asked Miss Thorne. "I don't think he considers himself unfortunate. He looked cheerful enough just now, dancing with Miss Maliphant."

Miss Hoad vouchsafed no reply to this; she moved off to where her father was talking to mine in a corner, and passing her arm within his, walked him off without the slightest ceremony to be introduced to the old lady with the handle to her name who had come over from our fashionable seaport.

I thought it was very rude, but Mr. Hoad was not quite as affable himself to-night as he was in the privacy of our own Grange parlor.

"I hate that kind of thing," said Miss Thorne to me, in her out-spoken way. "When are there ever men enough at a country dance unless you get in the riffraff from behind the shop counters? We come to meet our friends, not to whirl round with mere sticks."

I thought it was very nice of Miss Thorne, but I wished there were just men enough to dance with me.

The music struck up again and Joyce went off with her partner. I felt as though life indeed were altogether a disappointment; and it did not give me any pleasure to hear Miss Thorne commenting upon Joyce's beauty, nor laughing in her frank, good-natured way about the squire's attentions, any the more than it amused me to hear fragments of the gay descriptions with which Captain Forrester was making the time pass for mother.

But, after all, I began to despair too soon; it was only the fourth dance of the evening. Before it was over the squire came up to me.

"I have been so busy," said he, "I haven't been able to come before, but I hope you haven't given all your dances away?"

Although I was new to the ways of the world, an instinct within taught me to say, coolly, "Oh no, not all."

"What can you give me?" asked he. And he quoted three numbers further on in the evening. "I think, being old friends, we might dance three dances together," added he, with a smile.

"Oh yes," cried I. "I should like to dance them with you."

The squire was a beautiful dancer, although he was not a young man; or rather, although he was not what I then considered a young man. I fancied he did not smile at my enthusiastic reply. He even looked rather grave. I was too simple to think of not giving him my programme. I saw him glance at it and then at me. From that moment I did not lack partners, and as far as the company could provide them, good ones.

To be sure I jostled round the room with a raw youth or two, and guided a puffing gentleman through the maze, and let my toes be trodden upon by a tall gentleman with glasses on his nose, who only turned round when he thought of it; but on the whole I enjoyed myself, and it was all thanks to my host. I scarcely knew a man when I went into the room, and certainly, save for that one wild, delightful waltz, Captain Forrester had taken no account of me, although he had sat close to me half the evening, and one would have thought he would have noticed that I was not dancing. But then, of course, he was preoccupied. I could not make him out at all. All the evening I could not once catch him even talking to Joyce, and I am quite sure that when I went in to supper he had not asked her to dance once.

If I had been enjoying myself less I might have thought more of it, but I was too happy to remember it until the breathing-time came, when I went into the dining-room. Then, when I saw Captain Forrester sitting in one of the best places with that horrid old Miss Farnham, and Joyce at a side-table, with scarcely room to stand, and no one but my pet aversion, Mr. Hoad, even to get her something to eat, my blood boiled, and I could scarcely speak civilly to him.

And he seemed so interested too, so wrapped up in what the silly creature was saying, with that nodding old topknot of hers! I was thankful when he rose and took her outside to finish their discussion about the poor-laws in the seclusion of some corner of the drawing-room. I was very angry with him.

I looked suspiciously at the squire, who had taken mother in to supper and sat at the head of the table with her. Mother was smiling happily: she was proud of the honor that the squire was doing to her and hers. But I could not look kindly at the squire. It was infamous if, out of mere jealousy, he had tried to spoil two lives. Instead of being proud that he had done my sister the honor of opening the ball with her, instead of being grateful to him for his kindness to me, and pleased to see all the attention that he was paying to our mother amid the county magnates whom he might have preferred, I was eaten up with this new idea, and felt my heart swell within me as Joyce passed me presently with that calm and yet half-tired look on her beautiful face.

Midnight was long past, and it was nearly time to go home. In fact, father had said that it was time to go home long ago. He had made a new friend in the young parson, and seemed to have passed an hour happily with him, but the parson had left, and he had exhausted every argument that he would consent to discuss with the people whom he met in ordinary society and had been persuaded by Mr. Hoad to speak a civil word on commonplace subjects to his pet aversion Mr. Thorne, and now he was thoroughly sick of the whole thing, and would have no more to do with it.

He came up to mother and begged her to come home, but mother had heard the squire ask Joyce for another dance later on, and I knew very well that she would not leave till that was through; besides, she was the most unselfish old dear in the world, for all her rough words sometimes, and would never have consented to deprive us of an inch of pleasure that she could procure us.

Personally I was very grateful to her. I had a dance left with the squire myself, and besides the pleasure of it, I had been arranging something that I wanted to say to him. I was standing alone in the entrance to the conservatory when he came to claim it. I was looking for Joyce. I had missed her ever since supper. I had thought—I had hoped—that she was with Captain Forrester, but when Miss Thorne told me he was talking politics with Mr. Hoad in the drawing-room, I believed her, and was at a loss to understand my sister's absence. Could she be unwell? But I did not confide my doubts to the squire. He put his arm around me and swept me off onto that lovely floor, and I thought of nothing else.

I remember very clearly how well the squire looked that night—fresh and merry, with bright keen eyes.

"That's a pretty frock, Miss Margaret," said he, as we were waltzing round.

"Oh, I'm so glad you like it," answered I. "I was afraid it wasn't suitable."

In the excitement of the ball I had entirely forgotten all about my appearance, but now that the squire remarked upon it, I remembered how uncomfortable I had felt in it at first.

"Why not suitable?" asked he.

"Mother bought it at the great Exhibition in '52," said I.

But the real cause of the awkwardness of my feeling had arisen from the fact that I felt unlike myself in a "party frock," and not at all from any fear that the frock might be old-fashioned.

"Oh! and Miss Hoad considers that an objection, I suppose," smiled he. "Well, I don't. There's only one thing I don't like," added he, in his most downright manner. "I don't like the trinkets. You're too young for trinkets."

He had felt it. He had felt just what I had felt—that it was unsuitable for a girl like me to be dressed up.

"You mean the corals," said I; and my voice sank a little, for I was proud of the corals too, and pleased that mother should have given them to me.

"Yes," he answered. "They are very pretty; but," he added, gently, "a young girl's neck is so much prettier."

We waltzed round two turns without speaking. Then he said abruptly, "Perhaps, by-the-way, I ought not to have said that, but I think such old friends as we are may say anything to one another, mayn't we?"

"Why, of course," said I, rather surprised.

The speech was not at all like one of the squire's. I had always thought that he said just whatever he liked to any of us. But to be sure, until the other evening, he had never spoken very much to me at all.

I laughed—a little nervous laugh. I was stupidly nervous that night with the squire. "I think we should be very silly if we didn't say whatever came into our heads," said I. "I don't think I like people who don't say what they think. Although, of course, it is much more difficult for me to say things to you than for you to say them to me."

"Why?" asked he.

"Well, of course, because you're so much older," answered I.

He was silent. For a moment the high spirits that I had so specially noticed in him seemed to desert him.

"Well, what do you want to say to me that's disagreeable?" said he presently, with a little laugh.

"Oh, nothing disagreeable," declared I. "It's about your nephew, Captain Forrester."

"Oh!" said he.

His expression changed. It was as though I had not said what he had expected me to say. But his brow clouded yet more, only it was more with anger than sadness—the same look of anger that he had worn the other afternoon. He certainly was a very hot-tempered man.

"I don't think you are fair to him," said I, boldly.

He looked at me. He smiled a little.

"In what way not fair to him?" said he.

"Well, if it had been any one else but me," answered I, "and you had said all that you did say the other day in the Grange parlor, I think the person would have been set against Captain Forrester. Of course it made no difference to me, because I like him so much."

He winced, I fancied.

"You don't understand, my dear young lady," said he. "I merely wished that there should be no misunderstandings."

"I don't think there were any misunderstandings," answered I. "We always knew that Captain Forrester was not a man of property. He told us so himself."

"Well, then, that's all right," said the squire.

"We liked him rather the better for it," concluded I, prompted by a wicked spirit of mischief.

The squire did not reply to this. Of course there was nothing to reply to it. It was a rude speech, and was better taken no notice of. He merely put his arm round my waist again, and asked if we should finish the waltz. I was sorry for my discourtesy before we had done, and tried to make up for it.

Although the weather was still very treacherous in spite of the clear sky, couples had strayed out through the conservatory onto the broad terrace outside. I suggested to the squire that we should do the same. He demurred at first, saying it was too cold; but as I laughed at this, and ran outside without any covering over me, he came after me—but he passed through the entrance-hall on his way and fetched a cloak, which he wrapped round me. In spite of my naughtiness, he had that care for the daughter of his old friends.

The moon was shining outside. It made dark shadows and white lights upon the ivied walls and upon the slender gray pillars of the ruined chapel; within, beneath the pointed arches, black patches lay upon the grass, alternated with sharp contrasts of lights where the moonbeams streamed in through the chancel windows.

The marsh was white where the silver rays caught the vapors that floated over it, and dark beyond that brilliant path-way; there was a track of light upon the sea. We stood a moment and looked. Even to me it seemed strange to leave the brightness of within for this weird, solemn brightness of the silent world without. I think I sighed. I really was very sorry now for having made that speech.

We walked round the terrace outside the chapel. We scarcely spoke five words. When we came to the wood that shades the chapel on the farther side we stopped. The path that led into it lost itself in blackness.

"It's quite a place for ghosts, isn't it?" said I.

"Yes; it's not the place for any one else," laughed the squire. "Any one less used to dampness would certainly catch their death of cold."

"Oh, you mustn't laugh at ghosts," answered I. "I believe in ghosts. And I'm sure this wood must be full of ghosts—so many wonderful people must have walked about in it hundreds of years ago."

"So long ago as that?" said he.

He was determined to treat my fancy lightly. But his laugh was kindly. We turned back to the white moonlight, but not before I had noticed a tall, white figure in the black depths, which I should have been quite sure was a ghost if I had not been equally sure of the contrary. The figure was not alone. If it had been, I should have accosted it. As it was, I took the squire's arm and walked away quickly in the direction of the house. The music had struck up again. The swing of an entrancing Strauss waltz came floating out on the night wind.

"We must go in-doors," said the squire, not at all like a man who was longing to dance to that lovely air; "I'm engaged for this to Miss Thorne."

Poor man! No doubt he had had nearly enough by that time of playing the host and of dancing every dance; he wanted a few minutes' rest.

I too was engaged, but not to a very delightful partner. After one turn round the room with him, I complained of the heat, and begged him to take me outside. Of course we went towards the ruin.

Of the few couples who had come out, all had gone that way, because from that point there was a break in the belt of trees, and one could see to the marsh and the sea. But we went round the chapel to the wood on the other side.

"I say, it looks gloomy in there, doesn't it?" said the young man at my side.

"Yes," answered I, but I was not looking into the wood now.

I had glanced into the interior of the ruin as we had passed, and I had seen a tall black figure leaning up in the deep shadow against the side of the central arch that stood up so quietly against the soft sky. I felt quite sure that the "ghost," whom I had seen a few minutes before, was close by. I was nearly certain that I saw a white streak that was not moonlight beyond the bend of the arch.

I turned round and went down the lawn a few steps, my companion following. He began to talk to me, but I did not know what he said. I was listening beyond him to another voice. It fell sadly upon my ear.

"I've no doubt the girl was right," it said. "I'm sure she was right. I had never noticed it before, but his leading you out to-night before every one was very significant."

It was my sister's voice that answered, but she must almost have whispered the words, for I could not hear them at all.

The man spoke again.

"Yes; that's not very likely," answered he, with a soft laugh. "Of course, how could he help it? Oh, I ought to have gone away," he added; "I ought to have gone away as soon as I had seen you. But I couldn't. You see even to-night, when I have tried to keep away from you, you have made me come to you at last. And I didn't think that I was doing you any harm till now."

He emphasized the word "you." I did not notice it then, but I recollect it now.

Again my sister's voice said something; what, I could not hear.

"Do you mean that, dearest? do you mean that?" said he, softly. "That you would not marry him if you could help it, although he would make such a lady of you? Ah, then I think I can guess something!"

A fiery blush rose to my cheek. I was glad that in the white moonlight my companion could not see it. I ran quickly down the slope of grass onto the gravel walk. It was dreadful, dreadful that I should have listened to these words which were meant for her ear alone.

"Come," I called to the lad, who loitered behind; "come, it's cold, we must go in."

He followed me slowly.

"I believe there were a man and a girl spooning behind that wall," he said, with a grin.

How I hated him! I have never spoken to him from that day to this, and yet, was it his fault?

We went back into the ball-room. The waltz was over. I had a partner for the last one, but I did not care to dance it. I was watching for Joyce, and when I saw her presently floating round with her hand on Captain Forrester's arm, I thought I was quite happy.

But mother was not happy. She had thought that Joyce would dance the last dance with Squire Broderick. She said that father was tired, and that she wanted to go. And indeed his face looked very weary, and his heavy lips heavier than ever.

No doubt we were all tired, for the squire too had lost the cheerful look that he had worn all through the evening.

I sat and waited for Joyce, and I wondered to myself whether any one would ever make love to me with his heart in his voice.

CHAPTER XI

Time dragged heavily on my hands after the excitement of the squire's ball was over. It was not only that I had to go back to the routine of every-day life—for there was still the concert to look forward to, which gave us plenty of interest—but it was that during a whole fortnight I had been looking for news from Joyce, and that Joyce had said never a word. No; she had rather been more silent than usual, constrained and unlike her own serene and happy self; and I had been frightened, frightened at sight of the torrent that I had let loose, and doubtful whether, in spite of all his democratic theories, this handsome, courtly, chivalrous knight, who was my embodiment of romance, was really a fit mate for the humble damsel nurtured in the quiet shade.

Well, anyhow the torrent rolled on, whether it was really I who had set it free or not, and I was forced to stand aside and watch its course without more ado.

There had been plenty to watch. The village concert had come and gone; it had taken place a week after the squire's ball. Captain Forrester had worked us very hard for it towards the end. We had had practisings every afternoon, and I had rehearsed my solos indefatigably; but, save for singing in the glees and playing an accompaniment now and then, Joyce had taken no active part in the musical performance, and I had fancied that she had kept out of the way a great deal more than she need have done.

I could not understand her at all. She would not give Frank the ghost of a chance of saying a word to her alone; she shunned him as she shunned me.

On the night of the concert he was, of course, too much excited until the performance was over, to remember even Joyce at first; for he was one of those natures who throw themselves ardently into whatever they take up; and he was just as eager over this entertainment, of which he had accepted the responsibility, as though it were going to be given before a select company instead of before a handful of country bumpkins.

Well, he was rewarded for his pains. The concert was voted a brilliant success, and by a long way the best that had ever been given in the village.

"When stars are in the quiet skies," and "Robin Adair," which I sang "by request," as an *encore*, were greatly applauded, as were also the glees that we had so patiently practised; and though, of course, the crowning point of the evening was Captain Forrester's own song, poured forth in his rich, mellow barytone, we had none of us reason to complain of the reception that we got; and the stone walls of the old town-hall, that had stood since the days when the headsman was still an institution, responded to the clapping of the people.

To be sure, they wanted father to stand up and give them a speech, but he would have nothing to do with that on this occasion; he said it was one of relaxation and not of work; and he always refused to touch upon things that were sacred to him, for mere effect, or in anything but the most serious spirit. He wished them all good-night, and told them so.

I remember a curious incident that occurred that night. One of the American oil-lamps that lighted the hall took fire; a panic arose in the little crowd; the women pressed to the door. But Captain Forrester, calling out to the people in strong, reassuring tones to keep their seats, seized the lamp, carried it burning above the heads of the throng, and threw it down into the little court-yard without.

When the fright was over I missed father and Joyce. Him I found at once, sitting on the steps with two sobbing little ones on his knees—two little ones whose sisters had run out without them, and whose little hearts had been numbed with fear. Father would generally neglect any grown-up person in preference to a child. But Joyce I could not see.

I felt sure that she must have gone to look after Captain Forrester; but when presently he came back with his hand bandaged, and said that he had seen nothing of Joyce, I was really frightened. I discovered her sitting down in a dark corner of the court-yard, crying.

She said that she had been terrified by the accident, and had run out for safety before any one else. But her manner puzzled me. And for a whole week after that her manner continued to puzzle me.

Frank Forrester came every day to the Grange to see father. They had a new scheme on hand, an original scheme, a pet scheme of my dear father's— the scheme of all his schemes which he held most dear, and one which I know he had had for years, and had never dared hope would find favor with any one. It was a scheme for the succor of those poor children who had either no parents, or whose parents were anxious to get rid of them.

Of course I did not understand the workings of it at the time, it not being possible that I should understand the requirements of the case; but from what I can recollect, gleaned from the scraps of talk that fell from father and Captain Forrester, I think it was intended to pick up cases which were not provided for in the ordinary foundling hospitals, and to rescue those poor wretched little creatures whose parents were willing to part with them, from a life of sin and degradation.

The children were to be taught a trade, and were to be honorably placed in situations when they left the home.

Of course it was a vast scheme—how vast I am sure father cannot have grasped at the time; but although he must have had grave doubts of the possibility of its success, he was carried away for the moment by Frank Forrester's wild enthusiasm upon the subject, and was persuaded by him to try and put it into immediate practice.

I think he was more drawn to Frank than ever by this. I think he was drawn to every one who cared for children. But although the captain was very enthusiastic over this scheme, he found time to look at Joyce and to sigh for a word from her, for a chance of seeing her alone, and she would not give it him.

For a whole fortnight after that memorable evening of the squire's ball she had kept him sighing; at least, I think that she had, and I was very sorry for him.

To be sure, mother's eyes were vigilant—it needed some bravery to elude mother's eyes but then I thought that if one wanted a thing very much one would be brave.

Was Joyce cold-hearted? Was that why her face was so calm and so beautiful.

But one day, at last, the squire and his nephew came and went away together, and mother, thinking the visit was over for the day, had gone out on household errands. I was coming in from taking a parcel of poor linen to the Vicarage when Deborah met me in the hall.

"That there captain's in with Miss Joyce in the parlor," said she. "They didn't want no light, they didn't. But I've took 'em in the lamp just this minute."

She said this with grim determination, and went off grumbling.

Deborah wanted Joyce to marry the squire, and I fancy she suspected me of furthering her acquaintance with the captain.

I did not go in as Deborah suggested, not until close upon the time when I was afraid mother would come home.

Joyce was sitting in the big arm-chair with her hands clasped across her knees, gazing into the fire.

Captain Forrester sat at the old spinet—our best new piano was in the front parlor—and touched its poor old clanging keys gently, and sang soft notes to it in his soft, mellow voice. They were passionate love-songs, as I now know; but the words were in foreign tongues, and I did not understand them; no doubt Joyce did. He rose when I came in, and asked what o'clock it was.

I told him, and he laughed his gay, sympathetic laugh, and declared that at the Grange he never knew what the time was; he believed we kept our clocks all wrong. Then he said that he could not wait any longer for father that evening, but would come to see him in the morning. He went up to Joyce, and held out his hand. She shook herself, as though to rouse herself from a dream, and rose. This time it was no mistake of mine. Captain Forrester held Joyce's hand a long while.

"Good-bye—till to-morrow morning," said he, in a low voice.

She did not answer, and he turned to me.

"Good-night, Miss Margaret," he said, and there was a ring in his voice—an impressiveness even towards me—which seemed to say that something particular had happened.

When he was gone, I felt that I must know what it was. This barrier of reserve between two sisters was ridiculous.

"Joyce," said I, half impatiently, "have you nothing to tell me?"

She looked up at me. A flush spread itself all over her neck and face, her short upper lip trembled a little—it always did with any emotion.

"Yes," answered she, simply; "Captain Forrester wants to marry me."

I did not reply. Now that it had come to this pass as I wished, I was frightened, as I have said.

But Joyce was looking up at me with an appealing look in her eyes. I stooped down and kissed her.

"You dear old thing," I said; "I'm so glad. I hoped he had—I have hoped all along he would."

"I thought you wished it," she said, with child-like simplicity.

I laughed.

"Of course I knew from the very beginning that he would fall in love with you," I said.

"Oh, Margaret, don't say that!" pleaded she. And then, after a pause, with a little sigh she added, "I should have thought he would have been wiser than to fall in love with a country girl, when there must be so many town girls who are better fitted to him."

"Nonsense!" cried I. "The woman who is fitted to a man is the woman whom he loves."

"Do you think so?" murmured she, diffidently.

"Why, of course," I cried, warming as I went on, and forgetting my own doubts in laughing at hers. "A man doesn't marry a woman for the number of languages that she speaks, and that kind of thing—at least not a man like Captain Forrester. I don't know how you can misjudge him so. Don't you believe that he loves you?"

"Oh yes," she murmured again; "I think that he loves me."

I said no more for a while. Joyce's attitude puzzled me. That she should speak so diffidently of the adoration of a man who had addressed to her the passionate words which I had overheard, passed my comprehension.

I fell to wondering what was her feeling towards him. More than ever I felt that she had passed beyond me into a world of which I knew only in dreams. I had risen now, and stood over the fire.

"I always dreamed of something like that for you, Joyce," said I. "I always felt that you weren't a bit suited to marry a country bumpkin, but I never pictured to myself anything so good as this for you. Mother had grand ideas for you, I know. Oh yes; and you know she had, now," added I, in answer to a deprecatory "Oh, don't!" from my sister. "But I should have hated what she wanted; and I don't believe you would ever have consented. But Captain Forrester is not a landed proprietor; he cares for the rights of the people as father does. He is a fine fellow; and then he is young, and has never loved any one else," added I, dropping my voice.

I suppose I said this in allusion to the squire's first wife.

She did not say anything, and I knelt down beside her. "Dear Joyce," I whispered—and I do believe my voice trembled—"I do want you to be happy. And though I shall feel dreadfully lonely when you have gone away and left me, I sha'n't be sorry, because I shall be so glad you have got what I wanted you to have."

She squeezed my hand very tight.

"Oh, but I sha'n't be married, dear, not for ever so long yet," said she. "Why, you forget, we don't know what father and mother will say."

"Why, father and mother can only want what is best for you," answered I. And I believed it. Nevertheless, what father and mother, or at all events what mother thought best, was not what I thought best.

When Captain Forrester came the next morning, I knew before he passed into father's business-room that he was not going to receive a very satisfactory answer. He was expected; his answer was prepared, and I was to blame that it was.

That evening, after the captain's proposal to Joyce, the squire sent down a message to ask whether father would be disengaged; and if he were, whether he might come down after supper to smoke a pipe with him. We were seated around the meal when Deborah brought in the message.

"Certainly," answered father. "Say that I shall be pleased to see Mr. Broderick." But when she was gone out, he added, gruffly: "What the deuce can the squire want to see me for? I don't know of anything that I need to talk to him about."

He looked at mother, but mother did not answer. She assumed her most dignified air, and there was a kind of suppressed smile on her face which irritated me unaccountably. As soon as the meal was over, she reminded us that we had the orange marmalade to tie up and label, and we were forced to leave her and father together.

I went very reluctantly, for I wanted to hear what they had to say, and Deborah was in a very inquisitive mood—asking us how it was that the squire had not invited us up to supper at the Manor these three weeks, and when this fine gentleman from London was going to take himself back again to his own home.

I left Joyce to answer her, and found an excuse to get back again to the parlor as fast as I could. Father and mother sat opposite to one another in their high-backed chairs by the fire. Father had not been well since that night of the ball. I think he had caught a chill in the east wind and was feeling his gout again a little. I think it must have been so, or he would scarcely have remained sitting. Knowing him as I did, I was surprised; for I knew by his face in a moment that he was in a bad temper, and he never remained sitting when he was in a bad temper.

"Nonsense, Mary, nonsense!" he was saying. "I'm surprised at a woman of your good-sense running away with such ideas! Mere friendship, mere friendliness—that's all."

"Well," answered mother, stroking her knee, over which she had turned up her dress to save it from scorching at the fire, "it was not only his taking

Joyce out to dance first before all the county neighbors, but he took me into supper himself—and, I can assure you, was most attentive to me."

"Well, and I should have expected nothing less of him," said father. "The man is a gentleman, and you have been a good friend to him. No man, squire or not, need be ashamed of taking my wife into supper—no, not before ten counties!"

Mother smiled contentedly.

"Every one can't be expected to see as you do, Laban," said she. "I think it was done with a purpose."

"Oh! And, pray, what purpose?" asked father, in his most irritating and irritated tone.

Mother was judicious; perhaps even she was a little frightened. She did not answer just at first. I had slid behind the door of the jam-press in the corner of the room, and now I began putting the rows of marmalade pots in order. She had not noticed me.

"I think the squire wishes to marry our eldest daughter," said she, slowly; and then she reached down her knitting from the mantle-piece and began to ply her needles.

There was a dreadful silence for a minute.

"I have thought so for a long time," added mother. "I have felt sure that he must have some other reason for coming here so often besides mere friendship for two old people."

Father leaned forward in his chair, resting his hand on the arm of it, as though about to rise, but not rising.

"Well, then, if he has any other reason, the longer he keeps it to himself the better," said he, in a voice that he tried to prevent from becoming loud. "But we have no right to judge him until we know," added he. "You've made a mistake, mother. The squire isn't thinking of marrying again. He's no such fool."

"I don't see that he'd be such a fool to wish to marry a sweet girl that he has known all his life," remonstrated mother.

"He can marry no girl of mine, at least not with my consent," declared father, loudly, his temper getting the better of him. "My girls must marry in their own rank of life, or not at all. I have no need of the gentry to put new blood into our veins. We are good enough and strong enough for ourselves, any day. But come, old lady, come," he added, more softly, trying to recover himself, "you've made a mistake. It's very natural. Mothers will be proud of their children, and women must always needs fancy riches and honors are the best things in the world."

"Oh, I don't fancy that, I'm sure, Laban," answered mother. "But I can't think you would really refuse such a true and honest man for Joyce."

"Well, then, Mary, look here; you be quite sure that I shall never consent to my daughter marrying a man who must come down a peg in the eyes of the world to wed her," began he, raising his voice again, and speaking very slowly.

He looked mother keenly in the face, but he got no further than that, for I emerged from the jam-cupboard with a pot in my hand; and at the same time Deborah flung open the door and announced Squire Broderick. Mother put down her skirt quickly and father sank back in his chair. There was an anxious look upon the squire's face which puzzled me, but he tried to laugh and look like himself as he shook hands with us.

"You mustn't speak so loud, Maliphant, you mustn't speak so loud, if you want to keep things a secret," laughed he. "Marrying? Who is going to be married, if you please?"

Mother blushed, and even father looked uncomfortable.

"We were only talking of possibilities, squire, very remote possibilities," said he. "The women are fond of taking time by the forelock in such matters, you know. But now we'll give over such nonsense, and bring our minds to something more sensible. You wanted to see me?"

"Yes," answered the squire. "And I have only a few minutes. My nephew leaves to-morrow, and we have some little affairs to attend to."

"Your nephew leaves to-morrow!" cried I, aghast. They all turned round and looked at me, and I felt myself blush.

"He never said so when he was here this afternoon," I added, hurriedly, with a little nervous laugh.

"No, I don't suppose he knew it when we were here," answered the squire, evidently ignorant of the captain's second visit alone. "He had a telegram from his mother this evening, begging him to return home at once."

I said no more, and Squire Broderick turned to father. "Can you give me a few minutes?" asked he.

Father rose. It vexed me to see that he rose with some difficulty. He was evidently sadly stiff again, and it vexed me that the squire should see it. Without uttering a word, he led the way to his business-room.

I remained where I was, with the jam-pot in my hand, looking at mother, who sat by the fire knitting. There was a little smile upon her lips that annoyed me immensely.

"I think I ought to tell you, mother, that I was behind the jam-cupboard door while you and father were talking, and that I heard what you said," said I, suddenly.

"Well, of course I did not expect you to come intruding where you were not wanted, Margaret," said mother; "but I don't know that it matters. I'm not ashamed of what I said."

"Of course not," answered I; "and I've guessed you had that notion in your head these months past."

"I don't know, I'm sure, what business you had to guess," said mother. "It wasn't your place, that I can see."

"And I may as well tell you that I'm quite sure Joyce would never think of the squire if he did want to marry her," continued I, without paying any attention to this remark. I paused a moment before I added, "She couldn't, anyhow, because she's in love with another man."

Mother looked at me over her spectacles. She looked at me as though she did not see me, and yet she looked me through and through.

"Margaret," said she, at last, loftily, "I consider it most unseemly of you to say such a thing of your sister. A well brought up girl don't go about falling in love with men in that kind of way."

"A girl must fall in love with the man she means to marry, mother; at least, so I should think," said I.

And I marched off into the kitchen with the jam-pot that wanted a label, and did not come out again till I heard the study door open, and the squire's voice in the hall.

"Well, you'll come to dinner on Thursday, anyhow, and see him," he was saying; "it need bind you to nothing."

Father grumbled something as he hobbled across, and I noticed again how lame he was that day. The squire, seeing mother upon the threshold of the parlor door, stopped and added, pleasantly, "Maliphant has promised to bring you up to dine at the Manor, so mind you hold him to his word." Mother assured him that she would, and the squire went out.

"Well?" asked she, turning to father with a questioning look on her face, which was neither so hopeful nor so happy as it had been ten minutes ago.

"Well?" echoed he, somewhat crossly. Then his frown changing to a smile, he patted her on the arm, and said, merrily, "No, mother, no. Wrong this time; wrong, old lady, upon my soul. The time hasn't come yet when we are to have the honor of having our daughters asked in marriage by the gentry."

"Hush, Laban, hush," cried mother, vexed; for the kitchen door stood open, and Joyce was within ear-shot. And then, following him into the parlor, whither I had already found my way, she added, "Maybe I'm not quite such a fool as you think, and the time will come one day, although it's not ripe just yet."

"A fool! Who ever called you a fool, Mary? Not I, I'm sure," declared father. "No, you're a true, shrewd woman, and as you are generally right in such matters, I dare say you may prove right now; but all I want to make clear to you is that whatever time the squire's question comes—if it be a question of that nature—his answer will always be the same."

Mother said no more. She was a wise woman, and never pursued a vexed question when there was no need to do so. I, who was not so wise, thought that I now saw a fitting opportunity for putting in my own peculiar oar amid the troubled waters.

"I don't think you need trouble your head about it, father," I said. "Joyce will never marry Squire Broderick, even if he were to ask her. She's in love with Captain Forrester."

Father turned round with the pipe he was filling 'twixt his finger and thumb and looked at me.

"Margaret," said mother, "didn't I tell you just now that that was a most strange and unseemly thing to say?"

I did not answer, and father still looked at me with the pipe between his finger and thumb.

"In love with Captain Forrester, indeed!" continued mother, scornfully. "And pray, how do you know that Captain Forrester is in love with Joyce?"

"Well, of course," answered I, with a toss of my head, "girls don't fall in love with men unless the men are in love with them first. Who ever heard of such a thing? Of course he's in love with Joyce."

"Stuff and nonsense!" said mother, emphatically, tapping the floor with her foot, as she was wont to do when she was annoyed. "Captain Forrester and your sister haven't met more than half a dozen times in the course of their lives. I wonder what a love is going to be like that takes the world by storm after three weeks' acquaintance."

"There is such a thing as love at first sight," answered I, with what I know must have been an annoyingly superior air. It did not impress mother.

"A wondrous fine thing I've been told," was all that she said.

I turned to father, who had not spoken. "Well, anyhow, they're in love with one another," I repeated. "I know it as a fact, and he's coming here to-morrow morning to ask your leave to marry her."

"The devil he is!" ejaculated father, roused at last.

Mother dropped her knitting. I do believe her face grew white with horror.

"I always thought, Laban, it was a pity to have that young man about so much when we had grown-up girls at home," moaned she, quite forgetting my presence. "But you always would be so sure he was thinking of nothing but those politics of yours."

"To be sure, to be sure," murmured father.

"And he was always so pleasant to all of us," she went on, as though that, too, were something to deplore in him; "but I never did think he'd be wanting to marry a farmer's daughter. And I should like to know what he has got to marry any one upon," added she, after a pause, turning to me indignantly, as though I knew the captain's affairs any better than she did.

"His captain's pay," answered I, glibly, although I had been chilled for a moment by this remark. "And why should you consider him a ne'er-do-well because he earns his living in a different way to what you do? He kills the country's enemies, and you till the country's land. They are both honorable professions by which a man gets his bread by the sweat of his brow."

I looked at father; all through I had spoken only to him. He smiled and began to light his pipe. It was a sign that his mind was made up. Which way was it made up?

"Joyce is just the girl men do fall in love with," said I, wisely; "and as for her—well, you can't be surprised at her falling in love with a man whom you like so much yourself."

"Ay, I do like the young man," agreed father, stanchly. "I can't help it. They're precious few such as he whose heads are full of aught but seeking after their own pleasure."

"Well, if you like him so much, why are you sorry that he wants to marry Joyce?" asked I, boldly.

"I did not say that I was sorry, lass," said father, calmly.

My heart throbbed with pleasant triumph, but the battle was not over yet.

"Well, Laban, I don't suppose you can say that you're glad," put in mother, almost tartly, "after what I've heard you say about girls marrying out of their own class in life."

"Captain Forrester is not rich and idle," said I.

"No," answered mother, scornfully, "he is not rich, you're right enough there; but he is a good sight more idle than many men who can afford to keep a wife in comfort. I know your sort of play soldiers that never see an enemy."

"He's rich enough for a girl of mine," replied father. "As to his being idle, I hope maybe he's going to do better work saving the lives of innocent children than he could have done slashing at what are called the nation's foes."

"Yes, yes," said mother, a trifle impatiently. "I make no doubt you're right. I've nothing against the young man, but I can't believe, Laban, as you really mean to say that you'd give your girl to him willingly."

"Well," answered father, "I'm bound to say I'm surprised at the news; but we old folk are apt to forget that we were young once; and when I was a lad I loved you, Mary, so we mustn't be hard on the young ones. It's neither poverty nor riches, nor this nor that, as makes happiness; it's just love; and if the two love one another, we durstn't interfere."

"I don't understand you, Laban; indeed I don't," cried poor mother, beside herself with anxiety. "It's not according to what you were saying a few minutes ago, and you can't say it is."

Father was silent. I suppose he could not help knowing in his heart that the objections to Captain Forrester must be practically the same as those to Squire Broderick, with the additional one that he was almost a stranger to us. But his natural liking for the young man obscured his vision to plain facts. Father and I were very much alike; what we wanted to be must be. But when I look back at that point in our lives, I pity poor mother, who was really the wisest and the most practical of us all.

"Well, mother, the lass must decide for herself," said father. "She's of age; she should know her own mind."

"Joyce knows her own mind well enough," said I. "She has told Frank Forrester that she will marry him subject to your approval."

"I wonder she took the trouble to add so much as that," said mother at last. "Young folk nowadays have grown so clever they seem to teach us old folk."

There was a tremor in her voice, and father rose and went across to her, laying his hand on her shoulder.

"Meg, go and tell your sister to come here," said he in a moment. "You need not come back."

I was hurt at the dismissal, and I waited in the passage till Joyce came out from the interview; but her face was very white, and all that she would say was: "Oh, Margaret, let them settle it. I don't want to have any will of my own."

I was very much disappointed, and was fain to be agreeably surprised, when on the following morning I heard that, after mature deliberation, our parents had decided to allow the captain a year's probation.

I had been afraid that mother would entirely override all father's arguments; she generally did.

The affair was not to be called an engagement—both were to be perfectly free to choose again; but if at the end of that time both were of the same mind, the betrothal should be formally made and announced.

Mother must, however, have been very hard in her terms; for the young folk were neither to meet nor to write to one another, nor to have any news of one another beyond what might transpire in the correspondence that father would be carrying on with Frank on outside matters.

Frank told me the conditions out in the garden, when I caught hold of him as he came out of father's study. The whole matter was to be a complete secret, shut closely within our own family. This mother repeated to me afterwards, I guessed very well with what intent. But although Frank must have guessed at a possible rival in his uncle, he absolutely refused to be cast down.

The thought even crossed my mind that I should have liked my lover to have been a little more cast down. But no doubt he felt too sure of himself, even after the slight shock of surprise that it must have been to him to find his suit not at once accepted.

Nevertheless, as he passed out of the room where he had taken leave of Joyce alone, he bent forward towards me as I stood in the hall, and said, gravely, "Miss Margaret, I trust her to you. Don't let her forget me."

My heart ached for him, and from that moment it was afire with the steadfast resolve to support my sister's failing spirits and preserve for her the beautiful romance which had so unexpectedly opened out before her.

CHAPTER XII

Joyce and I sat in the apple orchard one May afternoon. It was not often we sat idle; but Joyce was going away on the morrow on a visit to Sydenham, and we wanted a few minutes' quiet together.

There was no quiet in-doors; mother was in one of her restless moods, and Mr. Hoad was with father. I supposed he was still harping on that subject of the elections, for I could not tell why else he should come so often; but I could have told him that he might have spared his pains, for that father never altered his mind.

However, on this particular occasion I was glad that he came, for I thought that it might save father from missing Frank too much—although, to be sure, they did not seem to get on so well as before Frank's coming; and I fancied that there was even the suspicion of a cloud on father's face when he closed the door after his man of business.

Who could wonder? Who would like Hoad after Frank Forrester? For my own part, I always avoided him, and that was why I had taken Joyce out-of-doors.

An east wind blew from the sea, and the marsh was bleak, though the lengthening shadows lay in soft tones across its crude spring greenness. The sun shone, and the thorn-trees that were abloom by the dikes made white spots along their straightness—softer memories of the snow that had so lately vanished, kindly promise of spring to come. Under the apple-trees, heavy with blossom, the air was blue above the vivid emerald of the springing grass, and all around us slenderly sturdy gray trunks and angular boughs, softened by a wealth of rose-flushed flower, made delicate patterns upon the sky or against the glittering sea-line beyond the marsh.

But a spring scene, with its frank, passionless beauty, its tenderness that is all promise and no experience, its arrogance of coming life, does sometimes put one out of heart with one's self, I think, although it should not have had that effect on one who stood in the same relation to life as did the spring to the year. Anyhow, I was not in my most cheerful frame of mind that day—not quite so arrogant and sanguine myself as was my wont.

Since the day when Captain Forrester had left the village three weeks ago, things had not gone to my liking. In the first place, I was not satisfied with this engagement of a year's standing, that was to be kept a profound secret from every one around. I thought it was not fair to Joyce. And then, and alas! I fear an even more active cause in my depression of spirits—Mr. Trayton Harrod had been engaged as bailiff to Knellestone farm!

Yes; never should I have expected it. It was too horrible, but it was true. Father and mother had gone up to meet him at dinner at the Manor two days after the captain's departure, and father had been forced to confess that he was a quiet, sensible, straightforward fellow, without any nonsense about him, and that there was no doubt that he knew what he was about.

It was very mortifying to me to hear father speak of him in that way, when I had quite made up my mind that he was sure not to know what he was about. But it seems that I was curiously mistaken upon this point.

Far from being a mere amateur at the business, he had been carefully educated for it at the Agricultural College at Ashford. His father had been of opinion that his own ventures had failed because of a too superficial knowledge of the subject—a knowledge only derived from natural mother-wit and practical observation, and he wished his son to labor under no such disadvantages.

I fancy Mr. Harrod's father had been, as the country-folk say, "a cut above his neighbors" in culture and social standing, and had taken to farming as a speculation when other things had failed. But of course this was no reason why his son should not make a good farmer, since he had been carefully educated to the business.

He was not wanting in practical experience either. He had done all he could to retrieve the fortunes of his father's farm, but the speculation was too far gone before he took the reins; and the elder Harrod had died a ruined man, leaving his son to shift for himself.

All this I had gleaned from talk between my parents and the squire in our own house; but it was mortifying, even though I had not guessed at that time that there was any real danger of his coming to Knellestone. For that had only been settled two days ago, and I could not help fancying that Mr. Hoad was partly to blame.

Of course there was no denying that father had been ill again—not so seriously ill as in the winter, but incapacitated for active life. He had not been able to mount his horse nor to walk farther than the garden plot at the top of the terrace for over a fortnight.

The doctor had suggested a bath-chair; but the idea of a farmer being seen in a bath-chair was positively insulting, and I would rather have seen him shut in-doors for a month than showing himself to the neighbors in such a plight. The idea was abandoned; but gradually, and without any sign, his mind came round to the plan which he had at first so violently repudiated—that of a bailiff for Knellestone.

I do not know whether it was really Mr. Hoad who had anything to do with his decision. He certainly had influence over father, and had been very often at the Grange of late, but it may have been merely the effect which Mr. Harrod himself produced. Anyhow, a fortnight or so after the dinner at the Manor, father announced to us abruptly at the dinner-table that he had that morning written to engage "that young man of the squire's" to come to Knellestone. His manner had been so queer when he said it that nobody had questioned him further on the matter; and as for me, I had been so thoroughly knocked down by the news that I do not think I had spoken to father since!

If my sister's departure had not been arranged—and in a great measure arranged by me—before this news had come, I am sure that I should not have suggested it; for it was the first time in our lives that we had been parted, and, reserved as I was, I felt that I wanted Joyce to be there during this family crisis.

She at least never allowed herself to be ruffled, and though this characteristic had its annoying side, there was comfort in it; and just at that particular moment we needed a soother, for the family was altogether in a somewhat ruffled condition.

Father was cross because of what he had been driven into doing with regard to the bailiff. Mother was cross because the squire had not proposed for Joyce, and Captain Forrester had. And I was cross—more cross than any one—because I was an opinionated young woman, and wanted to have a finger in the management of every pie.

It was a good thing that Joyce took even her own share in these matters more quietly than I took it for her. Nevertheless, even she was a little dismal that evening. How was it possible that she could be happy parted, without even the solace of correspondence, from the man whom she loved? I believe in my secret soul I set Joyce down as wanting in feeling for not fretting more than she did; but she *was* out of spirits, and mother had agreed with me that Joyce was pale, and had better choose this time for a visit to Aunt Naomi, which had been a promise for a long time. And now it was impossible to put it off.

Joyce came back from a dream with a little sigh, and turned towards me.

"Well, did you see Mr. Trayton Harrod this morning, Margaret?" asked she. "Deborah says he was here to see father. When does he come for good?"

"I don't know," answered I, shortly. "I know nothing at all about Mr. Trayton Harrod." Joyce sighed a little. "Deborah says he is a plain kind of man," continued she—"very tall and broad, and very short in his manners."

"He can't be too short in his manner for me," answered I. "He'll find me short too."

Joyce stretched out her hand and laid it on mine. It was a great deal for her to do. In the first place, we were not given to outward demonstrations of affection; and in the second place, Joyce knew that I abhorred sympathy, and that from my earliest childhood I had always hit out at people who dared to pity me for my hurts.

"Dear Margaret," said she, "I want you not to be so much set against this young man. Father said he was a straightforward, good sort of fellow, you know; and you can't be sure that he will be disagreeable until you know him."

"I don't suppose he is going to be disagreeable at all," declared I. "He may be the most delightful man in the world; I've no doubt he is. I only say that he is nothing to me. I shall have nothing to do with him, and I sha'n't know whether he is delightful or not."

"Well, if you begin like that, it *will* be setting yourself against him," said Joyce, bravely. She paused a moment, and then added, "I'm in hopes it will be a good thing for father. I've often thought of late that the work was too hard for him. Father's not the man he was."

"Father's all right," insisted I. "It's always the strongest men who have the gout. You'll see father will walk the young ones off the ground yet when it comes to a day's work. A man can work for his own—he works whether he be tired or not; but a hireling—why should a hireling work when he hasn't a mind to? It's nothing to him; he gets his wage anyway."

This theory seemed to trouble Joyce a bit, for she was silent.

"No," said I, "it'll be no go. He won't understand anything at all about it, and all he will do will be to set everybody by the ears."

"I don't see why that need be," persisted Joyce. "The squire says that he has been brought up to hard work, and that he has quite a remarkable knowledge of the country."

"Yes, what good did his knowledge of the country do him?" asked I, scornfully. "He managed his father's farm in Kent, and his father died a bankrupt. I don't call that much of a recommendation."

I had been obliged to come down from my high horse as to this friend of the squire's being one of his own class, an impoverished gentleman who wanted a living, for there was no doubt that he had been born and bred on a farm, and had been, moreover, specially educated to his work, but I had managed to find out something else in his disfavor nevertheless.

My sister was puzzled as to how to answer this.

"I did not know that that was so," said she.

"Of course it is so," repeated I. "That's why he must needs take a job."

"Poor fellow!" murmured Joyce.

"Nonsense!" cried I. "He ought to have been able to save the farm from ruin. It's no good pitying people for the misfortunes they bring upon themselves. The weak always go to the wall."

I did myself injustice with this speech. It did not really express my feelings at all, but my temper was up.

Joyce looked pained. "Perhaps the affairs of the farm were too bad to be set right before he took up the management," suggested she. "At all events, I suppose father knows best."

"I can't understand father," exclaimed I, hastily. "He seems to me to take much more interest in plans for saving pauper children than he does in working his own land."

"Oh, Margaret! how can you say such a thing?" cried Joyce, aghast. "You know that father is often laid by, and unable to go round the farm."

"Yes, yes, I know," I hastened to answer, ashamed of my outburst, and remembering that I was flatly contradicting what I had said two minutes before. "Nobody really has the interest in the place that father has, of course. That's why I don't want him to take a paid bailiff. When he is laid by he can manage it through me."

"I'm afraid that never answers," said Joyce, shaking her head; "I'm afraid business matters need a man. People always seem to take advantage of a woman."

I tried to laugh. "I wonder what Deborah would say to that?" I said, trying to turn the matter into a joke.

"Deborah doesn't attempt anything out of her own province," answered Joyce.

It was another of her quiet home-thrusts. She little guessed how they hurt, or she would never have dealt them—she who could not bear to hurt a fly.

"Margaret," began she again, her mind still set on that conciliatory project which she had undertaken, "do promise me one thing before I go. I don't like going away, and it makes me worse to think you will be working yourself up into a fever of annoyance at what can't be helped. Do promise me that you won't begin by being set against the young man. It'll make it very uncomfortable for everybody if you are, and you won't be any the happier. You can be so nice when you like."

I looked at her, surprised. It was so very rarely that Joyce came out of her shell to take this kind of line. It showed it must have been working in her mind for long.

"Yes, dear, yes," said I, really touched by her anxiety, "I'll try and be nice."

"You do take things so hard," continued she, "and it's no use taking things hard. Now, if you liked you might help father still, with Mr. Harrod, and he might be quite a pleasant addition to your life."

"That's ridiculous, Joyce," I answered, sharply. "You must see that he and I could never be friends. All I can promise is not to make it harder for him to settle down among the folk, for it'll be hard enough. However clever the squire may think him, he won't understand this country, nor this weather, nor these people at first, there's no doubt of that. He'll make lots of mistakes. But there, for pity's sake don't let's talk any more about him," cried I, hastily. "I'm sick of the man; and on our last evening too, when I've such a lot to say to you."

"What have you to say to me?" asked my sister, looking round suddenly, and with an uneasy look in her face.

"Oh, come, you needn't look like that," laughed I. "It's nothing horrid like what you have been saying to me. It's about Captain Forrester."

Her face grew none the less grave. "What about him?" asked she, in a low voice.

"Well, I'm going to fight for you, Joyce, while you're away," said I. "I don't think you've been over-pleased about having to go to Aunt Naomi, and perhaps you have owed me a grudge for having had a finger in settling it. It will be dull for you boxed up with the old lady and her rheumatism, but you must bear in mind that I shall be working for you here, better than, maybe, I could if you were by."

"Why, Meg, what do you want to do?" asked my sister, aghast.

"I'm going to get mother to make your engagement shorter," said I, getting up and standing in front of her, "and I'm going to make her allow you and Frank to write to one another."

"Oh, Meg, how can you?" gasped Joyce.

"Well, I'm going to," repeated I, doggedly. She did not reply. She clasped her hands in her lap with a nervous movement, and dropped her eyes upon them.

"Mother said that the year's engagement was so that you and Captain Forrester should learn to be quite sure of yourselves. Now, how are you to be any surer of yourselves than you are now if you don't get to know one another any better? And how are you going to know one another any better if you never see one another, and never write to one another?"

Joyce paused before she replied. She lifted her eyes and fixed them on the channel, of which the long, tortuous curves, winding across the marsh to the sea, were blue now with an opaque color in the growing grayness of the evening.

"Perhaps mother don't wish us to know one another any better. Perhaps she wishes us to forget one another," said she at last, slowly.

"I know mother wants you to forget one another, because she wants you to marry the squire," said I, bluntly, "but father doesn't."

"Oh, Meg, don't," whispered Joyce.

"Well, of course you know it," laughed I, a little ashamed of myself, "and you know that I know it. But you never would have married him, dear, so mother is none the worse off if you marry Captain Forrester, and you are not going to forget him because they want you to."

"No," murmured she. "But oh, Meg," she added, hastily rising too, and taking my hand, "I don't want you to say anything to them about it. It's settled now, and it's far best as it is. I had far rather let it be, and take my chance."

"What do you mean by taking your chance?" cried I. "You mean to say that you can trust to your lover not to forget you? Well, I suppose you can. He worships you, and I suppose one may fairly expect even a man to be faithful one little year. But, meanwhile, you will both of you be unhappy instead of being comparatively happy, as you would be if you could write to one another and see one another sometimes. Now, that seems to me to be useless, and I don't see why it need be. At all events, I shall try to prevent it."

"You're a good, faithful old Meg, as true as steel," said Joyce, tenderly, taking my hand; "and I suppose you can't understand how I feel, because we are so different. But I want you to believe that I would much rather wait. Indeed, I would much rather wait."

I gazed at her in silence. Once more there stole over me a strange feeling of awe, born of the conviction that Joyce had floated slowly away from me on the bosom of a stream that was to me unknown. Whither did it lead, and what was it like? What was this "being in love," of which I had dreamed of late—for her if not for myself? I laughed constrainedly.

"Well, I never was in love," said I, "and perhaps I never shall be. But I feel pretty sure that when a girl loves a man and he loves her, being parted must be like going about without a piece of one's own self. No, Joyce, you can't deceive me. I know that you want to see him every hour and every minute of your life, and that when you don't something goes wrong inside you all the while."

Joyce sighed gently, and drew her shawl around her. "You're so impetuous," sighed she. "Liking one person doesn't make one forget every one else."

"*Liking*, no," said I, and then I stopped.

The marsh-land had grown dark with a passing cloud, and the aspens on the cliff shivered in the rising wind. A window opened in the house behind, and Deborah's voice came calling to us across the lawn.

"Well, whatever you two must needs go catching your deaths of cold out there for, I don't know," cried she, as we came up to her. "And not so much as a young man to keep you company! Oh, there's two dismal faces!" laughed she, as I pushed past her. "Well, I was wiser in my time. The men never gave me no thoughts—good nor bad."

"No, you never got any one to mind you then as Reuben minds you now," cried I.

But Joyce stopped the retort by asking what we were wanted for.

"There's company in the parlor," answered she, speaking to me still. "The squire's come to bid Miss Joyce good-bye, and there's your friend Mr. Hoad."

I made no answer to this thrust, but as we passed through the passage, the door of father's room opened, and the voice of Mr. Hoad said, with a laugh: "No, I'm afraid you will never get any good out of him. A brilliant talker, a charming fellow, but no backbone in him. I was deceived in him myself at first, but he's no go. I should think the less any one reckoned on him for anything the better."

"You don't understand him," began father, warmly; but he stopped, seeing us.

My cheeks flushed with anger. There was a grin on Deborah's face, but my sister's was serene.

She could not have understood.

CHAPTER XIII

Joyce had been gone a week before Mr. Trayton Harrod arrived. I had preserved my gloomy silence on the subject of his coming, although I was dying to know all about it; and as father had given in to my mood by telling me no particulars, it so happened that I did not even know the exact day of his arrival.

It was a Monday and baking-day. There was plenty to do now that Joyce was gone, and I did not do her work as she did it. Mother was constantly reminding me of the fact. It did not make me do the work any quicker, or like doing it any better; but, of course, it was natural that mother should see the difference, and remark on it.

At last, however, the baking and mending and dusting was all done, and mother gave me leave to take a little basket of victuals to an old couple who lived down by the sea. I had been very miserable, feeling pitiably how little I had done at present towards fulfilling my promise to Joyce of trying to make things pleasant, and sadly conscious that I was not in mother's good books, or for that matter, in father's either, for which I am afraid I cared more. He had scarcely spoken a word to me all the week.

Poor father! Why did I not remember that it was far worse for him than it was for me? But as I ran across the lawn, with Taff yelping at my heels, I do not believe that I gave a thought to his anxieties, although I must have seen his dear old head bending over the farm account-books through the study window as I passed. I was so glad to have done with the house-keeping that I forgot everything else in the tender sunshine of a May afternoon that was flecking the marsh with spots of light, shifting as the soft clouds shifted upon the blue sky. How could any troubles matter, either my own or other people's, when there was a chance of being within scent of the sea-weed and within taste of the salt sea-brine?

I whistled the St. Bernard, and we set off on a race down the cliff. My hat flew off, I caught it by the strings; all the thickness of my hair uncoiled itself and rippled down my back. I felt the hair-pins tumble out one by one, and knew that a great curly, red mass must be floating in the wind; but I had a hundred yards to run yet before I came to the elms at the foot of the hill—and Taff was hard to beat.

Alongside the runnels that hemmed the lane, a ribbon, bluer than the sea or sky, ran bordering the green; it was made up of thousands of delicate veronica blossoms, opening merry eyes to the sun, and the red campion dotted the bank under the cliff, and the cuckoo flowers nodded their pale clusters on edges of little dikes. But I did not see the flowers just then; I ran on and on, jumping the gate that divides the marsh from the road almost as Taffy jumped it himself—on and on along the dike, without stopping, till I came to the first thorn-tree that grows upon the bank; and there, at last, I was fain to throw myself down to rest, out of breath and trembling.

What a run it was! I remember it to this day. It drove away all my ill-temper; and as I sat there twisting up my hair again, and laughing at Taff, who understood the joke just as if he were a human being, I had no more thought of anything ajar than had the white May-trees that dotted the marsh all along the brown banks of the dikes, and lay so harmoniously against the faint blue of the sky, where it sank into the deeper blue of the sea beyond.

Dimly, beyond the flaxen stretch of plain that was slowly flushing with the growing green, one could see the little waves rippling out across the yellow sands, with the sunlight flashing upon their crests; over the meadows red and white cattle wandered, and little spotless lambs played with their mothers on the fresher banks; tufts of tender primroses grew close to my hand, fish leaped in the still gray waters of the dike, birds sang in the belt of trees under the Manor-house, lapwing made strange bleating and chirping sounds amid the newly sprouting growth of the rushes that mingled softly with the faint gold of last year's mown crop; the cuckoo's note came now and then through the air. The spring had come at last.

I tied on my hat again and jumped up. I began to sing, too, as I walked. I was merry. What with Captain Forrester, and what with the trouble about the bailiff, and what with Joyce's departure, and the household duties falling upon me, I had not been out among my favorite haunts for a long time, and the sight of the birds and the beasts and the flowers was new life to me. I noted the marks of the year's growth as only one notes them who knows the country by heart; I knew that the young rooks were already on the wing, that the swifts and the swallows had built their nests, that the song-thrush was hatching her brood, and that a hunt along the sunny, sandy banks under the lea of the hill would discover the round holes where the little sand-martin would be laboriously scooping her nest some two feet deep into the soft ground.

I promised myself a happy afternoon when next I should have leisure, searching for plovers' eggs along the banks of the dikes where the moor-hen and lapwing make their homes; but to-day I dared not loiter, for the old couple for whom I was bound lived under the shadow of the great rock, where the marsh ends and the land swells up into white chalk-cliffs fronting the sea; and that was four good miles from where I now was. Taff and I put our best legs foremost, vaulting the gates that separated the fields, and crossing the white bridges over the water, until at last we came to where the dike meets the sea, and the Martello towers stud the coast.

I confess we had not always walked quite straight. Once my attention had been caught by the hovering of a titlark in the vicinity of a bank by the way-side, and I had not been able to resist the temptation of climbing a somewhat perilous ascent to look for the nest, whose neighborhood I guessed. It was on the face of a curious sort of cliff that lay across the marsh; one side of it sloped down into the pasture-land, but the other presented a gray, rugged front to the greensward below, and told of days when the sea must have lapped about its massive sides, and eaten its way into the curious caves where now young oaks and mountain-ash clove to the barren soil.

About half-way up the nethermost bank of this cliff I found the nest of the titlark beneath a heather bush. But in it sat a young cuckoo alone and scarcely fledged, while lying down the bank, about a foot from the margin of the nest, lay the two little nestlings of the parent bird. I picked them up and warmed them in my hand, and put them back in the nest, where they soon lifted their heads again. Then I stood a moment and watched. The young cuckoo began struggling about till it got its back under one of them, and, blind as it still was, hitched it up to the open part of the nest, and shoved it out onto the bank. Once more I picked the poor little bird up and put it back into its mother's nest. Then seeing that the cruel little interloper seemed to have made up its mind to try no more ejecting for the moment, I slid down the bank again and went on, promising myself, however, to look in upon this quarrelsome family on my way home.

This little adventure delayed us, but we ran a great part of the remainder of the way to make up for it, and reached old Warren's cottage somewhat out of breath, and I with red cheeks and hair sorely dishevelled by the journey. However, as we were old friends, we were soon restored by the kindly welcome that we got. Taffy lay down on the hearth with the great Persian cat, and I took my seat in the chimney corner, Mrs. Warren insisting on preferring the bed for a seat.

It was a funny little hut, nestled away under the shadow of the towering cliff, with the sea lapping or roaring within fifty yards of it, and the lonely marsh stretching away miles and miles to the right of it. No one knew why Warren had built it, but some fancied that he still had smuggled goods hidden away in the caves of the cliffs, and if so, he naturally chose a dwelling-place hard by, and not too much under the eye of man. It was a poor hovel, better to die in than to live in, one would have thought; but old Warren seemed to be of a contented disposition, and to enjoy his life well enough, although as much could not apparently be said of his wives, of whom he had had three already. The present one had lasted the longest, the former two having been killed off in comparatively early life (according to Warren) by the loneliness of their life and the terrors of the elements which they had witnessed.

Warren was a dramatic old fellow, and could tell many a story of shipwreck and disaster, and even (when pressed) of encounters between the revenue-cutters and the smugglers' boats, of dangerous landings on this dangerous bit of coast, and of nights when it was all the "boys" could do to get their kegs of spirits safely ashore and buried in the sand before morning. This afternoon he was in particularly good spirits. Something in the color of the land and the sea and in the direction of the wind had reminded him of a day when the fog had come up suddenly and had caused disaster, although, to my eye, the heavens were clear and fair as any one could wish. I soon drew from him the account of a terrible struggle between the Government officers and the smugglers, when the fog had given the latter a miraculous and unexpected triumph, and this led on to the tale—oft-repeated but never stale—of the wreck of the Portuguese "merchant," when the "lads" picked up the wicker bottles that floated ashore, and drank themselves sick with eau-de-cologne in mistake for brandy.

This was my favorite story; but it was hard to know whether to laugh or to cry when Mrs. Warren number three would shake her head sympathetically at the tearful account of the demise of Mrs. Warren number two, who "lay a-dying within, while the lads drank the spirits without," and old Warren was forced to take a drain himself to help him in his trouble.

The time always passed quickly for me with the funny old couple in their funny old hovel under the cliff, and it was late afternoon before I got out again onto the beach. Warren's memories had not been awakened by mere fancy; his prophecy was right. There was a heavy sea-fog over the marsh, blown up by a wind from the east. I gathered my cloak around me and set off walking as fast as I could. The mist was so thick that the dog shook himself as he ran on in front of me; the damp stood in great drops on the bristles of his shaggy coat and of my rough homespun cloak; it took the curl even out of my curly hair, which hung down in dank masses by the side of my face.

I could not see the sea, though I could hear it lapping on the shore close by; I could not even see the dike at my left, and yet it was not thirty yards away. I knew the way well enough, however, and the fog only made an amusing variety to an every-day walk. I started off merrily, avoiding the road, which was not the shortest way, and making, to the best of my belief, a straight line across the marsh, as I had done hundreds of times before. But a mist is deceptive, and I could not have been walking more than a quarter of an hour when I felt the ground suddenly give way beneath me, and I found myself disappearing into one of the deep ditches that intersect the marsh between the broader dikes.

I knew that there was brackish water at the bottom of the ditch, and though I did not mind a ducking, I did not care for a ducking in dirty water, and so far from home. By clutching onto the docks and teasels on the bank, I managed to hold myself up and get my heels into the soil, and then, with one spring, I landed myself on the opposite bank. My petticoats would not escape Deborah's notice, but my feet were dry, and even my skirts would not attract immediate attention.

But how had I got to the ditch? and where was I now? Yes, I must have borne farther to the left than I had intended; but it did not much signify— one way across the marsh was as good as another to me, and I had better keep to this side now, and go home under the lea of the hill. There would be the advantage that I might be able to find my little titlark again. I whistled, for I could not see the dog, and presently my call was answered by a loud barking close in front of me, and lifting up my face, I vaguely saw Taff chasing some larger object before him into the mist.

I knew at once that in coming to this side of the ditch I had landed myself among a herd of the cattle that had now taken up their summer quarters upon the marsh. I was not afraid of the cattle; I had seen them there ever since I had been a child, browsing in the warm weather; they were part of the land. But I wondered just where I had got to, and I stopped to think where the sea was, and where the dike. Without these two landmarks I was somewhat bewildered. The cattle closed around me. They, too, seemed to be doubtful about something, but they kept their eyes on me. I wished Taff would not bark so.

I turned round, and once more began walking briskly in the direction which I thought was the right one. A great brown beast stood just in front of me. I had not noticed him before, but he had come up over a mound of the uneven marsh-land and stood staring at me with head gently rocking. Up till now I had not had a moment's uneasiness, but I began to wonder whether the marsh cattle were always safe. I moved, and the bull moved too. Taff barked louder than ever, and the bull began to bellow softly. I was never so cross with the dog in my life, and I could not punish him, for I dared not take my eyes off the brown beast.

I moved forward till I had passed the place where the bull stood. But now it was worse than ever. The mist was so thick, and I had so entirely lost my way, that I dared not retreat backward for fear of falling into an unseen dike, and some of the dikes were deep at this time of the year. I began to run gently, but my heart failed me as I heard behind me the bull following, still bellowing softly. If I were only on the right road there must be a gate soon, but I feared I was not on the right road. Taff kept running round in front of me, hindering my speed. I felt that the creature was gaining on me. I don't think I was ever so frightened before. I don't remember that my presence of mind ever so entirely failed me as it did on that day. But my legs seemed as though they were tied together. I stood still, waiting, and then I think I must have fallen to the ground.

I knew that the bull must be close upon me, and it was no more than what I expected when I felt myself suddenly lifted up by the waist and flung to what seemed to me an immense distance through the air. For a moment I lay stunned. The bellowing of the bull, the barking of the dog, the murmur of the sea—all mingled in my ears in one great booming sound. Then slowly I became conscious that there was a human presence beside me in the fog. I opened my eyes. I was lying close under a five-barred gate. The bull was on the other side of it; Taffy lay whining beside me, and over me stood a big, tall man, looking down at me quietly.

"Are you hurt, miss?" said he.

I struggled into a sitting posture, and pulled myself up on my feet by the help of the gate.

"No; no, thank you," answered I. But my head was dizzy, and my arm ached dreadfully.

"I'm afraid I flung you over rather hard," said he. "But there wasn't time to do it nicely."

"You flung me over!" cried I, aghast.

"To be sure," answered he, "Did you think it was the bull?"

He gave a short laugh, scarcely a laugh, it was so very grim and quiet. But when he laughed his smile was like a white flash—I remember noticing it. I gazed at him. Angry as I was—and I was absurdly, childishly angry—I could not help gazing at this man, who could take me up like a baby and fling me over a five-barred gate in a twinkling.

He was very broad and strong, his eyes were dark brown, his hair was black and curling, and so was his beard. He had neither a pleasant face nor a handsome face—until he smiled. I was not conscious at the time of any of these details; but there in the fog I thought he looked very imposing.

"I'm afraid if it had been the bull he would have flung you farther, and hurt you more," said he. "You lay there very handy for him."

How I hated myself for having fallen to the ground!

"Come, Taff," said I, giving the dog a little kick, "get up."

The dog sprang to his feet with his tail between his legs. No wonder he was frightened and surprised. I had never done such a thing to him before. But I had a vague feeling that if he had not hindered me I should have got over the gate alone, and I was savage at the idea of having needed help from a man.

"Good-evening to you," said I, curtly, nodding my head in the direction of the man, but without looking at him again.

"Good-evening," answered he, raising his hat. "I hope you'll be none the worse for your fall."

I vouchsafed no answer to this speech, but strode on down the track as fast as my aching limbs and dizzy head would allow me to do. The sea murmured on the beach at my right. I could not see it for the fog, but I could hear it. After a while I think it must have lulled my anger to rest. The sea has always been a good friend to me, in its storms as in its calm. I like to see it rage as I dare not rage, and I like to see it calm as I cannot be calm. The restless sea has taught me as many things as the quiet marsh; they are both very wide. And that day I am sure it lulled my irritable temper.

Before long I began to think that I, to say the least of it, had treated my deliverer with scant courtesy. When I got to the farm that divides the marsh from the beach I turned round to see if he were following. The fog was beginning to lift. The distant hills of the South Downs rose out of the sea of vapor, and were as towering mountains in the mystery, lying dim and yet blue against the struggling light of the sunset behind. The white headland that I had left detached itself boldly against the sea-line—for the mist was only on the level land now, where it lay like a sheet a few feet above the marsh, so that the objects on the ground itself shone, illumined by the slanting rays of the sun, till each one had a value of its own in the scene. Through the golden spray of the sunlit vapor the red and the white cattle shone like jewels upon the brown land, where every little line of water was like a snake in the vivid light; and as I turned and looked towards the gray cliff, where I had climbed the bank after the bird's-nest an hour ago, the long line of hill behind, dotted with fir-trees and church-steeples and little homesteads, lay midway in the air through the silver veil.

I stood a while looking back. I do not know that I was conscious of the wonder of the scene, but I remember it very vividly. At the time I think I was chiefly busy wishing the stranger to come up that I might rectify my lack of courtesy. I saw him at last. He came in sight very slowly, and stood a long while leaning against the last gate lighting his pipe. I watched him several minutes, and he never once looked along the path to see if I was there. Why was I annoyed? I had dismissed him almost rudely. He did but do as he was bid. And yet I do believe I was annoyed; I do believe I was unreasonable to that point.

CHAPTER XIV

When I came into supper that evening my friend of the fog was standing beside father on the parlor hearth-rug. Directly I saw him, I wondered how I could have been such a fool as not to have guessed at once that that was Mr. Trayton Harrod. But it had never occurred to me for a moment; and when I recognized in the man to whom I had promised to be friendly, also the person who had presumed to take me by the waist and pitch me over a gate, all my bad temper of before swelled up within me worse than ever, and I felt as though it would be quite impossible for me even to be civil. And yet I had since promised somebody, even more definitely than I had promised Joyce, that I would do my best to make matters run smoothly.

On that very evening father had made an appeal to my better feelings. It seems that, while I had been out, Reuben Ruck and mother had had a real pitched battle. Mother had told him to do something in preparation for the arrival of the bailiff, which he had refused to do; and upon that mother had gone to father, and had said that it was absolutely necessary that Reuben should leave.

When I came home I had found father standing on the terrace in the sunset. It was a very unwise thing for him to do, for the air was chill. I wondered what had brought him out, and whether he could be looking for me. The little feeling of estrangement that had been between us since he had settled for the bailiff to come to the farm had given me a great deal of pain, and a lump rose in my throat as I saw him there watching me come up the hill. It was partly repentance for the feelings I had had towards him, partly hope that he was going to want me again as he used to do.

"Where have you been, lass?" said he, when I reached him. "You look sadly."

I laughed. The tears were near, but I laughed. My arm hurt me very much, and my head ached strangely; but I was so glad to hear him speak to me again like that.

"The mist has taken my hair out of curl," said I; "that's all. I have been down to the cliffs to take old Warren some tea. Did you want me?"

"Yes," answered he; "I want to have a talk with you."

"Well, come in-doors then," said I. "You know you oughtn't to be out so late."

We went into the study. Mother and Deb were getting supper ready in the front dwelling-room. There was no lamp lit; we sat down in the dusk.

"Your mother and Reuben have had a row, Meg," began father, with a kind of twinkle in his eye, although he spoke gravely.

"A row!" echoed I; "what about?"

"About Mr. Trayton Harrod," answered father; "she wants me to send Reuben away."

"Send Reuben away!" cried I, aghast. "Why, it wouldn't be possible. There would be more harm done by the old folks going away than any good that would come of new folks coming; that I'll warrant."

"That's not the question," said father, tapping the table with his hand. "Mr. Harrod has got to come, you know, and if the old folks don't like it, why, they'll have to go."

"There's one thing certain," added I, "Reuben wouldn't go if he were sent away fifty times."

Father laughed; the first time I had heard him laugh for a fortnight.

"Well, he'll have to be pleasant if he does stay," said he.

"Oh, you none of you understand Reuben," said I. "He's not so stupid as you all think. He'll be pleasant if he thinks it's for our good that he should be pleasant. He wishes us well. But he'll want convincing first. And," I added, with a little laugh, "maybe I want convincing myself first."

And it was then that father appealed to my better feelings.

"Yes, Meg," said he, "I know that. I've seen that all along, and maybe it's natural. We none of us like strangers about. But I thought fit to have Mr. Harrod come for the good of the farm, and now what we all have to do is to treat him civilly, and make the work easy for him." I was silent, but father went on: "And what I want you to do, Meg, is to help me make the work easy for him. It won't be easier to him than it is to us. If his father had not died beggared I suppose he would have had his own by now. It is a hard thing for children when their parents beggar them." It being dark, I could not see his face, but I heard him sigh, and I saw him pass his hand over his brow. "Mother is right," he added. "We ought to make him feel it as little as we can, and as Joyce is away, you're the daughter of the house now, Meg. I want you to remember that. I want you to do the honors of the house as a daughter should. What a daughter is at home a wife will be when she is married."

"I shall never marry," said I, with a short laugh. "But I'll behave properly, father, never fear."

"That's right, my lass," said father, who seemed to take this speech as meaning something more conciliatory than it looks now as I set it down. "He is coming to-night to supper. Mother means to ask him to come every night to supper. She would have liked to give him house-room, but that don't seem to be possible. So we mean to make him welcome to our board."

"All right," said I. "I suppose mother knows best."

"Yes," echoed father; "mother always knows best. She's a wise woman, that's why every one loves her."

Again I promised to do what I could to resemble mother—to conciliate Reuben, and to make myself agreeable to our guest. And yet, alas! in spite of all that, I could not conquer my petty feelings of ill-temper when I came into the parlor and found that the man to whom I intended to be polite was the man who had offended me by being polite to me. What a foolish girl I was! As I look back upon it now I am half inclined to smile. But I was only nineteen.

Mr. Harrod had his back towards me when I came into the room. But I could not have failed to recognize the broad, strong shoulders and the very black curly hair. I must have been the more changed of the two, for I had brushed and braided my locks, which curled all the merrier for the wetting, and I had put on another dress. Nevertheless, his eyes had scarcely rested upon me before his mouth broke again into that smile that showed the strong white teeth.

"I hope you're none the worse, miss," said he. "I was afraid you had got a bad shaking."

Deborah, who was bringing in the supper, looked at me sharply. Mother had not yet come in, and father was in a brown-study, but the remark had not escaped old Deb. She could not keep silence even before a stranger.

"I thought you looked as if you had been up to some mischief again," said she. "Your face is a nice sight."

I flushed angrily. I think it was enough to make any girl angry. It was bad enough to know that I was disfigured by a scratch on my cheek without having a stranger's attention attracted to it, and running a risk besides of a scolding from mother, who came in at the moment. Luckily she did not hear what Deborah had said. She was too much engaged in welcoming her guest, which she did with that gentle dignity that to some might have looked like a want of cordiality, but to me seems, as I look back upon it, to be just what a welcome should be—hospitable without being anxious. But when we were seated at the supper-table she noticed the mark on my face.

"It's only a fall that I got on the marsh," said I, in answer to her inquiry. "It isn't of the slightest consequence."

She said no more, neither did Mr. Harrod. I must say I was grateful to him. He saw that I wished the matter to be forgotten, and he respected my desire; but I have often wondered since, what construction he put upon my behavior. If he thought about me at all, he must have considered me a somewhat extraordinary example of a young lady, but I do not suppose that he did consider me at all. Of course I was nothing but a figure to him; he had plenty to do feeling his level in the new life upon which he had just entered.

I am sure that Mr. Harrod was a very shy and a very proud man. When mother said that she should expect him every evening to sup at the Grange, he refused her invitation with what I thought scant gratitude, although the words he used were civil enough; and when father spoke of his friendship with the squire, he said that he was beholden to the squire for his recommendation, but that he should never consider himself a friend of a man who was in a different station of life to himself.

I think in my heart I admired him for this sentiment, and father should also have approved of it; but if I remember rightly, mother made some quiet rejoinder to the effect that it was not always the people who were on one's own level that were really one's best friends. I recollect that she, who was wont generally to sit and listen, worked hard that evening to keep up the conversation.

Dear mother! whom with the arrogance of youth I had never considered excellent excepting as a housewife or a sick-nurse. County news, the volunteer camp, the drainage of the marsh, the scarcity of well-water, the want of enterprise in the towns-people, the coming elections—dear me, she had them all out, whereas father and I, who had undertaken, as it were, to put our best legs foremost, sat silent and glum. To do myself justice, I had a racking headache, and for once in my life I really felt ill, but I might have behaved better than I did.

Mr. Harrod began to thaw slowly under the influence of mother's kindness. She had such a winning way with her when she chose, that everybody gave way before it; and I noticed that even from the very first, when he was certainly in a touchy frame of mind towards these, his first employers, Mr. Harrod treated mother with just the same reverential consideration that every one always used towards her.

Margaret Maliphant | 123

In spite of it all that first evening was not a comfortable time. Father and Mr. Harrod compared notes upon different breeds of cattle and upon different kinds of grains; but there was a restraint upon us all, and I think every one was glad when mother made the move from the table and father lit his pipe. I have no knowledge of how they got on afterwards over their tobacco; when I rose from the table the room swam around me, and if it had not been for Deborah, who, entering on some errand at the moment, took me by the shoulders and pushed me out of the door in front of her, I am afraid I should have made a most unusual and undignified exhibition of myself in the Grange parlor. As it was I had to submit to be tucked up in bed by the old woman, and only persuaded her with the greatest difficulty not to tell mother of my accident, some account of which, as was to be expected, she wrung from me in explanation of Mr. Harrod's words in the parlor.

"I'd not have been beholden to him if I could have helped it," were the consoling words with which she left me; and as I lay there, aching and miserable, I became quite convinced that any comradeship between myself and my father's bailiff had become all the more impossible because of the occurrence of the afternoon.

CHAPTER XV

I got up the next morning just as usual. Nothing should have induced me to confess that there was anything the matter with me, although my arm was so stiff that it was with the greatest pain that I carried in the breakfast urn, and my head ached so from my fall that it was hard enough to put a good face upon it when mother remarked again upon the disfigurement that I had upon my cheek. But although I gave no sign, I was not used to being ill, and it did not improve my temper.

Things were not comfortable in the house, and I did nothing to make them better. To be sure, I kept my promise of talking to Reuben, but I'm afraid that I did not even do that in a manner to be of any use. I met Mr. Harrod as I passed out into the stable-yard, and he asked me how I did? That alone put me out.

To have been asked how I did by any one that morning would have annoyed me, but to be asked how I did by the man who was somehow connected with my doing ill annoyed me specially. I fancied it would have been in better taste if he had not remarked upon a body's appearance when she was looking her worst; and anyhow it seemed to me an unnecessary formality. I feel really ashamed now to write down such nonsense, but there is no doubt that such were my feelings at the time. I do not think that I even answered him by anything more than a "good-morning," but passed on as though I had the affairs of the world on my shoulders.

I found Reuben rubbing down the mare who was to go into town with father. She neighed as I came in, and stretched out her neck. I had no sugar, but she licked my hand nevertheless; and I remembered Reuben's compliment to me about my ability to win the love of beasts. It consoled me a little at a time when I thought I should always stand aloof, not only from the love but even from the comradeship of human beings. And it gave me courage to say what I wanted to say to Reuben. It was something to know that I was at least the old man's favorite.

"Reuben," I began, plunging boldly into the matter, "whatever made you behave so badly to father's bailiff when he came round the place?"

There had been a special cause of complaint that very morning when father had first taken Mr. Harrod round the farm, so I had a handle upon which to begin.

"Don't you know," I went on, "that this gentleman has got to be master over you?"

"Master!" repeated Reuben, stopping his work, and looking straight at me; "no, miss, I knows nothing about that."

I had used the word on purpose to draw out the whole sting at once.

"Yes," continued I, "he's going to be father's bailiff."

"Bailiff!" repeated Reuben, again putting on his most stolid air. "I knows nothing about that."

"Well," explained I, trying neither to laugh nor to be annoyed, "that means that he is going to manage the land and give orders the same as father, so that there'll be two masters instead of one."

Reuben continued rubbing down the mare's coat till it began to shine like satin.

"I've heard tell," answered he at last, "there's something in the Book that says a man don't have no call to serve two masters."

This time I did laugh outright. "Oh, that's different, Reuben," said I—"that's different; but these two masters will both be good, and both will want you to do the same thing."

"Do ye know that for sure, miss?" asked Reuben, again, and I had a lurking suspicion that he did not ask in a perfectly teachable spirit. "I've heard tell as when there be two masters, they always wants a man to do just the opposite things."

I paused a moment. I did not know what to answer, for it seemed to me as though there might be a great deal of truth in this.

But I said, bravely, "Oh no, Reuben."

Reuben scratched his head. "Well, miss, Farmer Maliphant, he have been my master fifteen year come Michaelmas, and he have been a good master to me. Many another would have turned me away because o' the drink. It was chill work at times down there on the marsh when I was with the sheep, and the drink was a comfort. I nigh upon died o' the drink, but Farmer Maliphant he have been patient with me, and he give me another chance when others would have sacked me without a word. And now I be what parson calls a reformed character."

"Well, you are quite right to avoid drinking, Reuben," said I, chiefly because I did not know what to say.

"Yes; but I don't mind tellin' you, miss," continued Reuben, confidentially, "that farmer he have more to do with making a pious man of me than parson had; not but what I respec's the Church; but bless you, parson wouldn't ha' given me nothing for giving up o' my bad ways, and where's the use of doing violence to yerself if ye ain't a goin' to get something by it?"

Reuben wiped his brow. This long and unwonted effort of speech was almost too much for him.

"Nay, parson he didn't offer me no reward," added he, "but farmer he did. He says to me, 'Reuben,' he says, 'if you give up the drink you shall stay on as long as I'm above-ground;' and three times I backslided, I did, and three times he give me another chance; and now as I'm a respectable party, and a honor to any club as I might belong to, I means to stick to my old master, and not be for going after follerin' any other mammon whatsomever."

I brightened up at this declaration.

"Well, I'm glad of that, Reuben," said I. "I'm sure we none of us want you to leave us after all these years."

"Lord bless you, I ain't a-going to leave," answered he, simply.

"Then that's all right," answered I. "If you have made up your mind to do as you're bid, I know father will be true to his word, and will never turn you off so long as he is alive."

"Ay, the master'll be true to his word," echoed the old man, nodding his head, "and I'll be true to mine, but I won't go follerin' after no new masters. One master's enough for me, and him only will I serve."

He gave the mare a smack upon her haunches, and turned her off; the light of reason faded from his face, and I knew that it was absolutely useless to say another word to him on the subject. I turned to go within, and in the porch, with a bowl in her hand, stood Deborah facing me, with an exasperating smile on her wide red face, and something more than usually aggressive in her broad, strong figure. I looked round and saw that the gate of the yard was open, and that Mr. Harrod, with his heavy boots and gaiters on, ready for work, stood just behind me. I could have cried with vexation.

"Mr. Maliphant is waiting," said he, going up to the animal that Reuben had just finished harnessing, and fastening the last buckle himself. "I'll drive the cart round to the front myself." And he took the reins and jumped up while Reuben, in gloomy silence, tightened up one of the straps. I went and opened the gates, and with a nod of thanks to me, Mr. Harrod dashed out.

I cannot tell whether it was the strap that he had fastened himself, or whether the one that had been Reuben's doing, but something galled the mare. She reared and began to kick. Without a smile upon his face, and without moving an inch, Reuben said, "Ay, it takes a man to hold that mare."

"You fool!" cried I, quite forgetting myself. "It isn't the man, it's the harness."

I flew down the gravel after the cart. The horse was still kicking violently. Every muscle on Mr. Harrod's dark face was set in hard lines.

"Leave her alone," cried he, as I approached; "don't touch her."

Something in his voice cowed me, and apparently cowed the horse also, for she was quiet in an instant, her sides only quivering with nervousness. I sprang to her and unloosed the cruel strap. She turned to me, and I held her by the bridle and patted her neck. Mr. Harrod got down and examined the cart. Fortunately it was not materially hurt.

"What can Reuben have been about to tighten that so," said I. "It was enough to madden any horse."

He did not answer.

"I'm afraid he was angry at your giving him an order," said I. "You must excuse him. He's an obstinate old fellow, but he is a good servant, and he has been with us many years."

"It's the most natural thing in the world that he should dislike me at first," answered Trayton Harrod, with that smile of his that was such a quick, short flash. "I rather like the sort of people who resent interference. But I don't suppose it was his doing for a moment. I buckled this up wrong."

He pointed to his part of the job. Father came up, and they drove off quietly together. I went back into the yard, musing on his words.

"I don't believe you'll find Mr. Harrod an unjust master, Reuben," said I.

Reuben took no notice; but Deborah laughed, and said, grimly:

"Well, he's a fine-grown young man, anyhow; and he'll know how to drive a mare, I don't doubt."

But I paid no attention to her words. I was wondering why Mr. Harrod had said that he rather liked people who resented interference.

CHAPTER XVI

A fortnight passed. I had seen little or nothing of Mr. Harrod till one afternoon when, with a volume of Walter Scott under my arm, I had taken my basket to get some plovers' eggs off the marsh. I had wandered a long way far beyond that part of the dike that lay beneath the village and was apt to be frequented by passers-by, and I had already about a dozen eggs in my little basket, when I heard some one whistling down behind the reeds on the opposite side of the bank.

It might have been a shepherd. There was a track across the level here, and none but the shepherds knew it; but somehow I did not think it was a shepherd. I sat down upon the turf, for the bulrushes in the dike had not yet grown to any height, and I did not want to be seen.

"Taff!" called a voice.

Yes, it was Mr. Harrod. I had missed the St. Bernard when I had been coming out, and had wondered where he had gone, for I had wanted him for a companion—Luck, the sheep-dog being out with Reuben. I wondered how it was that Mr. Harrod could have taken him.

I sat quite still among the rushes, where I had been looking for the birds'-nests. I did not want to be seen, and, as far as I remembered, there was no plank over the dike just here. But there was some one who knew the marsh better than I did. It was the dog. As soon as he got opposite to where I was, he began barking loudly, and then he ran back some hundred yards and stood still, barking and wagging his tail, and as plainly as possible inviting his companion to follow him.

Mr. Harrod must have loved dogs almost as much as I did, for he actually turned back, and when he came to where Taff stood he laughed. There was evidently a plank there, and I suppose he must have guessed that he was expected for some reason to cross over. He did so, and Taff followed. The dog tore along the path to me, and Mr. Harrod followed slowly. He did not seem at all surprised to see me. He came towards me with a book in his hand.

"I think you must have dropped this," he said, handing it to me. "We found it just down yonder."

He said "we." It must have been the sagacity of that wretched dog which had betrayed me, for there was no name in the book. I took it reluctantly; I was rather ashamed of my love of reading. Girls in the country were not supposed usually to be fond of reading. If it hadn't been for those good old-fashioned novels in father's library, mother would have considered the Bible, and as much news as was needed not to make one appear a fool, as much literature as any woman required. A love of reading might be considered an affectation in me, and there was nothing of which I had such a wholesome horror as affectation.

I took the book in silence—my manners did not mend—and stooped down to pat the dog. I wanted to move away, but I didn't quite know how to do it. Taffy wagged his tail as if he hadn't seen me for weeks. Foolish beast! If he was so fond of me, why did he go after strangers so easily?

"Taff knows the marsh," said I, for the sake of saying something.

"Famously," said Mr. Harrod. "He shows me the way everywhere. We are the best of friends."

I frowned. Was it an apology for having taken my dog?

"Taff will follow any one," I said, roughly.

It was not true, for Taff had never been known to follow any one before; and even as I said it, I wondered if Mr. Harrod were one of those whom "the beasts love," but he took no notice of my rudeness.

"What have you got there?" asked he, looking into my basket.

"Plovers' eggs," answered I. "There are lots on the marsh nearer the beach."

"Lapwings' eggs," corrected he, taking one in his hand.

"Oh no! plovers' eggs," insisted I. "They are sold as plovers' eggs in the shops in town as well as here."

"Yes," smiled he. "They are sold as plovers' eggs all over the London market also, but the lapwing—or the pewit, as you call it—lays them for all that. It is a bird of the plover family, but it should not properly be called a plover."

I bit my lip.

"Of course those are not all plovers' eggs," said I, taking up one of a creamy color spotted with brown, which was quite different to the gray ones mottled with black, that seemed to have been designed to escape detection on the gray beach, where they are generally found. "This is a dabchick's egg."

"I see you know more about birds than most young ladies do," said Mr. Harrod; "but I should call that a moor-hen's egg. And as for the gray plover, it is a migratory bird; it does not breed in England."

I suppose I still looked unconvinced, for he added, pleasantly, "Come, I'll bet you anything you like; and if we can be lucky enough to find a bird on the eggs, I'll prove it you now."

He turned round and began walking slowly along the bank of the dike, close to the water's edge. I gave Taff a friendly cuff to keep him quiet, for he was rather excitable, and it was necessary that we should be very wary if we wanted to surprise the bird sitting.

Mr. Harrod crept cautiously along, and I followed; I was as anxious now as he was, and by this simple means I was entrapped into a walk with my sworn enemy. A brown bird with a long bill got up among the reeds, and flew in a halting manner down to the water. It was a water-rail, and Mr. Harrod said so—for these birds are rarer upon the dike than the moor-hens and pewits, of which there are a great number, and I suppose he imagined I would not know it.

Something moved in the growing rushes at our feet; but it was only a couple of black moor-hens, who took to their heels, so to speak, with great velocity, and made little flights in the air with their legs hanging down and their bodies very perpendicular. We stood and laughed at them a minute, they were so very absurd out of their proper element; but when they took to the water they were pretty enough, the little red shields standing out upon their black foreheads as they jerked their heads in swimming.

I came upon a mother moor-hen presently tending her little brood; the large flat nest, built of dried rushes, lay in the overhanging branches of a willow-shrub, and she stood on the bank hard by. She did not fly or run away as other birds do when frightened, but stood there croaking as if in anger, and fluttering anxiously round the place where the six little balls of black down showed their red heads above the edge of the nest.

I held Taff by the collar, to prevent his doing any mischief, and we left the poor faithful mother undisturbed. We had not found any plovers' eggs since we had begun to look. They are always hard to find, being laid upon the open ground, sometimes on the very beach, where they almost look like little pebbles themselves, and sometimes in furrows and clefts of the earth, but always without any nest to mark the place. I suppose I had pretty well scoured this particular reach.

About a hundred yards farther on, however, the strange cry that distinguishes the bird we sought fell upon our ears; a cock lapwing flew up, his long feathery crest erect, and tumbled over and over in the air in the manner peculiar to his kind, uttering all the while the plaintive "cheep, cheep" that means distress and anxiety.

Mr. Harrod held out a warning hand behind him as he crept forward gently on tiptoe, and I was obliged to be silent, although I was particularly anxious to speak. Presently he beckoned to me to advance, and as I did so I saw the hen-bird running along the bank as close to the ground as possible, while in a furrow close by my feet lay the pretty, gray-spotted eggs that we were looking for.

Mr. Harrod turned and looked at me with a little smile, which I chose to think was one of triumph. "That proves nothing," said I. "I call that bird a plover, a green plover. I can't help it if you call it something else. Of course, I know there's another sort of plover; the golden plover, but no one could confuse the two, for this one has got a crest on its head which it lifts up and down when it likes."

"Oh, I beg your pardon," answered he. "I see you know all about it. It's only a confusion of terms."

I flushed and stooped down to pick up the eggs.

"No, don't," said he; "let the poor thing have them. You will see, she will fly back as soon as we have gone away."

We stepped back into the path, and surely, in a moment, the two parents met in the air, tumbling over together, and still uttering their plaintive cry. Then presently the hen-bird floated down again and returned to her patient duty; and soon her mate followed her also, and both were hidden among the rushes.

I turned round with a little laugh. I had thought I was annoyed; but the fact is, I was too happy to be annoyed.

The panoply of a tender gray sky, fashioned of many and many soft clouds, floating over and past one another, and lightening a little where the sun should have been, was spread over the placid ground; the sea was gray, too, beyond the flats, melting into the gray sky, the white headland in the distance, and the gray towers along the shore seemed very near and distinct; sheep wandered up and down the banks of the dike, cropping steadily; the air was soft and kindly. My heart beat with a sense of satisfaction that was unlike anything I had ever felt before; and yet many was the time that I had been out on the marsh on just such a soft day, among the birds and the beasts whom I loved.

"Listen," said I, presently, breaking the pleasant silence, as a loud, screaming bird's note, by no means beautiful, but full of delightful associations, came across the marsh. "The swifts are beginning to sing; that means summer indeed."

A little company of the lovely black birds came towards us, flying wildly in circles above the dike, sipping the water as they skimmed its surface, and then away again over the meadows.

"I wonder how it is that they are so black and glossy when they come over to us, and so gray and dingy when they go away?" said I.

"Have you noticed that as a fact?" asked he.

"Oh yes," I replied; and I am sure that I was very proud to be able to say so. "They come for May-Day, looking as smart as possible; and they don't look at all the better for their seaside season when they leave at the end of August."

"I expect they moult in those other countries to which they go when they leave us. But I haven't noticed very many swifts about here, anyhow. Perhaps the country is too wild for them."

"Well, we have plenty of swallows," said I, "and martins too. And I don't know why swifts should be so much more particular than the rest of their family. But I have a standing disagreement upon that point with our old servant Reuben. He swears that there are only eight pairs of swifts in the village, and that the same birds come back every year to the same place."

"That sounds rather incredible," said Mr. Harrod.

"So I say," rejoined I. "But he insists that he has counted the pairs, and that they are always the same number. And as, of course, there must be a pair of young to every pair of old birds when they leave us, he argues that the parent birds refuse to allow the young ones to inhabit the same place when they return. Reuben is as positive about it as possible," added I, laughing. "These swifts live under the eaves of the old church; and I do believe he greets them as old friends every year."

"I shouldn't venture to say that he was mistaken," said Mr. Harrod. "So many curious things happen among beasts and birds, and swifts are particularly amusing creatures. Reuben appears to be quite a naturalist."

I had quite forgotten my self-imposed attitude of defiance in the keen interest of this talk; but something in the tone of this remark roused it afresh.

"If that means some one who knows about birds and things, yes—he is," answered I, with a shake of my head—a foolish habit which I know I had when I wanted to be emphatic. "Probably a much better naturalist than people who learn only from books. He taught me all I know," added I, proudly, and not for a moment perceiving the construction that might be put upon this remark. "I used to be out here with him whole days when I was a child, and we both of us got into no end of scrapes for 'doing what we ought not to do, and leaving undone what we had to do.' Oh, but it was fun!" added I, with a sigh.

My companion laughed. "Delightful, I am sure," said he; "and it did you a great deal more good than sticking to books, I'll be bound."

He looked at me straight as he said this, as though he were taking my measure.

"I did stick to my books, too," cried I, quickly, anxious that he should not think me an ignoramus. "Mother was always very particular about that."

"Yes, yes, of course," said he. And then he added, with what I fancied was a twinkle of fun in his eye, "'The Fair Maid of Perth' is not every young lady's choice."

I blushed. Perhaps, after all, he did not think me ridiculous for reading novels. I was half angry, half ashamed, but it never occurred to me to wonder why I should care what this new acquaintance said or thought.

"We didn't read novels in lesson-time," said I, stiffly; "we didn't read many novels at all. Father and mother don't hold with novels for girls, and mother don't hold with poetry either, but father likes Milton and Shakespeare."

"I dare say they are quite right," said my companion. "But you are not of the same mind I suppose?"

"No," answered I, boldly, determined to be honest. "I think Sir Walter Scott's novels are lovely; and I like poetry—all that I can understand."

Mr. Harrod laughed. "I don't think I should have been willing to admit there was anything I couldn't understand when I was your age," he said.

I looked at him surprised. He talked as though he were ever so much older than I was, although he did not look more than six or seven and twenty. I forgot that even then there would be years between us. I always was forgetting that I was scarcely more than a child.

"I think that would be silly," said I, loftily. I forgot another thing, and that was that I had shown Mr. Harrod pretty constantly since he had been at the Grange, that I was not fond of admitting there was anything I could not understand, and that if there were any shrewdness in him, he must have set it down by this time as a special trait in me.

"Well, anyhow you understand the 'Fair Maid of Perth,'" added he.

"Yes," answered I. "The heroine is like my sister, beautiful, and dreadfully good."

I was ashamed directly I had said it: praising one's sister was almost like praising one's self.

"Indeed," said he; "that's not a fault from which most of us suffer, but then very few of us have people at hand ready and generous enough to sing our praises."

I might have taken the speech as a compliment, I suppose, but it seemed so natural to praise Joyce that I confess it rather puzzled me.

"You must miss your sister," added Mr. Harrod.

"Of course I do," cried I, warmly. "Luckily she isn't going to be away for long, or I don't know what mother would do. She's mother's right hand in the house. I'm no use in-doors."

"You always seem to me to be very busy," said Harrod.

"Oh no," insisted I; "it was father I used to help."

"Don't you help him now?" asked he.

"No," I answered, shortly; and as I spoke the recollection of my grievance swept over me, and brought the tears very close, "he doesn't need me."

Mr. Harrod did not say a word, he did not even look at me, and I was grateful to him for that; but I was sure that he had understood, and I grew more sore than ever, knowing that I had let him guess at my sore place. We walked on in silence.

"I used to love the Waverley novels when I was a lad," said he, changing the subject kindly.

"Don't you now?" asked I.

"I dare say I should if I read them, but I have to read stiffer books now— when I read at all."

"Books on agriculture! I suppose," said I, scornfully; "but father says a little practical knowledge is worth all the books in the world."

It did not strike me at the moment how very rude this speech was; but Mr. Harrod smiled.

"Your father is quite right, Miss Maliphant," said he. "Books are of little use till tested by practical knowledge; but after all, if they are good books, they were written from practical knowledge, you know, and perhaps it would take one a lifetime to reap the individual knowledge of all that they have swept together."

"I only know what father said," repeated I, half sullenly.

"Perhaps you don't remember it all," said he. "I think your father would agree with me this time; he is a very wise man, and I fancy I have stated the case pretty fairly."

"I should think he *was* a wise man!" I exclaimed, and I think my pride was pardonable this time. "All the country-side knows that."

"I know it," he answered. "One can't go into a cottage without hearing him spoken of with love and reverence."

"Yes; I never saw any one so sorry for people as father is," answered I. "I'm frightened of people who are ill and unhappy; but father—he wants to help them—well, just as I wanted to help the beasts and birds," I ended up with a laugh.

As I spoke the curious twittering note of the female cuckoo sounded in one of the trees upon the cliff, and immediately from four different quarters, one after the other, the reply came in the two distinct notes of the male bird. I stood still upon the path, and looked about me. The sound, and perhaps partly what I had just said, reminded me of one of the objects of my walk.

"I declare I had almost forgotten," I cried, and without another word of explanation I dashed up the bank of the cliff, Taff following.

Mr. Harrod stood below on the path. A few minutes more were enough to enable me to find the bush, which I had marked with a bit of the braid off my cloak on that memorable evening a few nights ago.

The lark's nest was still there. The cruel little cuckoo sat in it alone, while hovering in the air, close at hand, was the foolish mother waiting, with a dainty morsel in her beak, till I should be gone, and she could safely feed the vicious little interloper who had destroyed her own brood. The bodies of the little titlarks lay upon the bank. I jumped down to the path again and told Mr. Harrod the tale.

"I wish I had put the cuckoo out," I said. "I hate cuckoos—all the more because every one admires them." And I remember that all the way home I kept reverting to that distressing little piece of bird-tragedy.

We returned by the sea-shore. It was a longer way, but I declared that I must have a sight of the ocean on this soft, calm day. And soft it was, and calm and gray and mild. The sun was setting, but there was no sunset. Only behind the village on the hill the clouds lifted a little towards the horizon, and left a line of whiter light, against which the trees and houses detached themselves vividly; the marsh was uniform and sober.

When we had climbed the steep road and were at the Grange gates, Mr. Harrod held out his hand and said, as he bade me good-night, "I don't see why you shouldn't be of just as much use to your father as ever you were, Miss Maliphant. Please be very sure that no one ever would or ever could replace you to your father."

He spoke as though it were not altogether easy for him to do so; but there was a ring of honest kindliness in his voice that left me mute and almost ashamed. He held my hand a moment in his strong grip, but he did not look at me; and then he turned and almost fled down the road, as if he, too, were almost ashamed of what he had said.

And I had not answered a word. I stood there surprised, perplexed, and even a little frightened, surrounded by new and curious emotions, which I did not even try to unravel.

CHAPTER XVII

I do not suppose that I had the dimmest notion at the time that this man, whom I considered my foe, had sprung surely, and as soon as I saw him, into that mysterious blank space that exists in every woman's imagination, waiting to be filled by the figure that shall henceforth bound her horizon. I do not suppose that I guessed at my real feelings for a moment. If I had done so, I am sure that it would only have aggravated my hostile attitude, whereas my first most unreasonable mood was beginning slowly to lapse into one of friendly interest, and of eager desire to be of use.

It is poor sport keeping up an attitude of defiance towards a person who is entirely unconscious of one's intention; and whether Mr. Harrod was really unconscious of my intention or not, he certainly acted as if he were, and was, as far as his reserved nature would allow, so friendly towards me, that I could not choose but be friendly towards him in return. Anyhow, it is true that ere three weeks had passed, that began to happen which Joyce had so anxiously desired: Mr. Harrod and I began to make friends over our common interests.

A certain amount of defiance had begun to be transferred in me from him, whose coming I had so bitterly resented, to those who shared that resentment of mine.

Reuben was still sadly refractory. Luckily he was not much among the men; but where there's a will there's a way; and I'm afraid he had influence enough to do no good. And Deborah troubled me more. Although mother was for the bailiff, because he was the squire's friend, and also because, I think, she was really far more anxious about father's health than she allowed us to guess, and wanted him to be saved work—Deborah had not really allowed herself to be convinced as she generally was.

She was not unreasonable; she was too clever to be unreasonable, and she loved us all too dearly to resent any step which she chose to believe was for the good of any of us. But I am sure she never believed that this step was for the good of any of us. From beginning to end she never liked Trayton Harrod. And what specially annoyed me about her at this time was that she pretended to be trying to make me like him; and as I innocently began to change my own feelings, so I naturally began to resent this attitude in her.

On the very afternoon of which I am thinking, I resented Deborah's attitude. I had been in the kitchen making cakes (when Joyce was away it was I who had to make the cakes), and Deborah had taken advantage of the opportunity to follow up the line already begun by my sister, and to beg me, for father's sake, to forget my grievance and to be gracious to the young bailiff. As may be imagined, Deborah did not consider that she was bound to show any consideration in the matter of what she said to us girls.

"I know it comes hard on you, my dear," said she. "There's lots of little jobs you used to do afore, and no doubt did just as well, that'll be this young man's place to do now, and he won't notice whether you mind it or no. 'Tain't likely. But so long as he don't interfere with what we've got to do, we'll mind our own business and never give him a thought. You see, child, it's your father has got to say whether the young man's a-helping or a-hindering. Maybe he'll find out these chaps, that have learned it all on book and paper, don't know the top from the bottom any better nor he do himself. But that's for them to settle atween 'em, and it's none of our lookout."

I don't know why this speech should specially have irritated me, but it did. Even if I had begun to guess that I was growing to like Mr. Harrod better than I had intended to like him, I certainly should not have been glad that any one else should guess it. But the fact is that I believe I had lived the last fortnight without any thought, and that this speech of Deborah's roused me to an investigation of my feelings which was annoying to me.

"I have no intention at all of being rude, Deb," exclaimed I. "I leave that to you. I don't think it's lady-like to be rude."

Deb laughed.

"Oh, come now, none of your hoighty-toightyness!" exclaimed she. "Who carried on up-stairs and down when first squire talked about a bailiff to master at all? I haven't nursed you when you were a baby not to know when you're in a bad temper. It's plain enough, my dear."

"I know I have a bad temper," said I; "but I don't see that that has anything to do with the matter."

I suppose something in the way I said it must have touched old Deb, who had a soft heart for all her rough ways, for she said in her topsy-turvy way:

"Well, there—no more I don't see that it has. All I mean is that if you let him alone he'll let you alone, and no harm done. You'll have the more time for your books and for looking after your clothes a bit. You know I've

Margaret Maliphant | 139

often told you you'll never get a beau so long as you go about gypsying as you do."

"Deborah, how dare you!" cried I, angrily. "You know very well that—"

"That I wouldn't have a lover for anything in the world," I was going to say, and deeply perjure myself; but at that very moment mother opened the door and looked into the kitchen. She had her spectacles still on her nose, and an open letter in her hand.

"Margaret, I want you," said she, shortly, "in the parlor."

"I can't come just now, mother," answered I. "The cakes will burn."

"Deborah will see to the cakes," said mother, and I knew by her tone of voice that I must do as she bade me. "I want you at once."

I knew what it was about. Two days ago I had had a letter from Joyce. It gave me no news; she had got on with her tapestry; she had trimmed herself a new bonnet; Aunt Naomi's rheumatism was no better; she hoped that father's gout had not returned—no news until the very end. Then she said she had been to the Royal Academy of pictures in London, with an old lady who lived close to Aunt Naomi, and that she had there met Captain Forrester.

Certainly this was a big enough piece of news to suffice for one letter. But why had Joyce put it at the very end? and why did she hurry it over as quickly as possible, making no sort or kind of comment upon it? It was another of the things about Joyce that I could not make out. Why was she not proud of her engagement? Why did she never care to speak of it? I thought that if I were engaged to a man whom I loved I should be very proud of it, whereas she always seemed anxious to avoid the subject.

Of course it was horrible to be parted from him, but then it should lighten her burden to speak of it to some one who sympathized with her as I did. But I knew well enough why it was. It all came from that overstrained notion of duty. She had promised mother that she would not see Frank, and would not write to Frank, and would not speak of Frank, and she kept so strictly to the letter of this promise that she would not speak of him even to me.

When first I had read Joyce's letter I had been angry with her for a cold-hearted girl, but now I was not angry with her. I admired her, but I made up my mind that her passion for self-sacrifice should not wreck her life's happiness if I could prevent it. Face to face it was difficult to scold Joyce. There was a kind of gentle obstinacy about her which took one unawares, and was very hard to deal with. But in a letter I could speak my mind, and

I would speak my mind—not only to her, but, what was far more difficult, to mother also. So that when mother put her head in at the kitchen door and summoned me to the parlor, I guessed what it was about, and I knew pretty well what I was going to say. She put the letter into my hand and sat down, looking up at me over her spectacles as I read it, with her clear blue eyes intent and a little frown on her white brow. It was from Aunt Naomi, and it said that a young man named Captain Forrester had just been to call upon Joyce; she thought she noticed a certain confusion on Joyce's part during his presence, she therefore wrote at once to know whether his visits were sanctioned by her parents, as she did not wish to get into any trouble.

Oh, what a horrid old woman she was! "How could people be narrow-minded and selfish to such a point as that?" I said to myself. Mother watched me, and Deborah came into the room to lay the cloth. It was just curiosity that brought her.

"It's a ridiculous letter," said I, roughly, throwing it down with an ill grace, and looking defiantly, not at mother, but at the old woman, who regarded me with reproving eyes. "Why in the world shouldn't Joyce receive a visit from a gentleman—still more from the man she's going to marry?"

"She's not going to marry him, at least not with my free consent," said mother, putting her lips together in a set curve that I knew.

"Well, then, of course it will be a great pity, but I suppose it will have to be without your consent," said I, rashly.

"Well, I'm sure!" ejaculated Deborah, under her breath, and looking at me with something like remonstrance. Mother rose with dignity, and turning to the table she said, "Deborah, would you be so kind as to fetch in the cold ham?"

Of course Deborah knew that she was being sent out of the room that I might have a piece of mother's mind, and my own was a struggle between pleasure that Deborah should for once be set down, and anger that she should know the reason of her dismissal. She stayed a moment, setting the forks round the table to a nicety of precision; then, as she passed out of the room she gave me a friendly nudge, and looked at me a moment with a sort of humorous kindliness in her shrewd gray eyes.

Mother took up the letter again. "Do you know how Captain Forrester knew where Joyce was staying?" asked she.

"No, how should I know?" answered I. "Joyce told me that she had met him accidentally at the Royal Academy. I suppose he found out where she was. Where there's a will there's a way."

"But he undertook not to try and see her," remarked mother, severely. "His conduct is dishonorable."

"Well, you might make some allowances," cried I. "It shows he loves her; it shows she will be happy with him. And look here, mother," added I, in a sudden frenzy of frankness, "I believe that if I were to get the chance of doing anything to help to bring them together, I should do it."

Mother looked at me fixedly. "No, you wouldn't," said she at last. "You're headstrong and mistaken, but you're honest. You've taken your word you wouldn't interfere nor mention the matter to any one for a year, and you'll keep your word."

I knew very well that she was right, but I said boldly, "Joyce is my sister, I love her, I want her to be happy, and I shall do what I can to make her so."

Still mother looked at me. "You forget that I want Joyce to be happy too," said she. "If she is your sister she is also my daughter." There was a tremble in her voice, whether of anger or distress, I did not know.

"Of course I know very well that you care about her and her happiness," said I; "but perhaps you don't see what is best for it. How can old people, whose youth is past ever so long ago, remember how young people feel? They can't know what young folk need to be happy as well as others of their own age can."

"Maybe they can look ahead a bit better, though," said mother, without deigning to argue with me. "Be that as it may, I don't think I'll ask you to teach me what's best for my children's happiness. I may be all wrong, of course, but I mean to try and have my own way as long as I can, though I know very well we can't expect the duty and reverence we used to pay our parents when I was your age."

I felt that the rebuke was deserved, and I was silent.

"At all events, it's no business of yours," continued mother. "If the thing has got to be fought out, I would rather fight it out with Joyce herself. If she insists upon marrying the young man, I suppose she can do so. She is of age."

I did not answer her, but I laughed. The idea of Joyce insisting upon doing anything was too ridiculous. And, of course, mother knew this quite well, so that it was not quite fair of her.

Having once begun to laugh, the spell of my ill-humor was, however, broken, and it was in a very different tone of voice that I said, "Come, mother, you know very well that sister is far too gentle, and loves you far too much, ever to do anything against your wish, so that's ridiculous, isn't it?"

Mother smiled. "Yes, yes, she's a good girl," she said. "You are both of you good children, but you mustn't be so self-sufficient and headstrong."

"Well, I suppose I am headstrong," said I; "I'm sorry for it. But Joyce isn't. I do think she ought to be put upon less than folk who are. I believe if nobody fought Joyce's battles she'd let herself be wiped right out."

And sure enough, by the afternoon post there came a letter from Joyce which satisfied mother more than it did me. It explained that Captain Forrester had come to Sydenham uninvited and unwelcome; and it begged mother to believe that he would never come again.

CHAPTER XVIII

Thursday was the day for making the butter, and one Thursday in the beginning of June of the year I am recording, I walked along the flag-stones of the court-yard towards the dairy, that stood somewhat detached from the house. I hummed softly to myself as I went; I was happy. I could not have told why I was happy—for Joyce was away, and I should have been lonely. But the June was fair and pleasant, and I was young and strong.

Mother had a special pride in her dairy. The broad, low pans stood in their order on the dressers along the white-tiled walls, each of the four "meals" in its place; the household cream set apart, and other clean pans ready for the fresh setting. The warm summer breeze came through the trellised shutters, that let the air in day and night, and through the open door, around which the midsummer roses clustered thickly and the honeysuckle twined its sweet tendrils.

Beyond the door one could see the square of grass-plot, with the wide border running round it, in which old-fashioned flowers stood up against the brick wall; and over the wall one could see just a little strip of marsh and sea in the distance. Mother had not come in yet; but Reuben had churned before daybreak, and now Deborah stood lifting the butter out of the churn ready for the washing and pressing.

"Have you seen Reuben anywheres about?" said she, sharply, as I came in.

I knew by her voice that she was annoyed.

"Yes," said I; "I've just left him. Do you want him?"

"I want a few fagots for my kitchen fire; but nowadays there's no getting no one to do nothing," answered she. "Reuben was never much for brains, but he used to be handy; but now—if there's nothing, there's always something for Reuben to do."

"Dear me! How's that?" asked I.

Deborah was silent. She had said already far more than was her wont—for Deborah was not one to talk, and generally kept her grievances to herself.

"The butter'll want a deal o' pressing and washing this morning," said she. "The weather's sultry, and it hasn't come clean."

I was turning up my sleeves. "Dear me! Then it'll take a long time?" said I. I hated washing the butter; it was dull work.

"Sure enough it will," laughed Deborah, grimly. "What do you want to be doing? You haven't half the heart in the work that your sister has!"

"Ah no," I agreed. "I'm not so clever at it as Joyce is."

"You can be clever enough when you choose," said the old woman, sagely. "I dare say you could be clever enough teaching this Mr. Harrod his way about the farm if you were wanted to."

I looked up quickly. I think I blushed. Why did Deb say that? But why should I blush because she had said it?

"Indeed, I shouldn't think of trying to teach Mr. Harrod anything," said I, trying to laugh.

"What! Has he turned out sharp enough to please you after all?" asked she, with that peculiar snort which it was her fashion to give when she wanted to be disagreeable. "I thought you were of a mind that nobody could be clever enough over this precious farm, unless you was to show them how."

"Fiddlesticks!" said I.

It was very annoying of Deborah to want to put me in a bad temper when I had come in in such a good one.

"Have you seen your father?" asked she, presently.

"No," replied I. "Does he want me?"

"He was asking for you. Wanted you to go up and show this young chap the field where he wants the turnips put."

The bailiff again. What was the matter with Deborah, that she could not leave me and him alone?

"Mr. Harrod knows his way about the country quite well enough by this time to find it for himself," I said.

I did not look at Deborah, but I knew very well that her face wore a kind of expression of defiant mischief with which I was familiar.

"I'm sorry you're still set again the poor young man," said she, provokingly.

But there was a very different ring in her voice when she spoke again in a few minutes, and when I looked up I saw that an unwonted gentleness had overspread her hard, rough features.

"If you haven't seen your father since breakfast," she added, "maybe you don't know as he's had another o' them queer starts at his heart."

"No. What kind of thing?" asked I, frightened.

"Oh, you know; same as he had in the winter, only not so bad. There, you needn't be terrified," added she; "it's nothing bad much—only lasted a minute or two. He called and asked me for a glass of water, and I fetched the missis. He was better afore she came. But it's my belief he's neither so young nor so well as he was."

This was evident; but neither Deb nor I saw the joke—we were too serious.

"And it's my belief he's fretting over something, Margaret," added she, gravely. "So if this here new chap saves him any bother, I suppose folk should need be pleased."

I wondered whether Deborah meant this as an excuse for my being pleased, or as a rebuke for my not being pleased. I think now that she meant it as neither, but rather as a rebuke to herself. I took it to heart, however, and the tears rushed to my eyes.

Had I been really anxious to save father all possible worry over this innovation? Had I done all I could to help Mr. Harrod settle down in his place? I was not sure. I thought I would do more, and yet I thought I would not do more. Oh, Margaret, Margaret! were you quite honest with yourself at that time? I took up a fresh lump of butter and began washing it blindly.

"Come, come, you're not going the right way about it! You'll never get the milk out that way!" cried Deborah, coming up to me.

"No, no—I know," answered I, impatiently; and then, incoherently, "but, oh dear me! what is the right way?"

Deborah laughed, but gently enough. She was a clever old woman, and she knew that I was not alluding to the butter.

"Well, I don't rightly know myself," said she, without looking at me. "What you thinks the right way, most times turns out to be the wrong way; and when you make folk turn to the right when they was minded to turn to the left, it's most like the left would ha' been the best way for them to travel after all. I've done advisin' long ago; for it's a queer tract of country here below, and every one has to take their own chance in the long-run."

This speech of Deb's had given me time to choke down my ridiculous tears and put on my usual face again; for I should indeed have been ashamed to be caught crying when there was nothing in the world to cry about; and just as she finished speaking, mother's figure came past the window, walking slowly, Squire Broderick at her side.

"Oh dear me! whatever does squire want at this time o' day?" cried I, impatiently. "He shouldn't need to come so often, now Joyce is away."

Deborah looked at me warningly. The latticed shutters, although they looked closed, let in every sound; and indeed I don't know what possessed me to make the speech, for I had no dislike to the squire. I suppose I was still a little ruffled.

"You might keep a civil tongue in your head?" grumbled Deborah, angrily.

The squire was, I have said, a great favorite with the old woman, who was, so to speak, on the Tory side of the camp, although she would have been puzzled to explain the meaning of the word.

Mother was talking to the squire in her most doleful voice—a voice that she could produce at times, although she was certainly not by nature a doleful woman.

"It has upset me very much," she was saying, and I knew she was alluding to father's indisposition. "He says it is only rheumatics, and I hope it is; but it makes me uneasy. He's not the man he was, and I can't help fancying at times that he has something on his mind that worries him."

The very same words that Deborah had used; but what father should have specially to worry him I could not see.

"He gives too much thought to these high-flown notions of his, Mrs. Maliphant, that's what it is," answered the squire, testily. "It's enough to turn any man's brain."

"Oh, I don't think it's that. I think it cheers him up to think of the misery of the working-classes," declared mother, simply, without any notion of the contradiction of her speech. "I'm sure he's quite happy when he gets a letter from your nephew about the meetings over this children's institution. It's a notion of his own, you see, and he's pleased with it, as we all are with what we have fancied out. Not but what I do say it is a beautiful notion," added mother, loyally. "I pity the poor little things myself; no one more."

This was true. It was the only one of father's "wild notions" that mother had any touch of.

I noticed that the squire had frowned at the mention of Frank's name. He always did; I thought I knew why.

"Yes; that's all very fine, ma'am," he said, "but the trouble is that it won't make his crops grow. No; and paying his laborers half as much again as anybody else won't make his farm pay."

Mother looked at the squire anxiously.

"Do you think the farm doesn't pay?" asked she. "Do you suppose it's that as is making Laban fidgety?"

"How should I know, my dear lady?" answered the squire, in the same irritable way—he was very irritable this morning—"Maliphant knows his own affairs."

Mother was silent.

"Well, I hope this young fellow is going to do a deal o' good to the farm, and to my husband too," added she, cheerfully. "I look to a great deal from him, and I can't be grateful enough to you, Squire Broderick, for having settled the matter for us. He's a plain-speaking, sensible young man, and I like him very much."

"Yes, Harrod is a thorough good-fellow," answered the squire, warmly. "He *is* plain-speaking, too much so to his elders sometimes; but it's because he has got his whole heart in his work. He cares for nothing else, and you can't say that of every man that works for another man's money."

They had stopped outside the window, and had stood still there, talking all this while. I suppose mother forgot that Deb and I were bound to be inside doing our business, and that the lattice was open.

"I like him very much," continued she; "but I don't think Laban fancies him much, nor yet Margaret. Margaret set her face against his coming from the first, you see. It was natural, I dare say. She had been used to do a good bit for her father; and when Margaret sets her face against anything—well, you can't lead her, it's driving then. It's just the same when she wants a thing. You may drive and drive, but you won't drive her away from that spot. It's very hard to know how to manage a nature like that, Mr. Broderick, especially when you've been used to a girl that's as gentle as Joyce is. But there, they both have their goods and their ills. Far be it from their mother to deny that."

Squire Broderick laughed, and then mother laughed too, and they both came forward round the corner and in at the door. Mother started a little when she saw me, and the squire smiled curiously. But I did not smile; I was boiling over with anger.

"Why, Deborah, you have set to work early," said mother, without looking at me. "Why didn't you call me?"

"I didn't know as there was any need to call," answered Deborah, roughly, and I believe in my heart that she was the more rough because she didn't like mother's speech about me. "You've your work to do, ma'am, and I've mine. I supposed as you'd come when you wanted to, but that was no reason why Margaret and I should wait about, twirling our thumbs."

Mother did not reply. I felt the squire's gaze still upon me, and I looked up and gave him a bold, angry glance. I am sure that my eyes must have flashed, and I think that my lips were set in the hard lines that mother used to tell me made me look so ugly. I hated the squire to look at me, and he seemed to guess it, for he turned away at once, and afterwards I remembered how he had done it, and that somehow his face had looked almost tender.

But mother did not seem to care a bit that I should have overheard what she said; she began turning up the skirt of her soft gray gown, and rolling up her sleeves. Mother always wore gray when she did not wear the old black satin brocade that had belonged to her own mother, and which only came out on high-days and holidays. She had said she would never put on colors again when our little brother died many years ago; and I am glad she never did, for I should not like to remember her in anything but the soft tones that became her so well. Black, gray or white—she never wore anything else.

"The dairy is not what it is when Joyce is at home," said she, deprecatingly, to the squire.

"Well, to be sure, ma'am, I don't see what's amiss with it," declared Deborah. "It's hard as them as go away idling should be put above them as stay at home and work."

I looked at Deborah in surprise. She was not wont to set Joyce down.

"Why, the place looks as if you could eat off the floor. What more do you want, Mrs. Maliphant?" laughed the squire, coming up and standing beside me. "And I'm sure nobody could make up a pat better than Miss Margaret."

"Margaret has been more used to out-door work," said mother, at which Deb gave one of her snorts, I did not know why, except out of pure contradiction, for she had blamed my butter-making herself five minutes before.

"You seem to have plenty of cream," said the squire, walking round.

"Yes," answered mother; "our cows are doing well now, though Daisy will give richer cream to her pail than all the rest put together." Then she added, without looking at me, "Margaret, you need not do any more just now. Your father was asking for you. Go to him, and come back when he has done with you."

I wiped my arms silently, and turned down my sleeves. I had not said a single word since she had come in. She looked at me, but I would not return her glance. I was a wrong-headed, foolish girl, and when I thought that mother had been unjust to me I tried to make her suffer for it.

I walked straight out of the dairy without a word to any one, and it was not till I was outside that I saw that the squire had followed me. He was talking to me, so I had to listen him.

"Yes," I said, vaguely, in answer to him—for of course the remark, although I had not entirely caught it, had been about my sister, "yes, Joyce is very well; but she is not coming back just yet. I don't want her to come back just yet. I think it's so good for her to be away. When she is at home, mother wants her every minute. It isn't always to do something, but it's always to be there. And Joyce is good. She always seems pleased to have no free life of her own. But she can't really *be* pleased. *I* couldn't. Anyhow, it can't be good for her to be so dreadfully unselfish; do you think so?"

In my eagerness I was actually taking the squire into my confidence. He smiled.

"Miss Joyce always appeared to me to be very contented, doing the things about the house that your mother wished," said he. "You mustn't judge every one by yourself. People generally try to get something of what they want, I fancy. Your sister isn't so independent as you are."

"No," agreed I, gloomily, "she isn't. She's what folk call more womanly. I never was intended for a woman. Father always says I ought to have been a boy."

"I don't think women are all unwomanly because they're independent," said the squire. And then he added, in a lower voice, "I don't think you're unwomanly."

We had come round by the lawn, and we stood there a moment before the porch. The bees were busy among the summer flowers, and the scent of roses and mignonette, of sweet-peas and heliotrope, was heavy upon the air. The sun streamed down on our heads and upon the green marsh beneath the cliff and upon the sea in the distance. It was a bright, hot, June day. I was just going in-doors, when the squire laid his hand on my arm.

"Wait a minute, Miss Margaret, I want to say something to you," he said.

I looked at him, surprised. Was he going to ask me to intercede with Joyce for him? If so, he had come very decidedly to the wrong person. But something in his face made me look away.

"I won't keep you long," said he.

And then he paused, while I waited with my face turned aside.

"I don't think you'll take what I'm going to say amiss, Miss Margaret," he went on at last. "I've known you such a long time—ever since you were a little girl—that I don't feel as though I were taking a liberty, as I should if you were a stranger. I don't suppose you remember how I used to help you scramble out of the dikes when you got a ducking on the marsh after the rainfalls, and how I used to take you into the house-keeper's room at the Manor to have your frock dried, so that you should not get into a scrape? But *I* remember it very well, and the cakes that you used to love with the blackberry jam in them, and the rides that you used to have on my back after the school feasts."

He paused a moment, as though for an answer. I gave him none, but I remembered all that he alluded to very well.

"You don't mind my speaking, do you?" repeated he again.

"Oh no, I don't mind," answered I, with a little laugh.

"Having known you like that all your life, I care for you so much," continued he, "that I can't bear to see you doing yourself an injustice."

I looked at him now straight. I felt annoyed, after all, at what I knew he was going to say. But the kindness and gentleness of his face disarmed me.

"You mean that I don't behave well to my mother," said I, the flush of sudden vexation dying away from my face. "Mother doesn't understand me. I can't always be of the same mind as she is. I don't see why people need always be of the same mind as their relations; but it doesn't follow that they're ungrateful and heartless, because they are not. I've heard mother say that she doesn't believe that I care any more for her than for any tramp upon the high-road; but that isn't true."

The squire laughed.

"No; of course it isn't true," said he, "and Mrs. Maliphant doesn't think it."

"Oh yes, I think she does sometimes," persisted I. "She would like me to be like Joyce. But I shall never be like Joyce!"

"No," assented the squire, decidedly, "I don't think you ever will be. But it was not specially with reference to your mother that I was going to speak to you, although what I was going to say bears, I fancy, on what vexed her to-day."

I bit my lip. Was he going to refer to Mr. Harrod? He paused again.

"Your father is very much harassed and troubled, I fear, Miss Margaret," he said next. "I have noticed, with much grief of late, how sadly he seems to have aged."

"Do you think so?" said I. "I don't know what he should have to be harassed about."

"The conduct of a farm is a very harassing thing: it takes all a man's thought and care. And even then it doesn't always pay," said the squire, gravely.

I did not answer; I was puzzled.

"Your father is getting old," continued he, "and it is hard for a man, when he is old, to give as much attention to such things as in youth and strength."

"I don't think he is so very old," I said, half vexed; "but perhaps he doesn't care so much about farming as some people do. Perhaps he cares more about other things."

"Perhaps," said the squire, evasively. Then starting off afresh, he added, quickly, "I had hoped that this new bailiff would have relieved him of some anxiety; but I am afraid there are inconveniences connected with his presence which, to a man of your father's temperament, are particularly galling."

"Well, I suppose it's natural that a man who has been his own master all his life should mind taking a younger one's advice," said I, pretty hotly this time.

"Of course it is," agreed the squire; "but all the same, the farm needs a younger man's head and a younger man's heart in it before it'll thrive as it ought. And now I'm coming to what I wanted to say, Miss Margaret. *You* can do more than any one else to smooth over the difficulties. You must persuade your father to let Harrod have his own way. He's a headstrong chap, I can see that; and he'll do nothing, he'll take no interest, if he's gainsaid at every step. Nobody would. There are many kinds of modern improvements that are needed at Knellestone. Your father has always stood against them, because he fancied it wasn't fair to the laborers; but they'll have to come, and I know very well Harrod won't stay here long and not get them. No man who is honest to his employer would. Now, you must be go-between," he went on, still more earnestly, although speaking in a low voice. "You must get your father to see things reasonably, and you must be friendly to Harrod: show him that you take an interest in his improvements, and persuade him that your father does also. So he will, when he sees how they work. I can see that a vast deal depends upon you, Miss Margaret. You're a clever girl; you can manage it—*if you will*."

I turned my face farther aside than ever; in fact, I think I turned my back. I did not answer—I did not know what to answer.

"And you *will*, I know," added he, in a persuasive voice. "I quite understand that it isn't pleasant to you at first, but it will become so when you see that *you* can do a great deal to make things smooth when difficulties occur. I am sure it must be a great comfort to you to think of how much there still is in which you can help your father—quite as much as there used to be in the past, when you had it more your own way. No one else can help him as you can help him."

"Oh, I don't really think he wants help," said I—but rather by way of saying something than from conviction.

"Well, I think he wants more than you fancy," persisted the squire. "I would not for worlds cast a shadow over your young life, Miss Margaret," he went on, earnestly; "but I feel that it is the part of a true friend that I should, in a certain measure, do so. Your mother is a tender helpmeet and an admirable nurse, I know; but there are other things needed for a man besides physic and poultices. The time may come when he may turn to you for some things, and I think you should make yourself ready for that time."

He said no more. But after a few moments he held out his hand.

"Good-bye," said he. "Whenever you want a friend, I don't need to tell you that you have got one at the Manor."

He was gone, and I had stood there with downcast head, and had answered never a word. I did not at the time understand all that he had said, nor what he had meant by his doubts and his fears, although in after-years his words came back to me very vividly, as did also other words of Deborah's; but one thing was very clear to me even then, and that was that everybody—from Joyce and Deborah to mother and the squire—considered that I ought to make friends with the new bailiff, and that I had not yet done so sufficiently.

CHAPTER XIX

From that time forth I gave myself up unreservedly to following the squire's advice. Yes, I did not even shrink from any possible charge of inconsistency. Deborah might laugh at me if she liked, Reuben might look askance out of his stolid silence, mother might ponder; but I had been convinced; I knew what I had to do, and I would stand Trayton Harrod's friend. That was what I argued to myself. Was I quite honest? At all events I was very happy.

One morning—it must have been about a week after the squire's words to me—I had occasion to go out onto our cliff to plant out some cuttings that Joyce had procured and sent me from London. Reuben was in the orchard hard by, mowing the grass under the apple-trees. He did such work when hands were few. The orchard was only divided by a wall from the garden, and Reuben and I kept up a brisk conversation across it.

"I've heard say as Mister Harrod be for persuading master to have new sorts o' hops planted along the hill-side this year, miss," Reuben was saying.

"Indeed," said I. "Well, I suppose ours aren't a good sort, then."

"That's for them as knows to say," replied the old man. "The Lord have made growths for every part, and it's ill flyin' in the face of the Lord."

"Well, Mr. Harrod knows," declared I.

"Nay, miss, he warn't born and bred hereabouts. But I says to him, 'You ask Jack Barnstaple,' says I. 'He knows,' says I."

"You said that to Mr. Harrod, Reuben!" I exclaimed.

"Yes, miss," he answered, "I did."

"Well, then, I think it was very rude of you, Reuben. That's all I have to say."

"Nay, miss, I heard you say as how a stranger wouldn't be o' no good to master," grinned Reuben. "They don't understand."

"If I said that I made a great mistake," answered I, half angrily. "I think Mr. Harrod is a great deal of use."

"Well, miss, if he be agoing to have Goldings planted in instead of Early Prolifics, he won't get no change out o' the ground, that's what I say. They won't thrive for nobody, and they won't do it to please him."

Reuben shouldered his scythe as he said the last words, and went off to a more distant part of the orchard, and I set to work at my planting. I knew pretty well by this time that it was worse than waste of time taking Mr. Harrod's side against Reuben.

I wondered what he would have thought if he could have heard me taking his side. But I don't think he thought much about having a "side." He was too eager about his work.

I set to planting my cuttings busily—so busily that I did not hear steps on the gravel behind me, and looked up suddenly to see Mr. Harrod on the path beside me. He did not say anything, but stood a while watching me. At last I stood up, with the trowel in my hand, and my face, I do not doubt, very red and hot beneath my big print sun-bonnet.

"Did you meet Reuben just now?" asked I, rather by way of saying something.

"No," answered he; "I've come straight from your father's room. He wants you."

"Does he? Well, I can't go this minute. I must finish this job. I've neglected it for a week. What does he want me for?"

I kneeled down and began my work again.

"He and I have been discussing a new scheme," said Mr. Harrod, without answering my question.

"What, about co-operation, and children's schools and things?" cried I, with a smile. "Is he going to press you into it too?"

"Oh no; about the farm," answered he. "His possessions in hops are very small, and there's a fine and unusual chance just turned up of making money. I want him to take on another small farm—specially for hops."

"To take on another farm!" repeated I.

"Yes," said he; "but he doesn't take to it. I think he must have something else in his head. But the matter must be decided at once, for I hear there's another man after it."

"Where is it?" I asked, a secret glow of satisfaction at my heart to think he should come and tell me of this as he did.

"It's 'The Elms,'" he answered, "below the mill on the slope yonder."

I stood up and stopped my gardening to show I took an interest in what he was saying. "I know 'The Elms' well enough," I said, "but I didn't know it was to let."

"Yes," he replied. "Old Searle left his affairs in a dreadful mess when he died, and the executors have decided to sell the crops at a valuation, and let the place at once without waiting till the usual term."

"Dear me, what an odd thing!" said I. "I thought farms were never let excepting at Michaelmas."

"Never is a long word," smiled Mr. Harrod. "It is unusual. But I suppose the executors don't care for the expense of putting in a bailiff till October. Anyhow, they appear to want to realize at once; and it's a good chance for us."

"It's all hop-gardens at 'The Elms,' isn't it?' asked I.

"Yes, chief part."

"It seems to me it must either be a very poor crop, or they must want a good price for it so late in the season," said I, not ill pleased with myself for what I considered the rare shrewdness of this remark.

But Mr. Harrod smiled again. "The price will be the average of what the crops fetched during the past three years," said he. "That's law now. I should say about £36 to the acre. Leastways, that would be the price ready for picking, but there'll be a reduction at this time of year. That'll be a matter for private bargain."

"Yes," said I. "There'll be many a risk between now and picking."

"Of course," said the bailiff, half testily. "But it's just about the best-looking crop in these parts at the present time. They *will* plant those Early Prolifics about here. I suppose it's because they can get them sooner into the market. But they're a poor hop. Now, the plants at 'The Elms' are all Goldings or Jones."

"But they say the Goldings will never thrive in our soil," said I.

"*They*; who are *they*?" retorted Harrod. "They know nothing about it."

"No; I dare say you're right," I hastened to say. "Only hops are always considered risky, aren't they?"

"Everything is risky," answered he, more gently. "But as I have an interest in selling the crop to advantage if it turns out well, I don't believe your father could go very far wrong over it."

"Well, if you think it would be such a safe speculation, of course father ought to be persuaded to go in for it," said I.

"I really think so," answered Harrod, confidently.

"But perhaps he doesn't think he can afford the rent of it," suggested I, after a pause; "perhaps he hasn't the ready money."

"I can scarcely believe that, Miss Maliphant. Your father passes for a rich man in the county," answered he, with a smile. "No; he thinks the property is good enough as it has stood all these years; but, as a matter of fact, it would be a far more valuable one if it had better hop-gardens. Hops are the staple produce of the county, and I am sorry to say he doesn't stand as well in that line as many of the farmers about; he wants some one to give him courage to make this venture. Unluckily, he has not confidence enough in me, and Squire Broderick is away in London."

"Is the squire away?" asked I.

"Yes; I have just inquired, by your father's wish."

"I'll go and talk to father," said I, with youthful self-confidence, gathering up my tools, and too happy in feeling that I was the supporter of the man who but a fortnight ago I had sworn to treat as an open enemy to be troubled by any misgivings.

As I might have known, I did not do very much good. But what Mr. Harrod had said was true—father was in some way preoccupied. I think he had had a letter from Frank Forrester about the Children's Charity Houses Scheme, and it had not been a satisfactory one; for when I went into his business-room I found him busily writing to Frank, and I could not get him to pay any attention to me until after post-time. Then he let me speak.

"Meg, child," he said, when I had done, "I don't feel quite sure that you know a vast deal yourself about such things, but maybe you're right in one item, and that is, if I engage a man to look after my property, I ought to be willing to abide a bit by his advice. So we'll have a drop o' tea first, and then we'll go up and have a look at these hops of his."

And that is what we did. Mr. Harrod didn't come into tea, but we met him outside and walked up the hill together. It was still that bright June weather of the week before; we never had so hot and fair a summer I believe as that year. After our hard long winter the warmth was new life, and the long evenings were very exquisite. The breath of the lilac—just on the wane—of the bursting syringa, of the heavy daphne, lay upon the air, and was wafted from behind garden walls up the village street.

As we passed the old town-hall and came out at the end of the road, the white arms of the mill detached themselves against the bright sky where the sun, sinking nearer to the horizon, rayed the west with glory. Father stood a moment on the crest of the hill looking down into the valley, upon whose confines the broad meads of the South Downs swelled into rising ground again; a stream wound across the plain, that was intersected by dikes at intervals; far to the left lay the sea—a dim, blue line across the stems of the trees, breaking into a little bay in the dip of the hill where the valley met the marsh.

"The Elms" stood on the brow of the hill nearer the sea; the hop-gardens that belonged to it lay close at our feet. We went down the hill among the sheep and the sturdy lambs that leaped lightly still after their dams; father walked slowly in front, Mr. Harrod and I followed. The hop plantations covered the slopes, and swept across the valley to the other side. We left the house to our left above us, and went down into the valley.

The hops, according to their sort, had grown to various heights: some three feet, some less, and the women and girls from the village had been out during the last month tying them, so that they were now past the second bind.

Father and Mr. Harrod walked in a critical way through the lines of plants, examining them carefully. Here and there Trayton Harrod pinched off the flower of a bine that had been left on.

"It's very strange," said he, "that pruning and branching of the hops used not to be done some years ago. I read in an old book that the practice was first introduced since farmers noticed how hailstones, nipping off the bine-tops early in the summer, made the plants grow stronger."

They walked on again, Harrod showing father where the Jones hops grew, and where the Goldings, and arguing that, for purposes of early foreign export, the Jones hops easily took the place of the Early Prolifics, and came to a far finer, taller growth, while for later introduction into the market the Goldings were the best grown. Father stated the same objections that Reuben had stated—Trayton Harrod fighting each one vigorously, and coming off victorious, as he somehow always did.

We walked on through the gardens and then up by the house and back along the brow of the hill.

The sun had sunk below the horizon, and the crimson of the after-glow lay, a lump of fire, in the purple west, and sent rays of redness far into the heavens on every side, washing the clouds with a hundred tints from the brightest rose to the tenderest violet, the faintest green, the softest dove-color above our heads. Behind the village and its houses a row of dusky-headed pines stood tall or bent their trunks, bowed by the storm-winds, across the road; father stopped there a moment and looked at the glowing sky from between their red stems. The hills lay round the plain, wonderfully blue; the sunset gilded the quiet little stream upon the marsh till it looked like a streak of molten metal. He had not spoken a word, and now he sighed, half impatiently, as he turned homeward. I remember that Mr. Harrod left us at that point. He promised to be in to supper, and father and I walked on alone.

When we got to the dip of the road where the hill begins to go down towards the sea-marsh, we met Mr. Hoad coming up in his smart little gig, with his daughter Jessie at his side. I was for passing them with merely a bow, for they showed no signs of stopping, and I desired no conversation with either of them; but father stopped the gig.

"Hoad, can you spare me a few minutes?" asked he. "I should be much obliged to you. Miss Jessie, you'll come in and have a cup of tea," added he, courteously.

Miss Jessie said that she should be very pleased to come; but she did not look pleased, and for the matter of that I fear neither did I. I could not think why father should want Mr. Hoad's company again so soon; but I supposed it must be about that letter of Frank's. He had evidently seemed annoyed about it, although I did not know at that time why it was.

I took Jessie Hoad into the parlor while the two men went into the business-room. Mother was rather flurried when I announced, in my blunt way, that these visitors were going to stay to tea. The presence of a strange woman always *did* trouble mother a bit, and Jessie having been the head of her father's house since her mother died, she considered her in the light of a housewife. I knew that she was longing to have her best china out and the holland covers off in the front parlor. She was far too hospitable, however, to allow this feeling to be apparent, and she rose at once to welcome her guest.

"I'm very pleased to see you, Miss Hoad," said she; "I'm sorry Joyce is away."

"Oh, not at all; pray don't mention it, Mrs. Maliphant," declared Jessie, in her hard, high voice, sitting down and settling her dress to advantage. "Of course I'm sorry to miss Joyce, but I'm very glad to see you and Margaret."

My blood boiled to hear her call us like that by our Christian names, and to see the way she sat there with her little smart hat and her little nose turned up in the air, chatting away to mother in a patronizing kind of way, and keeping the talk quite in her own hands with all the town news she had to tell.

"Yes, the Thornes' is a beautiful house," she was saying, "all in the best style, and quite regardless of expense. I assure you the dessert service was all gold and silver the other night when father and I dined there. Of course it was a grand affair. All the county swells there. But the thing couldn't have been done better in London, I declare."

"Indeed!" answered mother. "I haven't much knowledge of London."

"No, of course not," said Jessie. "But you have seen the Thornes' house, I suppose?"

"No," answered mother. "We don't go there. My husband and Mr. Thorne don't hold together."

"Oh, indeed!" exclaimed Jessie; "that's a pity. He and his daughter are the nicest people in the county. But as I was saying to Mary Thorne, there's something very quaint in your old house, and I can't help fancying the new style does copy some things from the old houses."

"Oh, I can't believe that," said I, half piqued. "It wouldn't be worth its while."

She looked round at me, a little puzzled, I think, but any rub there might have been between us was put a stop to by the entrance of father and Mr. Hoad from the study.

Mr. Hoad was, if anything, in better spirits than ever; his eyes were bright, and he rubbed his hands as a man might do when anything had gone to his satisfaction. Father's brow, on the contrary, was heavy. We sat down to tea. Mr. Harrod came in a little late. He was about to retire when he saw that we had company; but mother so insisted on his taking his usual seat that it would have been rude to refuse, although I could see that he did not care for the society.

Mother introduced him to Miss Hoad, who just looked up under the brim of her hat, and then went back to her muffin as if none of us were much worth considering. There was altogether an air about her as though she wanted to get over the whole affair as soon as possible. And she did. That bland father of hers had not time for more than half the pleasant things that he usually said to us all before she whipped him off.

"It'll be quite too late to pay our call at 'The Priory' if we don't go at once, papa," said she, rising, and looking at a dainty gold watch at her waist. I suppose she did not trust the time of our old eight-day clock that stood between the windows, yet I'll warrant it was the safer of the two.

She turned to mother.

"I'm sorry to have to run away so soon," said she, with an outward show of cordiality, "but you see it's very important to leave cards on people like the Thornes directly after a large party. And if I don't do it to-day I must drive out again on purpose to-morrow."

"Have you been dining at Thorne's, Hoad?" asked father.

"Yes," answered the solicitor. "He's a rare good-fellow, and he gave us a rare good dinner."

Father did not say a word, and the Hoads took their leave.

"I'll let you have that the first thing in the morning," said Mr. Hoad, as he shook hands with father.

Father nodded, but otherwise made no remark. When the visitors were gone he turned to Mr. Harrod: "I've made up my mind to rent 'The Elms,'" said he, shortly. "We'll drive into town to-morrow and see Searle's executors about it."

"That's right, sir," said Harrod, cheerfully. "I feel sure it will turn out a sound investment."

"'The Elms!'" exclaimed mother. "Are you thinking of that, Laban?"

"Yes," answered he. "Harrod advises it."

"Well, of course I shouldn't like to set myself against Mr. Harrod," said mother, half doubtfully. "But I should have thought our own farm was enough to see after. It seems a deal of responsibility and laying out of money."

"There's no farm to speak of at 'The Elms,' ma'am," answered Harrod. "It's all hop-gardens. That's why I advised Mr. Maliphant buying it."

"Dear," said mother, nowise reassured. "Isn't that very risky? I've always heard of hops as being riskier than cows, and I'm sure they're bad enough, though Reuben will have it they're nothing to sheep at the lambing."

Harrod had frowned a little at first, but now he smiled. "There's a risk in everything," he said. "You might break your leg walking across the room."

"You'll live up at the house, Harrod," put in father. "I've been sorry there's been no better place for you up to the present time."

"Oh, I've done very well," laughed the young man; "but it'll be best I should go over there now. It's only a step for me to get here of mornings."

"Well, I'm glad of *that* at any rate," said mother. "Father's quite right. It wasn't fitting for you as our bailiff not to have a proper place. And now you'll have it. Meg, you and I must go up and see as everything's comfortable. And we must get a woman in the place to see after him. Old Dorcas's niece might do. She's a widow—she'd want to take her youngest with her, but you wouldn't mind that," added she, turning again to Harrod. Her mind was full of the matter now. So was mine. We were quite at one upon it, and discussed it the whole evening. Nevertheless, I found time to wonder now and then how it was that it was only after his talk with Mr. Hoad that father had made up his mind to take on "The Elms." It rather nettled me. Mr. Hoad could not possibly know as much about farming as did Trayton Harrod.

However, the thing was done, that was the main thing. Mr. Harrod had had his way, and I tried to flatter myself that I was in some way instrumental in procuring it.

CHAPTER XX

The time was coming near when Joyce was to come home, and I had done positively nothing in the matter in which I had promised to fight her battle. It is true that she had begged me not to fight her battle, but I wanted to fight it, and I was vexed with myself that I had so allowed the matter to slide. In the one tussle that I had had with mother, I had been so worsted that I felt, with mortification, my later silence must look like a confession of defeat.

The fact is that I had been thinking of other things. Trayton Harrod and I had had a great many things to think of. He had started a new scheme for the laying on of water.

Our village abounded in wells; they, too, were the remnants of the affluence of the town in by-gone days, but they were all at the foot of the hill.

Trayton Harrod wanted to bring the water from the spring at the top of Croft's hill, in pipes through the valley, and up our own hill again. He wanted to form a co-operation among the inhabitants for the enterprise. If this was impossible, he wanted father to do it as a private undertaking, and to repay himself by charging a rental to those people who would have it brought to their houses. But he met with opposition at every turn. The inhabitants of Marshlands were a stubborn lot; they did not believe in the possibility of the thing; they did not care for innovations; they had done very well all these years with carts that brought the water up the hill and stored it in wells in their gardens, and why not now? He had not gained his point yet, either in one way or in the other, and I had been very busy fighting it for him; that was how it had come to pass that I had forgotten Joyce's business.

Mother and I sat in the low window-seat of the parlor straining our eyes over the mending of the family socks and stockings by the waning light of the June evening. Mother had missed Joyce very much. I had not been all that a daughter should have been to her since I had been in sole charge; I had been preoccupied, and she had missed Joyce much more, I knew very well, than she chose to confess. Knowing this as I did, I thought the moment would be well chosen to speak of what should affect Joyce's happiness; I thought her heart would be soft to her. But on this point I was mistaken. Mother did not alter her opinion because her heart was soft. She could be very tender, but she was most certainly also very obstinate.

I opened the conversation by alluding to the letter which father had had from Captain Forrester.

"That scheme of his for poor children doesn't seem to be able to get started as easily as he hoped," I said. "I'm sorry. It would have been a beautiful thing, and father will break his heart if it falls through."

"He seems to think the young man hasn't gone the right way to work," said mother. "I could have told him he wasn't the right sort for the job."

I tried to keep my temper, and it was with a laugh that I said, "Well, if anything could be done I'm sure he would do it, if it was only for the sake of pleasing Joyce."

Mother said nothing. She prided herself upon her darning, and she was intent upon a very elaborate piece of lattice-work.

"He would do anything to please Joyce. I never saw a man so much in love with a girl," I said.

"Have you had great experience of that matter?" asked mother, in her coolest manner. "Because if you have, I should like to hear of it; girls of nineteen don't generally have much experience in such matters."

"I can see that he is in love well enough," said I, biting my lip. Then warming suddenly, I added: "I don't see why, mother, you should set your face so against the young man? You want Joyce to be happy, don't you?"

"Yes," said mother, quietly. "I want her to be happy."

"Well, it won't make her happy never to see the man she loves," cried I; "no, nor yet to have to wait all that time before she can marry him. I've always heard that long engagements were dreadfully bad things for girls."

Mother smiled. "I waited three years for your father," she said, "and I'm a hearty woman of my years."

"Perhaps you were different," suggested I.

"Maybe," assented mother. "Women weren't so forward-coming in my time, to be sure."

"I don't see that Joyce is forward," cried I.

"No, Joyce is seemly behaved if she is let alone. She'll bide her time, I've no doubt," said mother.

"Then, my dear, it's to be hoped you won't love a man just yet," said mother, as she went out of the room.

And that was all that I got by my endeavor to further my sister's cause with mother. I think, however, I soon forgot the annoyance that my failure caused me; it was driven out of my head by other and more engrossing interests.

Mother and I had been up at "The Elms" that very day getting things in order for Mr. Harrod. We had found a tidy widow woman to wait on him, and mother had put up fresh white dimity curtains from her own store to brighten up his little parlor. When he came in to supper he was full of quiet delight. I forget what he said; he was not a man of many words; he was always wrapped up in his business; but I recollect that, however few they were, they were words of affectionate gratitude to mother for a kind of care which he seemed never to have known before, and I know that I was grateful to him for them—so sensitively responsible is one for the actions of another who is slowly creeping near to one's heart.

Harrod sat some time with mother on the lawn discussing the qualities of cows; she wanted father to give her a new one, and she wanted Harrod to find her one as good as Daisy, if such a thing were possible. He listened with great patience to her reminiscences of past favorites, and promised to do his best; but I could see that there was something on his mind.

I fell to wondering what it was. I fell to wondering whether Trayton Harrod ever thought of anything else but the work he had to do, the dumb creatures that came his way in the doing of it, and the fair or lowering face of the world in which he did it. I soon learned what it was. It was something that had been discussed many times, but it had never been discussed as it was discussed that evening.

Father came out with his pipe a-light; his rugged old face wore its dreamy and contented expression. He had evidently been thinking something that had given him pleasure; but I do not think it had to do the farm. But Mr. Harrod went to meet him, and they strolled down den together, and stood for about ten minutes talking hard by the re the golden gillyflowers and the purple iris bloomed side by side.

, you know what I have told you, Mr. Maliphant," said Harrod. r can make the farm pay so long as you hold these theories. Your horter hours and receive higher wages than anybody else's; and, t, you absolutely refuse to have any machinery used. It'll take long to get in your hay and your wheat as it will take the other can you possibly compete with them?"

I felt the hidden thrust, and it was the more sharply that I replied, "You're so fond of Joyce, I should have thought you wouldn't care to make her suffer."

Mother gave a little sigh. She took no notice of my rude taunt.

"The Lord knows it's hard to know what's best," said she. "But I'd sooner see her pine a bit now than spend her whole life in misery, and there's no misery like that of a home where the love hasn't lasted out."

The earnestness of this speech made me ashamed of my vexation, and it was gently that I said: "But, mother, I don't see why you should think a man must needs be fickle because he falls in love at first sight. I don't see how people who have known one another all their lives think of falling in love. When do they begin?"

"I don't know as I understand this mighty thing that you young folk call 'falling in love,'" said mother. "I was quite sure what I was about when I married your father."

"Well, now, mother, I don't see *how* you can have been quite sure beforehand," argued I, obstinately. "You have been lucky, that's all."

"Nay, it's not all luck," said mother. "It isn't all plain sailing over fifty or sixty years of rubbing up and down; and they'd best have something stouter than a mere fancy to stand upon who want to make a good job of it."

"I don't see what they are to have stouter than love to stand upon," s? I. "And I always thought love was a thing that came whether you wou' not, and had nothing to do with the merits of people."

It was all a great puzzle. Did mother make too little of love, ' make too much?

"That's not love," said mother; "that's a fancy. I misdou' undertake to show patience and steadiness in one thing, b learned it in anything else."

"What has Frank Forrester done, I should like to kr that she was too hard on him.

"Nothing, my dear," answered mother, lacon·

And I sighed. It was very evident there wo' and that if there was to be any relaxation in ' Joyce, it must come through father, and no

She rose and moved away, for the ' see to work.

"If I loved a man I'd take my char.

Margaret Maliphan.

"I don't want to compete with them," said father—"not in the sense of getting the better of them. I merely want the farm to yield me sufficient for a modest living; I don't need riches."

"Well, and you won't do it in the way you are going on," said Harrod, calmly. "You won't do so, unless you allow me to stock the farm with the proper machines, and to get the proper return of labor out of the men."

"What is the proper return?" asked father, his eye lighting up. "That I should get three times the profit the laborer gets? I'm not sure of it. My capital must be remunerated, of course; but I am not sure that that is the right proportion." His heavy brows were knit, his hair was more aggressive than ever, his lower lip trembled.

Harrod stared. He had not yet heard father give vent to his theories, and he stared.

"And as for machines," continued father, "I don't choose to have them used, because I consider it unjust that hands should be thrown out of work in order that I may make money the faster. My notions may be quixotic, but they are mine, and the land is mine, and I choose to have it worked according to my wish."

"Certainly, sir," answered Harrod, stiffly. "Only, as I'm afraid I could not possibly make the farm succeed under these conditions, I would prefer to throw up my situation."

"Very good," said father; "that is as you wish." And he moved on into the house.

Mother looked at Mr. Harrod a moment as though she were about to beg him to take no notice, and to recall his hasty resignation. Her eyes had almost a supplicating look; but apparently she seemed to think that her appeal would be best made to father, for she hurried after him through the open door.

Trayton Harrod and I were left alone on the terrace. His mouth was set in a hard curve that was all the more apparent for his clean-shaven chin; his eyes seemed to have grown quite small. I was almost afraid to speak to him. He stood there a moment, with his hands in his pockets, looking out across the marsh where the coming twilight was already beginning to spread brown shades, although there was still a reflection of the distant sunset upon the clouds overhead. He looked a moment, and then he turned to go; but I could not let him go like that.

My heart had gone down with a sudden, sick feeling when he had said he must leave Knellestone. I can remember it now. I did not ask myself what it meant. I suppose I thought, if I thought at all, that it was anxiety for the welfare of the farm; but I remember very well how it felt.

"Oh, Mr. Harrod, you don't really mean that!" said I, hurriedly.

"Mean what?" answered he, without relaxing a muscle of his face.

"That you will give up your work here."

"Indeed I do," answered he, with a little hard laugh, showing those white teeth of his. "A man must do his work his own way, or not at all."

I did not know what more to say. But he did not offer to go now; he stood there, with his hands in his pockets and his back half turned to me.

"Do you think so?" said I, at last, doubtfully.

"Well, if I can't do my work here so that it should be to your father's advantage, I'm cheating him, Miss Maliphant—that's evident, isn't it? And I have a particular wish to be an honest man." There was bitterness in his voice.

"I see that," said I. "Only, if you go away the work will be done much less to father's advantage than if you stay—even though you can't do it just as you wish."

"That has nothing to do with me," answered Harrod, in his hardest voice. "I should harm my reputation by remaining here."

A wave of bitterness swept over me too at that.

"I see," I replied, coldly. "You are considering your own interest only. Well, we have no right to expect any more. You have only known us a short time."

He did not speak, and I walked forward to the palisade that hedged the garden, and leaned my arms upon it, looking out to the sea. After a little while he came to my side.

"Well, you see," said he, in a softer voice, "a man is bound to consider his own interests to that extent at least—so far as doing his work honestly is concerned. I consider a man a thief who doesn't do what he has to do to the best of his lights."

"I quite understand that," answered I. "I quite understand that it would be more comfortable for you to go away."

"I should be very sorry to go away," replied he, simply. "I like the place, and I like the work, and I like the people."

"Then why do you go?" asked I, bluntly.

"A man must have his convictions," repeated he, doggedly.

I looked up at him now.

"Yes," I said, firmly. "Father has his convictions too. They are not your convictions, but he cares just as much about them. You ought to make allowances for that."

"I make every allowance for it," answered he; "only, I don't see how the two lots can mix together."

"You said just now that a man must do his work his own way, or not at all," I went on, without heeding him. "But I don't see that."

This time Mr. Harrod did more than smile, he laughed outright. I suppose even in the short time that we had been friends he had learned to know me well enough to see something amusing in my finding fault with any one for obstinacy. But I was not annoyed with the laugh; on the contrary, it restored my good-temper.

"Well, I don't see why you shouldn't go a little way to meet father," insisted I, boldly. "Of course he won't give in to you about everything; it isn't likely he should. But you might do a great many things that he wouldn't mind, which would make the farm better; and then, when he saw they made it better, and that the laborers went on just as well, maybe he would let you do a few more. I can't discuss it," added I, seeing that Harrod was about to speak, "because I can't understand it. But I see one thing plain, and that is that folk think the farm wants doing something with that father doesn't do—and if so, you're the man to do it."

I paused. Had I not followed the squire's instructions well? Had I not done my very best to "smooth over difficulties?"

"I don't think that I am the only man who could do it, by any means," answered Harrod. But he said it doubtfully—pleasantly doubtfully.

It made me bold to retort with greater determination: "Well, *I* think so, then. And if you say you are comfortable here, if you say you like the place—and the people," added I, hurriedly, "why don't you try, at least, to stay on and help us?"

He did not reply. We stood there what must have been a considerable time looking before us silently. The wane of the day had fallen into dusk, the brown had settled into gray, now that the gold of the sunset reflections had faded; the marsh-land was very still and sweet, the sheep were not even white blots upon it, so entirely did the tender pall harmonize all degrees of hue, so that the kine seemed no longer as living beings, but as mysterious shapes bred of the very land itself; even the old castle, so grand and solid in the day-time, was now like some phantom thing in the solitude—every curve and every circle defined more clearly than in sunlight, yet the whole transparent in the transparent gloaming of the air.

The most solid thing in all this varied uniformity, this intangible harmony, was a clump of trees in the near distance that told a shade blacker than anything else; for the turrets of the distant town lay only as a faint mass of purple upon the land, the little lights that twinkled in it here and there alone betraying its nature; long, living lines of strange clouds, that were neither violet nor gray nor white, lay along the blue where sea and sky were one.

"Before you came," said I, at last, in a low voice, "I used to think that I could help father as well as any *man*. I thought that I understood very nearly as much about farming as he did. I thought I could do much better than a stranger, who would not understand the land or the people. But now I think differently. I see how much more you know than I had dreamed of. You have made me feel very foolish."

"I am sorry for that," said he. "It was far from my intentions—very far from my thoughts."

He said no more, neither did I. Perhaps, to tell the truth, I was half sorry for what I had said, half ashamed of even feeling my inferiority, more than half ashamed of having confessed it to any one. Ashamed, sorry—and yet—

Mother called us to go in-doors.

"If your father asks me to remain, I will remain, and do my best," said Trayton Harrod, as we walked slowly up the lawn.

And the glow that was upon my heart deepened. It was a concession, and wherefore was it made?

CHAPTER XXI

For two days not a word was spoken on the sore subject between father and Mr. Harrod, and on the evening of the second day the squire returned from town.

Father and I had gone down on the morning after the quarrel to see the sheep-shearing at the lower farm. By a corruption of the name of a former owner the country-folk had come to call it "Pharisee Farm," and Pharisee Farm it always was. It lay on the lower strip of marsh towards the castle, with the southern sun full upon it. As we came down the hill I heard steps behind us, and without turning I knew that Trayton Harrod was following us. Father gave him good-day quite civilly, and I held out my hand. I do not know why I had got into the habit of giving my hand to Trayton Harrod; it was not a usual habit with me.

"It has turned a bit cooler, Mr. Maliphant, hasn't it?" said Harrod.

"Yes," answered father; "but we must be glad we have had the rain before we had to get the hay in."

"That we must," replied Harrod. "The hay looks beautiful."

We were passing along through the meadows ready for the scythes; they stretched on every side of us. Meadows for hay, pastures for sheep, there was scarcely anything else, save here and there a blue turnip-field or a tract of sparsely sown brown land, where the wheat made as yet no show. The one little homestead to which we were bound made a very poor effect in the vast plain; there was nothing but land and sea and sky. A great deal of land, flat monotonous land, more monotonous now in its richness and the brilliant greenness of its early summer-time than it would be later when the corn was ripe and the flowering grasses turning to brown: an uneventful land, relying for its impressiveness on its broad simplicity, that seemed to have no reason for ending or change; above the great stretch of earth a great vault of blue sky flecked with white vapors and lined with long opal clouds out towards the horizon; between the land and the sky a strip of blue sea binding both together; sea, blue as a sapphire against the green of the spring pastures. Far down here upon the level we could not see the belt of yellow shingle that from the cliff above one could tell divided marsh and ocean:

right across the wide space it was one stretch of lightly varied tints away to the shipping and the scattered buildings at the mouth of the river.

We walked on, three abreast. Our talk was of nothing in particular; only of the budding summer flowers—yellow iris, and meadowsweet along the dikes, crowfoot making golden patches on the meadows, scarlet poppies beginning to appear among the growing wheat—but I don't know how it was that, in spite of father's presence, there was a kind of feeling in my heart as though Trayton Harrod and I were quite on a different plane to what we had been two days ago; I don't know why it was, but I was very happy.

The sheep were gathered in the fold when we reached the farm, and Tom Beale, the shepherd, was clipping them with swift and adroit hands. Reuben and his old dog Luck were there also; they were both of them very fond of having a finger in the pie of their former calling, but I think there was no love lost between them all. Luck could be good friends enough with Taff, but he never could abide that smart young collie who followed Tom Beale's lead; and as for Reuben, he was busy already passing comments in a low voice to father on the way in which Beale was doing his work.

Father humored the old man to the top of his bent—he was very fond of Reuben—but Beale went his way all the same, and sent one poor patient ewe after another out of its heavy fleece, to leap, amazed and frightened, among the flock, unable to trace its companions in their altered condition. One could scarcely help laughing, they looked so naked and bewildered reft of their warm covering, and just about two-thirds their usual size.

"Ay, the lambs won't have much more good o' their dams now," chuckled Reuben. "They're forced to wean themselves, most on them, after this, for there are few enough that knows one another again."

"They do look different, to be sure," laughed I.

"You might get your 'tiver' now, Reuben Ruck," said Beale, "if you have a mind to give a hand with this job. They're most on 'em tarred."

The "tiver" was the red chalk with which the sheep were to be marked down their backs, or with a ring or a half-ring round their necks, according to the kind and the age. A shepherd had been tarring them on their hindquarters with father's initials, each one as it leaped from out of its fleece.

The work went on briskly for a while, and we were all silent watching Reuben mark the two and three and four year olds apart.

"It's a pity there aren't more Southdowns among the flock," put in Harrod at last.

I turned round and looked at him warningly. It was a mistake, I thought, that under the strained relations of the moment he should choose to open up another vexed question.

"Southdowns!" echoed Reuben, who was listening. "You'd drop a deal o' master's money if you began getting Southdowns into his flocks."

I bit my lip, furious with the old servant for his officiousness, but to my surprise father himself reprimanded him sharply for it, and, turning to his bailiff, led him aside a few steps and discussed the question with him at length. My heart glowed with pleasure as I overheard him commission Harrod to go to the fair at Ashford next week and see if he could effect some satisfactory purchase. I was quite pleased to note Reuben's surly looks. How sadly was I changing to my old friends! And yet so much more pleased was I to see the honest flush of satisfaction on Harrod's face as father left him, that I felt no further grudge against the old man, and nodded to him gayly as I followed father across the marsh.

When we reached the bottom of the hill we met the squire. He was coming down the road full tilt with the collie who was his constant companion, and before we came within ear-shot I could see that his face was troubled. I knew him well enough now to tell when he was troubled.

"Why, Maliphant, what's this I hear?" said he, as he came up to us.

Father leaned forward on his stick, looking at the squire with a half-amused, half-defiant expression in his eyes.

"Well, Squire Broderick, what is it?" asked he.

"I hear in the village that you have leased 'The Elms,'" answered the other, almost severely.

I happened to be looking at father, and I could see that his face changed.

"Yes," he said, quietly, "I have. What then?"

The squire laughed constrainedly.

"Well," he began, and then he stopped, and then he began again. "'Tis a large speculation. What made you think of it?"

"Mr. Harrod advised father to take on 'The Elms,'" I put in, quickly. I was vexed with the squire for saying anything that was a disadvantage to Trayton Harrod in the present state of affairs.

"Harrod!" cried the squire. He began beating his boot with his stick in that way he had when he was annoyed. "I thought it was Hoad," he said at last beneath his breath.

Margaret Maliphant | 173

Father's eyes were black beads. "Pray don't trouble yourself to think who it was who advised me, squire," said he. "If it's a bad speculation nobody is to blame but myself. I am entirely my own master. I was told 'The Elms' was to be had, and I chose to take it. My hop-gardens were not as extensive as I wished."

He had raised his voice involuntarily in speaking. A man passing in the road turned round and looked at him.

"Hush, father," whispered I.

It was one of his own laborers, one of father's special friends.

"Wait a bit, Joe Jenkins, I'm coming up the road. I want a word with you," said father.

He held out his hand to the squire, but without looking at him, and then went on up the hill. I stayed a moment behind. The squire looked regularly distressed.

"Your father is so peppery," he said, "so very peppery."

"Well, I don't understand what you mean," said I, but not in allusion to his last remark. "Why isn't the thing a good speculation?"

"Oh, my dear young lady, it's very difficult to tell what things are going to turn out to be good speculations and what not," answered he. "At all events, I'm afraid you and I would not be able to tell."

It was very polite of him no doubt to put it like that, but I did not like it: it was like making fun of me, for of course no one had said that I should be able to tell.

"I understood that you thought a great deal of Mr. Harrod's judgment," said I, coldly.

"So I do, so I do," repeated the squire, eagerly. "I believe it to be most sound."

"Well, anyhow, father won't have it much longer, sound or unsound, unless things take a different turn," continued I, with a grim sense of satisfaction in hurting the squire for having hurt Harrod's case with father.

"Why, what's up?" asked he.

"They have had a quarrel," explained I, carelessly. "Mr. Harrod wanted father to reduce the men's wages, and to make them work as long hours as they do for the other farmers hereabouts, and of course father wasn't going to do that, because he thinks it unjust."

"I knew it would come—bound to come," muttered the squire beneath his breath.

"And then he wanted him to buy mowing-machines for the haymaking," continued I, "and you know what father thinks of machines. So he refused, and then Mr. Harrod said that if he couldn't manage the farm his own way he must leave."

"Dear! dear!" sighed good Mr. Broderick. And dear me, how little I realized at the time all that it meant, his taking our affairs to heart as he did! "This must be set straight."

"I tried my best," concluded I. "It's no good talking to father; but Mr. Harrod promised me that he would take back his word about leaving if father asked him to."

The squire looked at me sharply. "Harrod promised you that?" he asked.

"Yes," repeated I, looking at him simply, "he promised me that."

The squire said no more, but his brow was knit as he turned away from me.

"I'll go and see Harrod," said he. "Can you tell me at all where I shall find him?"

"He's down at Pharisee Farm at the sheep-shearing," said I. "He and Reuben are having a quarrel over Southdowns. He wants to have Southdowns in the flock. But if he goes away there'll be no Southdowns needed."

Mr. Broderick made no answer to this, he strode on down the road. But when he had gone a few steps he turned.

"By-the-bye, will you tell your father," he said, "that my nephew came down with me last night? I believe he wants to see him on some affair or other. No doubt he'll call round in the afternoon."

He went on quickly, and I stood there wondering. Frank Forrester back again at the Manor! Did he suppose that Joyce had returned? Did he hope to see her? Poor fellow! He little knew mother.

"Father," said I, as I joined him on the hill, "do you know that Captain Forrester has come down again?"

He stopped, he was a little out of breath; I even fancied that his cheek was flushed.

"You don't say so!" said he. "He gave me no idea of it in his letter. No idea at all."

A light had kindled in his eye.

"When does your sister come home?" he asked.

"She was to have come next week," answered I. "But I suppose mother will put it off now."

"Yes, Meg," said he, with a twinkle in his eye, "I suppose she'll put it off. And yet the lad is a good lad, but mother knows best, mother knows best."

We turned up the road, and as we came to the corner of the village street we saw two figures coming along towards us. One of them was Mary Thorne and the other was Captain Forrester. I had not known the Thornes were back at the Priory: they had left it for the London season.

The two were laughing and talking gayly. She came forward cordially as soon as she saw me and held out her hand. Her round, rosy face shone with merriment, and her brown hair caught the sunlight. She spoke to me first while Frank was shaking father warmly by the hand.

"How are you, Mr. Maliphant?" cried he. "It's delightful to see you again. You see I could not keep away. I had to come down and get a fresh impetus, fresh instructions."

Mary Thorne laughed. "Oh, he talks of nothing else," said she. "He's quite crazed over this wonderful scheme, I can assure you, Mr. Maliphant."

Father's brow clouded, and to be sure I could not bear to hear her talk like that, though why, I could not exactly have told.

"And so we made it an excuse to snatch a couple of days from balls and things, and come down here for a breath of fresh air," she continued.

I wondered why she said "we." But Frank explained that.

"Mr. Thorne is quite interested in the affair, I can assure you, Mr. Maliphant," said he. "He's going to put a splendid figure to head our subscription list."

Father did not say a word. His shaggy eyebrows were down over his eyes.

"Oh, well, father never is stingy with his money; I must say that for him," said Mary. "He'll give anything to anything." Then turning to me, she added: "We're going to squeeze in a garden-party next week, before we run up to town again. They say one must give entertainments this electioneering-time. At least that Mr. Hoad says so, and he seems to have done a great deal of this kind of thing from what he says. We did two dinners before we went up to London, but a garden-party is jolly—it includes so many. You'll come, won't you? All of you. You're just about the only people I care to ask, you know."

She ran on in her frank, funny way—always quite transparent—not noticing father's scowl and Frank Forrester pulling his mustache, and trying to catch her eye. If she had she would have turned the matter off; she was no fool, but what she had said was what she thought.

Father answered before I could speak. "My eldest daughter is away, Miss Thorne," he said, "and I'm sorry to say Margaret must refuse your kind invitation. My girls are farmer's children, and are not used to mixing with folk in other stations of life."

I felt the color fly to my face, for it was a discourteous speech, and not even perfectly honest, for Mary Thorne had met us at the squire's house although we *were* only farmer's daughters. It mortified me to have father do himself injustice before Frank Forrester.

But Mary took it charmingly. For a moment she looked astonished, then she said, with a merry laugh: "Ah, I see what it is, Mr. Maliphant; you're a Tory. I beg your pardon, I forgot you were the squire's friend. I'm dreadfully stupid about politics. I'm quite ashamed of myself."

Father seemed about to reply, but was stopped by a merry laugh from Frank, whom Mary, however, silenced by a pretty little astonished stare.

"Oh, pray don't apologize," said she to father. "Only don't you try to tell me another time that your daughters are not used to good society. I know better," added she, smiling at me. "I know who was voted the best dancer at the squire's ball. And as for your eldest daughter—well, we know how many heads *she* has turned with her beauty."

She glanced up teasingly at Captain Forrester as she spoke. She was a little woman, and had to glance up a long way; but although he laughed, his face was troubled; and I could see he was trying to catch my eye.

"Well, good-bye," said Mary to me. "I'm sorry you mayn't come."

I took the hand which she offered, but when she held it out afterwards to father he only bowed with laborious politeness. I think I blushed with annoyance as we turned away, but he made no allusion to the meeting; only his brightened humor of five minutes ago had evaporated, and his features were working painfully.

"I shall go and fetch little David Jarrett, Meg," said he. "The sun is warm now, and it'll do him good to lie a bit in the garden. Go home and tell mother."

I went, and a quarter of an hour later he carried the boy in—a poor little delicate fellow, whose father had knocked him down in a drunken fit, and who had been a cripple ever since. We had heard of the misfortune too late to be of much use; for continued want of proper nourishment on a sickly frame had caused the accident to set up a disease from which the poor child was scarcely likely to recover; but all that could be done father had had done, and he was his special favorite among many friends in the younger portion of the community. We spread a mattress on the garden bench and laid him there, and mother sent me out with port-wine and strengthening broth for him, and father spent all the afternoon beside the little fellow, reading and talking to him.

Beyond alluding to Captain Forrester's arrival when mother spoke of it, he made no mention of his young friend or of what had hurt him in the passing meeting with him. But when Frank came, as promised, in the evening, the storm broke.

He came in just as if he had not been away from us these two months; just as kindly, just as interested in all we had been doing, just as easy and charming. But when, I fancied a trifle diffidently, he opened up the subject of the charity scheme, father suffered no misunderstanding to abide.

"I know Thorne is an old friend of your family's, my lad," he said, "and I understand that you can't throw off an acquaintance of your youth; but as to this affair, I want to make it quite clear that I'll have no influence of his to start the school with. If I could help it I'd have none of his money. I can't help that, and the 'big figure' must stand; but I'll have none of him, or the likes of him, on any committee that may be formed, not while I'm in it."

Father always became vernacular when he was excited.

"Very well, sir," smiled Frank. "It's your affair, and I must be led by you. I think you're mistaken. You miss the valuable help of a large and influential class, and why you should forbid manufacturers to remedy an evil which they may have been partly instrumental in increasing, I don't know. But you have your reasons, and I am in your hands."

"Yes, I have my reasons," repeated father, laconically.

And then the conversation became general, and Frank, with his usual amiable courtesy, drew Trayton Harrod into it, as far as the somewhat morose mood of the latter would allow. He seemed to have taken no fancy to the new-comer, and responded but surlily to his interested questions upon the country and country matters.

Frank Forrester was always interested in everything; always seemed to be most so in the subject which he thought interested the particular person to whom he was speaking. But Harrod would betray no enthusiasm on his own pursuits to an outsider. He was very surly that night. I think he was not well. Mother taxed him with it. As I have said, she took a motherly interest in him always. He allowed that he had a bad headache, and rose to leave. I recollect that she went up-stairs to fetch him some little medicament. Father, too, followed him out into the hall. They stood there some five minutes talking, during which time I am afraid that I tried more to listen to what they were saying than to what Frank Forrester took the opportunity to say to me.

I brought my mind to it, however, and told him what I could about Joyce. There was so little to tell; there was always so little to tell about Joyce—nothing very satisfactory to a lover in this instance.

And I was forced to allow what he half gayly asserted—that mother was none the more cordial to him than she had been in the past. He did not seem to be cast down about it, he only asserted it. He did not seem to be in any way cast down. He looked at me with those wide-open brown eyes just as confidently and gayly as ever, and bent towards me with his tall, slim, lissome figure, and took my two hands in his and told me to tell Joyce that he had come hoping to see her for a moment, even though it had been but in mother's presence.

"She forbade me to see her against your mother's wishes," said he, "but openly there would have been no harm."

I felt quite sure that he loved her just as much as ever, and I willingly promised to give his messages to her.

But I hurried over the little interview; I wanted to get out into the hall before Harrod left, and I shook hands with Frank hastily as I heard mother coming down-stairs with the physic.

I was too late, nevertheless. Frank had kept me for a last word, and the front door closed as I came out of the room. I went up to bed in a bad temper.

CHAPTER XXII

Trayton Harrod did not leave Knellestone. I think we had to thank the squire for that. Father and he being so proud and obstinate, they would never have come to an understanding alone, nor would either certainly have accepted me for a mediator.

I don't know whether Mr. Broderick persuaded father to ask his bailiff to remain, or how the matter was arranged. I only know that a few days after the squire's return I met Harrod down at the haymaking on the eastern marsh, and that he told me he was not going to leave us. I remember very well how he told it me with a smile; not that quick flash which I have sometimes noticed before as being characteristic of him when moved to sudden mirth, but a kind of half-smile that had something triumphant in it.

"Yes," he said, looking round on the meadows that were ready for the scythe, "we shall have a mowing-machine on them before the week's out."

That was all; but the words told me he was going to remain. I know I looked up with an answering smile of satisfaction, but it faded as I saw Jack Barnstaple's gloomy eye fixed on me. The very silence of a faithful servant reproved me for my disloyalty. For in my first content I had forgotten that satisfaction to such a speech *was* disloyalty to father, to the horror of machines that had always been my creed till now.

"I'm sorry—" I began, but then I stopped, confused. I was too honest to tell a lie. How could I say that I was sorry he had triumphed? He turned and said some word to the laborer, and I had time to lose my sudden blushes. Had he noticed them? I think I scarcely cared. I was strangely happy.

All that day I was happy. In the eventide we followed the last wagon up the hill. Tired horses, teased to madness by the ox-fly in the heat, tired men shouldering their forks, tired women in curious sun-bonnets, and girls not too tired yet to laugh with the lads, went before, and we two followed afterwards, not at all tired of anything—at least I speak for myself.

A long line of flame marked the horizon behind the hill and upon the red sky, the houses of the village, the three roofs and the square tower of the old church, the ivied grayness of the ancient gate-way, and the solitary pines that marked the ridge here and there, all lay dark upon the brightness, their shapes defined and single. Close behind us the sea was cool and fragrant. Upon the hem of the wide soft sands that shone in sunset reflections, a regal old heron had fetched his evening meal from out of the little pools that the sea had left, and unfolding his huge pinions, sailed away in a queer oblique and apparently leisurely flight to the tall trees that were his inland home. We left the haymakers to take the road, and followed the heron across the marsh.

A wheat-ear's nest that I found in a furrow and carried home with its five little dainty blue eggs gave rise to a discussion about the rarity of these pretty little structures compared with the numbers of the tiny builders who are so plentiful in harvesting that the shepherds make quite a perquisite from the sale of them; an old hare that the bailiff started from its form on the unbeaten track made him wonder at the unusual size of these marsh inhabitants, and as we came along the dike where the purple reeds were already growing tall, I remember his noticing how changing was their color on the surface as they swayed in great waves beneath the breeze, how blue one way, how silver-gray the other; I recollect every word that we spoke.

It was commonplace talk enough, but it was the talk that had first begun to bind us together, and now there was beginning to be something in it that made every word very much the reverse of commonplace to me. What was it?

I did not ask myself, but I knew very well that since that night when Trayton Harrod had promised to try and remain on Knellestone, because I had asked him to do so, that something had grown very fast, so fast that I was conscious of a happy state of guilt, and wondered whether old Deborah knew anything about it as she watched me bid the bailiff good-bye at the gate while she was picking marjoram on the cliff-garden above our heads.

I know that at first I was angry because of her keen little dark eyes and her short little laugh, and I loftily refused to discuss either with her or with Reuben the advantages of Mr. Harrod's remaining on the farm, or the indignity of having machinery at Knellestone and Southdowns on the marsh. There was no delay about either of these matters. Mr. Harrod was a prompt man. I recollect the very day he bought the sheep—yes, I recollect it very well. It was a very hot day, one of the first days of July. He had had the mare—my restive mare—put into the gig, and had started off very early in the morning to Ashford market. It was a long way to Ashford market, but you could just do it and get back in the day if you started very early, and if you had a horse like my mare to go. There was a haze over the sea and even over the marsh; down in the hayfield, where I had been all the morning, the heat was almost unbearable. When five o'clock came I went in to mother in the parlor.

"It's such a nice evening for a ride, mother," said I. "I think I'll just take that pot of jelly over to Broadlands to old Mrs. Winter. She'd be pleased to see me."

Mother looked up, surprised. "I thought you didn't care for riding that old horse," said she.

"Well, I *can't* have the mare, so it's no use thinking of it," I answered.

"You can't have her to-day, because the bailiff has got her, but you can have her to-morrow," said mother. "And it's full late to start off so far."

I walked to the window and looked out. "I think I'll go to-day," said I. "It may blow up for rain to-morrow. As likely as not we shall have a storm. It's light now till after nine."

"Very well," said mother; "you can please yourself. You'd better take some of that stuff for the old body's rheumatism as well."

So I put on my habit and set out. It was quite true that the old black horse did not go so well as the mare, but for some reason best known to myself I had a particular desire to ride to Broadlands that particular afternoon.

I let the poor beast go at his own pace, however, for the heat was still very great; the plain was opal-tinted with it, and the long, soft, purple clouds above the sea horizon had a thundery look. I jogged along dreamily until I was close beneath the old market-town upon the hill. Somehow the memory of that winter drive with Joyce, when we had first met Captain Forrester, came back to me vividly. I don't know how it was, but I began to think of how he had looked at her, of how he had bent towards her hand just a moment longer than was necessary in parting from her. I wondered if those were always the signs of love. I wondered if a man might possibly be in love and yet give none of those signs.

I rode on slowly, watching the rising breeze sweep across the meadows, swaying the long grass in a rhythmic motion like the waves of a gentle sea. I had passed the town by this time, and had come down the little street paved with cobble-stones, and through the grim old gate onto the marsh again. The river ran turbidly by, between its mud banks and across its flat pastures to the sea a mile beyond. Above the river the houses of the town stood, in steps, up the hill, flanked by the dark gray stone of the old prison-house, and crowned by the church with its quaint flying-buttresses; the wall of the battlements hemmed the town; beneath it lay the marsh and then the sea.

This was all behind me; around and in front was the faint, gray flat land, scarcely green under the creeping haze of heat, with the breeze undulating over the long grass, and the light-house, the brightest spot on the scene as it shone white through the mist, on the distant point of beach.

I took the shortest way, avoiding the regular road, and was soon lost upon the grassy sea. The soft, bright monotony of the landscape was scarcely broken by a single incident, save for the Martello towers that stood at regular intervals along the coast, or the sheep and cows that were strewn over the pasture-land lazily cropping and chewing the cud; there was not a house within sight, and even the low line of the downs had dipped here into the flatness of the marsh.

I tried to whip the horse into a canter, but the poor beast felt the heat as I did, and I soon let him fall again into his own jog-trot. It was not at all my usual method of riding, but that day I did not mind it so much; I had my thoughts to keep me busy. They were pleasant thoughts—if so vague a dream was a thought at all—and kept me good company. The dream was a dream of love, but I am not sure whether that time Joyce was the heroine. I think, if I had been asked, that I should have said that there was no heroine to my dream—that it was far too vague, too entirely a dream to have one.

I rode on for another hour across the hot plain before I came to the village of Broadlands. It lay there sleepily upon the bosom of the marsh, with scarce a tree to shelter it from the fierce midsummer sun or the wild sea winds, and until my horse's hoofs were clattering up the little street I scarcely saw man, woman, or child to tell me that the place was alive. But around the Woolsacks some half-dozen men lounged, smoking, and a fat farmer in a cart had stopped in the middle of the road to exchange a few observations on agricultural news. It was the inn at which Trayton Harrod must have put up in the middle of the day for dinner.

This farmer had evidently returned from market. I wondered how long it would be before Trayton Harrod would also come along the same road and stop at the Woolsacks for a drink. I don't think I deceived myself as to there being a little hope within me that I might meet him somewhere on the road. But I reckoned that he could not possibly be as far on his homeward route yet a while, for he probably had had much farther to come than the farmer in the cart, and had not reached the market so early.

I trotted on up the street to Mrs. Winter's cottage, which stood at the extreme end of the village, looking out along the Ashford road. I am afraid that all the time I was in the cottage—although I gave all mother's messages, and inquired with due attention after every one of the old lady's distinct pains—my eyes were ever wandering along that dusty road and listening for horse's hoofs in the distance.

But Mrs. Winter noticed no remissness on my part—she was too pleased to see me, too glad to have news of mother, who had been her friend and benefactress these many years past. I took her a pair of stockings that I had knit for her in the long winter evenings, and I can remember now the matter-of-fact way in which she received the gift, and how, when I said that I hoped they would fit, she answered, with happy trustfulness, "Oh yes, miss; the Lord he knows my size."

We drank tea out of the white-and-gold cups that had been best ever since I could remember, and then she kissed me and bade me be going lest the darkness should overtake me.

I laughed, and declared that the long twilight would more than last me home; for I did not want to be going until I was sure that Mr. Harrod was on my road; the vague hope that I had had of meeting him had grown into a settled determination to wait for him if I could. But the old lady would not be pacified by any assurances that I was not afraid of darkness; and to be sure there was a strange shade in the air as I got outside and mounted the black horse again.

When I got beyond the village again I saw what it was—there was a sea-fog creeping up the plain. Such fogs were common enough in the hot weather, and gave me no concern at all; but I saw with some dismay that the sun must have set some time, for the twilight was falling in the clear space that still existed above the mist.

I looked back upon the road. Surely he could not have passed. I could not bear to give up the hope of this ride home with him, and yet I scarcely dared loiter lest mother should grow anxious. I put the beast to a gentle trot and rode forward slowly. I knew of no other way that Harrod could have taken, and I felt sure that he had not passed that cottage without my knowledge.

But the mist thickened. I could not see before me or behind; it was not until I was close upon it that I could tell where the path branched off that led across the meadows to the town. It did not strike me at the time that I was foolish to take it; I only wondered whether Harrod would be sure to come that way. I only thought of whether I should recognize the sound of the mare's trot, for that was the only means by which I could be sure of his approach before he was close upon me.

I rode on slowly, listening always. I rode on for what seemed to me to be a very long time. The mist was chill after the hot day, and I had no covering but my old, thin, blue serge habit, which had seen many a long day's wear.

The fog gathered in thickness, and darkened with the darkness of the coming night. I began to think that, after all, I had made a mistake in taking the short-cut. Perhaps Mr. Harrod had kept to the high-road, as safer on such a night; perhaps thus I should miss him. I was not at all afraid of the fog, but I was very much afraid of missing the companion for whose sake I had come this long ride on a hot day. And with the fear in my mind that I might miss him, I did a very foolish thing—I turned back upon my steps. I put the horse to a canter, and turned back to regain the high-road. I rode as fast as I could now, urging the beast forward; but though I rode for a much longer distance than I had ridden already since I left Mrs. Winter's cottage, I saw no trace of the road.

I stood still at last and tried to determine where I was. My heart was beating a little. Presently—through the stillness, for the air was absolutely lifeless—I heard the sound of voices. I listened eagerly. But, alas! there was no sound of horse's hoofs: the wayfarers, whoever they were, were on their feet. Mr. Harrod could scarcely be one of them. I stopped, waiting for them to come up. They were tramps. Their figures looked wavering and uncertain as they came towards me through the mist. They walked with a heavy lounging gait, smoking their clay pipes.

"Can you tell me if I'm in the right way for the high-road?" said I, as they came within ear-shot.

They stopped, and one of them burst into a laugh and said something afterwards in an undertone to his companion.

"You're a long way from wherever it is you're bound for," said he; and as he spoke he came up to me and took hold of the horse's bridle.

Something in his face displeased me. I gave him a sharp cut across it with my whip. He yelled with rage, but he let go the bridle; and another cut across the horse's neck sent him forward with his hind-hoofs in the air. I had never known him answer like that to the whip before. I think he can have liked the look of the men no better than I did.

Before I knew that there was a dike before me, I found myself safely landed on the other side of it; and it was only then that I pulled the poor old beast up and looked round. Of course I could see nothing: the mist would have been too thick, even had the growing darkness not been sufficient to obscure any object not close at hand. But I could hear no voices, and I felt that I was safe.

How a girl, with nothing but a little whip in her hand, had prevailed against two strong men—even though she was on a horse and they on foot—I did not pause to consider. I was safe; but the little adventure had frightened me, and I thought I would try to get home as fast as I could.

But how? I was absolutely uncertain where I was. I had crossed a dike, which I should not have done; but one dike was much like another, and that was no guide. I could see nothing, and I could hear nothing.

Nothing? Yes; as I listened I did hear something. It was the sound of distant waves lapping gently upon the beach. I must indeed have strayed far from the high-road if I had come near enough to the sea to hear the sound of its waves. I stopped and waited again. I thought I would wait until those men had got well ahead. Then, after a while, I put the horse across the dike again, and went forward slowly, straining every nerve to determine whether the sound of the sea was growing louder or less in my ears.

I felt sure after a while that it was growing less, and yet I could not be absolutely certain, for there was a strange feeling in my head; and I was soon obliged to acknowledge to myself that I was getting very sleepy. The mist, I knew, was apt to make people sleepy if they were out long in it; but I had often been out in a sea-fog before, and I had never felt so sleepy. I wondered what o'clock it was. I struggled on a little longer, but I felt that unless I were to walk I should fall off the horse, so I got down and led him on by the bridle. For another reason it was better to walk—I was chilled to the bone.

I turned the end of my habit up over my shoulders, and although it was wringing wet, it served as a kind of poultice; but I cannot say that I was either cheerful or comfortable. The night was perfectly still, the mist perfectly dense. Once a hare, startled I suppose by the sound of the horse's hoofs, ran across in front of me, and retreated into his form; but I think that that was the only time I saw a living thing.

I got so used to the silence and loneliness that when at last another sound began to mingle with the monotonous tread of the weary beast, I scarcely noticed it. Perhaps it was because it was only an increase of the same sound: it was the tread of another weary beast. But whether that was the reason, or whether it was that I was gradually growing more and more sleepy, certain it is that the sound grew to a point, and then began slowly to fade away again before I was quite conscious of its existence. Then suddenly I realized what it might be, and with all the strength of my being I shouted through the mist.

Once—twice I shouted, and then I stood still and listened. The sound of the hoofs and the wheels—yes, the wheels—still went on faintly. My heart grew sick, and again I shouted into the night; this time it was almost a cry. The wheels stopped. I shouted again, and there came back a faint holloa that told me how much fainter still must have been my own voice through the fog.

I leaped onto the horse, and urged him forward as near as I could tell in the direction of the voice. And all the time I continued shouting.

Thank Heaven! I heard the answering cry clearer and clearer each time. At last—at last I saw a horse and gig just discernible through the steaming darkness.

"Who is there?" cried a voice; and—how can I describe my happiness?—it was the voice of Trayton Harrod.

I don't think I answered. I think there was something in my throat which prevented me from answering; but he must have recognized me at once, for he gave vent to an exclamation which I had never heard him use before—he said, "Great heavens!" Then he got down out of the gig, and came towards me quickly.

"Miss Margaret!" he exclaimed. "How did you ever get here?"

I had recovered my usual voice by this time, and I replied, quietly enough, to the effect that I had been on an errand to Broadlands, and had lost myself coming home in the fog.

"Lost yourself! I should think you had lost yourself," ejaculated he, half angrily. "I was uncertain of my own road before you called, but I know well enough that you are entirely out of the beaten track here."

"Oh, then I'm afraid I shall have made you miss your way too," said I, apologetically.

I don't know what had come to me, but I was so glad to see him that I could not bear he should be angry with me.

"That doesn't signify in the least," said he. "It's you of whom I am thinking. I am afraid you must be cold and tired, and I fear we shall be a long while getting home yet." He was close to me now. "You had better get into the gig," said he; "I'll tie the horse to it."

He held out his hands to help me down, and I put mine in his.

"Why, you are chilled to the bone," murmured he. "You'll take your death of cold."

He lifted me from the horse, for indeed I was numb with the penetrating damp, and led me to the gig. Then he took the horse-cloth which lay across the seat and wrapped it round me as tightly as he could.

"Haven't you a pin?" he asked.

I tried to laugh but I could not; something stuck in my throat.

"I thought women always had pins," he added.

Then I did laugh a little; but I must have been very much tired and overwrought, for the laugh turned into a sort of sob. I could only hope he did not notice it. He made no remark, at all events; he only wrapped the rug as closely as he could around me, and took hold of my hands again, as though to feel if they were any warmer. He held them in his own a long time; he held them very fast. The blood seemed to ebb away from my heart as I stood there with my hands in his. My face was turned away, but I felt that his keen dark eyes were fixed upon mine, concernedly, tenderly. A strange, new happiness filled my whole being; I did not know what it meant, but I knew that I wanted to keep on standing there like that, in spite of the cold and the dampness and the dark; I knew that what I felt was sweeter than any joy that had come to me before in my life.

But Trayton Harrod took away his hands. He passed his arm round my waist, and holding me by my elbows so as not to displace the plaid which he had wrapped so carefully around me, he helped me up into the gig. I let him do just what he liked. I, who had been so defiant and proud before, and who thought that I scorned such a thing as a beau, I was letting this man behave to me just as Captain Forrester might have behaved to Joyce; I was as wax in his hands. I did not think of that at the time; I do not know that I ever thought of it. It only strikes me now as I write it down.

I sat there without saying a word while Harrod fetched the horse and tied him to the back of the gig. I was not conscious of anything, save that I was perfectly contented, and waiting for him to come up and sit beside me. All my fatigue had disappeared, all my desire to be home, all my remembrance of mother's anxiety.

But why should I dwell further upon all this? If any one ever reads what I have written, they will understand what I felt far better than I can describe it. Every one knows that love is self-absorbed, and, save towards the one being for whom it would sacrifice all the world, utterly selfish. And what I was slowly beginning to feel was love.

We moved away into the misty night. Mr. Harrod did not speak for some time. He was busy enough trying to find out which was the right way. We had no clew. The sound of the sea, it is true, had grown faint in our ears, so that we were farther inland; but, excepting for the dike which I had crossed after my meeting with the tramps, we had no landmark to tell us where we were.

Harrod thought he remembered the dike; but how far it was from the high-road that we wished to reach, we could neither of us exactly determine. The tract of country was a little beyond our usual beat, or we should have been less at a loss. But there was no sign or sound yet of the market-town through or by which we must pass before we reached our own piece of marsh-land.

There was no doubt about it that we were lost on the marsh, and all that we could do was to jolt slowly along, avoiding dikes and unseen pitfalls, and waiting quietly for the day to show us our whereabouts. Luckily, in these midsummer nights the hours betwixt dusk and dawn are but short. Only Harrod seemed to be concerned about it; he kept asking me whether I was warm; he kept begging me not to give up and go to sleep. I suppose he was afraid of the fever for me. But for my own part I felt no inconvenience; I was not cold, and I had no more inclination to go to sleep.

I do not remember that we talked of anything in particular; I do not remember that we talked much at all. I think I was afraid to speak; I think I was afraid that even he should speak; the silence was too wonderful, and the vague sense of something unspoken, unguessed, was sweeter than any words. It was the deepest silence I have ever felt; there wasn't so much as the sound of a bird, or of a stirring leaf, or of the breath of the sleeping cattle; even the gentle moaning of the sea was hushed now in the distance; it was as though we two were alone in the world.

Sometimes I could see that smile of Mr. Harrod's flash out even in the darkness as he would turn and ask if I was quite warm, and sometimes he would merely bend over me and wrap the rug—tenderly, I fancied—more closely around me. Ah, it was a midsummer-night's dream! But at last nature was stronger than inclination—I was young and healthy—and I dropped asleep. When I awoke, a promise of coming light was in the east, the sea was tremulous with it, and long purple streaks lined the horizon. Overhead the sky was fair, although the thick, white fog still lay in one vast sheet all around us. Out of it rose the market-town straight before us, dark and sombre, out of the shining sea of mist.

We were trotting now along the beaten track towards it, and Mr. Harrod was urging on the weary mare with one hand, while the other was round my waist. The gig was narrow for two persons, and I suppose I should have risked being thrown out in my unconscious state if he had not done so. He took away his arm as soon as I stirred, and I shook myself and looked at him. Had my head been resting on his shoulder? and if it had, why was I so little disturbed?

"I am afraid I have been asleep," said I.

"Yes," answered Mr. Harrod, "you have been asleep. I hadn't the heart to rouse you again, you were so tired. But we shall soon be at home now."

"Why, we've got back into the track!" I exclaimed.

"Yes," laughed he. "When the town began to appear through the mist it was a landmark to me, though I believe I tumbled over the path at last by a mere chance."

He said no more. We were soon out into the high-road again, and climbing the street of the town. We were the only stirring people in it, and this made me feel more conscious of my strange adventure than all the hours that I had spent alone on the marsh with my companion.

For the first time I began to wonder what mother would say. Once out of the town, we sped silently along the straight, familiar road that led towards our own village. The mist was beginning slowly, very slowly, to clear away, and the hills upon which our farm stood loomed out of it in the distance. In the marsh, on either side of us, the cattle began to stir like their own ghosts in the white vapor, and gazed at us across the dikes with wondering, sleepy eyes.

The stars were all dead, and above the mist the quiet sky spread a panoply of steely blue, while out above the sea the purple streaks had turned to silver and sent rays upward into the great dome. Hung like a curtain across the gates of some wonderful world unseen, a rosy radiance spread from the bosom of the ocean far into the downy clouds above that so tenderly covered the naked blue—a radiance that every moment was more and more marvellously illumined by that mysterious inward fire, whose even distant being could tip every hill and mountain of cloudland with a lining of molten gold. Unconsciously my gaze clung to the spot where a warmth so far-reaching sprung from so dainty a border-land of opal coloring; and when at last the great flame was born of the sea's gray breast, I felt the tears come into my eyes, I don't know why, and a little sigh of content rose from my heart. I was tired, for the sunrise had never brought tears to my eyes before.

"I hope you'll be none the worse," said Harrod, glancing at me uneasily, and urging the horse with voice and hand; "but I'm afraid your parents will have been sadly anxious anyhow."

Alas! I had not thought of it again. I sat silent, watching where the familiar solid curves of the fortress upon the marsh began to take shape out of the fog.

"If I hadn't met you I should have been out on yonder marsh now," I said.

I thought he would have said something about being glad he had met me, but he did not. He only answered, "I ought not to have allowed you to fall asleep."

I laughed at that. "If it had not been for you I should be asleep now on that bank where I first heard you," I declared. "And I should have got my death of ague by this time, I suppose."

Still he said nothing. There was some misgiving on his mind which no words of mine removed. I felt it instinctively. Even when I said—and as I write it down now I marvel how I *could* have said it—even when I said, softly, "Well, I regret nothing. I have enjoyed myself," he did not reply.

I wondered at it just for a moment, but no mood of his could damp my complete content. Even though, as I neared home, I began to be more and more uneasy about my parents' anxiety, no cloud could rest on the horizon of this fair, sweet dawn of day. I could not see beyond the barrier of that ever-widening, ever-brightening curtain of glorious light; but there it was, making glad for the coming of the blessed sun that would soon fill the whole space of heaven's free and perfect purity.

The coldness of the sky and of all the world was slowly throbbing with the wakening warmth. What was there beyond that burning edge of the world, beyond that sea of strange, exultant brightness?

We began to climb the hill, and on the garden terrace stood my father. He was waiting for me just as he had waited for me on that night in May when he had told me to be friends with Trayton Harrod.

CHAPTER XXIII

Mother never scolded me at all for my adventure, and of course I was much more sorry than I should have been if she had done so.

As I stood there in the cool, gray dawn, with my wet habit, the dewdrops still standing on the curls of my red hair, my face—I make no doubt—pale with distress, and my gray eyes at their darkest from the same cause, I suppose I looked rather a sorry spectacle, and one that melted her heart; anyhow, I know that she put her arm round me and gave me a hasty kiss before she pushed me forward to meet father. For a moment I felt something rise in my throat, and I suppose I ought by rights to have cried. But I did not cry; I was too happy in spite of it all, and luckily neither father nor mother was of those people who expect one to cry because one is sorry.

As I have said, they neither of them said a word of rebuke. I gave my explanation, and it was accepted; father only declared that it was a very good thing Trayton Harrod had met me when he did; and mother only remarked that "least said soonest mended." I suppose they were both glad to have me safe home. And that drive with father's bailiff, which had meant so much to me, was thus buried in sacred silence.

It was the day that Joyce was to come home. As I dressed myself again after the couple of hours' sleep, which I could not manage to do without, I remembered that it was the day for Joyce to come home. How was it that I had not thought of it? How was it that I had not thought of it all yesterday, nor for many yesterdays before it?

I was conscious that even my letters to my sister had been fewer and more hurried than they were at the beginning of her absence. I was angry with myself for it, for I would not have believed that any length of absence could have made her anything but the first person of importance in my life. But of course now that she was home again, everything would be as before.

I felt very happy to think that I was to see her again. I begged the gig to go down to the station and meet her myself. The mare was used to me now, so that even Joyce would not be nervous. Her face lit up with her own quiet smile as she saw me, breaking the curves of the sweet mouth, and depressing, ever so little, that short upper lip of hers, that always looked as if it had been pinched into its pretty pout. She looked handsomer than ever; I don't know whether it was because it was so long since I had seen her, but I thought she was far more beautiful than I had ever imagined. I pitied poor Frank more than ever for having to wait so long for a sight of her.

"Why, Meg," said she, as she came out with all her little parcels, "how tanned you are! I declare your hair and your face are just upon one color."

I laughed aloud merrily.

"Well, if my face is the color of my hair, it must be flame indeed," I cried. "But I've been out haymaking, you see, all the time that you, lazy thing, have been getting a white skin cooped up in a London parlor. Oh, my dear! I wouldn't have been you."

"No, you wouldn't have liked it," answered she. "I was pleased to be of use to poor old aunt, but it was rather dull, and I must say I'm glad to be home."

"Everybody has missed you dreadfully," said I. "As for mother and Deb, they can't tell me often enough that I can't hold a candle to you."

"Oh, what nonsense, Meg!" murmured she. "You know well enough they don't mean it."

"My dear, I don't mind," cried I. "I know it well enough, and I can do my own bit of work in my own way all the same. But mother has missed you and no mistake," added I, "though as likely as not she won't let you guess it. She wanted you home long ago, only then Captain Forrester came down again."

A troubled shade came over Joyce's face, as I had noticed it come once or twice before, at mention of her lover's name.

"He came down for a few days a week ago, you know," I added. "I told you so, didn't I?" I was not quite sure whether I had even remembered to give that great piece of news.

"Oh yes, you told me," replied Joyce, in a slow voice.

"He inquired a great deal after you, of course," I went on. "He asked me to give you a great many messages."

She did not answer. A blush had crept up on her dainty cheek, as it was so apt to do. But we had reached the hill, and I jumped down and walked up it, giving her the reins to hold. And when we got to the top, Deborah was there hanging clothes in the back garden ready to catch the first sight of us along the road, and Reuben at the gate looking half asleep because he had been out the best part of the night with Jack Barnstaple, looking for me in the fog. There was no time for any more private talk.

Mother, it is true, did not come to the gate, that not being her way, and when we got inside, you might have thought Joyce had been no farther than to market from the way in which she received her; but that meant nothing, it was only Maliphant manners, and father said no more than, "You're looking hearty, child," before he took me away to write out his prospectus for him because his hand was stiff.

It was not till late in the evening that I got time to have a chat with Joyce in the dear old attic bedroom that she and I had always shared, and I was anxious for a chat. She had brought back two new gowns for us, and apart from all I had to say to her, I wanted to see the new gowns. I had never cared for clothes till quite lately; I used to be rather ashamed of a new frock, as though folk must think me a fool for wearing it, and had been altogether painfully wanting in the innocent vanity which is supposed to be one of a young girl's charms. But lately it had been different. I wanted to look nice, and I had my own ideas of how that was to be achieved. Alas! when I saw the gowns, I knew that they did not meet my views.

Joyce was settling her things—laying aside her few laces and ribbons with tender care; she opened the heavy old oak press and took out the gowns with pride. I think that she was so busy shaking them out that she did not see my face; I hope so, for I know it fell. The gowns were pale blue merino, the very thing for her dainty loveliness, but not, I felt instinctively, the thing for a rough, ruddy colt like me.

"Won't they spot?" said I, diffidently.

"That's what mother said," replied she, a little sadly; "but, dear me, they're our only best frocks; we sha'n't wear them o' bad weather."

I am so glad I said no more, for she had brought me a book from London— it was a novel by a famous author of whom we had heard; the author was a woman, and I had expressed a great wish to read it in consequence. I was very pleased to think that Joyce should have remembered it. I recollect that I kissed her for it, and I thought no more about the frocks, I only felt that it was nice to have sister home. I had not known until now how much I had missed her.

"I wonder how we shall all get on when you go away for good and marry that young man of yours?" said I. "It don't seem as if the place were itself somehow when you are not there."

"Time enough to think of that when the day comes," answered Joyce, I thought a trifle sadly.

"Well, yes, maybe," said I, doubtfully; "and yet it isn't so very far off, you know. And if only you had a little more determination in you it might be a great deal nearer."

"You seem to be very anxious to get rid of me just as soon as you have got me home," said she, with just the merest tone of wounded sensibility in her voice.

Of course I laughed at that—it wasn't really worth answering. But I could have said that since three weeks ago, I had learned that which made me think it harder than ever that Joyce should be separated from the man she loved. I had not thought much of her or her concerns of late, but now that she was close to me I felt very sorry for her. When Joyce had gone away I had been conscious of a curious feeling of inferiority with regard to her as though she knew some secret which was to me sealed, but now—now I felt that there was a rent in the cloud that divided us; I felt that I could look into her world, I felt that I was on her level. And it was only with a more delicate feeling of sympathy than formerly that I began to give her some of the messages with which Frank had intrusted me.

I could not exactly pretend that he had looked very miserable, but I could assure her of his continued ardent devotion to her, and this I did most fervently. Somehow, when I had entered upon this task I began to feel that it was rather a queer compliment to assure a girl that her lover was not forgetting her, and I asked myself why I felt obliged to do it.

She listened quietly to all that I repeated to her of the short interview, but when I began to speak of my endeavors to induce mother to cut the term of the engagement short, she interrupted me with that serene air of determination which I knew there was no gainsaying.

"Meg," she said, "I want you never to do that again. I want you to understand once and for all that if things don't come naturally, it's because I believe that they oughtn't to come at all. If Frank cares for me as he says, he will care for me just as much at the end of a year, and I had rather wait and see."

I looked at her open-mouthed.

"I think you're a queer girl," I said at last. "I shouldn't have thought you wanted to punish yourself for the sake of putting a man to a test. But I suppose I don't understand. That's the sort of way mother talks, and I know it's very wise, and all that; but, dear me, I think it's all stuff wanting to sit down and wait till the wave comes over you. I'm sure that if *I* wanted a thing very badly I should love to fight for it—I should *have* to fight for it."

Joyce sighed a little sigh, and sat down by the window, looking out into the deepening twilight.

It was close upon midsummer, and the evenings were exquisitely long and luminous, the twilight stretching almost across to the dawn. After the heat of the day, lovely soft gray mists rose in transparent sheets off the marsh below us, and floated upward towards the hill. It was not a thick fog, as it had been the night before, but just a ghostly veil thrown across the land, above which lights twinkled amid dark houses on the distant hill. There was not a breath of wind, and in the silence the lapping of the sea came faintly to our ear. Joyce looked out into the mist.

"Of course," continued I after a while, "I'm not engaged to a man, and so I don't know what I should do if I were."

"I think you would do what you do in other matters," answered Joyce. "I think you would try very hard to get your own way. But then you and I are not alike."

No, we were not alike, I felt that. And I supposed that my sister was right, and that the only difference lay in my being more obstinate.

"I don't think that a woman ought to fight to have her own way," added she, in a low voice.

I considered a moment before I understood what she meant. "Do you mean to say that if any one fights, it ought to be the man?" asked I. "Well, you *are* an unreasonable girl! Good gracious me! When Frank lifts a finger you are angry with him."

Joyce smiled a faint smile like the gray mists below.

"I don't think you know *what* you mean nor *what* you want," added I, impatiently.

Without taking any notice of my short tone, she said, gravely, "I know that it will be all as it is ordained."

When Joyce talked about things being as they were ordained, it always put me in a horrible temper; and it was either this or some little feeling of awkwardness in my mind about Harrod which made me reply very shortly when she began asking me presently about the new bailiff.

From some motive entirely incomprehensible to myself, there arose within me a sudden dislike to the idea that Joyce should guess at my liking for him. And so when she asked what he was like, I replied, gruffly, "Oh, like many other men—plain and very obstinate."

This was true, but the impression that I gave in saying it was false; I knew that perfectly well, but I was too proud to change it, although in my heart I felt ashamed that I should be guilty of any sort of deception towards my dear, simple Joyce, and when I was really so glad to have her back again.

She looked distressed for a moment, but then she brightened up and said, gayly, "Well, many a good-fellow is plain, and as for being obstinate, that should be to your liking."

"So it is," said I. "Of course."

"I hope father and he get on nicely. I hope he isn't obstinate with father."

I laughed. "Oh, birds of a feather, you know," said I. "We're all obstinate together. But we none of us waste words, so we get on first-rate."

Joyce sighed a little. "Mother said what a good-fellow he was, but father wouldn't say a word about him to me," she said. "Of course he never does. But I don't think he's looking well. He has aged so of late."

I looked at her defiantly. So many people had said the same thing during the last few months.

"Good gracious, Joyce!" I cried. "You're always saying that. Father's hale and hearty enough. Folk are bound to grow older. And I can tell you one thing, he's not half so touchy as he was. He and squire haven't had more than two rows since you left. That's a very good sign."

"Yes, I *am* glad of that," agreed Joyce. "The squire's too good a friend to quarrel with. And though of course I know the quarrels never meant anything, they used to make me uncomfortable, Meg, and worse than ever when you used to follow father's way. It didn't seem pretty in one of us girls, dear. Something's good for mere manners. We don't think enough of them."

I was silent. My manners were certainly of the worst when my heart did not go with them. But I was conscious that I was not quite the same girl as I had been when my sister left. Even to the squire I was different; since his talk to me on the garden terrace I had felt no inclination to be anything but gentle to him.

"Of course, if father quarrels with the bailiff it's as bad for his own health as if he quarrelled with the squire," went on my sister, concernedly.

"Why, dear me, Joyce, who said he quarrelled with him?" cried I. "I only said they were both obstinate. Father wouldn't think of quarrelling with his bailiff."

I took off my dress and hung it up, and shook out my red mop of hair before I said another word.

Then I added, "And I think Mr. Harrod is very considerate towards father. He's far too good a fellow not to be respectful to an old man." I felt bound to say that much for honesty.

"Well, then, you do like him?" cried Joyce.

"Who said I didn't?" answered I. "He's a downright honest fellow, with no nonsense about him."

It wasn't quite what I felt about Trayton Harrod, but it was as near as I could get to the truth, and it seemed to give Joyce some idea of my liking him, for she turned round with a brightened face, and laid her hand on my shoulder.

"Oh, Meg, you can't think how pleased you make me by saying that," she murmured, softly; "I have been afraid you would just set your face against the poor man out of mere obstinacy, and make things unpleasant for everybody. You do sometimes, you know. And when you never mentioned him in your letters, I made sure that was the reason. I thought you were just making yourself as disagreeable as ever you could to show you hated his coming to Knellestone."

"Well, you must think me a dreadful old cross-patch," laughed I, awkwardly.

"You *are* tetchy when you have a mind to be, you know, though you can be so bright when you're pleased that one's forced to love you. That's just the pity."

"Well, of course, I *did* hate a bailiff coming to Knellestone," answered I; "but now that I see how much cleverer he is about farming than we are, I'm pleased."

"I see," said Joyce. "Then he *is* clever?"

"Oh yes," answered I. "He's clever."

Joyce paused.

"Well, then," she said, diffidently, "I hope before long you'll be real good friends. I have often thought, Meg, that the folk here aren't bright enough for you. I believe if you weren't set down in a country village you'd be a real clever girl."

I laughed, not ill pleased.

"Oh no, Joyce," said I. "I expect what you and I think clever wouldn't really be so."

"I know more than you think," said Joyce, sagely, nodding her pretty head with an authoritative air. "I don't mean book-learning clever, I mean mother-wit. And do you know, Meg, I do so hope that Mr. Harrod being here may make a difference to you! But you don't seem to have seen much of him yet."

"Oh yes," said I, evasively. "He comes in to supper most nights; and of course one meets out-doors now and then in a country place."

"Well," concluded Joyce, with a sort of air of resignation, "of course it wasn't to be expected you'd be great friends just at once. It's a great deal to be thankful for you don't quarrel."

"Oh no," said I; "we don't quarrel."

And then we both said our prayers and got into bed.

But for a long while I lay awake thinking—wondering why I had pretended that I did not like the new bailiff, and whether I really was a clever girl; and—shall I confess it?—hoping a little that the pale blue dress would become me. And then, as I fell asleep and far into my dreams, the memory of my ride with Trayton Harrod shone through the mist, and I thought again of that bar of silver promise across the dawn beyond which I had not been able to see.

CHAPTER XXIV

Two whole days passed without Mr. Harrod coming to the Grange. I dare say nobody else noticed it; I dare say *I* should not have noticed it if—if I had not thought that he would come to inquire how I did after our adventure. I was always supposed to resent being asked how I did: and here I was, quite hurt because a young man whom I had known not three months had omitted to do so.

I took covert means of finding out that father and Reuben had seen him, and that he was well; and I am quite sure that I blushed with pleasure when, on the morning of the third day, mother said that she was certain the white curtains at "The Elms" must be getting soiled, and suggested that I should carry up a new pair. Harrod was becoming quite a favorite with her, or she would never have taken so much trouble for his comforts—it was no necessary duty on her part. I blushed, but I did not think that any one had noticed it.

When mother had left the kitchen, however, with the key of the linen press, I saw that two little black eyes were fixed on me with a merry twinkle. They made me angry for a moment, I don't know why; but it was a shame to be angry with old Deb, especially when her dear old red face was so kindly and affectionate: it was not always wont to be so.

"Well, well, I'm glad to see folk are for forgiving that poor young man for being bailiff at Knellestone," said she, with good-humored banter. "When I see'd what a fine masterful chap it were, I had my doubts it ud end that way."

"What way, if you please?" asked I, haughtily.

Deborah laughed. "What do you say, Joyce?" said she, turning to my sister, who was intent upon some one of the household duties that she was so glad to be back at. "They aren't quite so hard on the young man as they were for going to be, are they?"

"I don't quite understand," said Joyce, with perfectly genuine innocence. "Why should mother be hard upon him? It isn't his fault if he's father's bailiff. Besides, I'm sure mother sees how useful he is to father."

Deb laughed louder than ever. "There, bless you, my dear," said she; "you never could see round a corner; but you've more common-sense than the lot of 'em. Why should folk owe the man a grudge, to be sure? All the same, your mother'll spoil him afore she's done with him. Curtains, indeed! I never knowed a bailiff as needed 'em before."

Mother came back at that moment with the things, and I hastened to beg Joyce to accompany me up to "The Elms" after dinner. Somehow, although in my heart I knew that I was longing to see Trayton Harrod again, a sudden shyness had come over me at the thought of meeting him, and I wanted Joyce to be there.

Joyce, however, would not come; she begged off on the score of many household jobs that had got behind-hand in her absence, and mother said that I might just as well go alone and get the thing done with Dorcas's help, for that of course the bailiff was sure to be out at that time of day.

So alone I was forced to go. Most likely, as mother said, Mr. Harrod would be out; but I took Taff with me—a dog was better than most human beings; and with Taff at my heels I felt my self-consciousness evaporate.

I crossed the lane and skirted the brow of the hill behind the pine-tree lane; the mill-arms faced the village with a west wind, but the breeze had dropped since morning, and the air was heavy and thunderous. I thought I would go round by the new reservoir and see how the work was getting on. Mr. Harrod would very likely be there: it was that one among his new ventures about which at the moment he was the most excited, and the pipes were just about to be laid; even if I met him he was not obliged to know that I was going to "The Elms."

My heart began to beat a little as I drew near the group, but the bailiff was not there; only old Luck, the sheep-dog, ambled towards me wagging his tail, and I knew that Reuben could not be far off. Sure enough, there he was among the men, who were just leaving off work, talking to Jack Barnstaple.

"I want to know whatever he needs to come stuffing his new-fangled notions down folk's throats as have thriven on the old ones all their lives?" the latter was saying. "We don't understand such things hereabouts. We haven't been so well brought up. He'd best let us alone."

"Yes, I told him so," said Reuben, sagely, shaking his stately white head, that looked for all the world like parson's when he had his hat off; "but these young folk they must always be thinking they knows better than them as has a life's experience. But look 'ere, lads, we hain't been educated at the Agricultural College at Ashford, ye know."

"Blow the Agricultural College," muttered Jack Barnstaple.

"Yes; and so he'll say when he finds out he's none so sure about these Golding 'ops. And so master'll say when he finds as he's dropped all his money over pipes and wells as was never meant to answer."

"What do you mean by that, Reuben?" said I, coming up behind him. And I am sure that my cheeks were red, and my eyes black, as father would declare they were when the devil got into me. "What was never meant to answer?"

Reuben looked crestfallen, for of course I know he had not expected me to be within hearing, and the other men began to pack up their tools for going home.

"Well, miss, it don't stand to reason that a man can expect water to go uphill to please him," said Reuben, with a grim smile.

"Water finds its own level, Reuben," explained I, sagaciously; "Mr. Harrod told me that, and father said so too. The spring is on yonder hill, and if the pipes are laid through the valley to this hill, the water is bound to come to the same level."

I saw smiles upon the men's faces, and Reuben shook his head.

"There's nothing will bring water uphill saving a pump, miss," said Jack Barnstaple, gloomily. He always said everything gloomily—it was a way he had.

"Nay," added Reuben, looking at me with those pathetic eyes of his that seemed to say so much that he can never have intended; "it may be a man or it may be a beast, but some one has got to draw the water uphill afore it'll come. It may run down yonder hill, but it won't run up this un of its own self. 'Tain't in nature."

"Well, Reuben, I advise you to keep to talking of what you can understand," said I, crossly. "I should have thought you would have had sense enough to know that Mr. Harrod must needs know better than you."

A faint provoking smile spread over Reuben's lips. "Young folk holds together," said he, laconically. "'Tis in nature."

I flashed an angry glance at the old man, but I saw a lurking smile—for the first time in my experience—on the face of stolid Jack Barnstaple, who had lingered behind the others. My face went red, as red as my red hair, and I stooped down to caress the dog. What did the man mean? what had Deb meant that morning in the kitchen? But I raised my head defiantly.

"Well, I think you had just best all of you wait and see," said I, severely. "You'll feel great fools when you find you have made a mistake."

I was alluding to the water scheme; but it struck me afterwards that the men might have misunderstood me. But it was too late to correct the mistake, and without another word I ran down the hill to the path that led to "The Elms."

My cheeks were hot with the consciousness that I had a secret that could be guessed even by Reuben Ruck; the consciousness made my heart beat again very fast; but it need not have done so: as was to have been expected, Mr. Harrod was not at home.

Dorcas and I put up the curtains together, and then I was left alone in the little parlor while she went to make me a cup of tea. It was the first time I had been alone in that room—his room.

A bare, comfortless, countryman's and bachelor's room, but more interesting to me than the daintiest lady's parlor. By the empty hearth the high-backed wooden chair in which he sat; beside the wide old-fashioned grate the hob upon which sang the kettle for his lonely breakfast; in the centre of the rough brick floor the large square oaken table at which he ate; on the high chimney-piece the pipes that he smoked, the tobacco-jar from which he filled them, a revolver, and an almanac; on the walls two water-color drawings, one representing an old gentleman in an arm-chair, the other the outside of a country house overgrown with wistaria; standing in the corner a handsome fowling-piece, which I had seen him carry; in the bookshelf between the windows the books that he read.

I wandered up and looked at them: a curious assemblage of shabby volumes, although at that time they embodied to me all that was highest in culture. That was ten years ago, and I was in love. Had it not been so I might have remembered that father's library was at least as good.

Milton, a twelve-volumed edition of Shakespeare, a Bible, a Pilgrim's Progress, a volume of Cowper's Poems, a volume of Percy's Reliques, Adam Smith's Wealth of Nations, Chaucer's Canterbury Tales, Sir Walter Scott's Novels, Byron, Burns, some odd volumes of Dickens, and then books on Agriculture, the authors and their titles strange to me; this is all I remember. A mixed collection—probably the result of several generations, but not a bad one if Trayton Harrod read it all and read it well.

I looked at it sadly. Save the Walter Scott Novels, the Burns Poems, the Bible, and the Pilgrim's Progress, I knew none of them excepting by name, and not all of them even then. I felt very ignorant and very much ashamed of myself; for I never doubted that Harrod read and knew all these books, and how could a man who knew so much have anything in common with a girl who knew so little? I resolved to read, to learn, to grow clever. Joyce had said that I was clever, Joyce might know; why not?

I took the volume of Milton down and sat upon the low window-seat reading it. It was rather dreadful to be immediately confronted with Satan as an orator, for I had never been used to consider him as a personage, but rather as a grim embodiment of evil too horrible to be named aloud. But the rich and sonorous flow of the splendid verse fascinated me and I read on, although I didn't understand much that I read.

My thoughts wandered often to notice that the square of carpet was threadbare, and that I must persuade mother to get a new one; or to gaze out of the window upon the sloping bosom of the downs whereon this house stood lonely—a mark for all the winds of heaven; in the serene solitude the sleepy sheep strayed idly—cropping as they went—white blots upon the yellow pastures. And all the while I was listening for a footstep that I feared yet hoped would come, longing to be away and yet incapable of the determination which should take me from that chance of a possible meeting. But, long as I have taken to tell it, the time that I waited was not ten minutes before a heavy foot made the boards creak in the passage and a hand was on the door-knob. I started up, my cheeks aflame—the volume of Milton on the floor. But when the door opened it was Squire Broderick who stood in the opening. I don't think the red in my face faded, for I was vexed that he should see me there, and I fancied that he looked surprised.

"Oh, do you know if Harrod is at home?" asked he.

"No, he's not," answered I, glancing up at the clean windows; "and I've been putting up fresh curtains meanwhile."

"They look delicious," said the squire, with a little awkward laugh, not quite so hearty as usual. "What care you take of him!"

"Mother is a dreadful fidget, you know," murmured I.

"And at the same time you took a turn at Harrod's library," smiled he, picking up the volume which lay near my foot. "Milton! Rather a heavy order for a child like you, isn't it?"

I flushed up angrily. A child!

"Do you understand it?" asked he.

I struggled for a moment between pride and truthfulness. "No," said I, "not all. Do you?"

He smiled, that kind, sweet smile that made me ashamed of being cross.

"Come, I'm not going to confess my ignorance to you," he laughed. "I'm too old;" and he took hold of my arm to help it into the sleeve of my jacket, which I was trying to put on.

But at that moment Dorcas brought in the tea, and of course I was obliged to stay and have some, and even to hand a cup to the squire to please her; country-folk stand on ceremony over such things, and I did not want to offend Dorcas.

"You'll stop in to-night and see Joyce, won't you?" said I, for want of something to say, for I felt more than usually awkward. "She looks better than ever. She hasn't lost her country looks."

"I am glad of that," said he, glancing at me, although of course he must have been thinking of sister; "they're the only ones worth having." And then, although he promised to come in and welcome her home, he went back to our first subject of talk.

"As you're so fond of reading, you ought to get hold of a bit of Shakespeare," said he.

"Should I like that?" asked I. "I like poetry when it sounds nice, but I like the Waverley novels best."

"But Shakespeare is novel and poetry too," said the squire. "I'm no great reader of anything but the news myself, but I like my Shakespeare now and again."

"Father keeps all those nice bound books in the glass-case," said I, "and I don't believe mother would let *me* have them."

The squire laughed. "Your mother thinks girls have something better to do than to read books," smiled he. "Reading is for lonely bachelors like Trayton Harrod."

"He's no more lonely than you are, Mr. Broderick," said I, "and yet you always seem to be quite happy."

He did not answer, and I was sorry for my thoughtless words, remembering that brief episode in his life when he had not been lonely.

"So you think I am always quite happy?" said he at last.

I blushed. Somehow the question was of a more intimate kind than the squire had ever addressed to me before, for although he had spoken familiarly to me on my own account, he had never allowed me to know any feeling of his own. I was afraid he must be going to speak to me about Joyce.

"Oh yes," I replied, lightly; "I think you're one of the jolliest people I know."

"Well, you're right, so I am," said he, gayly; "and I'm blessed in having rare good friends. But it does sometimes occur to me to think that I am pretty well alone in the world, Miss Margaret."

He looked round at me in his frank way, but I noticed that the hand which held his stout walking-stick trembled a little. I blushed again. It was very unusual for me, but he made me feel uncomfortable; I did not want him to tell me of his love for my sister, for I felt that if he did I *must* tell him of her secret engagement to his nephew, and that would be breaking my promise to my parents. Suddenly an idea struck me; I thought I would take the bull by the horns.

"You should marry," said I, boldly.

He looked at me in blank astonishment.

"Of course," added I, "there's no one hereabouts that would be good enough for you—unless it might be Mary Thorne, and she is only a manufacturer's daughter. You must have a real lady, of course. You should go and spend a bit of time up in London, and bring back a nice wife with you. Wouldn't it brighten up the country-side!"

I marvel at myself for my boldness; I, scarcely more than a child, as he had said, to a man so much older than myself! But the squire did not seem in the least offended, only he looked very grave.

"You don't approve of people not marrying in what is called their own rank of life, I see," he said presently, with a twinkle of humor in his eye.

"No," said I, gravely; "I agree with father."

"Ah!" said the squire, with the air of a man who is getting proof of something that he has affirmed. "I told Frank so the other day. As a rule, the farmer class consider it just as great a disadvantage to mate with us as we do to mate with them."

I bit my lip. So he did consider it a falling down for a gentleman to marry a farmer's daughter! Well, let him just keep himself to himself, then. But what business had he to go meddling with Frank's opinions? I was very angry with him.

"I think you're quite right," I said, shortly. "They do."

"It takes a very great attachment to bridge over the ditch," said he, meditatively.

There came a time when I remembered those words of his, but at the moment I scarcely noticed them. I thought I heard a footstep on the gravel without, and my fear of being surprised by the master of the house came back stronger than ever, because of the presence of the squire.

"I must be getting home now," said I, hastily. "I'm afraid there's a storm coming up;" and even as I spoke, a deep, low growl echoed round the hills.

The squire fully agreed that there was no time to be lost if one did not want to get a drenching, and on the slope outside we parted company, he promising once more to come up in the evening and see Joyce.

The bailiff was not within sight. I had got over my visit quite safely; but, alas! I am not sure that I was relieved. I walked homeward as fast as I could, for heavy drops had begun to fall, and flashes of light rent the purple horizon. The sun had set, leaving a dull red lake of fire in the cleft, as it were, of two purple-black cloud-mountains; above the lake a tongue of cloud, lurid with the after-glow, swooped like a vulture upon the land, where every shape of hill and homestead and church-spire lay clearly defined, and yet all covered as if with a pall of deathly gloom.

The storm advanced with terrible swiftness. By the time I had crossed the hop-gardens and was climbing the opposite lane, it had burst with all its strength, and was tearing the sky with seams of fire, and emptying spouts of rain upon the land. I was not afraid of a storm, but certainly I had never seen a fiercer one.

I ran on, forgetful for the moment of everything but the desire to be home, and thus it was that I did not notice footsteps behind until they were alongside of me, and Mr. Harrod's voice was saying, almost in my ear, "Miss Maliphant!"

The voice made me start, but the tone of it sent a thrill through me.

"I should have thought that one piece of foolhardiness was enough for one week," added he, with a certain look of feeling, veiled under roughness, that always seemed to me to transform his face.

"I took no harm from the other night," said I.

"Well, you may thank your stars that you didn't," answered he; "and you certainly will get wet through now."

I laughed contentedly. "*That* won't hurt me," I said. "I've been up at 'The Elms' to put up fresh curtains." I hadn't meant to tell him, but a sudden spirit of mischief, and I don't know what sort of desire to know the effect of the speech on him, prompted me.

"To 'The Elms!'" cried he, in a disappointed tone. And then, in a lower voice, "To put up the curtains for me."

"Yes," answered I, demurely, "mother sent me?"

What he would have answered to that I don't know; for at that moment the sky seemed suddenly to open and to be the mouth of a flaming furnace full of fire, far into the depths of the heavens; it was the hour that should have been twilight, but it was dark, save when that great sheet of blue light wrapped the marsh in splendor; then the brown and white cattle huddled in groups on the pastures, the heavy gray citadel on the plain, the wide stretch of sea that, save for the white plumes of its waves, was ink beyond the brown of its shallows, the wide stretch of monotonous level land, the rising hill, with the old city gate close before is—all was suddenly revealed in one vivid panorama and faded again into mystery. The thunder followed close upon the lightning—a deafening crash overhead.

"By Jove!" said Harrod. "That's close. I hope you're not frightened of a storm."

"Frightened!" repeated I, scornfully.

"Some girls are," said he, half apologetically, looking at me with admiration.

"Not I, though," I laughed.

But as I spoke my heart stood still. We had climbed the hill and had reached a spot where the trees overshadowed the road, nearly meeting overhead; a fiery fork crossed the white path in front of us, there was a kind of crackle in the wood, and a blue flame seemed to dart out of the branch of an elm close at hand.

"Great God!" ejaculated Trayton Harrod under his breath, and he flung his arm around me and dragged me to the other side of the path.

I had said an instant before that I was not frightened, and I had spoken the truth; but if I had said now that I was not frightened it would have been because the sweet sense of protecting strength, which this danger had called forth, had brought with it a happiness stronger than fear.

"Can you run?" said he. "We must get away from these trees."

I could not speak, something was in my throat, but I obeyed him. We ran till we reached the abbey, where it stood in the great open space of its own graveyard, and there we drew aside under the shadow of the eastern buttress, protected a little by the projecting arch.

"You're wet through," said he, laying his hand upon my arm.

I laughed again, not in the sort of exultant way I had laughed when he had asked me if I was afraid of lightning, but in a low, foolish kind of fashion.

"It won't hurt me," murmured I. "Nothing hurts me. I'm so strong."

"Oh yes, you're the right sort, I know," said he; "but all the same, you ought to have stayed at 'The Elms' till it was over. If I had been there I should have made you stay."

How angry those words would have made me a week ago! But now they thrilled me with delight, and with that same tender fear and longing of fresh experience that had haunted me ever since the night upon the garden cliff. Could he really have "made" me do anything?

"I shouldn't have stopped," I said; "no, not for any one. I'm not afraid of a storm." But I think there was very little of my old defiance in the tone. He laughed gently, and I added, "I don't see any use in waiting here."

I advanced forward into the open, but as I did so a fresh flash rent the clouds and illumined the ground all about us, revealing darkest corners in its searching light. He took me by the hand and drew me once more into the shadow—not only into the shadow of the buttress this time, but of the ruined roof of a transept, where only the lightning could have discovered us.

"Not yet," he said, gently; and although there was no need for it, he still held my hand in his.

My foolish heart began to beat wildly. What did it mean? Was that coming to pass about which I had wondered sometimes of late? I wanted to get away, and yet I could not have moved for worlds. I waited with my heart beating against my side.

But he did not speak, he only held my hand in his firmly, and I felt as though his eyes were upon me in the dark. I may have been wrong, but I felt as though his eyes were upon me.

All at once in the ivied wall above our heads an owl shrieked. We started asunder, and I felt almost as though I must have been doing something wrong, so hard did my heart thump against my side.

"Fancy that poor old barn-owl being able to frighten two sensible people," laughed Trayton Harrod. "But upon my word I never heard him make such a noise before."

I made no reply. I came out once more into the path, and, turning, held out my hand.

"The storm is over," I said. "Good-night."

"Oh, I must see you home," said he. "It's getting quite dark."

He walked forward with me, but the spell was broken, only my heart still beat against my side.

"You'll come in to supper?" said I, when we reached the gate. I felt myself speaking as one in a dream. The only thing that I was conscious of was a strange and foolish longing that he should not go away from me.

He did not answer for a moment, but then he said: "I'm afraid I mustn't. I'm drenched through; I shouldn't be presentable."

I had forgotten it; we were, in truth, neither of us presentable.

"Well, you must come to-morrow," said I, in as matter-of-fact a tone as I could muster. "Mother expects you, and my sister is home now."

He stepped forward in front of me and opened the front door, which always stood on the latch. The brightness from within dazzled me for a moment as he stood aside to let me pass, and there in the brightness stood Joyce.

How well I remember it! She had on a soft white muslin dress, that fell in straight, soft folds to her feet, and made her look very tall and slender, very fair and white. The light from the lamp fell down on her shining golden hair; her blue eyes were just raised under the dark lashes, gentle and serene. Suddenly, for the first time in my life, there flashed upon me a sense of the contrast between myself and her.

I stood there an instant in my dripping old brown frock looking at her. Then I turned round to introduce Mr. Harrod. But the house door had closed behind me again. He was gone.

CHAPTER XXV

Trayton Harrod did come to supper the next day.

I remember that mother upbraided him for having been so many days absent, and that he made some kind of an excuse for himself; and I remember that I blushed as he made it, and felt quite awkward when he shook hands with me and asked if I had taken any cold of the night before. But I was happy—very, very happy. I was happy even in fancying that I saw a certain self-consciousness in him also, in the persistence with which he talked to mother, and in something that crossed his face when our eyes met, which was almost as often as his were not fixed on Joyce, where she sat in her old place by the window.

Every one always was struck with Joyce at first, and I had been so anxious that Harrod should duly admire her that I had purposely refrained from saying much to raise his expectations, so that no doubt his surprise was as great as his admiration; and I had never seen my sister look handsomer than she did that night.

There was a little increased air of dignity about her since she had been to London, and had been thrown a little more on her own resources, which sat with a pretty style upon her serene and modest loveliness. She looked people in the face as she never used to do, raising her eyes without lifting that little head of hers that was always just slightly bent, like some regal lily or drooping tulip. She talked a little more, and she blushed seldomer.

She did not talk much to Mr. Harrod, but then he was very busy explaining his scheme of water-supply to Mr. Hoad, who had dropped in to supper. But she talked quite brightly to Squire Broderick when he came, as he had promised, to bid her welcome home, and shone in her very best light, just as I had wished she should shine—the beautiful hostess of our home.

It was a happy evening, typical of our happy home-life, that, flecked as it may have been by little troubles, as the summer sky is flecked with clouds, was yet fair and warm as the bright July days that followed one another so radiantly.

Ah me, how little I guessed that night that there were not many more such happy family parties in store for us when we should sit around that board united, and without a gap in the family circle! It is good that we cannot see into the future. No gathering cloud disquieted me that night; no fears for myself nor for any of those whom I loved; I was absorbed in that one throbbing, all-engrossing dream which was slowly beginning to fill my life.

Absorbed, yet not quite so much absorbed but that I could feel sorry for my sister's sake that one who had been there was now absent: where Frank Forrester had been Trayton Harrod now was. I could not honestly say to myself that I wished it differently, but I was sorry for Joyce. She, however, did not seem to be depressed, she was very bright; the gladness she had in being at home again gave her beauty just that touch of sparkle which it sometimes lacked.

It was a warm evening, and when supper was over we drew our chairs around the low porch that led onto the lawn, and took our ease in the half-light. It was very rarely that we sat thus idle, but sometimes, of summer evenings, mother was fond of a bit of leisure herself, and she never made us work when she was idle. The scent of the sweet-peas and the roses came heavy upon the air; the dusk was still luminous with lingering daylight, or with heralding a moon that had not yet risen.

"I hear you have got Southdowns into your flock, Harrod," said the squire. "I hope you won't have any difficulty with them. I feel confident they ought to do, but when I tried the experiment it certainly failed."

"Perhaps they weren't carefully looked after," answered Harrod. "Of course you have got to acclimatize animals just as well as people, and the more carefully the more delicate they are."

"Ah, I dare say it may be a matter of management," agreed the squire. "I hadn't a very good shepherd at the time."

"I don't leave it to a shepherd," said Harrod. "Shepherds are clever enough, and there are plenty of things I learn from them and think no shame of it; but they know only what experience has taught them, and these shepherds have no experience of Southdowns. Besides, they are a prejudiced lot, and they set their faces against new ventures."

The squire laughed, a laugh in which Mr. Hoad—subdued as he always was by Mr. Broderick's presence—ventured to join.

"Yes, you're right there," he said. "You get it hot and strong, I dare say, all round. They snigger at you pretty well in the village for this water scheme of yours, I can tell you, Mr. Bailiff."

My cheek flamed, and Mr. Hoad went down one step lower still in my estimation.

"I dare say," said Harrod, shortly, and he said it in a tone of voice as much as to say, "and I don't care."

"But it's a very clever thing, isn't it?" asked dear old mother, in her gentle voice. "I never could have believed such a thing was possible."

I could have said that Reuben declared it was not possible, but I would not have told on Reuben for worlds.

"It's not a new discovery," answered the squire, who had taken no notice of the solicitor, and took mother's question to himself, "but it's a very useful one."

"I wonder you haven't thought of using it before for the Manor," put in father. "You must need a deal of water there."

I felt a glow of satisfaction at seeing father stand up for Harrod; for, as far as I knew anything of their discussions, I had fancied he was not very keen upon the scheme.

"I had thought of it," answered Mr. Broderick; "but I didn't think I could afford it. I didn't think it would pay for one individual."

I fancied father was vexed at this. He began tapping his foot in the old irritable way, which I had not noticed in him of late; for, as I had remarked to Joyce on her return, I thought he was far less peppery than he used to be, and I fancied it was a good sign for his health.

"Neither do we think it will pay for one individual," said he. "We intend to make many individuals pay for it."

He said "we" and I was pleased.

"Well, of course I shall have the water laid on to the Manor, and am grateful to the man who started the thing," said the squire, in a conciliatory tone; "but I'm a little doubtful as to your making a good job of it all round. Marshlands folk are very obstinate and old-fashioned."

"Oh, they'll come to see which side their bread's buttered on in the long-run," declared Harrod, confidently.

But Mr. Hoad smiled a sardonic smile, and the squire added: "I'm afraid it will cost you a good bit of money meanwhile, Maliphant. However, as I sincerely hope you are going to make your fortune over these new hop-fields, it won't signify." It was, to say the least of it, an indiscreet speech, not to say an unallowable one; for I believe there is nothing a man dislikes so much as having his affairs talked of in public. It was not at all like the squire, and I could not help thinking, even at the time, that Harrod must have in some way nettled Mr. Broderick, although I was very far from guessing at the cause of the annoyance.

Father rose and walked slowly down to the edge of the cliff. I could not tell whether he did it to keep his temper or to conceal his trouble, for I fancied he looked troubled as he passed me.

"The hops are a splendid crop now," said Harrod, without moving, as he lighted a fresh pipe. He never allowed himself to show if he were vexed.

But the squire did not reply. He rose and followed father. I'm sure he was sorry for what he had said. It was the solicitor who answered.

"It ought to be a fine crop," he said. "Maliphant paid a long price for it."

"How do you know what price he paid for it?" asked Harrod, sharply.

I fancied Mr. Hoad looked disconcerted for a moment, but he soon recovered himself.

"Well, to tell the truth, he did me the honor to ask my advice," he replied, with a sort of smile that I longed to shake him for. "No offence to you, Mr. Harrod, I hope," he added, blandly. "I know Maliphant holds your opinion in the highest reverence; but—well, I'm an old friend."

My blood boiled in the most absurd way; but Harrod was far too wise to be annoyed, or at any rate to show it. He only remained perfectly silent, smoking his pipe.

Father and the squire came up the lawn again; I wondered what they had said to each other. The evening was fresh and fragrant after the rain of the night before upon the hot earth; the dusky plain lay calm beneath us; the moon had just risen and lit the sea faintly in the distance; nature was quiet and sweet, but I felt somehow as though the pleasure of our evening was a little spoiled. Mother tried to pick up the talk again, but she was not altogether lucky in her choice of subjects.

"Why, squire, the girls tell me the right-of-way is closed across that bit of common by Dead Man's Lane," said she. "Do you know whose doing it is?"

Father turned round sharply.

"It never was of much use," said Mr. Hoad, answering instead. "The way by the lane is nearly as short, and much cooler."

"It depends where people are going whether it is as short," said father. "It's a flagrant piece of injustice. Do you know who's to blame for it?"

Mr. Hoad looked uneasy, and did not reply; and the squire burst into a loud laugh.

"Why, the Radical candidate, to be sure," said he, with a pardonable sneer in his hearty voice. "Those are the men for that kind of job."

"Mr. Thorne!" exclaimed mother. "No, never!"

"Ay," said father under his breath; "a man who can rob his fellow-creatures in big things won't think much of robbing them in little things!"

"You shouldn't run down your own party, Maliphant," laughed the squire. "Thorne is no particular friend of mine, but robbery is too big a word."

"I understand he's a very charitable man," said mother, who always would have fair play.

"Yes," echoed Joyce. "You don't know, father, what a deal of good Mary Thorne does among the poor."

Father rose; he was trembling. I saw a fire leap in his eye.

"It's easy to give back with your left hand half of what you robbed with your right," said he, in a low voice, that yet resounded like the murmur of distant thunder; "but it isn't what those who are struggling for freedom will care to see in their representative."

"Oh, I don't believe in a Radical party—here anyhow," said the squire, abruptly; "not even if you began to back the candidate, Maliphant."

"I shall not back the candidate," said father, grimly.

"No," laughed the squire. "He has done for himself with you over this right-of-way."

"When I see a man who declares he is going into Parliament on the people's side deliberately try to rob the people of their lawful possessions, I feel more than ever that the name of Radical is but a snare," said father.

His face had grown purple with emotion; his voice quivered with it; his hand shook.

I saw mother look at him anxiously, and I saw a sullen expression settle down upon Mr. Hoad's detested face.

"Now, Laban, don't go getting yourself into a heat," said mother, in her quiet, sensible voice. "You know how bad it is for your health, and it's unpleasant for all parties besides."

"I can't make head or tail of the Radicals myself," began the squire, who, it must be remembered, spoke ten years ago. But mother interrupted him.

"Come, come, squire," said she, in the pretty familiar way in which she always addressed him, "we'll have no more politics. The girls and me don't understand such talk, and it isn't civil to be leaving us o' one side all the evening."

He laughed, and asked what we wanted to talk about, and at the same time Mr. Hoad came forward to take his leave.

He smiled, shaking hands with mother, but his smile was a sour one, and I noticed that he scarcely touched father's hand.

"I suppose Hoad is in a bad temper because you won't take up Thorne's cause," said the squire, as soon as the solicitor had passed up the passage.

Father gave a grunt of acquiescence, and the squire turned to us with most marked and laudable intent to obey mother and change the talk.

"Have you heard the news?" he asked. "Young Squire Ingram is to be married to Miss Upjohn. I heard it yesterday riding round that way."

Mother looked up eagerly. The subject was one quite to her own mind, but the news was startling.

"Never to Nance Upjohn of Bredemere Farm?" asked she.

"The very same, Mrs. Maliphant," replied the squire. "Folk say they are to be married at Michaelmas."

"Heart alive!" ejaculated mother, lapsing into the vernacular in her excitement. "Isn't old squire in a fine way?"

"I believe he doesn't like it," agreed Mr. Broderick, evasively.

"Why not, pray?" asked father, rousing from his reverie.

I always noticed that once he had been brought to arms upon the real interest of his life, he was the more ready to take fire upon secondary subjects, even remotely connected with it. No one answered him, and he repeated his question.

"Why not, pray? The Upjohns come of as good a stock as we do, though they haven't been so long upon the soil."

"To be sure," put in mother, quickly. "And I've been told she's as well schooled as any town miss. I don't mean to say she isn't good enough for the young squire, only I've heard say the old gentleman is so terribly particular."

"Yes, indeed, she's as well-behaved and pretty a young woman as you could find anywhere," declared Mr. Broderick, warmly. "Old Ingram can have no objection on anything but the score of connection."

"Connection! What's that?" exclaimed father. "If the girl comes of a different stock to the lad, why must it needs be of a worse one? Faith, if I were neighbor Upjohn, 'tis I would have the objection."

"Nonsense, Laban," said mother, half annoyed.

"No; I wouldn't let any girl of mine wed where it was made a favor to receive her," continued father, hotly.

"There are plenty among the gentry too that would make it no favor at all to receive a nice young woman just because she came of another class," added mother, with a vexed manner. "There's good honest folk all the world over, and bad ones too."

"Right you are, old woman," answered father, after a moment's hesitation, with generous repentance. "There's some among them that I'm proud to shake by the hand. But all the same, a prejudice is a prejudice, and a class is a class."

"You'd best come in-doors," said mother, still annoyed. "It's getting chill, and you've been out too long already, I believe."

He rose with the habit of obedience, and we all stood up, but he tottered as he walked. I saw Harrod, who was beside him, stretch out his arm.

He did not take it, he walked in bravely, the others following—all but myself and the squire. I saw he was troubled—I saw he wanted to speak to me, and I did not like to move.

"Your father is so emphatic, so very emphatic," he murmured; "but I hope, Miss Margaret, that you do not misunderstand me."

I looked at him a little surprised. I could not see how it could signify to him whether I misunderstood him or not. If it had been Joyce it would have been different.

"Oh no, I don't misunderstand you," said I, a little hurriedly, for I wanted to get in-doors. "It was quite clear."

I was vexed with the squire. I was angry with him for having seemed to make light of Harrod's knowledge and of Harrod's schemes.

I thought it was not fair of him before father—and when he had always bidden me fight the bailiff's battles for the good of the farm. So I answered, a little proudly, "You can't grumble if father and I have our pride of class as well as you yours."

"No, I don't grumble," said he, with a smile, and yet I fancied with something half like a sigh too. "Only I, personally, have very little pride of class."

"I'm glad to hear it," said I, and I ran in-doors.

I wanted to say good-night to Trayton Harrod. But in the parlor there was nobody but my sister, leaning up against the open casement and looking out into the fragrant summer night.

"What are you doing?" I asked, abruptly. "Where are they all?" And as I spoke I heard a step die away on the gravel outside.

"I have just let Mr. Harrod out," answered she, "and I came to close up the windows. I think mother has gone up-stairs with father. I don't believe he is well."

I did not answer. It was Joyce's place again, now that she was home, to close the front door after the guests. But it was the first time that Harrod had left the Grange without bidding me good-night. When Joyce asked me where the squire was I did not care. It was she who hastened out to meet him and made mother's apologies; it was she who let him out as she had let out the bailiff.

It needed a sudden scare about my dear father to bring me back to myself. He had had a bad fainting fit—the worst we had ever seen him in. It was the bell ringing up-stairs, and mother's frightened voice calling, that waked me from a dream. And the evening ended badly, as I had had a silly presentiment that it would end.

CHAPTER XXVI

The next morning the sun shone, and the world was as gay as ever. Father declared himself well and hearty; complained of no pain and betrayed no weakness, was merry at the breakfast-table over a letter of Frank Forrester's, and withdrew with it as usual to his study, where he spent more and more time opposite the portrait of Camille Lambert, and left farm matters more and more to his bailiff.

For me the sun shone the more brightly because of a short, delightful ten minutes with Trayton Harrod, in which we said nothing in particular, but that chased away the tiny shadow of disappointment that had crossed the horizon of my sweet, dawning experience, and banished it—disgraced and ashamed—into oblivion.

It was a very short ten minutes. Miss Farnham and the vicar's wife had been to call, and the Hoad girls had come to ask us to go to a ball at the town-hall. "Oh, do come," they had said, "and bring the bailiff;" and my dignity had flamed into my cheek, and I had been grateful to mother for promptly refusing for us, and even to old Miss Farnham for declaring that we were more sensible than most girls, and weren't always on the watch for new occasions to pinch in our waists. Miss Farnham, I recollect, had declared afterwards that it was only a dodge to catch father.

It was after the guests had left, and while we were waiting for mother to get her bonnet on for a drive, that Harrod and I got those short ten minutes to ourselves.

Joyce had gone to Guestling to lunch with some friends, and mother had proposed to Harrod to drive us over to fetch her, so that at the same time she might look at a cow which he had found for her there for sale.

We set forth, Harrod driving mother in the cart with the steady old black horse, and I riding Marigold alongside.

I saw as soon as we set out that he was just a little shade out of spirits. It troubled me at first, but I soon guessed, or thought I guessed, what it was about.

"Wasn't that Mr. Hoad I saw up atop of the hill with you and Laban?" asked mother, just after we had set out.

Harrod nodded.

"What does the man want meddling with farming?" asked mother. "I shouldn't have thought he was a wiseacre on such-like."

Harrod shrugged his shoulders; he evidently didn't intend to commit himself.

"Mr. Hoad wouldn't wait to hear if other folk thought him a wiseacre before he'd think he had a right to interfere," laughed I. "Those smart daughters of his came inviting Joyce and me to a ball just now."

"You're not going?" asked Harrod, quickly.

"No, no," answered mother. "I don't hold with that kind of amusement for young folk. There's too many strangers."

"Why don't you want us to go?" asked I, softly.

He didn't reply; he whipped up the horse a little instead.

"Miss Farnham declared our going would have been made use of to try and draw father into the election against his will," said I. "But she's always got some queer notion in her head."

"Well, upon my word, I don't believe there's much these electioneering chaps would stick at," declared Harrod, contemptuously. "I declare I believe they'd step into a man's house and get his own chairs and tables to go against him if they could."

Mother laughed, but Harrod did not laugh.

"And if they can't have their way, there's nothing they wouldn't do to spite a fellow," added he.

"Why, what has Mr. Hoad been doing to spite you?" asked mother.

"Nothing, ma'am, nothing at all," declared the bailiff. "There's nothing he could do to spite me, for I don't set enough store by him; and I should doubt if there's any would be led far by the words of a man that shows himself such a time-server."

He spoke so bitterly that I looked at him in sheer astonishment.

"I thought Mr. Hoad seemed to have taken quite a fancy to you last night," said mother.

Harrod laughed harshly.

"Yes," he said; and then he added, abruptly, "There's some folk's seemings that aren't to be trusted. They depend upon what they can get."

"Good gracious!" said mother. "Whatever could Mr. Hoad want to get of you?"

"Excuse me, ma'am, I don't know that he wanted to get anything," declared Harrod, evidently feeling that he had gone too far. "I know no ill of the man. I don't like him—that's all."

Mother was silent, but I said, boldly, "No more do I."

And there talk on the subject ended. It was not until many a long day afterwards that I knew that Hoad—moved, I suppose, by Harrod's argument against father on the previous evening—had tried to persuade him to help in some sort against his employer in the coming political struggle. He little knew the man with whom he had to deal, and that no depreciatory remarks which spite might induce him to make to father upon his farming capacities would have any influence upon father's bailiff. Only I was glad I had agreed with him in not liking Mr. Hoad. It got me a reproving look from mother, but it got me a little smile from him, which in the state of my feelings added one little grain more to the growing sum of my unconfessed happiness.

It was a long way to Guestling. Away past "The Elms" and its hop-gardens, and many other hop-gardens again, where the bines were growing tall and rich with their pale green clusters; away between blackberry and bryony hedges that the stately foxglove adorned, between banks white with hemlock; away onto the breast of the breezy downs, where the hills were blue for a border, and solitary clumps of pines grew unexpectedly by the road-side.

The west became a sea of flame beyond the vastness of that swelling bosom, just as it had been almost every evening through that glorious summer, and set a line of blood-red upon the horizon for miles around, firing clots of cloud that floated upon lakes of tender green, and hemming other masses with rims of gold that were as the edges of burning linings to their softness.

Mother was almost afraid of it. She declared that she had never seen a sunset that swallowed up half the heavens like that, and she wondered what it boded; for even after we had turned and left the west behind us the clouds that sailed the blue were red with it still.

When we got near to Guestling we were overtaken by Squire Broderick on his roan cob. I think he had intended to ride farther but he seemed so delighted to find mother out-of-doors that he could not detach himself from our party.

"Why, Mrs. Maliphant," I remember his saying with that half-respectful, half-affectionate air of familiarity that he always used to our mother, "if you knew how becoming that white bonnet is you would put it on oftener. It's quite a treat to see you out driving."

Mother declared that only business had brought her out now; and I remember how the squire told her she would never find a new friend to take the place of an old one, not if Harrod were to find her a cow with twice the good points of poor old Betsey. And while Mr. Broderick was paying sweet compliments to mother, Harrod and I exchanged a few more of those commonplace words, the memory of which made me merry, even when presently I was obliged to drop behind and ride alongside of the squire.

I had something to say to him, and as it related to the bailiff, I was not unwilling to drop behind. The night before he had made light of those schemes and improvements on the farm of which I was beginning to be so proud, and I had not thought it fair of him to try and set his own protégé in a poor light before father. I meant to tell him so, and this was the opportunity.

"Mr. Broderick," said I, driving boldly into my subject, "why did you talk last night as if things were going badly on the farm? You told me a while ago that all the farm wanted was a younger head and heart upon it—somebody more ambitious to work for it. Yet now one would almost fancy you mistrusted the very man you recommended, and wanted to make father mistrust him."

I saw the squire start and look at me—look at me in a sharp, inquiring sort of way.

"I did not intend to give that impression," he said.

"Well, then, you did," said I, wisely shaking my head. "Any one could have seen it. You were quite cool about the water scheme. Why, father took his part against you."

"I think you exaggerate, Miss Margaret," murmured he.

"Oh no, I don't," I insisted. "And if I am rude, I beg your pardon; but I think it a pity you should undo all the work I have been doing. Besides," added I, in a lower voice, "it's not fair. You said you were 'afraid' he was spending too much money, and you 'hoped' he would make a fortune over the hops. It didn't sound as if you believed it would be so."

"Well, so I do hope a fortune will be made," smiled he.

"Ah, but you said it as if it might have been quite the contrary," insisted I.

"Did I?" repeated he, humbly.

"Yes," declared I. "If you don't think Mr. Harrod manages well, you should tell him so; you are his friend."

The squire was silent, moodily silent.

"Ah, who can tell what is good management in hops?" sighed he at last. "The most gambling thing that a man can touch. All chance. Twelve hours' storm, a few scalding hot days, and a few night-mists at the wrong moment, may ruin the most brilliant hopes of weeks. I have seen fortunes lost over hops. A field that will bring forth hundreds one year will scarcely pay for the picking the next. No man ought to touch hops who has not plenty of money at his back."

"Do you think father knows that hops are such a tremendous risk?" I asked.

"Oh, of course he must know it," answered the squire.

And there he stopped short. I did not choose to ask any more. It seemed like mistrusting father to ask questions about his affairs. But I wondered whether he was a man who had "plenty of money at his back."

"I think Harrod is a safe fellow, and a clever fellow," added the squire. "A cool-headed, hard-headed sort of chap, who ought not to be over-sanguine though he is young."

The words were not enthusiastic, they were said rather as a duty—they offended me.

"Oh, I am sure you would not have recommended him to father unless you had had a high opinion of him," said I, haughtily. "And I am glad to say that father has a high opinion of him himself, and always follows his advice. I do not suppose that anything that any one said would prejudice father against Mr. Harrod now. In fact we all have the highest opinion of him."

With that I touched Marigold with the whip and sent her capering forward to the cart. Mother started, and reproved me sharply; but at that moment we drew up at the farm gates, and she turned round to beg the squire would spare her a few minutes to give his opinion also upon the contemplated purchase. Harrod looked round, and I was angry, for she had no right to have done it. I do not know how the squire could have consented, but he did so, though half unwillingly, and demurring to Harrod's first right.

"The squire is such a very old friend of ours," I murmured, half apologetically, to the bailiff on the first opportunity. "Mother has so often asked his advice."

"Yes, yes, I quite understand," replied he. And then he added—I almost wondered why—"I suppose you remember him ever since you were a child?"

"Oh yes," laughed I; "he used to play with us when we were little girls and he was a young man."

"A young man!" smiled Harrod. "What is he now?"

"I should think he must be nearly thirty-five," said I, gravely. "And you know he's a widower."

"Indeed! Well, he's not too old to marry again," smiled Trayton Harrod, looking at me.

"That's what mother says," answered I. And then I added—and Heaven knows what induced me to do it, for I had no right to speak of it—"Some folk think he's sweet on my sister."

It was unlike me to babble of family secrets. I glanced at my companion. There was a little scowl upon his brow; it was usually there when he was thinking, and he was ruffled still with vexation at mother's unusual want of tact. He looked after her where she was talking with the squire.

"Oh, is it to be a match?" he asked, carelessly.

"Oh, dear no," laughed I. "Joyce—"

I was going to say, "Joyce cares for some one else," but luckily I remembered that solemn promise to mother just in time.

"Joyce doesn't even think he likes her," I added instead.

He turned to me and broke into a little laugh. I thought it almost rude of him, and wondered whether he, too, thought that a farmer's daughter was not worthy of marriage with a squire.

But he was looking at me—he was looking at me with a strange look in his eyes. Yes, there was no mistaking it—it was a look of admiration, a look of almost tender admiration, and as I felt it upon me a blush rose to my cheek that so rarely blushed, and the power of thinking went from me; I only felt his presence.

I don't know how long we stood thus; I suppose it was only seconds before he said, "I believe you would put that sister of yours before you in everything, Miss Margaret."

I made an effort to understand him, for I think I was in a dream.

"Yes, she's so beautiful!" I murmured.

"Beautiful!" echoed he.

There was something in the tone of his voice that made me lift my eyes to his face. His gaze was fixed on the gate of the farm-yard. I followed his gaze. Joyce had entered and was coming towards us. This was where we had arranged to meet.

She shook hands with Harrod and then with the squire, who joined us with mother. We all went together into the cow-shed.

I don't remember what remarks were made upon Betsey's proposed successor; I don't even remember if we bought her or not. I don't think I was in the mood to attend much to the matter. I was roused from a brown-study by a curious remark of Trayton Harrod's.

Mother had found occasion to ask him whether the woman whom she had provided for him at "The Elms" made him comfortable, and was pleasant-spoken. It had been on her mind, I know, ever since he had been there.

"She does her work," answered the bailiff. "I don't know if she's pleasant-spoken. I never speak to her."

"That's not the way to get the best out of a woman," laughed the squire. "We poor bachelors need something more than bare duty out of our servants." He said it merrily, and yet I did not think he was merry.

"I want no more than duty," repeated Harrod. "Talking, unless you have something to say, is waste of time."

"You'll have to mend your manners, my lad, if ever you hope to persuade any young lady to become your wife," laughed the squire again.

"I never should hope to do any such thing," answered Harrod. "I shouldn't be such a fool." And with that he walked away out of the farm-yard and began untying the cart for the homeward journey.

Mother looked after him, puzzled for a moment. Then, nodding her head at the squire, she said, softly: "Ah, that's what all you young men say till you've fixed on the girl you want. You're none so backward then."

I fancied the squire looked a little uncomfortable, but he said, lightly: "Do you think not, Mrs. Maliphant? Well, nothing venture, nothing have, they say. Harrod has had his fingers burned, I suppose. A bit sore on the subject, but he'll get over it. He's a nice lad; though, to take his word for it, his wife wouldn't have a very cheerful life of it!"

"Well, we needn't take his word for it," said mother. "And, good gracious me! it's fools indeed that would want to wed upon nothing but sugar. There'd be no grit in love at all if we hadn't some duties towards one another that weren't all pleasant. 'Tis in the doing of them that love grows stronger. I've always thought you can't smell the best of roses till you get near enough to feel the thorns."

This speech of mother's comes back to me vividly now, but at the time I was scarcely conscious of it.

Trayton Harrod's words—"I shouldn't be such a fool"—were ringing in my ears. What did he mean by them? I looked round after him and saw that my sister had strolled across to where he was waiting by the cart. It was natural enough—it was time to be getting homeward. But as I looked I saw him bend towards her just a little and say something. The expression of his face had softened again, and the scowl on his sunburnt brow had faded, but his lips were pressed together so that they were quite thin instead of full, as they appeared in their normal shape; and I wondered why he looked so, and why what he said made the blush, that was now so much rarer than it used to be, creep up Joyce's cheek till it overspread her fair brow and tipped her delicate little ears with red.

An uncontrollable, unreasonable fit of anger took possession of me. I flew across the yard to that corner where Marigold was tied beside the dog-cart.

"I suppose you read a great deal of evenings?" Joyce was saying.

And Harrod answered, shortly, "No, I don't so much as I used to do. I am too much taken up with other things."

Simple words enough, but they set my heart aflame, yet left me sick and sore.

I undid the mare with a rough hand, and, before she had time to see what I was about, I set my foot in the stirrup and sprang into the saddle. She was used to my doing that, but she was not used to my doing it in that way.

She reared and kicked. My thoughts were elsewhere, and it served me right that, for the first time in my life, she threw me.

I heard a scream from mother, and the next moment I felt that a man's arm had helped me up from the ground.

I was not hurt, only a little stunned, and when I saw that it was Trayton Harrod who had picked me up, I broke away from him and staggered forward to mother.

"I'm not hurt, mother, not a bit," said I, and then I burst into tears. Oh, how ashamed I was! I who prided myself on self-control.

But she put her arm round me and laid my head on her shoulder, and her rare tenderness soothed me as nothing else in the world could have done. I kept my face hid on her neck, as I had done when I was a little child, and used to be quite confident that she could cure every wound.

Yet it was only for a moment.

"I had better ride, and lead the mare," I heard the squire say in a low, concerned voice. "She won't be fit to mount again, or even to drive the cart."

I lifted my head.

"Oh, indeed, Squire Broderick, I'm not in the least hurt," said I, as cheerfully as I could, for I was grateful for those kindly tones. "I can ride Marigold home perfectly well."

"No, my dear, that you won't," said mother, all her decision returning now that her alarm was over. "I've had quite enough of this fright for one day."

Joyce returned from the farm with a glass of water, and Harrod by her side with some brandy that he had begged at the doctor's house hard by. I drank the water but I refused the brandy, and scoffed at the notion of the doctor coming out in person. Then I got into the cart. I insisted on driving, and as the horse was the quiet old black Dobbin, mother consented. Joyce sat behind, and Harrod rode after upon Marigold.

The squire showed signs of joining our caravan at first; but as I turned round and assured him once more that I was perfectly well, and begged him to continue his road, he was almost obliged to turn his horse back again in the direction in which he had been going when he overtook us. But he still looked so very much concerned that I was forced to laugh at him. I think it was the only time I laughed that day.

The drive home was soothing enough across those miles of serene pasture-land whose marge the sea was always kissing, and where the sheep cropped, in sleepy passiveness, beneath faint rosy clouds that lay motionless upon the soft blue; the vast dreamy pastures, browning with autumn tints of many planes of autumn grasses that changed as they swayed in the lazy breeze, were hemmed by a winding strip of beach, pink or blue, according as the sun was behind or above one, and to-night bordered beyond it by a stretch of golden sand, over which rows upon rows of little waves rippled with the incoming tide. We drove along the margin of the beach; the yellow sea-poppies bloomed amid their pale, blue-green leaves upon every mound of shingle, and not even the distant church-spires and masts of ships, that told of man's presence, could disturb the breathless placidity that no memory of storm or strife seemed to awaken into a throb of life.

Margaret Maliphant | 227

But suddenly upon the vast line of wide horizon, where the sea melted into the sky with a little hovering streak of haze, a throb of light stirred; at first it was but a spot of gold upon the bosom of the distance, but it was a spot that grew larger, though with a soft and rayless radiance unlike the dazzle of the sun-setting; then out of the breast of it was made a red ball that sent a path of gilded crimson down the sea, and tipped the crest of every little wave that crept towards us with a crown of opalescent light; it was the sun's last kiss welcoming the moon as she rose out of the sea.

It was a rare and a beautiful sight, and to me, who loved the world in which I lived so well, it should have brought joyousness. And yet it did not please me. I would rather have had it chill and stormy, with a thick fog creeping up out of the sea—a fog such as that through which Trayton Harrod's tall figure had loomed the first time that I had met him, just on this very tract of land.

CHAPTER XXVII

On the day following I met Frank Forrester in the lane by the vicarage.

I verily believe I had forgotten all about him during the past few days, but that very morning I had remembered that he was most likely at the Priory for that garden-party to which father had so annoyingly forbidden us to go; and I vowed in my heart that, by hook or by crook, my sister should see him before he left the neighborhood. It was a regular piece of good-luck my meeting him thus; but I thought, when he first saw me, that he was going to avoid me. He seemed, however, to think better of it, and came striding towards me, swaying his tall, lithe body, and welcoming me even from a distance with the pleasant smile, without which one would scarcely have known his handsome face. I was glad he had thought better of it, for I should certainly not have allowed him to pass me.

"Holloa, Miss Margaret," said he, when we were within ear-shot; "this is delightful. I was afraid I shouldn't get a chance of seeing any of you, as I am forbidden the house. How are you?"

"I am very well," said I, looking at him.

I fancied he had grown smarter in his appearance than he used to be; there was nothing that I could take hold of, and yet somehow he seemed to me to be changed.

"Why weren't you at the garden-party yesterday?" asked he. "It was quite gay."

"Yesterday! Was it yesterday?" said I, half disappointed. "We weren't allowed to go, you know. We wanted to go very much."

He looked at me in that open-eyed way of his for a moment, and then he shifted his glance away from my face and laughed a little uneasily.

"Was I the cause?" he asked.

"Oh, dear no," cried I, eagerly, although in my heart I knew well enough that, with mother, he had been. "But you know father never did like the Thornes. They belong to that class that he dislikes so. What do you call it—capitalists? Why, he hates them ever so much worse than landed proprietors, and they are bad enough."

I said this jokingly, feeling that, as of course Frank sympathized with all these views and convictions of father's, he would understand, even though he might not himself feel just as strongly towards those members of the obnoxious class who had been his friends from his youth upward. But a shadow of annoyance or uneasiness—I did not know which—passed over his face like a little summer cloud, although the full, changeful mouth still kept its smile.

"And Mr. Thorne has done something special to vex him," I continued. "He has closed the right-of-way over the common by Dead Man's Lane. So now father has forbidden us to go to the house."

The slightest possible touch of scorn curled Frank's lip under the silky brown mustache.

"That's a pity," said he.

"Well," said I, "you would feel just the same, of course, if these people didn't happen to be old friends of yours, and they never were friends of father's. He disliked them buying the property from the very first."

"It makes things rather uncomfortable to drive a theory as far as that," laughed Frank.

Of course it was what I often felt myself, but somehow it vexed me to hear him say so; if he was the friend to father that he seemed to be, he had no business to say it, and specially to me.

"Well, anyhow, it's the reason we didn't go to the garden-party," said I, shortly. And then I repeated again, and in a pleasanter tone, "But we wanted to go very much, of course."

"Ah yes," answered he, glancing at me and then away again, and referring, I suppose, to the pronoun I had used, "your sister is home again now. Of course I heard it in the village. What a pity you couldn't come! We had a dance afterwards—altogether a delightful evening, and you would have enjoyed it immensely. Besides," he began, and then stopped, and then ended abruptly, "every one missed you."

I laughed. "That means to say every one missed Joyce," I said. "I am not so silly as to think people mean me when they mean Joyce—some people, of course, more particularly than others."

It was rather a foolish remark, and he took no notice of it.

"Your sister is well, I hope," was all he said.

"Oh yes, she's well," I answered.

And then there was an awkward pause. I wondered why in the world he did not ask any of the innumerable questions that must be in his mind about her, and yet I felt that it was natural he should be awkward, natural that he should not want to talk to me about her.

I did not know exactly what to say, and yet I would not let this golden opportunity slip.

"You must come and see for yourself," said I, boldly, without in the least considering what this course of action laid me open to from mother. "She's prettier and sweeter than ever, Joyce is, since she's been to London."

He turned quickly, and looked at me with his wildest gaze.

"Come and see her! Why, Miss Margaret, you know that's impossible!" ejaculated he.

"You came to see us the last time you were in Marshlands," said I. "You don't come to see Joyce, you come to see father. Father would be dreadfully hurt to think you were in Marshlands and didn't see him. He doesn't know you are here." This was true, but whether father would have wished me to run so against mother's wishes, I did not stop to think.

"Your sister was not at home when last I came to the Grange," said he, softly.

I almost stamped my foot with vexation at the lack of recklessness in this lover of Joyce's, whose ardent devotion I had begun by envying her once upon a time. But I reflected that it was both foolish and unfair to be vexed, because Frank Forrester was only keeping to the word of his agreement.

"You come to see father, not to see Joyce," I repeated, dogmatically. "Father doesn't seem to be happy about the way that notion of his is turning out."

"That notion?" repeated the young man, in an inquiring tone of voice.

I looked at him.

"Yes," said I. "I don't know exactly what it is, but something or other that father and you have got up between yourselves."

Still he looked puzzled.

"Some school, or something for poor children," explained I, I think a trifle impatiently.

"Oh, of course, of course," cried Frank. "I didn't quite understand what you were referring to, and one has so many of those things on hand, so many sad cases, there is so much to be done. But I remember all about it. We must push it. It's a fine scheme, but it will need a great deal of pushing, a great deal of interest. It's not the kind of thing that will float in a day. Your father, of course, is apt to be over-sanguine."

I did not answer. It crossed my mind vaguely that three months ago it had been father who had said that Frank was apt to be over-sanguine; or rather, who had given it so to be understood, in words spoken with a kindly smile and some sort of an expression of praise for the ardor of youth. "It's to the young ones that we must look to fly high," he had said, or words to that effect.

"Well, you must come and talk it over with father," said I, somewhat puzzled. "He thinks a great deal of you."

"Ah! And so do I think a great deal of him, I assure you," cried Frank. "He's a delightful old man! So bright and fresh and full of enthusiasm! One would never believe he had lived all his life in a place like this, looking after cows and sheep. There are very few men of better position who can talk as he talks."

I suppose I ought to have been pleased at this, but instead of that it made me unaccountably angry for a moment. I thought it a great liberty on the part of a young fellow like Captain Forrester to speak like that of an old man like my father. But one could not be exactly angry with Frank. In the first place, he was so pleasant and good-natured and sympathetic that one felt the fault must be on one's own side; and then it would have been waste of time, for he would either never have perceived it, or he would have been so surprised that one would have been ashamed to continue it.

However, I tried to speak in an off-hand way as I said, "Yes, he doesn't often get any one here whom he cares to talk to, so of course he is very glad of whoever it is that will look at things a bit as he does." And then, afraid lest I should have said too much, and prevent him from coming to the Grange after all, I added, "But he's really fond of you, and if he thinks you have been so near the place and haven't been to see him, I'm afraid he'll be hurt."

Frank looked undecided a moment, and I glanced at him anxiously. Truly, I was very eager that day to secure a companion for my father.

"Father is depressed," I added. "I don't think he's quite so cheerful and hopeful as he used to be, and I am sure you would do him good."

Frank laughed. "Very well," said he, turning down the lane with me, "if your mother is displeased, Miss Margaret, let it be on your head."

"Oh, I'm not afraid of mother," I said, although in truth I was very much afraid of her. "She will be pleased enough if you cheer up father. And if you tell him some good news of his plan about the poor little children, you will cheer him up."

"He mustn't set his heart too much upon that just at present," said Frank, in a cool, business-like kind of way. "There's a deal of hard, patient work to be done at that before it'll take any shape, you know."

"Yes, I understand," said I; "but who is going to do the work?"

He looked a bit put out for the moment, but he said, cheerily: "Ah, that's just it. We must find the proper man—the man for the place—then it'll go like a house on fire." And then he turned and fixed his brown eyes on me, as was his wont, and said, "But how is it that this bailiff hasn't roused your father's heart in his own work more, and made him forget these outside schemes?"

I flushed with anger; I thought the remark unjustifiable.

"I hear he's a clever fellow," continued the captain. "That's it, I suppose. He prefers to go his own gait. Although they tell me"—he said this as if he were paying me a compliment—"they tell me you can twist him round your little finger."

"Who are they?" cried I, my lip trembling. "They had best mind their own business."

He laughed gayly. "The same as ever, I see," he said. "But you might well be proud of such a feat. He struck me as a tough customer the only time I saw him."

I set my lips tight together and refused to answer another word; but when we had left the pines, and turned out of the lane into the road, I was sorry for him, and forgave him; for glancing at him, I saw that his cheek was quite pale.

"I'm dreadfully afraid of your parents," laughed he. "Your mother won't deign to shake hands with me, and your father will be hurt because I haven't brought a train of little London waifs at my heels."

Of course it was neither the prospect of mother's cold welcome nor the thought of father's disappointment at the stagnation of the scheme which had really made his cheek white. I understood things better than that; it was that he was going to see Joyce, whom he had not seen for three months. I was sorry for the poor fellow, in spite of his having offended me.

On the top of my original plan, which had only been to get him to the Grange, another took sudden shape. It was a Thursday—dairy morning. But as we had come down the street I had seen mother's tall back beside the counter of the village grocer's shop, and I determined to risk Deborah's presence, and to bring Frank straight in through the back door to the milk-pans and Joyce's face.

Luck favored me. Deborah had gone outside to rinse some vessel not quite to her mind, and Joyce stood alone with a fresh pink frock and a fresh fair face against the white tiles, kneading the butter with sleeves upturned. I left Frank there, and ran on to Deborah, who showed signs of returning.

"Whatever does that dandified young beau want round about again?" said she. "I thought he had taken those handsome calves of his to London to make love to the ladies."

I must mention that Frank always wore a knickerbocker suit down at Marshlands—a costume less in vogue ten years ago than it is now, and an affectation which found no favor in Deborah's sight. To tell the truth, it did not please me that day; nothing about him quite pleased me, yet indeed I think he was the same as he had always been. But I was not going to let myself dwell upon anything that was not in the captain's favor, and certainly I was not going to let Deborah comment upon it. After all, as I had once said to mother, he was my sister's lover, not mine; but he was my sister's lover, and as such I should stick up for him through thick and thin.

"He's come to see father," said I, shortly.

"That's the first time I knew that the way to your father's room was through the dairy," grinned Deborah. "But look here, Margaret"—and here old Deb grew as solemn as a judge—"you'd no business to bring him in there when your mother was away. You know very well you hadn't. You'll get into a scrape." How much Deb really knew about the particulars of Joyce's engagement I have never found out, but that she guessed what she did not know was more than likely.

"Why not?" asked I.

"Why not? Because he's a slippery young eel, that's why not," said Deborah. "If Joyce cares for him, the sooner she leaves off the better. But it's my belief she's got more sense in her head than some folk give her credit for."

"Of course Joyce cares for him," cried I, angrily, "and he's not slippery at all. He can't come courting her when mother forbids him the house. But it's very unkind of mother, and that's why I brought him. I don't care if I do get into a scrape for it. You're a hard-hearted old woman to talk so. But I suppose you've forgotten what it was to be young—it's so long ago."

"I remember enough about it to know how many men out of a dozen there are that are fit to be trusted, my dear," smiled Deborah, grimly. "And my old ears haven't grown so queer yet but they can tell a jig from a psalm tune."

"I don't think you go to church often enough to know them apart," sneered I; for Deb was not as conspicuous for piety as Reuben, and was wont to declare that when she listened to parson her head grew that muddled and stagnated she couldn't tell her left hand from her right.

"Ah, I'm not like some folk as likes to go and be told o' their sins," said she, alluding, as usual, to the unlucky Reuben. "I know mine well enough, and on the Sabbath I likes to put up my legs and give my mind to 'em in peace and quiet. But I'm not afraid I shall hear the Old Hundredth if I go into the dairy just now," grinned she, catching up the milk-pail, which she had been scrubbing viciously, "so I'll just go back and finish my work."

I laid my hand on her arm to detain her, but at that moment Trayton Harrod appeared round the corner from the garden.

"Where's Reuben?" asked he, with a thunder-cloud upon his brow.

"That's more than I can tell you," answered Deb, shortly. "I'm not the man's keeper."

"What's the matter?" I asked.

"Some malicious persons have been taking the trouble to break the pipes that have just been laid across to the new reservoir," he answered. "They were not yet covered in. But I'm determined to find out the offenders."

"Well, you needn't come asking after Reuben, then," said old Deb, with rough stanchness, "The man mayn't be much for brains, but he ain't got time to plan tricks o' that sort."

"I'm not suspecting Reuben," answered Harrod, "but I look to Reuben to help me to find out who's to blame."

"Well, if there's wrong been done against master, so he will," declared Deborah again. "Reuben's a true man to his master, say what you may of him. You'd best not come telling any tales of Reuben to me."

"No, no," replied Harrod, hurriedly, "I want to tell no tales of Reuben nor any one else, but I must get to the bottom of the matter;" and then turning to me, he added, "I must see your father at once."

He moved across the yard to the outer door, but midway he stopped, listening.

The voices in the dairy had attracted his attention. I think he was going to ask me who was there, when suddenly Joyce came out of the door, her cheeks red, her eyes wet with tears.

As soon as she saw him she ran quickly by, and round the corner of the yard to the front of the house; but I knew by the way that he glanced at me that he had seen that her eyes were full of tears. He did not speak, however, neither did he look after her. He first glanced across to the dairy, but Frank Forrester did not show himself, and he strode across to the gate of the yard and let himself out into the road.

"I'll see your father another time," he said to me as he went past.

I went round the corner, meaning to follow Joyce, but remembering that Frank must be in a very uncomfortable position, and that I was rather bound to see him through with it, I went back and found him bidding Deborah tell me he would come again in the evening.

"The master'll be busy all the evening," she said; and her inhospitality decided me to make a bold move.

"Father is at liberty now," I said. "Please come this way." And he had no choice but to follow me round to the front.

Luckily for me, father was there alone, reading his newspaper in the few spare minutes before dinner; neither Joyce nor mother was visible. He welcomed Frank even more cordially than I had hoped.

"How are you, lad?" he cried, heartily. "Why, I didn't know you were near the place at all. When did you come?"

Frank sat down in his usual place, and the two talked together just as if they had never parted. All Frank's cautiousness, not to say half-heartedness, about father's scheme seemed to have evaporated, now that he was in his presence, just as if he were afraid or ashamed not to be as enthusiastic as he was. As I listened to them I couldn't believe that he had told me ten minutes before that father was "apt to be over-sanguine," and that he must not "set his heart too much" upon the matter. On the contrary, it seemed to be Frank who was sanguine, and father who was suggesting the difficulties of working; father, moreover, who used almost the very phrase about its being necessary to get the proper man to work the details, and Frank who declared, as he had declared before, that *he* would be the man. How was it that, as soon as his back was turned, the fire seemed to die out of him? Was he like some sort of fire-bricks that can absorb heat, and give it out again fiercely while the fire is around them, but that grow dead and cold as soon as the surrounding warmth is withdrawn?

But it was very pleasant to see them there talking as merrily as ever. Merrily? Well, yes, with Frank it was "merrily," but with father I don't think it had ever been anything but earnestly, and now I fancied that there was even a tinge of hopelessness about him which had not been there of old. Yet he smiled often, and treated Frank just in that half-rough, half-affectionate way that he had always had towards him—something protecting, something humorous, almost as though he traced in him a streak of weakness, but could not help being fascinated by the bright kindliness, the sympathetic desire to please in spite of himself.

Perhaps it was so with all of us—with all of us, excepting mother. She had never felt the fascination, she had always seen straight through the mirror. And as she had always been inexorable, so she was inexorable that day.

Father, in his eagerness about the interest that he had at heart, had forgotten all about Joyce, all about the reason why Frank Forrester should not be at the Grange. But I had not forgotten it; I knew mother would not have forgotten it, and I stood, with a trembling heart, listening for her step upon the stairs within.

She came at last, and one glance at her face told me that Frank's presence was no surprise to her; that she knew of it, and knew of it from Joyce. Her lips were pressed together half nervously, her blue eyes were smaller than usual; and she rustled her dress as she walked, which somehow always seemed to me a sure sign of displeasure in her. She did not hold out her hand to him, although he advanced with every show of cordiality to greet her as usual.

"Oh, Mrs. Maliphant, you are angry with me for coming here," cried he, in a half-humorous, half-appealing voice, that he was wont to use when he wanted to conciliate. "You're quite right. What can I say for myself?"

He did not say that I had persuaded him. I liked him for that, but I said it for him.

"*I* brought Captain Forrester here, mother," said I, in my boldest manner, trying neither to blush nor to let my voice quaver. "I knew father would want to see him, and he is in Marshlands for only one day."

"Captain Forrester is always welcome in my house," said father, and his voice did shake a little, but whether from annoyance or distress it was not possible to tell. But mother said nothing. She kept her hands folded in front of her. It was Joyce who spoke—Joyce, who had followed mother down the stairs and out into the porch.

"Father, I have been telling mother," said she, coming very close to him, "that I knew nothing of Captain Forrester's coming here to-day. I did not wish to see him."

She kept her head bent as she said the words, but she said them quite firmly, although in a low voice. Certainly Joyce, for a gentle and diffident girl, had a wonderful trick of courage at times. I admired her for it, although to-day she angered me; she might have allowed her love to shine forth a little—for her lover's sake if not for her own.

"All right, my girl," answered father, without looking at her. "I understand."

And then he turned again to Frank. "You'll stay and have a bit of dinner with us?" he said.

I was grateful to him for saying it, for things were altogether rather uncomfortable. The honesty and frankness of our family is a characteristic of which I am proud, but it certainly has its uncomfortable side. Fortunately Captain Forrester's pleasant and easy manners were second nature, and cost him no trouble. They came to the aid of us all that day.

"Oh, Mrs. Maliphant does not echo that kind invitation of yours," said he. "I know I have deserved her wrath. A bargain is a bargain." He put out his hand again. "But she will shake hands with me before I go?" he added.

Who could have resisted him? Mother put out her hand.

"You're welcome to our board, captain, if you will stay," said she.

"Thank you, that is kind of you," answered he, with real feeling in his voice. "I mustn't stay, I am due elsewhere, but I appreciate your asking me none the less."

He turned to me and shook hands with me warmly. Then he stopped in front of Joyce.

She did not lift her eyes; she put her hand silently into his out-stretched palm without, so far as I could see, the slightest tremor. He pressed the soft long fingers in his for a moment, and then he turned away without speaking.

Father and he went along the passage together, talking; and it was father who showed him out of the front door.

I was sorry that I had persuaded him to come to the Grange. Harrod had seen Joyce in tears, and would wonder what was the cause; and was it worth while to have gone through the very uncomfortable scene which had just taken place for anything that had been gained? It was Joyce's own fault, but it showed me how idle it was to hope to move her in any line of conduct which she had laid out for herself.

CHAPTER XXVIII

The next morning I was still more sorry that I had brought Frank to the Grange.

Mother very rightly upbraided me for it, and in a way that showed me that she was more than ever determined that Joyce should not marry Captain Forrester if she could help it. She said that Joyce was beginning to forget this dandy love affair, and that it was all the more annoying of me to have gone putting my finger in the pie and stirring up old memories. I declared that Joyce was not forgetting Frank at all, and told mother I wondered at her for thinking a daughter of hers could be so fickle, and for supposing that her manner meant anything but the determination to keep to the unfair promise that had been extracted from her.

Ah, dear me, if I could have believed in that other string that mother had to her bow for Joyce! But although the squire came to the Grange just as often as ever, I could not deceive myself into thinking his coming or going made any difference to my sister, whatever might be his feelings towards her. If Joyce had not encouraged her lover, as I thought she ought to have done, that was not the reason. I told myself that the reason was in the different way in which we looked at such matters; but I was sorry I had brought Frank to the Grange.

With my arrogance of youth, I might have got over mother's scolding if I could have persuaded myself that I had done any good; but I could not but think that I seemed to have done nothing but harm. Joyce was almost distant to me in a way that had never happened before in our lives; and when I tried to upbraid her for her coldness, she choked me off in a quiet fashion that there was no withstanding and left me alone, sore and silent and angry. Oh, and there was a worse result of that unlucky visit than all this, although I would not even tell my own heart of it.

Joyce, as I have said, was moody and silent all the next day. To be sure, the weather had turned from that glorious heat to a dull gray, showery fit that was most depressing to everybody. It had most reason to be depressing to Trayton Harrod, who had his eye on the crops even more anxiously than father had himself. The rain had not as yet been heavy or continuous enough to do more than refresh the parched earth, but a little more might make a serious difference to the wheat and the hops, of which the one harvest was not yet all garnered, the second nearly ready for picking.

This, and the annoyance about the broken water-pipes—in which matter he had failed to discover the offenders—were quite enough, of course, to account for the cloud upon the bailiff's brow as I came across him that evening on the ridge of the downs by the new reservoir. I ought to have remembered this; I ought to have soothed the trouble; I should have done so a fortnight ago. But I was ruffed, unreasonable, unjust.

"Well, have you discovered anything more about that ridiculous affair?" I asked, nipping off the twig of a bush in the hedge pettishly as I spoke.

"What affair?" asked he, although I knew that he knew perfectly well what I meant.

"Well, about those water-pipes that you fancy the men have stamped upon to spite you," laughed I, ill-naturedly.

He pressed his lips together. "I think I guess pretty well who was at the bottom of it," he said. "But the work is finished now and in working order, so I shall say no more about it."

I knew very well that if he could have been certain of his facts he would have said a great deal more about it, and in my unreasonable ill-temper I wanted to make him feel this.

"Guessing isn't enough," I replied. "But if you could be sure, it would be far better to let the man know that you have discovered him. You'll never get anything out of these Sussex people by knuckling under to them."

I was sorry for the words as soon as I had said them, for it was an insulting speech to a man in his position; but I wouldn't show any humility.

"Thank you," he answered, coldly. "I must do the best I can, of course, in managing the Sussex people. But, anyhow, it is *I* who have to do it."

I would not see the just reproof. "Well, if any one is to blame in this it isn't poor old Reuben," I declared, stoutly; "he's obstinate, but he isn't mean. It *might* be Jack Barnstaple. I don't say it is, but it *might* be. It isn't Reuben."

"I am quite of your opinion," answered he. "But as you say, guessing is of no avail, so we had best let the matter drop."

He turned to go one way and I the other. But just as we were parting, Reuben appeared upon the crest of the hill with Luck at his heels. They were inseparable companions. Luck was the one sign of his former calling that still clung to poor old Reuben. But he was very old, older than his master; both had done good work in their day, but both were nearly past work now.

"That dog will have to be shot soon," said Trayton Harrod, looking at the way the poor beast dragged itself along, stiff with rheumatism, which the damp weather had brought out. "I told Reuben so the other day."

"Shot!" cried I, with angry eyes. "No one shall shoot that dog while I have a word to say in the matter."

And I ran across to where Luck was coming to meet me, his tail wagging with pleasure.

"Poor old Luck! poor old fellow!" I murmured, stooping to caress him. "They want to shoot you, do they? But I won't allow it."

"Shoot him!" growled Reuben, looking round to the bailiff, who had followed me. "Shoot my dog?"

"He's not *your* dog, Reuben," I said. "He's father's, although you have had him for your own so long. And father will have a voice in the matter before he's shot. Don't be afraid. He sha'n't be shot. We can nurse him when he needs nursing, and he shall die peaceably like a human being. He deserves as much any day, I'm sure. He has worked as well."

Taff was my special dog, and it was true that Luck had always, as it were, belonged to Reuben, but now that I fancied him in danger, all my latent love of the weak and injured rose up strong within me, and I fought for the post of Luck's champion. Perhaps my mood of unreasonable temper had just a little to do with it too.

"You are mistaken," said Trayton, coldly. "The poor beast is ill and weary. It would be a far greater kindness to shoot him."

"Well, he *sha'n't* be shot, then, so there's an end," cried I, testily, rising to my feet and looking Harrod in the face.

"Oh, very good; of course it's not my business," said he.

He turned away up the slope. But the spirit of annoyance was in Reuben as it was in me that day.

"I came to have a bit of a look at the 'op-fields, master," said he. "The sky don't look just as we might choose, do it?"

"This rain is not enough to hurt," growled Harrod, without looking round.

"No, no; we might put up with this so long as it don't go on," agreed Reuben, slowly. "We want a bit of rain after all that dry weather. You didn't get your water-pipes laid on in time for the dry weather, did you, Master Harrod? begging your pardon," asked the old man, slyly.

"No; some mischievous persons took a childish delight in putting them out of order," said the bailiff, turning round sharply; "but I have my eye on them."

"They're dreadful brittle things, them china things, for such work," said Reuben, in a slow, sleepy voice. "I doubt you'll never get the water to go just as you fancy. They do say there's another broke down by Widow Dawes," he added, with a grin.

Harrod turned round, with a muttered imprecation.

"But there, I'm thinking you won't want no water round about for some while to come, mister. The Lord'll do it for ye."

"I tell you the weather hasn't broken up, man. This rain is nothing," growled Harrod again, striding up the bank as he spoke.

"Right, right," agreed Reuben, nodding his head; "we must trust the Lord, we must. Though, for my part, I'd sooner trust Him with anything rather than a few gardens of 'ops." Reuben sighed as he looked out across the valley that was so rich now with the tall and graceful growths. "They're a fine sight now," said he, "but the Lord can lay 'em low." And with that comforting reflection, he turned his back on me and went down the path.

Luckily for Reuben, I had not leisure just then to think of him or his words; my thoughts were elsewhere. Trayton Harrod had reached the top of the slope. He was nearly out of ear-shot. I watched his figure grow longer and longer upon the softening sky, that was slowly clearing with the coming twilight.

How could I bear to let him go from me like that? Was it for this that we had had those good times together, those happy, happy hours, that lived in my memory like stars upon a bright sky? Was it for nothing that he had held my hands in his and tuned his voice to gentleness in speaking to me? Was it for nothing that my heart beat wild and hot, so full of longing, so full of devotion? Oh, and yet it was I who had made this foolish quarrel! How could I have allowed my unreasonable temper to get the better of me like that? It was my fault, all my fault! What devil had taken possession of me to fill my heart with wicked and unjust fancies, to imbitter all that was but a little while ago so sweet?

My heart was heavy, the tears came into my eyes. If he loved me he would forgive me, I said to myself, and I forgot all of what I had been wont to consider proper pride, and ran after him.

"Mr. Harrod," I called. He turned at once and waited for me.

"You're going to London one of these days, aren't you?" I said, breathlessly, for I had run up the bank.

"One day before the hop-picking begins," he said, hurriedly, impatient to get on; "but not before the harvest is all in."

He turned, walking on, and I walked by his side.

"Well, when you go, I want you to do something for me," I said. "I want you to buy some books for me."

"Buy some books!" ejaculated he. "What books?"

"I don't know," I answered. "I have saved some money, and I want to buy some books with it. But I don't know what books. I thought you would advise me."

He laughed. "I don't think I'm at all the proper person to advise you what books to buy. I'm not much of a reader myself. I've got my father's books, and have had some pleasant hours with them too, but I don't know if they're the best kind of books for a young woman to read. No, I'm not the proper person to advise you, I'm sure. You'd better ask the squire."

"The squire!" cried I, vexed. "And pray, why should I ask the squire?"

"Well, he's an older friend of yours than I am, and far better suited to advise you," answered Harrod. "And he would do anything for you, I'm sure."

Was it possible that Harrod might be under a delusion? Somehow it gave me pleasure to think that it might be possible.

"The squire is no friend of mine," said I. I was ashamed of the words before they were spoken, they were so untrue; but I spoke them under the smart of the moment.

"How can you say such a thing?" said Harrod, sternly.

"I don't mean to say that he wouldn't do anything for any of us," I murmured, ashamed. "I only meant to say that he would be more likely to do it—for Joyce."

I felt his eyes turn upon me, and I raised mine to his face. It was quiet, all trace of the temper that had been there five minutes ago had vanished; but his eyes, those steely gray eyes, looked me through. But it was only for a moment. Then the shade upon his brow melted away, and the hard lines of his mouth broke into that parting of the lips which was scarcely a smile yet lit his whole face as with a strong, sharp ray of light.

There never was a face that changed as his face changed; not with many and varying expressions as with some folk—for his was a character reserved almost to isolation, and if he felt many things he told but few of them, either tacitly or in words—but with a slow melting, from something that was almost akin to cruelty into something that was very much akin to good, honest tenderness. It was as the breaking of sunlight across some rugged rock where the shadow has hidden every possible path-way; when the sunlight came one could see that there was a way to ascend. Judging with the dispassionateness of distance, I think that Harrod feared any such thing as feeling. Life was a straightforward and not necessarily pleasant road, which must be travelled doggedly, without pausing by the way, without stopping to think if there were any means by which it might be made more agreeable. Life was all work for Trayton Harrod.

And as a natural consequence, if he had any feelings he instinctively avoided dwelling on the fact; therefore he mistrusted any expression of them in others. He was cruel, but if he was cruel to others he was also cruel to himself.

That evening, however, the sunshine broke out across the rock. It melted the last morsel of pride in me. He turned away his eyes again without a word, after that long, half-amused, half-reproachful, and wholly kind look. It puzzled me a little, and yet it gave me courage.

"I think I'm in a very bad temper to-day," said I, with a little awkward laugh. "I think I was very rude to you just now."

"Rude!" echoed he, turning to me quickly. "Why, when were you rude?"

"Just now, about the hops and everything."

He laughed aloud, quite merrily. "Good gracious! surely we are good friends enough to stand a sharp word or two," cried he.

I was silent. Harrod walked very fast, and talking was difficult. When he reached the top of the hill he held out his hand, and said, in a cheerful, matter-of-fact voice, "Good-night; I must be getting along to Widow Dawes as fast as I can."

I stood watching him as he ran down the slope. At any other time I should have been just as much excited as he was about the breakage of the pipes, but that night there was a dull emptiness about things for which I had no reason.

The west was still clouded, and in the plains the struggling rays of the sinking sun made golden spray of the mists that the rain had left; but to the eastward the sky was clear of showers.

The mill was quite still, its warning arms were silent; it stood white upon the flaxen slope, where the short grass was burned to chaff by the rare summer heat—white and huge against the twilight blue. Behind it—slowly, slowly out of the blue sea—rose the golden August moon.

I turned my back to the clouds and faced the golden moon.

CHAPTER XXIX

And now let me pause a while and think. Ten years have passed since the time of which I write. I am a woman, twenty-nine years old—a woman in judgment as well as in years, for many things have happened since then which have taught me more than the mere passage of time. And I can see clearly enough now that what I am going to tell happened through no fault of others; my pain and my disappointment were the result only of my own mistake; let me state that as a fact—it will be a satisfaction to my own conscience. I never had any excuse for that mistake. I was a foolish, passionate, romantic girl, and out of the whirlwind of my own love I conjured up the answering love that I craved; but it was never there—it was a phantom of my own making.

A month had passed since Joyce had come home, since that night when Trayton Harrod and I stood under the abbey eaves in the lightning and the storm—a long, long summer's month. The hay had all been gathered in long ago, and the harvest was golden and ready for the reaping; the plain that had once been so green was growing mellower every day; the thick, reedy grass that blooms with a rich dark tassel upon our marsh made planes of varied brown tints over the flatness of the pastures—the whole land was warm with color; the gray castle lay sleeping upon the flaxen turf, with the gray beach beyond; the white sheep cropped lazily what blades they could find; between the two lines of tall rushes yellow and white water-lilies floated upon the dikes, and meadowsweet bloomed upon their banks; the scarlet poppies had faded from the cornfields, and the little harvest-mouse built her nest upon the tall ears of wheat.

Every sign told that the summer would soon be fading into autumn; the young broods were all abroad long ago; the swallows and the martins were preparing for a second hatching; the humming of the snipe, as his tardy mate sat on her nest, made a pleasant bleating sound along the dikes near to the sea; the swift, first of all birds to leave us, would soon be taking her southward flight; on the beach the yellow sea-poppies bloomed amid their pale green leaves.

There had been the same little trouble over the bringing of reaping and threshing machines onto the farm as there had been over the mowing.

Poor father did not appear to be reconciled to these innovations, although he seemed to have made up his mind to give in to Trayton Harrod up to a certain point; he had not, however, wavered an inch on the subject of the length of the laborers' working-hours; on that he and the bailiff still preserved an ill-concealed attitude of hostility.

I did what I could to preserve the peace, so did mother, so did we all; but I don't think that father grew to like Trayton Harrod any better as time went on. I think he respected him thoroughly. More than once, I recollect, he took occasion to observe that he was an upright and honorable man, and yet, somehow, he scarcely seemed even to thoroughly trust him.

I know, at least, that one morning about this time he called me into his study and bade me ride into town at once with a letter for Mr. Hoad, which I was to deliver privately into his own hands, letting nobody know my errand. Three months ago how proud I should have been of this trust, which might have been given to the man who had been called in to supplant me! But now I did not like it; it filled me with apprehensions, with misgivings, with anger at the slight to him.

"Are you afraid to go, Meg?" father had asked, seeing me hesitate. "I'll go myself."

The word must have lit up my gray eyes with the light that he was wont to laugh at, for he put down his stick and sank into his chair.

"There," said he, patting my cheek, "I thought she hadn't lost her pride."

And neither had I; but the strangeness of the request, and the strangeness of Mr. Hoad's face as he read the letter, set me thinking most uncomfortably all the way home. Nor was it only on that occasion that I had need to ponder somewhat anxiously on matters that were not my own.

A Sunday morning about this time comes back to my mind. Father had been up to London during the week on one or two matters of business. It was an event in those days for a farmer to go up to London. To father it was specially an event, for he always had been a more than usually stay-at-home man. But there must have been some special reason that took him up; he had seemed disquieted for some time.

I had fancied that it was purely on account of that scheme that Frank Forrester had not yet succeeded in floating, and I was angry with Frank for that cooling down which I have noticed as happening in him whenever he got away from the fiery influence. I was angry with Joyce for not keeping him up to his first ardor, angry with mother for not allowing them to correspond, so that she might do so. But after all, I don't believe that father's uneasiness was entirely owing to Frank Forrester, for his journey to London was suddenly decided upon one afternoon after he and Mr. Hoad had had a long talk together in the business-room. Father had seen Harrod afterwards, and had then announced his proposed journey at the tea-table.

He had been away only two days; but although he said that he had been made a great deal of by the old friend with whom he had stayed, and though he declared that Frank was just the same as ever, and it was therefore to be supposed that they had been as good comrades as usual, father looked none the better for his little change. As we all stood up in the old church to say the Creed, I remember noticing how ill he looked.

It was not only that he bent his tall, massive figure over the desk, leaning heavily upon it with both hands, as if for needful support; it was not even that his cheeks were more sunken, and that he bowed his head wearily; it was that in his dull eyes and set lips there was an air of suffering, of dejection and hopelessness, that was pathetic even to me who should have known nothing of pathos at nineteen. It struck me with sad forebodings, and those words of the squire's a few weeks before came back to my mind.

I glanced at mother's face—beautiful and serene as ever—with the little net-work of delicate wrinkles spread over its soft surface, and the blue eyes content as a young girl's beneath the shadow of the thick white hair. It was what Joyce's face might grow to be some day, although at that time there were lines of character about the mouth which my sister's beauty lacked; it was what my face could never grow to. But surely neither of those two had any misgivings. "And the life of the world to come," repeated mother, gravely, saying the words a little after everybody else in a kind of conclusive way. But, somehow, I wondered whether she had really been thinking of what they meant, for she sat down again with almost a smile upon her lips and smoothed out her soft old black brocade without any air of undue solemnity.

I glanced at Joyce. Her eyes were bent down looking at her hands—large, well-shaped, useful hands, that looked better in the dairy or at her needle than they did in ill-fitting kid-gloves; her face was undisturbed, the lovely little chin resting on the white bow of the ribbon that tied on her fresh chip-bonnet. It was before the days when it was considered respectable to go to church in a hat.

I, too, had a white chip-bonnet—Joyce had brought them both from London, together with the blue merino frocks, which we also wore that day; but I did not look as well in a chip-bonnet as Joyce did.

I glanced along the row of pews. At the end of the one parallel with ours across the aisle sat Reuben in his clean smock, his fine old parchment-colored face set in the quiet lines induced by sleepiness and the suitable mood for the occasion. Deborah, as I have said, came rarely to church; she always declared that a deafness, which I had never noticed in her, made the coming but a mere form, for "what was the use if you couldn't extinguish the parson?" But Reuben was a pious and constant attendant, and looked better in keeping with the place than did the owner of two keen gray eyes, just beyond him, that I noticed were fixed upon my sister's face.

They were withdrawn as soon as I turned my head, although they did not look at me, but I paid no further attention to the service that day, and for all the good I got of the sermon I might as well have stayed at home.

And yet we had a fine discourse—or so father said as we came out of church—for it was from the curate of the next parish, that young Mr. Cyril Morland, to whom he had taken such a fancy, and it was for the ragged schools, and touched on father's subject in father's own way. If I had cared to look round at him again I should have seen that his weary eyes had regained all their usual fire, and that his head was raised gazing at the impassioned young speaker.

But I did not look at father again. I sat with my eyes fixed on the old tombstone at my right, on which reposed the mail-clad figure of an ancient knight; and, for aught I knew or cared, the preacher might have been the sleepy old vicar himself, clearing his throat and humbly enunciating his well-worn sentiments. I don't remember just what my thoughts were—perhaps I could not have put them into words even then; but I know they were not of God, nor of the poor little wretched children for whom our charity was asked. When the plate came round at the end it awoke me from a dream; ah me! it was not a good dream nor a happy dream. I wondered if people were often so wicked in church.

When the service was over father went round to the back and took up little David Jarrett, whom he had carried into church. The little fellow was supposed to be better, but he did not look as though he would be long for this world, and I think he grew nearer every day to father's heart.

The vicar's young wife spoke to him as he went out in father's arms.

"You've got a very kind friend, David," she said to the child, in her weak, whining voice. "I hope you're very grateful."

A smile came over the little pinched face. The boy did not reply, but he put his arm round father's neck to make the burden easier, and looked into his eyes.

"I'm going to take you to the Grange to-day for a bit of roast beef, David. What do you say?" asked father.

"I should like to go to the Grange," said David, without making any allusion to the roast beef.

"Come, you youngster," said the squire, coming down the path with Mary Thorne, and speaking in his hearty, healthy voice, "isn't that leg of yours well enough yet for you to walk alone and not trouble a poor old man?"

The child flushed scarlet, and father said, in a vexed tone, "I'm not so very old yet, squire, but I can carry a poor little cripple a couple of hundred yards."

The squire had spoken only in joke, and he said so; it was his way, for in reality he was as kind a man as father himself, but I don't think father forgave him for quite a little while.

"Well, did you see anything of that good-for-nothing nephew of mine up in London?" asked the squire again.

We were all standing round in a little group, as folk are wont to do coming out of church, when they rarely get time to meet on week-days. Mother was talking to that aggressive old lady, Miss Farnham; Joyce stood at her side. I could not see Harrod anywhere, but it was just like him to have disappeared; he hated a concourse of people.

"Oh, come, Mr. Broderick, I don't think you ought to take away a poor fellow's character when he's absent," laughed Mary Thorne, in her jolly way. "Here's Miss Maliphant," added she, pointing at Joyce, "might be prejudiced against him by it, and he thinks a very great deal of what Miss Maliphant's opinion of him may be, I assure you."

She said it in a good-natured, bantering kind of way, but not at all as if she guessed at the real relations that existed between Joyce and her childhood's friend.

The squire frowned, and mother turned away from Miss Farnham.

"Now, Miss Thorne, I should take it very kindly if you wouldn't bring my girl into it," said she. "I'm an old-fashioned woman, and I don't hold with jokes of that sort."

Mary looked rather surprised, but it was just like mother to speak up like that; she never was afraid of anything or anybody, although she did seem so gentle.

"Ah, I often have my suspicions that Mrs. Maliphant is a good old Tory at heart," said the squire, trying to turn the matter off lightly.

"No, no, squire, don't you try to make more out of my words than's in them," declared mother, shaking her head. "I never was for politics. I make neither head nor tail of them."

Of course everybody laughed at this, and the squire added, "I'll be bound Frank won't show himself till after we have got my friend Farnham in for the county."

"He said nothing about coming down," said father, who had withdrawn from the group since the Thornes had joined it, and stood by the old stone wall, on which he had rested little David; "but I don't think that's the reason."

"He'd have been down before now to torment me about those new stables unless there were something particular keeping him away," went on Mr. Broderick. "He keeps writing to me about them, but I tell him I'll have the men and women housed before the dogs and horses. There are two new cottages wanted on the estate, and they're going to be done first."

"Ah, you're a decent sort of landlord; they're few enough like you," declared Miss Farnham, nodding her ever-bugled head before she turned up her black silk gown over her white petticoat, and trudged off across the church-yard; "and that's a sight better than going about making mischief, as some seditious folk must needs do."

This was a parting thrust at father, but he did not seem to have even noticed it.

"Mother, I'll just take the little chap home," said he. "You get hold of Mr. Morland, and ask him to come and have a bit of dinner with us, will you?"

The squire looked after him. "You oughtn't to let him carry that child about, Mrs. Maliphant," said he. "He's not the man he was."

"Oh, squire, what a Job's comforter you are, to be sure!" sighed mother, half fretfully. "Why, I think Laban's quite himself again since the summer weather has come in. He's a bit cast down to-day, I've noticed it myself; but that's in his spirits. I don't think that trip to London did him any good. Those railways are tiring things, and then I can't help fancying he's a bit disappointed about this notion of his for getting the charity school, or whatever it is. He's so set on those things. I tell him it's a pity. He wears himself out and neglects his own work. And no offence to you, squire, that young nephew of yours isn't so smart about it as he might be. I always warned Laban against putting too much trust in him. Not that he has said anything, but if matters were going as he wants, he would have had something to say, you see. The young man seemed just as eager about it as my old one once upon a time, but young folks haven't the grit."

Mother made the whole of this long speech in a confidential manner to the squire, but I heard every word of it. So must Joyce have done, for she and Mary Thorne had been talking, and were standing side by side, but she gave no sign at all, although Mary said, with a loud laugh: "Is that Frank you're talking of? Why, dear me, you don't expect him to hold long to one thing, do you? The squire knows him better than that. As jolly an old chap as ever was, but never of the same mind for ten minutes together; at least," added she, quite gravely for her, "not about things of that sort. Dear me, I know at least five things he has taken up wildly for the time being, and wearied of in six months."

The squire smiled a little maliciously. "There's a bit of truth in that," he agreed, "though I don't know that I could have told it off so glibly. Oh, Miss Mary, Miss Mary, what a wicked tongue you have got!"

I fancied she looked distressed. "Come, who was it stood up for him just now?" cried she. "You can't call black white because you happen to like a person."

He laughed. I couldn't help thinking that he was very well pleased with what she had said, and I thought it was very unkind of him. As for me, I was furious with the girl. I had always liked her before, but that day I positively hated her. What business had she to go telling tales about Frank?

It never occurred to me for a moment that she might possibly have a reason for wanting to set Joyce against Frank, for making her think that his liking for people as well as for pursuits was of a very transitory nature.

I went home in a very bad temper. Why was I so specially angry now every time that Joyce was lukewarm where her absent lover was concerned? I had often secretly accused her in my heart of being lukewarm before. She was not of a forthcoming temperament; she never had expressed her emotions freely, and she never would do so; it was not in her nature.

Why did it trouble me more now than it used to do? Why did it trouble me so much that, when I reflected that Joyce had not said a single word during the whole of that scene, I could not find it in my heart to speak to her?

A month ago I should have scolded her for letting mother awe her into silence—I should have laughed at her for her timidity. But that day I could not.

I let her go up-stairs alone into our little bedroom to take off her bonnet, and found an excuse to lay mine aside down-stairs.

I heard the Rev. Cyril Morland talking the management of the ragged schools over with father, and considering his suggestions of improvement. At any other time I should have been proud to notice the deference that he showed to the old man. I should have liked to listen to the comparison of their ideas and plans. But then I was afraid.

The pity of suffering, the zeal for succoring it, seemed to me so much more akin between the curate and father than they had ever really been between him and Frank.

I could not bear to acknowledge it, yet I could not but instinctively feel that it was so.

I did not guess at possible rocks and quicksands of creeds that might be ahead in any intercourse between father and his new friend, but I felt that in him was the spirit of endurance and self-sacrifice which, girl as I was, I could not but fear was lacking in the sympathizing, sympathetic nature of my sister's lover. It was only since he had been at the Grange the last time that I had begun to fear it; but after that, that waxing and waning in the heat of his enterprise was apparent even to me.

I felt that mother was right when she said that you knew where you were with a man who had troubled himself to put some of his ideas into practice, and could not blame her for being glad that father had put his scheme into the hands of one who had shown that he could work as well as talk. I could not blame her; she had no reason for making excuses for Frank Forrester; on the contrary, she had every reason for wishing father to see him in what she called his true colors, so that their intercourse should be at an end.

But I—I had a reason best known to myself for wishing to strengthen every little thread that could bind Frank to father and the Grange. And even though this fervent young curate should turn out to be that man of whom Frank himself had spoken—he who was the "right man to do the work"—I could not like him. How could I like any one who showed signs of taking Frank's place with father?

I sat silent at the board, and well deserved mother's just reproof afterwards for my lapse into the old, ill-mannered ways out of which she hoped I was growing.

I was cross—I was cross with Joyce; but it was unjustly so, and I felt it. When I had said my prayers that night I went up and kissed her where she lay with her golden heaps of hair upon the white pillow.

CHAPTER XXX

There is no season so bad but there are some fine days in it, and there is no time so heavy but it has some happy hours. That stormy summer-time had its happy hours, although I must needs tell also of its clouds.

The earth was the same, although the eyes with which I saw it saw another image before they reached it, and sometimes the sense of its eternal beauty came to my spirit with a soothing song, and whispered of an enduring life that was beyond the changes and chances of varying weathers, bidding me be still and wait. I don't know that I was still, I don't know that at that time I was content to wait; but those voices that were so familiar made me glad as nothing else did, and, though I knew it not, made me strong.

The wind that breathed soft from over the downs, heavy with the scent of the hops; the wind that smote salt upon my cheek with the fresh sea-brine; the lap of the waves upon the sand's soft lip, or their fretful flow upon the steeper beach whence they would suck the pebbles back again to the ocean's heart; the rush and rustle of birds in the air—rooks, or starlings, or fieldfares in great congregations that blackened the sky; the clouds hastening over the blue that lay so wide a covering over the wide level land, and made the red roofs of the town purple beneath their touch; the rippling of a breeze in the ash-trees, and the moaning of it in the pines; the pattering of rain, the lowing of cattle; the hundred notes of birds, and sounds of beasts upon the land; the throbbing sunlight, and the cold moon—all these things, and many, many more, spoke to me, gay or pitiful, in tones that I had learned from my childhood up, and told me of that wide sea of life that was there for me, whether I would or not, beyond the present, beyond selfish longings, beyond happiness or unhappiness.

Yes, I think something of all this came to me even then, although I could not have told it in words, as I try to do now—ten years afterwards.

It was late August—the last of the harvesting. I had gone down to those wheat-fields upon the marsh that lie almost alongside of the beach.

The day's work was nearly done, the reapers were binding up the last sheaves, and only a few solitary gleaners were still busy where the hated machines had left off their monotonous grind. I don't know how it was the men had done work so early that day, for it was an hour off sundown yet, but I think it was the very last field they had to reap upon father's land.

Trayton Harrod had been there, but I had not spoken to him all the afternoon, and now, as I stood looking at him from afar through the late golden sunshine, and one of those strange showers of cobwebs that sometimes fall about this time of year upon our Sussex levels, I saw the squire upon the path hard by that led to the beach. I had seen him coming down the road before with his bailiff, but had scarcely noticed him then—he was such a familiar figure in the landscape. Only when he was comparatively close at hand something occurred to me with regard to him.

I gave up a foolish wish that I had had to walk up to the village with Trayton Harrod after work was done, and jumped the dike, beyond which only a narrow strip of pasture-land was between me and the road. I remember how I stopped to pluck meadowsweet and flowering willow as I stepped across, that I might just climb the bank not too long before the squire should have reached that point.

"Been harvesting, Miss Margaret?" said he, in, I fancied, rather a preoccupied manner. "We have all got plenty of that to do just now, haven't we?"

The squire had more of it to do than we had, for he had more wheat, and the ugly weather having given place that week to a fresh burst of summer, all we who still had crops on the ground were anxious to take advantage of the unexpected good-fortune. I did not reply; I was thinking how to begin what I had to say, and I took my knife out of my pocket, and stooped to cut a tall teasel that was turning brown on the dike-side, and a spray of ruddy dock that grew beside it.

"The weather is splendid now for harvesting," said I, finding the squire did not speak again, "and Mr. Harrod says the crop of wheat will be finer than he once thought."

"Why shouldn't he have thought it would be fine?" grumbled the squire, looking in the direction where our bailiff stood in the wheat-field talking to the bailiff from the Manor. "We have rarely had such a hot summer."

The field was hot and golden, the hill behind cool and dark.

I pulled one of the heads of dock to pieces in my hand, and said, "He says that a hot early summer doesn't always do good; it sucks the juices out while the straw is milky, and impoverishes the strength of the plant."

The squire laughed, and I grew scarlet with vexation.

"Why, you'll be quite a farmer under Harrod's auspices," he said. "You were nearly fit to manage the farm before he came, and I'm sure you'll soon be able to turn him off."

"No, indeed," said I, trying to speak quietly. "I'm only just beginning to learn that I know nothing."

"Ah! Well, they say that's the first step to growing clever," he replied. "And, joking apart, of course Harrod's a very able fellow, and can teach us both a lot of things, I've no doubt, though he does have queer notions at times, I'm bound to say. He is a business man, and no mistake."

"Of course Mr. Harrod is a good man of business," said I, haughtily. "We all know that. That's why you recommended him to father, I suppose."

Whenever the squire was rough on Harrod for his energy—which somehow seemed to me to be rather often of late—I always reminded him that he had recommended him for that very quality. I don't think he liked to be so reminded. I don't know why, but I am sure he did not like it.

"Mr. Broderick," I said, striking a bold tangent, "when is Captain Forrester coming down again to the Manor?"

He looked at me, surprised.

"I don't know, I'm sure," he said. "He never used to come at all. He has never been at the Manor before for so long a time as he was here this spring."

"No, perhaps not," I said.

He looked at me sharply, and remembering the warning he had given me against any intimacy between my sister and Frank, it occurred to me that he might be to blame for Frank's long absence.

This thought made a sudden flame of anger leap up within me towards the squire. I could not help being angry with him if he were doing anything to keep Joyce and Frank apart. I longed to tell him so, but with that promise to mother at my back I did not dare.

"He might come for the election," said I. "I think he ought to come for the election."

The squire laughed again.

"On which side do you suppose he would throw in his interest, Miss Margaret?" he said.

I saw that I had said a silly thing, and flushed. Of course if Frank put any interest in the election it would be on the side that was not the squire's.

"But, upon my soul, I scarcely know myself," added he. "The lad is a slippery sort of fellow."

This speech pleased me no more than the former one. It pleased me none the more because it awakened a certain uneasiness that I had felt myself about Frank. Girl as I was, I, too, had fancied he was not always the same; but I stood up for him.

"I think it's very unfair of you to say that of your own nephew," I said.

The squire fixed his blue eyes upon me with an amused expression.

"Why, Miss Margaret, you're a very stanch champion of that young scapegrace," said he. "What makes you so bold at fighting his battles, and so eager that he should come back again to the Manor?"

"I fight his battles because I think you are unjust," I said. "And I want him to come back because father looks to him to help him in his work."

"Oh, I see," said the squire, somewhat doubtfully. "But you mustn't fancy that he is so necessary to your father as all that. I am sure my friend Maliphant is far too wise a man to set much store by the talk and opinions of a young and idle fellow like my nephew. He is far more likely to value the advice of a man such as this new parson over at Iden. I am glad to see they have struck up quite a friendship together. I wish he wouldn't wear such a long coat, but I can see that he is an honest chap in spite of it."

At any other time I might have been willing to enter into a discussion as to the merits of the Rev. Cyril Morland, but at that moment I was only annoyed with the squire for having noticed father's liking for him. However, he gave me no more time for further talk. Whether I had said anything to annoy him, or whether he was really busy, I don't know; but he bade me good-bye abruptly, only asking me, if I should meet Harrod, to tell him that he would call round at "The Elms" and see him later on.

I strolled down to the sea-shore that hemmed the margin of the marsh, and sat down upon the beach to listen to the wash of the water upon the pebbles as the tide went out. It was one of those serene evenings that are made for dreaming; the sea was calm, and melted into the sky, with a little haze upon the horizon; streaks of varied shades crossed it in lines, brown upon the shallows, palest green beyond, blue where the water deepened, and darker still where the shadow of passing clouds fell upon its bosom. A fishing-boat, with brown sail flapping idly, lay becalmed in the offing; a steamer crossed the distance. The light-house at the end of the long, faint pink line, that was the far point that swept out into the ocean, seemed scarcely to be on land at all, but a mere speck of white in a veil of haze at sea; even the shipping in the harbor, but two miles away, had a phantom look, although the distant cliffs to my right could not but be stable and stately even in that languid atmosphere.

It was all so peaceful and pleasant that I forgot the storms that oftentimes raged upon it, and although I was not actively happy I was passively content, involuntarily wrapped around by the soothing influence of the world that had been all the world to me until six months ago.

I began thinking of the days—not so very long past—when I knew no excitement so great as to be out with the fisher-lads fishing for mackerel. Mother would not allow me to go out when it was very stormy, so it was days of comparative calm that I remembered, and one night in special when I had leave to go out with Reuben and an old fisherman by torchlight. It was in the month of November—a cold, clear night—and we fished for herring. There had been just enough of a swell not to make the adventure tame, but the stars had shone calmly, and the haul had been a good one. At the time, I had thought much more about the haul of fish than about the stars, but now I remembered that the stars had shone calmly. A longing came over me to be once more on the sea.

The old fisherman with whom I had been out that night was dead, I knew; but there were others whom I had known, and with a sudden impulse I got up from the shingle, and began walking towards the fishing village hard by. It was but a handful of little low cottages, with a rough inn in the middle—a wild, strange place, alone on the border of the marsh with the wind and the sea.

I met one of my friends coming along the beach; he was going for his shrimping-net, for the tide was going out, and in another hour the work would begin. He came slouching along, with his old faded blue jersey rolled up around his waist, and his woollen cap cocked over his eyes to keep out the slanting rays of the late sun.

"Good-day to you, Eben," I called out. His name was Ebenezer, but everybody called him Eben. "Are you going to take up the nets this afternoon, or it is too calm?"

The old fellow—not so very old, but weather-beaten into an appearance that might mean any age from forty to sixty—pursed up his dry lips and looked out over the water. The yellow sail of the fishing-boat yonder had swelled out; there was a little breeze getting up.

"We might put out," he said, "though it's touch and go if it'd be worth while. Do you want to go out?"

"Yes, I should like to go," said I. "It's a long while since I've been on the water."

Eben looked at me. I don't know if he saw anything in my face different from what used to be there, but he said, quite sympathetically, "Well, 'tis mopin' work being always on dry land."

I laughed. "I'd rather have the land than the sea all the year round," I said; "but I should like to taste the salt again."

"I've my shrimpin' to do," said he. "And we can't go afore the turn o' the tide, anyhow."

"All right," answered I. "I'll wait a bit."

"There won't be more than a handful of codling and p'r'aps a sole," declared the old man, doubtfully.

"Never mind," answered I.

"How's the old chap up at the farm?" said he, as he was moving off. One might have imagined that he meant Reuben, but I knew well enough that he meant father.

"Father's well," I said.

"He have got a bailiff to look after the place now, haven't he?" asked Eben. "Don't work very well, do it?"

"Why, yes; it works all right," said I.

I did not ask whether it was Reuben who had said it did not work, but of course I knew, and wondered what I could do to punish Reuben for it.

"He's a nice-spoken chap," added the man. "I've seed him about here many's the time, and he's always spoke civil to me. Ain't that him coming along now?"

I turned round sharply. Yes, walking along the beach towards us was Trayton Harrod. He too was taking a rest after his day's work. The glare on the shingle dazzled me so that I could not see him, for the sun was behind me, sinking towards the hill, and shone onto the face of the pebbles, making the long stretch of beach shine rosy gray. Was he coming towards us? No, most likely he had not recognized me talking to the fisherman. Should I go to meet him? I had the squire's message to deliver. But I thought I would not go. Of late there had come upon me a resolve to wait until he should seek me. Foolish and useless effort of pride! Was I even true to it? He turned across the beach back again to the road, but in the direction of the cliff.

"Well, I'll be back again in an hour or so, Eben," I said. "You'll know by that time whether you mean to go out or not."

He nodded, and shouldered the pole of his big square net. I stood and watched him wade into the water. But when he had distanced me by some couple of hundred yards, plodding through the rippling waves, and pushing the big square net in front of him, then I turned and crossed the shingle back to the short brown turf, where the rabbit-warrens are thick upon the uneven ground, and the blue bugloss and sea-gillyflower bloom sparsely upon the dry soil.

I had suddenly resolved to use up the spare hour in a sharp walk to the cliffs. I did not know, or did not confess to myself, that I had any special object in view in coming to this determination; but I think my heart beat a little as I walked, wondering whether some one else was advancing in the same direction behind me. I walked without turning, however, till I came to certain pools in the beach that tides no longer reach—pools housed behind banks of shingle, and scarcely even remembering the sea their mother; quiet havens where rushes grow and moor-hen make their nests, and the stately purple heron comes for his meal at dawn and sunset.

One flew across from trees inland, obliquely, slowly sailing, just as I reached the last of these seeming remnants of a primitive world, and stood bathing his feet on the shallow lip, erect and imposing, the only inhabitant fitted to the spot. He did not see me nor move, even though I stooped down as I neared him to pluck a bunch of the yellow sea-poppies that bloomed amid the very pebbles.

The beach stretched blue now in front of me as I raised my head, for the sun was before me—nearing the edge of the hill; I looked back along the way, that was pink, but Trayton Harrod was not in sight, and with something that was very like disappointment at my heart, I went on again, following the dike, that now ran not far from the shore, until I came to where it widens into a channel between a greensward on one side and the high ridge of shingle on the other. Its end is in a deep pool sheltered beneath the hood of a gray cliff—a cliff adorned at its base with the blackberry and ash, and whitening at its top into the chalk that here begins to give its glistening frontal to the gales of the turbulent sea.

Upon a bank of bracken that September promised to gild with amber, I sat down to rest. Poor foolish child! How faint was my heart when my hope was vain—how wild when I saw it fulfilled! For he came at last, leisurely, reading as he came.

I had not been mistaken: for him too this was a favorite spot, this corner forsaken of the world, but loved all the more of the sleepy marsh and of the sleepless sea, of the raging winds of heaven and of the tender summer sunshine.

"Why, Miss Margaret!" said he, as he came up, with something of surprise, but also—ah yes—something of pleasure, in his tone. "Fancy finding you such a long way from home!"

"Oh, I often come here," I said. "It is but a step."

I was longing to remind him that it was but just yonder on the marsh that I had met him for the first time, but I could not. "What is that?" I asked, abruptly, instead, as a bird flew out of one of the caves that the sea once filled, and hovered over our heads. It hung there some forty feet aloft, winnowing the air gently; then fell like a stone upon the field. "A hawk, I call it," added I; "but I know you have some strange name for it."

When we were together we went back naturally, I think, with one accord to our little altercations about the names and manners of beasts and birds; it was on such little things that the first good beginning of our friendship had been built. It set me at my ease that day.

"It's a kestrel, not a sparrow-hawk," said Harrod. "It's a pity keepers ever mistake them. The kestrels are useful birds. They kill mice. That was a mouse it got now."

"What is your name for it?" I repeated.

"Windhover," he answered.

"Ah yes, it's a pretty name," I said.

And we went on discussing the habitations of the bird, and how it loved to dwell in old buildings; and as we talked we climbed the flight of rough steps, hewn, winding up the face of the rock, and stood on the bald top, with the wind fresh in our faces and nothing but sea, sea all around, in the midst of which we almost seemed to stand as on an island. The little struggle with the breeze did me good, and the familiar way in which he went from one subject to another of our every-day interests put stormier thoughts for a moment out of sight.

As we walked back along the beach—colorless now that the sun had sunk, with the silvery curves of the gull's white wings bright upon the blue waters—the sympathy that he sought from me once more, as of old, upon the things of his ambition, the daily and engrossing interest of his work, all made me happy again, as I had not been happy for many a day, and I think that for the moment I scarcely thought of anything better than that this sympathy should go on like that forever.

A flight of starlings, beginning with companies of fifties, till, as day waned, the army counted thousands, blackened the sky. Flying towards us, with wings perpendicular and wide-spread, they were a dark cloud high in the air; but presently, as though by silent command, they changed their course, and in the twinkling of an eye the cloud became a mere patch of faint gray upon the sky, although the birds were still as close to us as before; they had but altered the poise of their bodies, and the wings, presented horizontally, made only little lines where before they had been black blotches. But once more they varied their flight, the sky darkened again, the compact mass became a long, sweeping curve that, with one great rush and rustle, descended across the belt of trees that clothe the Manor cliff above the marsh, and with a roar of wings and a very Babel of chirping that was like the noise of a mountain torrent, they buried themselves completely out of sight in the bank of tall reeds and bulrushes that here clothe the dike-banks.

"It's a parliament," said Harrod. "Now, I wonder what they have got to talk about. If the truth were ever known, I dare say they know more about co-operation than we do."

He laughed, and so did I.

"You see I've got co-operation on the brain, Miss Margaret," he said. "I've set my heart upon making your father see what an advantage it would be for the farmers."

"I thought that was one of his own favorite things," said I.

"I'm afraid that's not exactly the sort I mean," replied he. "He means co-operation between laborers or artisans to thwart their employers—or at least to get on without them. I mean co-operation between land-owners to keep their goods up to the prices that will repay them for their outlay."

"Oh, I'm afraid that is a very different thing," murmured I. I felt in my bones that father would never take part in it.

"Yes, I know," he answered. "But I want to see the squire about it. I hope to bring him round to my views. I am to meet him to-night." He looked at his watch. We had not noticed how the twilight was falling.

"Well, you hurry on and meet the squire," said I, just a trifle nettled at the way he said it. "*I'm* going out in the boat with old Eben."

"That'll make you very late," said Harrod.

"I mean to go," said I, obstinately.

He looked at me and smiled, shaking his head a little, reprovingly. The smile made me forget everything.

"Won't you put the squire off a little to come out with me?" I begged, wistfully. "It's so beautiful on the sea."

He hesitated a moment, and I ran down to the shore, where old Eben was waiting for me. But before I had reached it I heard Harrod's firm, light step following me.

"Is this the right time to take up nets?" he asked of the fisherman.

"Women always thinks it's the right time to do a thing when they wants it," said Eben. "But I've knowed missie a little one," he added, stolidly.

He was going to call his "mate" for the other boat, two being necessary to do what they called the "seining"—that is to say, the drawing in of the net from opposite angles—but Harrod stopped him.

"I'll go out in one boat with the young lady, if you'll take the other," he said.

My heart grew big. Eben asked him if he knew anything about the work, very doubtful as to the competency of a mere pleasure-seeker, but suddenly his face lit up.

He looked from me to Harrod.

"It works all right, eh?" he asked of me.

I thought he had lost his wits, until suddenly it occurred to me that those were the words I had used when he had suggested that the new bailiff did not "work well" at the farm. What did he mean? I think I grew red as I jumped into the boat, and was glad that it was so dark that nobody could see me—for the twilight was dying fast, and the stars were coming out faintly. It was cold on the water after the hot day. Harrod rowed, and once, as before, he took a warm garment and wrapped it about my shoulders; this time it was his own coat.

We sat there a long hour, throwing pebbles at the net to make the fish sink down in it, and rowing hither and thither to gather it in. Now that he was at it, Harrod was keen upon the sport; I think he was always keen upon all sport. But eager as I had been a while ago to see the fish brought in once more, I was not a bit eager now; though the "take" was not a good one, I was not a bit disappointed.

The stars shone brighter every moment as the sky grew darker; they shone calmly. I looked up at the vault—deep and blue, with the perfect blue of a summer's night, and studded over so thick and bright with those thousands of wonderfully piercing eyes. Half an hour ago I had thought I wanted no more than that quiet sympathy of friendship—but now, did I want no more? I scarcely knew myself.

But the stars shone calmly. They shone as we crossed the solitary marsh and roused the timid night-jar upon the road-side. He uttered his weird and plaintive note like the speechless cry of some sorrowing soul, and fluttered away in short little flights along the path-way till he reached the dark wood under the cliff; and there he hid himself from our sight, still sending his mournful appeal at intervals through the darkness.

No wonder that the country-folk hold the bird in horror, and still imagine that its presence in the neighborhood of any dwelling is an omen of coming death or misfortune. One could fit the cry with words if one would, so far is it from the senseless utterance of a senseless creature, so near to the pathetic appeal of a human soul.

But the stars shone, and not even mother's just upbraiding, nor a certain silent surprise on my sister's countenance, which troubled me far more, could take away from me the good hours which had been mine, could make the stars stop shining in the great fathomless blue.

CHAPTER XXXI

A week or more had passed by since the night when I had drawn the nets. It was the first of September, and my birthday. I was nineteen years old. A hot, fair day; all the cloudiness and rain of a fortnight since forgotten in bright sunshine and in the scent of the roses, that were making their second bloom.

I was hardly up in the morning before Joyce brought me a little gift which she had been busy preparing for me; it was a handkerchief that she had embroidered for me herself. It must have cost her all her leisure. I had often laughed at her, telling her that a piece of needle-work was far more beautiful to her than all the lovely things that God had made in the world; but that day I wondered why it was that Joyce loved to work a handkerchief for me when I had never cared to sit long enough in-doors to do such a thing for her in all my life. I turned and kissed her. I hoped she did not see that there was a tear in my eye. I turned away very quickly so that she should not do so; but I know that there was one.

Father and mother gave me a black silk dress. It was a sign that I was now quite grown up, and I think I appreciated it more on that account than for its own particular value; certain ideas about "looking nice" were slowly beginning to develop in me, but they were not altogether associated with a black silk dress, although indeed this was a very good one, soft and rich, as much like mother's own old-fashioned one as could be obtained in those more modern days.

Deborah too had her little gift for me, although with a comment upon the absurdity of such things; and even Reuben found a word to say on the subject. Ah me, why was I not contented, as I had always been contented before, with these tender signs of the quiet affection which had filled my life up till now? When father gave me one of his rare kisses before the others came in to dinner, and bade me be a good girl and a happy one, I was ashamed to think that there was anything else in the world that I wanted besides his love and care.

We sat down rather silent to the meal. Even though it was my birthday, nobody was in good spirits. Father had ridden up to "The Elms" that morning, and I suppose he was tired; he was often tired with a very slight exertion nowadays. And the weather was hot. Mother declared that the weather was so hot that her marrow-bone was melted to a pulp. She never could abide the hot weather, and always had the strongest figures of speech ready to hand to express its effect upon her.

"I should think it'll kill off all the old folk in the village," said she.

"Oh no, mother," I laughed; "it's the frost kills off old folk. This will do them good. It ought to do little David Jarrett good too."

Father shook his head sadly. "Mother, I want you to send the poor little lad some more broth," said he. "I've been round to see him this morning. He won't be long for this world, and while he's in it I want him to have all that his own mother ought to get him and don't."

Mother promised to take him the broth herself, and then she asked, what I had been dying to ask ever since father had come in, whether he knew when the bailiff was expected back from London, whither he had gone on farm business some three days ago.

"Dorcas expected him home to-day," said father; "but she didn't know what time."

"Well, I shall be right glad to see him," declared mother. "I don't believe he's been near the place this week past; and as for the squire, why, I can't but think there must something have happened to him."

"Nonsense, Mary; what should the squire want to come for, save now and then for friendship?" said father. "He hasn't got work upon the place, and I'm sure we're not such good company all the year round as to tempt folk to come here to do nothing. We're working men and women, and have no time for talk."

Mother laughed. "Well, Laban, I have seen you get time to talk over some things," said she. "It's natural, I'm sure. And when it's the Rev. Mr. Morland, that knows something about doing good, I'm pleased myself. Not but what you used to have many a nice chat with the squire too, times ago, before you got so set upon other things."

This was all a hit at Frank, I knew; but father did not answer. He tapped his fingers impatiently on the table-cloth, waiting for his helping of pudding, and at that moment a dark figure passed across the lawn to the porch, and my heart went thump upon my side as mother declared gladly that it was Mr. Trayton Harrod, and bade Joyce go bid him welcome.

"Now, Laban," said she, "you won't go and be tetchy with the man, will you? He has done you a world of good with the farm, and you might be beholden to him for it, instead of being so worriting as you have been of late."

Whether father was "tetchy" or not I never knew. It was my place to leave him alone with his bailiff when they had to talk business; and, moreover, I did not want to meet him there among so many; I had a craving for just one quiet word.

I went and sat outside on the lawn, just under the big square window-seat of the dwelling-room. There was a seat there in the shade, and I took a book and waited. I heard the voices of the two men inside rising and falling in eager discussion; then mother's voice in gentle remonstrance, for she had not left the room when Joyce and I did, and a moment later I heard father pass out, still talking, and Harrod after him. Mother came to the window and opened it wide just above where I was sitting, and then went out also; the room was empty.

I fell to wondering how it was that men who all seemed to me good and admirable could differ so very materially; father, the squire, Trayton Harrod—all good in their own way, and none agreeing; father's warmest welcome for a new-comer, who did not really give him what the others did.

Yes, I felt *that*, although I recognized Frank Forrester's fascination, and declared to myself that he had fascinated, and always would fascinate, my sister Joyce.

She came into the room above my head just as I made this reflection. She was singing to herself. I wondered how it was that she could sing. If she really loved Frank, could she sing like that now that he was away, that she could never see him, never have any news of him? If she really loved Frank? Something that was like an iron hand seemed to grip my heart and turn me sick. Could I have sat there singing to myself when the man I loved was far away? No, I knew that I could not. Even now, I felt as though I should never sing again; never sing again as I had sung that bright May morning when I had raced along the dike with Taff, before I had ever met Trayton Harrod. Yet he was here, within hail; the word that I wanted of him might be spoken any day. Even a week ago, on the sea, under the stars, had it not been near to being spoken?

I was not unhappy, but I could not have sung as Joyce was singing. I kept quite still under the window; I did not want her to know I was there, I did not want to speak to her, I wanted to think.

Involuntarily there came to my mind that time on the cliff, the night before she went away to Sydenham, when I had told her that she was overrating her own strength—that she would never be able to live without Frank. I had not met Trayton Harrod then, but now I knew that what I had said was true: "When a girl loves a man she wants him every minute of her life, and something goes wrong in her heart all the time that she is parted from him."

It would be true for me, but was it true for Joyce? Was it only that we were different?

I sat still and Joyce went on singing. She was singing "Annie Laurie"—one of the songs that I used to please father and the squire with when the long winter evenings made time.

But suddenly she stopped. Some one had come into the room; it was Harrod. I knew it before he spoke. And he did not speak for a long while, for such a long while that I wondered.

"You're not looking well, Miss Maliphant," he said at last. "The heat tells on you."

"Oh, indeed," answered she, in a low voice, "I'm quite well. I never have such a color as Margaret has, you know."

"But I think you work too hard in the house. You don't get out-doors enough."

She laughed a little shy laugh.

"I like working," said she. "I'm not so fond of out-doors as Meg is."

He said no more, and presently I heard the rustle of brown paper. I had noticed when I met him in the hall that he had a small parcel in his hand.

"How did you like London?" asked Joyce. "It must have been very hot there."

"It was," replied he. "I didn't like it at all. I'm heartily glad to get back. But I found a minute to run up to Regent Street to look at those shops you told me of. I bought this. I want your opinion on it."

I wondered what it was. A smothered exclamation came from Joyce.

"You like it," asked he, in a pleased tone.

"Oh yes, I think it's lovely," answered she, "lovely!" I had never known Joyce so enthusiastic over anything.

"Well, Miss Maliphant, will you—" he began, and then he stopped.

I raised myself a little on the seat lest I should miss the words. But no words came; and then suddenly it struck me that I was playing a mean part, listening here to what was not meant for my ears, and I rose, rustling the leaves of the shrubs as I went by. Even then there was no sign from those two within the room. What ailed the man? He was not wont to be so awkward. And I felt that Joyce was blushing; it made me furious. I moved on, meaning to go in, but the next words arrested me.

"At least," said Joyce, "I think it would be lovely for a lady to wear in town."

Then it was some article of dress.

"I see you don't really admire it," replied Harrod, in a disappointed voice. "I was afraid I shouldn't know how to choose such a thing properly. I'm sorry. I was thinking—" He made a long pause, and then he added, abruptly, almost savagely: "Well, I was thinking of offering it to your sister. I hear it is her birthday."

A blush crept over my cheek, even out there where there was no one to see me. But I could not have told whether I was pleased or not.

"Oh, do, do please give it to her, then," cried my sister, eagerly. "I'm sure she'll be pleased. I'm sure she would like to have it. Don't think of what I said."

She was quite distressed. Why was she so much distressed over it?

"I don't think it's really worth giving to any one," said he, with a laugh; and then he said something quite commonplace, I forget what, and I heard him throw down the parcel and go out of the room.

What did it mean? His behavior was scarcely even polite. I waited a minute, wondering; I thought I heard a little sob through the window. I hastened in-doors and into the parlor. Yes, Joyce turned away hastily as I came in, and I could see that she dried her eyes furtively; she had been crying.

"Whatever is the matter, Joyce?" cried I, I'm afraid, crossly enough. She turned her face round to me smiling. I felt a throb of shame. Only that very morning tears of tenderness had come into my eyes, as I thought of the pleasure she had taken in sitting hours together to do fine embroidery for me when she might have been in the fields! But before I could say any more, and before she could answer, mother came in.

"Joyce," said she, "here's Mr. Hoad with his daughters, and father wants us to make 'em welcome to tea. I'm sure we're not fit to make any one welcome to-day—the butter coming so bad, and all the ironing to do, and the best-parlor not turned out this week past. But whatever father says is right, of course, so I suppose they must stay."

Joyce looked up with her patient, gentle eyes.

"Of course we will make them welcome," said she. "I'll set the drawing-room straight." And she and mother went out together to see to the washing of the best teacups, and the uncovering of the best furniture.

I had not said a word. Mother and Joyce no doubt found it natural enough that I should not speak, for they both knew my aversion to the Hoad family. But at that moment I was not thinking of the Hoads. I was thinking of nothing but Joyce and Harrod, and the parcel which still lay on the table. Mother had not noticed it.

As soon as she and my sister were gone out, I darted towards it and opened it. Had he not said that it was meant for me?

It contained a delicate rose-colored silk shawl, strewn with little white flowers, and finished with long fringes—a soft, quaint garment that reminded one of one's grandmothers even then, and was choice and dainty enough for the sprucest of them.

It was perfectly suited to Joyce, who always had something of the air of an old picture; but to me—commonplace, workaday me, with my red hair—how could he have thought of such a thing?

I held it in my hand a long time, looking at it and wondering. It was not that I was surprised that he should give me a present; to tell the truth, I had looked for a present from him, but I had thought it would be a book—a book like one of those in his father's old library that I had so much envied. How was it that he had chosen a thing so unsuited to me, and so well suited to Joyce?

I was still standing there, with the soft, pretty folds crushed up in my hand, when the door opened suddenly and Trayton Harrod stood on the threshold. I had no time to put the shawl away; I remained there with it in my hand—awkwardly. And he did not say a word to help me out of the difficult position; he only looked at me in a morose sort of fashion. I was obliged to make the best of it.

"I beg your pardon," I stammered; "but Joyce said—that is to say—" I stopped, blushing furiously. I had meant to be quite frank, and to confess that I had overheard the conversation, but my courage failed in his sight.

He did not speak, and I felt very foolish. Why did he stand there, silent, with that frown upon his wide brow, that frown that never used to be there!

"It's a very beautiful shawl," I said, timidly, "and it would look lovely, I am sure, upon some grand lady who drives in her own carriage."

"Yes," said he, speaking at last; "things aren't pretty if they don't suit."

"Well, of course, finery is *not* in our line; at least not in—in my line," I stammered.

I added the last words so low that I don't think he heard them. He almost snatched it out of my hand.

"No, thank Heaven, it's not," he answered. "So we'll say no more about it."

But when he took it from me, there came over me a wild, foolish longing to have the thing. What at another time I should have laughed at possessing, I wanted now more than all the books that I had envied, more than any other gift in the world. And it belonged to me; he meant it for me, it was mine and I would not part with it.

"Oh, please, please, Mr. Harrod," I cried, "don't misunderstand me. I am very much obliged to you for having thought of my birthday. I like it very much indeed. I—thank you with all my heart."

I stretched out my hand for it again, but he only looked at me. I fancied there was a sort of surprise in his gaze.

"Of course, of course," he murmured at last, as if he were pulling himself together. "I'm afraid it will be of no use to you, Miss Margaret, as you say it is not a suitable gift; but if you will take it, of course you are welcome."

I took it; but a chill fell upon my heart.

"You did not remember my commission when you were in London, Mr. Harrod?" I asked, with, I am afraid, something of bitterness in my voice.

"No," he answered, quickly. "Did you give me a commission? I'm very sorry if I forgot any wish of yours."

"A commission to buy me some of those books that you have in your library," I said.

I saw him bite his lip as though vexed. Perhaps he *was* vexed to think that he had forgotten something which might have given me pleasure. But if he was, he was too proud to confess it.

"Oh, that was no commission," he said, with a little cold laugh. "You know I would not take it. I told you I was not the person for such a job. I advised you to ask Squire Broderick."

I tossed my head. "Yes, and I think I answered you that the squire was no such friend of mine that I should ask favors of him," I replied, hotly. My temper was rising, but luckily he had more self-control than I had; he saved me from making an exhibition of myself.

"I ought not to have forgotten any request of yours," said he. "I'm sorry. If you'll give me the names of the books you want, I'll write to-night."

I thanked him, but I said I did not know the names of the books, which indeed was true enough; and we turned the talk round to every-day things, until luckily some one came into the room.

But there was some one else who knew the names of books, and who, moreover, remembered that I cared about them. It was Squire Broderick. He came in that evening with a case of twelve little volumes of Shakespeare's complete works under his arm.

"I know you're very keen about reading, Miss Margaret," said he, with his sunny smile. "I've often thought of you trying to puzzle out Milton's 'Paradise Lost' up there on the old window-seat at 'The Elms.' But I think you'll find this easier reading than 'Paradise Lost,' and more amusing."

I blushed a fire-red, for they were all standing by: father, mother, and Joyce, and Trayton Harrod. I almost fancied that I saw a suspicion of a smile break round his mouth as the offering was made.

I am afraid that I scarcely even thanked the squire audibly for it. I can only hope that that fiery blush appealed to him somehow as a recognition of his kindness to me, and not as what it really was. Good Mr. Broderick! How far too good to me always! Even to this day it hurts me to think that perhaps I hurt him.

But something in the way father shook him by the hand, and something in his voice as he said, "Oh, Meg, it isn't every girl has such a kind and thoughtful friend," made up, a little, I hope, for my curtness, although indeed the squire went away as soon as he had given his gift, and with something in his face that was not quite like his usual cheeriness. I am afraid that neither father's warmth of manner nor mother's thanks, hearty as they were, were enough for him. Could he have been wishing that it had been Joyce's birthday, that the gift might have been made to her? For no one had been so enthusiastic as Joyce over my good-fortune.

"The very thing for you, dear," she had said, after the squire was gone, taking up the books and looking at them admiringly. "Isn't it, Mr. Harrod?"

Harrod agreed warmly that there was no doubt about their being the very thing for me, and every one declared that I was a very lucky girl. But no one knew anything about that pale pink shawl, with the white flowers, that had fallen into my hands in so strange a manner. I don't know why, but I kept that gift a secret from every one. And to this day it lies in the same folds, in the same piece of gray-blue paper in which it was originally given me.

Did I think myself a very lucky girl?

CHAPTER XXXII

Frank Forrester did not come down to Marshlands for the elections. He did not come, but he was very near coming.

I met Mary Thorne and the Hoad girls out canvassing two days before. Mary would have passed me with a nod, but Jessie Hoad had something to say.

"I don't think it's at all nice of your father not to let you help us canvass for Mr. Thorne, Margaret Maliphant," said she, tartly. "Father says he can't make it out at all. He always understood that Mr. Maliphant would support the Radical cause, and now that for the first time they have got a candidate who has some chance of getting in, he won't have anything to do with him."

"I suppose my father knows what he is about," answered I, proudly.

"Does he?" retorted she. "It's more than any one else knows, then."

I bit my tongue in my efforts to keep it from saying something rude, yet I am afraid the tone was not quite conciliatory in which I retaliated. "His friends seem to know well enough to trust him! You've only got to ask the people round about to hear whose advice they would soonest follow on the country-side."

It was true, but I should not have said it.

Jessie turned to Mary Thorne. "We ought to have her with us," said she. "The funny thing is she's right enough. The laborers hereabouts do look to Farmer Maliphant in the most extraordinary way. He don't hold any meetings, or work at the thing like other folk work. But there's the fact, and that's why it's so aggravating of the man to hold aloof. What does he do it for, eh, my dear?" asked she, looking at me again.

"I don't know," I said, sullenly; "I'm not clever enough to understand father's motives. I only know that he says that Parliament's no good."

Jessie was going to retaliate, but the other stopped her.

"Come, don't bother any more about it, Jessie," said she, with the frank, good-natured smile that had always drawn me towards her, in spite of my father. "We're not going to get Farmer Maliphant's vote nor his support either, and what's the good of going on at it?"

"Oh, my dear, going on at it is the only way to get anything; and one doesn't like to be beaten without knowing the reason why. However, we shall have some one down to-night who will make a finer speech at the meeting than ever Farmer Maliphant would have made, even if he had consented to give us a glimpse of those grand deep notions of his."

Mary Thorne laughed in a sort of self-conscious way; I wondered why.

"Who is coming to speak at the meeting?" I asked.

"Why, Squire Broderick's nephew, Captain Forrester, to be sure," laughed Miss Hoad. "He'll make an effect on the people, I'll be bound. So fascinating and so handsome. I've never heard him speak, but father says he's awfully enthusiastic, and all that kind of thing."

I felt myself grow red or pale, I don't know which. I had wanted him to come, but I had not thought it would be in that way. Yet it was what I should have known must happen if Frank came down to the elections at all.

"I'm sure he will make a splendid speech," said Mary Thorne, with a sort of pride. "I told father it would be everything if we could get him to come down."

"He has been a long while making up his mind," said Jessie.

"Well, it is awkward for him, you see," said the other. "He naturally doesn't care to go against his uncle."

"It's worse to go against one's principles," declared Jessie, loftily.

"I quite understand it," declared Mary, loyally. "He mightn't mind it if the squire weren't such a dear old fellow, but it is awkward, and I consider it a great mark of friendship that he should do it for us."

"Is he going to stay at the Manor or at the Priory?" I put in, bluntly.

"Oh, at the Priory with us, of course," replied she. "And I must send the carriage for him in an hour. So, please, we must get on, Jessie, or I shall never be home in time."

She held out her hand to me, and of course I took it, as I took also Jessie Hoad's when she offered it, but I was not comfortable.

Why was Frank always going to stay at the Priory now, and why was he willing to risk hurting his uncle's feelings solely for the sake of doing an act of friendship to the Thornes? I could not understand it, any more than I could understand why Mr. Hoad should be so extravagantly anxious that Thorne should succeed. Miss Jessie was not in the habit of troubling herself about things that, as she would have expressed it, "didn't pay"; yet here she was putting herself to all manner of inconvenience to go canvassing with Mary Thorne, while Mr. Hoad was scouring the county for votes and spending his evenings writing flaming articles for country papers, or making emphatic speeches at country meetings.

I might have thought about it more than I did if I had not had the more interesting matter of Frank's arrival to occupy me. Would father let us go to the meeting that we might hear Frank speak? Would mother let Joyce have a word with him? How were they to meet, and most important of all, how would Joyce behave towards him? I flew home to tell her, but she was not in the house. Deb did not know where she was.

Deb only gave vent to a loud fit of laughter when I told her that Captain Forrester was coming down to speak at the meeting, and that I wanted to give my sister the news. She made me angry—it was no good speaking to Deb. I caught up my hat again, and rushed off, seized with a sudden inspiration to take a walk that evening and find myself at the station at the time that Frank Forrester would arrive. In common civility he could not do less than offer me a lift up in the carriage which would have been sent to meet him; and anyhow, I could not fail to get a few words with him.

Yes, I would talk to him of Joyce; I would tell him that her manner was deceptive; I would tell him how reserved we all were; how different to himself; how rarely we showed what we really felt; I would tell him that her cold manner the day when I had taken him to the Grange was but from her desire to be loyal to the promise she had sworn our parents, that in truth she loved him; I would tell him how changed she was—for indeed it was true. I would try and not be shy; I would try and give him fresh heart.

I sped away over the downs and along the hill, Taff following me uninvited. It was a long way to the station, and I was afraid of missing the train. Ah, I had missed it! Just as I was crossing the last strip of level road before reaching the rails, I saw the Priory carriage bowling towards me on its return journey. "What a pity!" said I to myself. But it came near and nearer, and at every bit that shortened the distance between us I became more and more sure that Frank was not in it; there was only one person, and that person was Mary Thorne.

She stopped the carriage as she saw me. Her face was very pale, and I saw that she held the yellow envelope of a telegram in her hand.

"Oh, Miss Maliphant, do you think it would really be quite impossible to persuade your father to address the meeting for us to-night?" she said, hurriedly. "We are disappointed of Captain Forrester, who was to have spoken." Her lip trembled a little.

"I hope he's not ill?" I said.

She did not answer at once.

"I hope nothing has happened to him?" I repeated.

I saw her fingers close tightly over the yellow envelope until they were quite white.

"Yes," she said, slowly. "He was riding in a steeple-chase not far from here; he has been thrown. They say—" Her lip trembled again. She could not go on.

"But he's not much hurt, not badly hurt?" I cried, in a fury of anxiety. "Do speak!"

She looked at me sadly, but a little surprised; and no wonder. I did not know how loud or how eagerly I had spoken till I saw the coachman look round.

"Father is so fond of him," I said. "I should be so sorry if he were hurt."

"They say only slightly injured; no cause for alarm," she answered. "But one never knows."

She turned away her head. I knew very well that she was crying. I ought to have been sorry; I was only angry.

"Oh, I dare say it's a mere excuse," I said, ill-naturedly. "Men are so clever at excuses. He has got scratched just enough to say so. He didn't want to come."

She turned round. Her eyes were dry again. But she must, indeed, have been a good-natured girl, for there was no trace of anger in her face.

"You don't know him; that's not his way," she said, quietly. And then she added, "You'll try and persuade your father, won't you?"

"I'll give him your message," I answered. "But I know perfectly well he won't speak."

"Well, then, we must do the best we can without him," she said. "It's too late to get any one else. I must get home quickly. Good-night."

She drove on and left me standing in the road. Another time I might have thought it rude of her; but then I noticed nothing, I thought of nothing, just as she, probably, thought of nothing, but that Frank Forrester was hurt. And for my own part, I thought of nothing so much as that Joyce would—*must be*—heart-broken.

Taff, seeing me standing there as though turned to stone, leaped upon me, barking. I took no notice of him, but he roused me, and I tore up the hill as fast as I could to carry my grewsome message. Instinctively, I felt that this, at last, must rouse my sister to show her true feelings, and if there were a mask on her face, that this at last must strip it off.

I did not want to see Deborah, and I did not stop to go in by the front door. I climbed the hedge and crossed the lawn to the parlor window. Through the tangle of traveller's-joy and frail old-fashioned jasmine that framed it around, I looked into the room. Father and Trayton Harrod sat by the fireless hearth smoking their pipes, and at the table was Joyce, with the inevitable basket of family darning; her profile was turned towards me, listening intently, with eyelids raised and needle poised idle in her hand, to something the bailiff was saying.

What was there in anything there to vex and sour and wound me? Yet I went in hastily, letting the door slam behind me.

"Good gracious me! Fancy sitting in-doors this lovely fine evening!" said I. "We sha'n't have so many more of them that we need waste one. The summer is nearly over."

"Why, what's the matter, Meg?" asked father. "Let folk please themselves, child."

"Oh, dear, yes; they can please themselves," I answered.

"Is that all you came in-doors to say?" laughed he again.

Harrod was busy filling his pipe, ramming in the tobacco with a stern hand, while Joyce bent forward again over her work.

"No," answered I, promptly. "I came with a message for you, father, from Miss Thorne. She wants you to oblige her by speaking at the Radical meeting to-night."

A cloud gathered on father's brow. "Speak at the Radical meeting!" echoed he. "What ails the girl to make such a request, or you, Meg, to bring it? You know very well I shall speak at no meeting."

"I told her so," said I, curtly; "but she would not take my word."

"This is some of Hoad's work," he said, excitedly. "Why can't the man understand that he won't bully me into doing what I don't intend to do? I don't intend to support James Thorne. I don't consider James Thorne an honest man. Why can't he leave off worrying?"

This speech was not at all like father. There was an amount of irritability, almost of pettiness, in it, which was quite foreign to him; and his saying that Hoad couldn't "bully" him into anything struck me as odd even then, though the more weighty matter that was in my mind made me chiefly impatient to hear my own voice.

"Well, it isn't Mr. Hoad this time, father," said I, hastily. "I'm sure he knew nothing about it. Captain Forrester was to have spoken."

Joyce did not raise her head, but I saw a little frown trouble her smooth brow.

"Forrester!" echoed father. "No, no! You're mistaken, child. I should be disappointed, grievously disappointed," he added, tapping the fingers of one hand on the knuckles of the other, "to think he should be led astray to throw himself in with that lot. Are you quite sure of it, Meg?"

"I am quite sure he *was* going to speak," said I; "but—"

"Ah, I'm sorry, I'm very sorry," repeated father. "But he's young— easily misled. I must have a talk with him. I didn't know the lad was in these parts."

"He's not," said I. "He was to have come, but he has had an accident; he has been thrown from his horse in a steeple-chase."

"God bless my soul!" cried father, starting up from his chair. "Why didn't you say so? Not killed?"

My eyes were on Joyce's face. She had looked up anxiously, but she had not changed color one bit.

"No, not killed," answered I, slowly; "but I don't know how badly hurt. The telegram didn't say."

"Poor lad, poor lad! murmured father, concernedly, as he sat down again. But still Joyce did not speak. She looked serious and distressed, and a faint pink flush had deepened on her cheek, but there was no horror in her eyes.

"Men shouldn't ride in steeple-chases," said Harrod. "It's the most dangerous of all riding—and only for amusement, after all."

"I should have thought Captain Forrester was such a splendid rider that he could have managed any horse," said Joyce.

"Oh, it's not always a matter of mere management in a steeple-chase," said Harrod. And I do believe my sister was actually opening her mouth to reply to him, when I said, sharply, "Joyce, mother wants you," and by that means got her out of the room.

"Poor lad!" I heard the old voice murmur again as I closed the door.

"Father's sorry," said I, as I turned round and faced my sister.

"Yes," said she; "of course. Who could help being sorry?"

"Some folk seem to be able to help it very well," laughed I. "*I* couldn't have sat there discussing with another man how my lover had nearly come by his death! At least I can scarcely fancy that I could. Of course I'm not engaged to be married to anybody, so perhaps I don't know how I should feel."

Joyce looked at me aghast. "Good gracious, Meg!" said she, in a half-frightened whisper, "what is the matter?"

I suppose my face had told her something of what I was feeling; I suppose it had become white, and the gray eyes were black in it, as father used to declare they were wont to become when I was angry.

"The matter?" cried I. "Oh, there's nothing the matter. Only I was a little surprised to see how coolly you took the news of Frank's accident."

"Why, what was I to say?" said she. "I am very sorry, and I sincerely trust that it is nothing serious."

"Well," answered I, scornfully, "I should think you would feel as much as that if Joe Millet had been run away with by the old dray-horse, or even if Luck were to have a fit. I'm sure I should. I was afraid you would be very unhappy when I brought you that bad piece of news. I was afraid you would be quite upset. I didn't know whether I ought to tell you before a stranger, but I needn't have troubled myself. You took it very well. Perhaps poor Frank would have been a little hurt to see how well you took it."

"I don't know what right you have to speak to me like that, Meg," said my sister, in a low voice. "How do you know what I feel? People aren't all alike. You take things very hard. You must have everything your own way, or else you fight and struggle. But I'm not like that. I believe that whatever happens is all for the best. Why can't you let me take things my own way?"

"Good gracious me!" cried I; "take them your own way by all means, only you might argue till you're black in the face, but you'll never get me to believe that it's all for the best whether the man one cares for breaks his neck or not."

"Oh, Meg, you know I didn't mean that," murmured Joyce, in a low, disheartened voice. The tears gathered over those clear blue eyes of hers, that were as untroubled waters whose transparent depths could be fathomed at a glance. There was never anything mysterious about my sister's eyes; they were simple as a little child's, but, unlike a child's, they had ceased to wonder.

The tears irritated me, but they made me ashamed of my unreasonable temper, and I said, quickly, with sudden change of mood: "Well, I'm a cross-patch of course; but you know it was enough to make anybody angry to see you sitting there so meek and patient when I knew you must be dying of anxiety. And all for nothing but to please two dear old people who have forgotten what it was to be young and eager. But you must write to Frank at once."

"He knows very well how sorry I am," said Joyce.

I think my face must have darkened again, for she added, almost humbly, "You know I never could write letters, and I had rather not vex mother."

"Then you'd rather let that poor fellow think you didn't care whether he was dead or alive than show mother you've got a mind and ten fingers of your own?" I cried.

"He must think what he likes," said Joyce, in her most quietly obstinate voice; "I don't want to write." And that was all I could get from her.

"Very well, *I'll* write, then," I said, with ill-concealed anger. "I like writing letters, and I am not afraid of mother."

I flew up-stairs; I did not dare trust myself to say another word, but on the first landing I looked down and saw her head upturned towards me. There was a pitiful look in the blue eyes.

"Don't think me heartless, Meg," she murmured.

"Oh no; I understand," said I, wearily. "I dare say you're quite right. I dare say it's much better not to take things too hard."

After all, she might be right. She had said, "How can you know what I feel?" And, indeed, how could I possibly know? "How could one ever know what anybody else felt?" I repeated once more, as if to convince myself of it; and I am afraid, I am sadly afraid, that my own voice broke a little. "I know I'm not always happy, and perhaps it's because I take things too hard."

CHAPTER XXXIII

Girls such as we were got little time for sentimental brooding, however, and though up-stairs in the little attic where Joyce and I had always slept, I threw myself on the bed and looked sadly out across the marsh with eyes that saw none of its plaintive placidity, mother soon waked me from day-dreams, and called me down-stairs to active employment that did its best to drive love and its torments from my mind.

The squire was ill; he had taken a bad cold out partridge-shooting, and mother was making him some of her special orange-jelly as a salve for his cough.

Those who were interested in the Conservative success at the elections were much concerned at the squire's illness just at this time; and Mr. Hoad, who had, it seems, been round that afternoon, had been heard to declare that it was all to "our" good that the squire should not have been able to hold forth at the rival meeting that evening.

But mother did not regard the matter in that light, and I believe she told Mr. Hoad so. I was not present; it had happened at the time I had been gone to the station, but according to Joyce, she had told him so very plainly. Mother, as I have often said, was as loyal to squire as if he had been her own son, and on this occasion so, I believe, was father also. Looking back to that time, I seem to remember the sort of rough stand-aloofness which had characterized father's attitude towards the squire, giving place of late to a curious sort of half-unwilling consideration and tenderness.

When mother called me from my bedroom to the kitchen, she was full of the squire's illness. "I hope it's nothing serious," she kept saying; "and that he won't go worrying himself any way about this accident to his nephew."

"Oh, you have heard about it, have you?" answered I. "Well, I don't see why the squire can't afford to worry a little about it, I'm sure. And I'm certain he does; anybody with any heart in them would." I said it bitterly, but I did not anger mother.

"Well, there, Margaret," she said, abruptly, "you know I never did like the young man, and I can't pretend to break my heart over this. I'm sorry he's come to harm, of course, but I can't help feeling glad Joyce takes it as she does. We can't expect her to forget all at once, but please God she *will* forget, and things perhaps be even as I hoped for."

"I can't think how you can suppose it would please God your daughter should be a fickle, shallow-hearted creature, I'm sure," said I, hotly.

"You and I never were of one mind over that matter, were we?" smiled mother, quite good-temperedly. "But the day'll come when perhaps you'll say I was right. You're but a child yet; you know nothing about such things saving what you've got out of books, and that ain't much like it. Perhaps you may come to know what it is yourself one day, and then you'll tell the difference between the real stuff and the make-believe."

A child! Was my waywardness, my impetuosity, my passionate longing only childishness? Now that I am a woman, I wonder whether mother was partly right in her simple intuition? Only partly: I did know something about "such things."

"I don't believe Joyce hasn't taken it to heart," said I, doggedly.

"Well, her eyes aren't so heavy as yours by a long way," answered mother. "I don't know what's come to *you* of late. You used not to be mopy. Nobody could say it of you whatever else they might say. You had your tantrums, and you always have been a dreadful one for wearing out your clothes, but mopy you were not. But I'm sure you fret more over this business than Joyce herself does. I've no patience with you. As for any work you do for me, I'd as soon have your room as your company. I like to see a body put her heart into whatever comes to hand, if it's only boiling a potato. You take my word for it, my girl, it's the only way to be happy."

The tears came into my eyes, for I knew very well that mother was right. I turned away that she should not see them, for I was ashamed of tears, but she did see them nevertheless.

"There, there," she added, kindly; "I don't want to rate you. Be a good girl, and look more like yourself again. Half-hearted ways won't bring anybody on; and as for your complexion, well, you used to have a skin that I could boast of. 'Red hair she may have,' I used to say, 'but look at her skin.' And now it's no better than curds and whey. Come, get the muslin and strain off that jelly."

I did as I was bid, but I'm afraid not with my whole heart. Had it come to that, that anybody could say of me, Margaret Maliphant, that I had taken to moping after anybody?

"You shall take it up to the Manor yourself and leave it with the house-keeper, as soon as it's set, in the morning," said mother, tasting the liquid to see that it had just enough flavoring in it. "You can say it's from an old friend, and then it won't hurt her feelings."

We finished the job and set it down to cool before we went in to tea. Joyce was there, with her hair smoothed and her face fresh, and I had red cheeks from stooping over the fire, and red eyes from something else that I would not remember. But I forced myself to look Harrod boldly in the face, asking what had become of father, and learning that they had been up to "The Elms" together, and that the walk had been too much for him.

"Mr. Maliphant will take things so hard," added the bailiff, and the words sounded sadly familiar to me.

Father came in presently and handed me a letter addressed to Frank.

"Take that up to the Manor presently, Meg," said he; "and get the address and ask for news."

"Margaret is going up in the morning with some jelly for the squire; I suppose that'll do," said mother. "I don't expect it's near so bad as it was made out. Those things are always worse in the telling, and these young beaus are just the ones to get a sorry tale abroad about themselves."

"Hush, hush, mother; that's not like your kind heart," said father, reproachfully; and mother laughed, and said she had meant no harm to him, and Joyce looked down on her plate uncomfortably.

But I heard nothing, and as soon as I had swallowed my meal I got up and went out. I recollect with what relief I welcomed Reuben on the terrace with his old dog, and began to talk of commonplace simple things. Feeling hurt me too much, and Reuben did not foster feeling.

"Dear old Luck," said I, stooping down to pat the dog, who looked up at me with tender eyes out of his dusky black and white face, and would have wagged his tail if there had been a long enough piece of it to wag. "I hope there has been no more talk of shooting you. We couldn't spare the sight of you about the farm."

"Nay," said Reuben, shaking his head; "when the dog goes, Reuben'll go too. No mistake about that. He's been my luck, and when they take him they take me."

"Ah, well, you aren't either of you going yet a while," said I, consolingly. "There's lots of life in you both."

"Ay, miss, ay," grinned the old man, well pleased. "We sent the sheep home last night, Luck and I; didn't we, old boy? Beale he have taken his sweetheart on a spree somewhere out Eastbourne way, and he asked me to see to the folding. I'm spry in the summer-time, and I was pleased enough. But I wouldn't have none o' them ondependable, skittish young uns. Not I."

"Whom do you mean?" I asked.

"Nay, I place no dependence on young things," repeated he, doggedly. "They're sure to have their eye on a bit of fun somewheres, and they be allays for trying new dodges. Now, Luck he's safe and he's sure. He's got sperience, Luck has. He knows."

He nodded his head to and fro with an air of profound wisdom, and I burst out laughing.

It did me good. I had not laughed that day.

"What? You mean the young sheep-dog, I suppose?" I said.

"Ay, miss," answered Reuben. "A 'andsome young chap enough, but ondependable." He paused, waiting for me to speak, but I saw whither he was drifting, and was silent. "There's others besides dogs as is ondependable!" he added, slowly. "Such as we durstn't understand the ways o' them that are learned. Nay, would we presume? But there's others as is ondependable. Poor master! But the Lord knows what is best for us all."

"Well, He is sending us glorious weather for the crops, anyway," said I, with determined cheerfulness. "It's quite too hot for me."

"Ay, so be it for the 'ops, miss," grinned the old man.

"I don't believe it," cried I.

He took me by the arm and led me forward to the edge of the cliff, whence we could see the marsh in its whole wide expanse. The day, as I had said, had been very hot, but the sun had set now—it was full seven o'clock, and the long twilight had begun her peaceful reign, exquisite in sober tints and fragrant coolness of silent air. The plain was slowly sinking into mystery, but silver-gray upon the bosom of the dikes, clearly defining their long, straight lines wherever they crossed the marsh; ribbons of white mist unrolled themselves in the dim light.

"They're thicker than that back yonder," said he, "where the 'op-gardens be."

"Well, what harm do the mists do?" laughed I. "The hops haven't got the rheumatics."

"Nay, miss, but the mists, this 'ot weather, and the scalding sun atop'll spoil 'em worse nor they'll 'arm my old bones. They'll be as brown as brushwood."

Reuben delivered this speech in a low tragic whisper, and with the most ominous of expressions, holding my arm the while.

"Oh, Reuben, you always were a gloomy creature," said I. "I believe you like making the worst of things."

"Nay, it's the Lord's doing," said Reuben, piously; "but if he had a-planted Early Perlifics they would ha' been all safe and garnered by now."

"Well, it isn't you that'll be afflicted if the hops fail, Reuben," said I, tartly, "so you needn't be so pious and resigned over it;" and with that I walked off back into the house.

What Reuben had said had set me thinking. I wondered whether it was neither altogether distress at Frank's accident, nor fatigue from the walk, that had made father depressed at tea-time. He was not in the dwelling-room, neither was mother. There were papers strewn over the table, and an inkstand with pen aslant across it stood in the midst. The papers were evidently accounts, and somebody had been working at them.

I supposed it might be Trayton Harrod, for he was still there, contrary to his wont; but he was not seated at the table. He was standing up before the big, empty fireplace, and in one of the deep spindle-railed chairs at the side sat my sister Joyce. I fancied that he moved a little as I came in, but I was not sure.

"Where's father?" asked I, sharply.

I looked at Joyce, but she did not reply.

"Your father is in the study, I believe," said Harrod. "He was here doing some work with me, and did not feel so very well. I believe your mother is with him."

"Oh, I suppose the news of Captain Forrester's accident upset him," said I. "He is so very fond of him."

There was silence. The fact of Joyce's not speaking somehow exasperated me.

"Do you think that was the reason, Joyce?" asked I.

"I don't know, I'm sure," she answered.

And when she spoke I saw why it was she had not spoken before: she had been crying.

"Dear me!" said I, half frightened. "Is he so bad as that?"

Again she did not answer; it was Harrod who replied for her. "No, no, Miss Margaret," he said; "I assure you it's nothing of consequence."

Margaret Maliphant | 287

Which did he mean? Father's illness, or Joyce's distress?

"I must go and see," said I. But I did not move. I was anxious about father, and yet I had not the courage to go and leave those two together. I stood looking at them. Joyce sat just where she had sat that cold spring evening not six months ago, when she had told me that Frank Forrester had asked her to marry him. She even sat forward and clasped her hands over her knees, as she had clasped them then; only there was no bright fire now in the hearth to illumine her golden hair; the hearth was empty, but there was a curious sense of gold in the twilight.

In the flash of a moment the scene came back to me; the strangeness of it; the absence of the glow of romance that I had dreamed of when I had first dreamed of romance for my beautiful sister. I had not guessed then that it was the lack of that golden glow that had chilled me. I had wanted it so; I had felt that, outwardly, everything was fitting for it to be so, and I had chosen to believe that it was so; but now I knew very well that it had never been so.

The fire was dead to-night, but the sense of the glow was there—too, too brightly.

"I must go and see about father," I repeated, in a kind of dull voice. I wondered to hear the sound of it myself.

"Don't *you* go, Meg," said Joyce. "I haven't washed up the tea-things yet, and Deb is busy. I must make haste. I'll look in as I go past."

Her voice had recovered its serenity, and she spoke brightly and sweetly. "Very well, I'll come, too, in a minute, and help you," answered I, going through the hollow pretence of looking for something that I didn't want.

She got up and glided across the room, and out of the door, with that soft way she had. Harrod had sat down again to the table and the papers.

"What's the matter with Joyce?" I asked, bluntly, almost before the door had closed.

He looked at me with those honest eyes of his. I could see that he scorned to make any pretence, any evasive answer.

"I have been speaking to her of something that distressed her," he said. "I should not have done it. I am sorry. I did not think it would have distressed her."

It was on the tip of my tongue to ask what it was. I don't know whether it was natural good-feeling and politeness that prevented me, or whether I simply dreaded the answer. I tried to think that the "something" related to

Frank Forrester's accident, but I did not ask. "I did not think it would have distressed her" might point to that explanation, as of course Harrod knew nothing of any relations between her and the captain. It might, but there was an undefined fear within me that it did not.

Harrod dropped his eyes again on the papers on the table, and took up the pen. An insane, wicked desire came upon me to hurt him for innocently hurting me.

"Mr. Harrod," said I, roughly, "Reuben has been talking to me outside. He thinks the hops are looking very badly."

He laid down the pen, and looked up, with an underlip that quivered a little.

"Reuben's opinion is not so infallible as I fancy you suppose, Miss Margaret," said he, trying to smile. "Your father has been round the property, and is, I fancy, quite as well able to judge of it as Reuben Ruck."

"Oh, did father think the hops looked well, then?" asked I.

I thought Harrod winced.

"Hops are a very difficult growth," he answered. "I don't suppose a perfect crop is gathered more than once in twenty years. A hundred chances are against it; your father knew this well enough when he went in for the speculation. He is a reasonable man."

I knew that this was intended as a reproof to me, and I knew that I deserved it. I had prided myself on being wise and calm over the business affairs of the farm, as I should have been if I had been father's son instead of his daughter; I had prided myself that Harrod considered me so by talking things over with me as he often had done. But of late I had not been reasonable. I knew it; I knew that I was straining the very cord that I most counted upon, perhaps even to breaking-point. I knew it, I could have bitten my tongue out, and yet my wounded feelings got the better of me and carried my tongue away. I stood there ashamed, sick at heart. I wanted to make it up, I wanted to be forgiven, but I did not know what to say.

And while I was thinking what to say, the door opened, and father and mother came in. Father's face was pale, and he walked uncertainly.

"There, there, that'll do, Mary," he said, testily. "I'm all right now. The weather is a bit oppressive, that's all. I want to finish this bit of business with Harrod, if you'll leave us quiet."

Mother knew better than to say a word. Father sat down in the chair which Harrod got up to give him, and mother and I went out of the room.

My chance of reconciliation that evening was over.

I had to listen to mother's very natural distress about father's fresh indisposition, and her expressions of annoyance at its having been brought on, as she supposed, by the piece of news about "that young good-for-nothing." Then I had the tea-things to wash up with Joyce, and the clean linen to put away. And when all our work was done Trayton Harrod had gone, and I went up into the little attic whence mother had called me in the early evening, and sat down again in the dark to have it out with myself about all the puzzling events of this puzzling day.

Joyce had not yet come up to bed; I was all alone. The twilight was dead; the stars shone above—thousands of stars looking down upon me with a story of courage and hope in their bright eyes—I wonder whether I understood it!

Deborah came in with a candle. She had forgotten to give us one. I was sorry she brought it.

"Lord bless my soul, Margaret, you startled me," said she. "Whatever are you doing? Why don't you get to bed?"

"Joyce hasn't come up yet," I said.

She put down the candle, and came up to me and took hold of me by the shoulders.

"You've been frettin'," said she, sharply, looking down into my eyes. "Now, whatever is that for?"

"How dare you say such a thing?" answered I, pulling myself away. "I've not been fretting. I've nothing to fret about."

"Well, I don't know as you have," answered she; "but you've been fretting for all that. I've seen it for weeks past. What's it for?"

She stood there above me, with her arms akimbo, and her keen, round, dark eyes fixed upon me. It never occurred to her that I was not going to tell her what it was for.

"You've been frettin'," repeated she. "And what call you have to fret because Joyce's beau goes and falls off his horse is more than I can understand."

"I tell you I'm not fretting," repeated I, emphatically. "Of course what should it matter to me? I was surprised that Joyce took it so coolly. Some folk are so quiet. I suppose they feel just the same, but I'm sure you'd never know it. It's a mercy for them they don't make so much noise."

"Oh, that's where it is," said Deb, sagely, as if she had guessed a secret. "You're so set on Joyce frettin' over that young spark. But, Lor' bless my soul, Joyce don't care for him. She never have cared for him, so as to say, properly. She was took at first by his being such a fine fellow and seemin' so fond of her. 'Twas natural enough. And you was so set on it you made her believe she liked him better nor she did. But that ain't what's going to wash. She never loved the fellow."

"It's not true," cried I, with flaming eyes. "She did love him always, and she loves him just as much now."

Deb was not a bit put out by my impetuous sally. She only shook her head quietly, and repeated, "No, she don't. And a precious good thing, too, seeing he's so like to forget her and mate with his own class."

"You're talking nonsense, Deb," cried I, hotly. "Mate with his own class, indeed! We're as good as he any day."

"That may be," answered Deb, calmly, "but he don't think so. He were keen upon her pretty face at first, but he's cooled down now, and sees it wouldn't be a wise thing for him to do. It's a precious good thing Joyce don't care for him."

"I tell you Joyce does care for him," reiterated I, savagely.

"Now, I wonder whatever makes you so set upon Joyce being in love with that young man," said the old woman, looking at me sharply, and without paying the slightest attention to my passionate vindication of my sister's constancy.

"Oh, I know, you want her to marry the squire and be a lady, as mother does," retorted I. "But you needn't bother. The squire'll never propose to her."

"No, you're right there," laughed Deb, with a loud laugh that both puzzled and irritated me. "He won't. I don't rightly see as he could propose to any one in this house till folk are minded to give him a civil word now and then. But that ain't no reason why you should want your sister to wed where she don't love. Nay, Margaret, there's somethin' under that as we don't know of. What is it, eh?"

I looked at Deb defiantly, but her round black eyes were full of a rough and simple sympathy. I knew Deb well enough to recognize the signs of it, and my sore, struggling pride gave way. I forgot all about having insisted a minute ago that I had nothing to fret about, and that I was not fretting. Just as I had used to do when I was a child and mother had whipped me for messing my frock, I put my head upon her broad bosom and began to cry.

Deb offered me no caress; she didn't know how, and she knew well enough I should be ashamed of my unusual behavior later; but after a few minutes she said, grimly: "I thought as much. Bother the men!"

I dried my eyes at that, and between a laugh and a sob I said: "Why should you say that? What have they to do with it?"

"What have they to do with it?" cried Deb. "Why, everything. They always have. Folk may say it was the woman made Adam to sin, but she's been punished for it ever since if she did, and it's just about time it should stop. Men are at the bottom of every trouble that comes our way, though we ought to be ashamed to say so. If it's not loving of 'em, it's hating of 'em, and that's just as bad. What I want to see is a man a-worriting *his* life out for one of us. They take it so easy, they do. But there, dearie me," smiled the old woman, "I weren't always so wise; and you mark my words, if folk go fixin' their hearts on what's not meant for them, they can't expect to be easy nor comfortable no ways. Ah, I'm not talking stuff, I can tell you. Old Deb isn't such a fool as she looks. You wouldn't think I'd ever had a lover, would you, my dear? But I had, once upon a time. I was a smart, bright lass, though I never was pretty, and the lads they were all fond of me. There was one of 'em fond of me for many a long year, just as patient as could be. He was better to do than I was, and would ha' been a good match for the likes o' me. But, Lord, I must needs go snubbin' of 'im, nasty uppish-like as I always was. Ah, many's the time poor mother has told me I was a fool for my pains. I might have had him if I had liked. But I never so much as cared to think he was coming after me. He was a good body for a friend—as you might say, a walking-stick of a summer evening, and there was an end."

"Well, but you couldn't have married him if you didn't like him, anyway, Deb," said I, interested in spite of myself by the story.

"Ah, I should have liked the man well enough if there hadn't been somebody else by, my dear," said Deb, "and that's just the pity. But one fine day there comes along a stranger lad, a lad as I didn't seem to want to snub—well, not for more than the first week. It was hop-picking time, and we used to be in the fields together all day. He never took particular account of me, more than for a joke and a laugh with the rest; but, my dear, he was as the light o' my eyes to me from morning till night again. I'm not ashamed to tell you now, it's so long ago. I dare say they all saw how it was; I dare say I was the jest o' the field. It don't matter now. I don't know as I much minded then, so long as I could get a word from him. He had always been kind and civil, helping me with the poles over the bin when they were too long and heavy for me to lift; and one day I was ailing and couldn't do my work, and he picked for me, and spoke so as I thought he meant courtin'. But, Lor' bless your soul, he didn't. It was only his nice, pleasant way. Afore the hopping was over I saw him kissing Bess Dawe down by 34 tower of a Sunday evening. The girls told me they'd been trysting it all the time, and he was going to wed her."

"Poor Deb," murmured I, softly, "poor Deb!"

"Oh, it's all past and gone now, child," laughed the old woman. "I've forgotten it, I think. It served me right enough for going for to fix my fancy on a man that didn't want none of me."

"I don't see how you could help that," said I, passionately. "I don't see how it's loving at all unless folk can't help it. And how were you to guess he wouldn't want you? It was cruel, cruel!"

"Nay, child, it weren't cruel. It were just natural, just as it had for to be," said Deb, quietly. And then, in her most matter-of-fact tones, she added, "But it were a rare pity I hadn't wedded the other one, for he'd have made me a good husband."

"Oh, how can you talk so?" cried I. "Why, you wouldn't have loved him."

"Maybe it ain't seemly for a woman to love," said Deb, considering. "The run of women marries the men because it's comfortable, and I'm thinkin' it's the best way. When a woman begins loving she do fret so over it. But the men, they takes it cool and easy, and does their work atween whiles."

"Well, I'm very glad you didn't do it that way at all events, Deb," said I.

"Ah, you wouldn't have had a sour old thing to rate ye if I had," laughed Deb. "But, Lor', I'm content enough. If I'd had a 'ome I'd have had cares, and a man alongside the whole blessed time, which I never could abide. But the Bible do tell us man ain't made to bide single, don't it? That's as much as to say a girl durstn't throw away her chances. And so that's what old Deb's story was for."

"If you mean to say Joyce is to marry the squire for fear Frank mightn't be faithful to her, all I have got to answer is, you're a horrible old woman, and I won't be a party to any such thing."

"Well, of all the obstinate, contrairy-headed, blind-eyed young women that ever I see'd in my whole life!" began Deb, planting her arms akimbo and looking me full in the face.

But she got no further in what seemed very much like the beginning of a sound rating of me. Joyce was coming up-stairs. The old boards cracked even under her light footfall. She was very late. Mother had been keeping her talking. Deb just nodded her head at me with an expression of anger, disappointment, impatience, and warning mysteriously mixed, and went down-stairs without so much as a good-night to my sister.

It was the last I ever heard from her on matters relating to the sentiments and affections. Such an upheaval of her busy, business-like temperament I should have thought not possible; it never was possible again to my knowledge, and the strange revelations in that apparently rough nature remain a marvel to me to this day.

CHAPTER XXXIV

The elections were over. They had passed quietly enough, and Mr. Farnham was returned for our division of Sussex, as Squire Broderick had always said he would be. As far as I recollect, it was as every one had expected, and I don't even remember that any one was particularly disappointed excepting the Thornes themselves and Mr. Hoad.

He, I remember, came to see father the very next day on business, and whether it was the "business" or the Radical failure I don't know, but his face wore that expression of mean vindictiveness which I had always instinctively felt it could wear, although I had never actually seen it as I saw it that day. He was closeted some time with father in the study. I met them in the hall as they came out; I was just starting for the Manor with the basket of jelly.

"Ah, we should have won it if you had helped us," the solicitor was saying. "And I must say, Maliphant, it doesn't seem to me to be right to hold aloof when energy is required in the cause."

Father's underlip swelled portentously; it was the sign of a storm within him; but he controlled himself and did not reply.

He turned to me instead, and said: "Are you off to the Manor, Meg? Well, ask the squire if I shall come and spend an hour or two with him to-night, as he's laid up."

The disagreeable expression deepened on Hoad's face. "Ah, your friend the squire'll be in fine feather," said he to father. "It's a precious good thing for him and his friend Farnham that that smart young nephew of his didn't come down and address the meeting the other night. He's an influential chap, and he's an honest fellow; he sticks by the ship."

Father looked towards me, and said, quietly, "Well, be off, my girl."

It seemed to bring Mr. Hoad to his senses. He turned to me with that particular smile which I so much disliked, and said: "Ah, Squire Broderick is a great friend of Miss Margaret's; we all know that. It's not always the young and handsome that succeed with the fair sex, and we can't blame a lady if she should put in her oar on the side it suits her to trim the boat."

"Don't talk nonsense to my girl, Hoad, if you please," cried father, angrily. "She doesn't understand that kind of stuff."

I didn't wait to hear any more. I lifted the latch and went out; but I heard Hoad laugh loudly, and as I closed the gate I heard him say: "Well, good-bye, Maliphant. You understand me about the loan? I'm glad the hops are looking well; but I'm afraid I can have nothing to do with any such negotiations as you propose about them."

I walked down the road with my little basket on my arm, pondering this sentence and Hoad's attitude altogether. It puzzled me. It almost seemed as though he wanted to pay father out for something. But what? Why should the election matter so very much to Mr. Hoad? And in what way could he pay father out?

I could not understand, but I hated Mr. Hoad worse than ever, and none the less for his vulgar banter about squire and me. I suppose he thought girls liked such stuff, but he was oddly out of it in every way.

But neither Mr. Hoad nor his words were long in my thoughts, I am bound to say. My head was so full of other things—of things that seemed all the world to me, because they concerned, and vitally concerned, that poor little, throbbing, aching piece of selfishness, Margaret Maliphant—that I had little thought left for anything else. The day before had left a vivid impression on me; it seemed almost like an era in my life.

The way in which Joyce had received the news of Frank's accident, the strange and puzzling scene with Deborah, and last but not least, the chance discovery of my sister and Harrod in the parlor, and the manner in which Harrod had answered me about it, inducing me, to my bitter regret, to try and quarrel with him in return—was it not enough to distress such a girl as I was then, living so much on sentiment and emotion?

All the morning I had been hoping to see Harrod, to have a little word with him that should set matters straight again between us; at all events, set them where they were before. Only two days ago I had been so happy with him on the ridge of the open cliff, I had felt so confident that my companionship was sweet to him, and now ajar again! What was the reason? And even as I asked myself that question, I saw Joyce sitting in the low chair by the fireplace, with the tears on her long lashes, and the dusky light upon her golden hair.

I was so intent upon my dream that I did not see the chief figure of it walking towards me until he was close at my side. My heart leaped within me for gladness; here was my opportunity. The demon—I *would* not give it its name—fled in the presence of a happy humility that surged up within me, and made me almost glad to have put myself in the wrong, that I might say so and be forgiven.

Ah, what was this terrible unseen power, that rode rough-shod over every sense that had ruled me up till now? How was it that I fell so passively, so imperceptibly, beneath its might? how was it that I did not struggle? how was it that I had forgotten to be proud?

I think that there was a smile on my face as I looked up into Harrod's. I know there was a smile in my heart, but it must have faded away very quickly, for his was quite cold. My courage sank.

I don't know what I feared, but I felt as if some unknown evil were going to happen. Yet, if I had been cool enough to notice him critically, I should have seen that he was not thinking of me.

"Has Hoad been with your father?" he asked.

"Yes," I answered. "He has only just left him."

"I suppose he is very much annoyed about the failure of this election," he said.

"I don't know," answered I, not caring at all about the election. "I don't know why he should mind so very much."

"Oh, I do," growled Harrod, striking his left hand smartly with a newspaper which I now saw he held in his right. "The vil—"

He stopped himself, and set his teeth.

"Yes, he *was* angry, I suppose," added I, recollecting the man's face. "But—" I wanted to say, "But don't let us talk of Mr. Hoad," and I hadn't the courage.

"Well, I wish you would try and keep the paper out of your father's way to-day, if you can," added he, more quietly. "There's something in it I'm afraid might distress him."

At any other time this speech would have filled me with curiosity and probably alarm, but just now I was so intent upon that idea of humbling myself and "putting matters straight" that I scarcely even noticed it.

"I suppose he doesn't often read it before the evening, does he?" added Harrod.

"Sometimes he does," said I. "I'll do my best. What is there in it— something bad about hops?"

The preoccupied look changed into one of simple annoyance and anger.

"I'm afraid it is," said I, blundering, and trying to find my way to the explanation that I wanted. "But never mind. As you said yesterday, hops are always very difficult things, and father must know that quite well. It was very stupid of me to say what I did yesterday about them, Mr. Harrod. I was talking foolishly. But I do know better than that, you know."

I spoke gently, but the frown deepened almost into a scowl on the bailiff's face.

"What on earth makes you think hops have anything to do with the matter?" cried he.

His lip trembled in that dreadful way I have noticed in him before. It was very slight, so slight that any one else might not have noticed it, but to me it was horrible—it terrified me. Yes; and two months ago I had never seen him look so—I did not know it was possible.

"I beg your pardon," said he, in a low voice; "but indeed the subject that I referred to in the paper has nothing at all to do with agriculture of any sort."

I did not say anything. I could not have spoken a word. He stood a moment with his face turned from me, and then he said "Good-day," abruptly, and walked down the road.

Without looking after him I went on my way. I had forgotten where I was going; a great weight hung at my heart. Yet nothing had happened. I had stupidly harped on a matter which, I might have seen, annoyed him; he *had* been annoyed, and he had been sorry for it. What was there in that? Nothing. No, it was not that anything had happened, it was that nothing had happened; it was that every little thing that occurred day by day showed me more clearly that nothing could happen, that I had no hold, that the ground was slipping away from under my feet.

I walked mechanically forward, I was giddy, the air danced around me, and my heart went beating about in its cage. I kept repeating to myself that I had not said what I had meant to say, that if I had said what I had meant to say all would have been well. I felt instinctively that I had not touched at the root of the matter; but I did not know that I could not have touched at the root of the matter, that I should not have dared to go within miles of it.

And still I went on under the leafy trees, with that unexplained hunger within me, until, as in a dream, I stood upon the broad steps of the Manor gate-way. Was it forgiveness that I wanted of him? He would only have wondered to hear me say that it was needed. What was it that I wanted?

I rang the great bell, which sounded so emptily through the hall. The sound called me back to myself, but even as the words of the message that I had come to deliver formed themselves upon my lips, a sudden resolve formed itself within my heart.

When the door opened, instead of merely giving my message, I asked if the squire was at home. I dare say the man was astonished. It did not occur to me to think whether he was or not; I had not had enough experience of the world to think much of such a matter; and my purpose burned too bright in me for such reflections.

I was shown through the great hall, which Frank Forrester had so cleverly decorated with flags and garlands on the night of the county ball, to the long room beyond that looked out onto the fine lawn through three great deep-embrasured windows that enclosed the landscape in their dark oak frames. I leaned upon one of the faded cushions of the window-seat and looked out to the garden. It was laid out in a large square of lawn, with a broad old-fashioned flower-bed flanking it on either side; but to the belt of trees towards the marsh it was free, and through the trees one had glimpses of the wide, sad land, with the sea in the distance, that we saw from the Grange; to the right of the lawn was the ruin of the thirteenth-century chapel, the tall, slender arch of the chancel, and the graceful little turret of the bell-tower standing out against the elms and sycamores.

How well I remembered that night of the ball, when we had strayed out into the moonlight—the squire and I—and when I had envied Joyce for having a lover! Yes, I had wondered to myself whether I should ever have a lover who would speak to me like that in the moonlight with his heart in his voice.

Joyce's white dress had fluttered in the shade of that dark ruin—cold as the shrouds of the ghosts who might have peopled it. I remembered that now, as though it had been an evil omen. But then nothing had seemed to me cold. I had envied Joyce for having a lover. Did I still envy her her lover?

A step sounded in the hall, and I stood up holding my basket with the jelly in it; my heart was beating a little with the strangeness of the place, for of the squire I was not afraid.

The dark oak room was getting a little dim; I had not been able to get off in the morning, it was afternoon—late afternoon, because Harrod had detained me. A shadow over the sky without made very dark corners in the old wainscoting, that the heavy tapestry curtains made darker still. Everything was dark and old-fashioned, with a solid serviceable goodness, in the squire's house. There were bits of delicate satinwood furniture, as

I knew, in the citron-colored drawing-room with its canary hangings, but here, in the room where the squire sat, everything was for use.

I took it all in at a glance; the shelves that lined the walls—books and books and books for him who declared he did not read—the carved settee by the hearth, the old leather arm-chair whence he must just have risen, the large table strewn with newspapers and pamphlets, driving-gloves, hunting-crops, dog-collars, and all kinds of strange implements that country gentlemen seem to require. An old Turkey carpet covered the floor, and a heavy curtain kept the draught from the door; it was a comfortable winter room, dim and hot on this warm September evening.

As I looked I remembered another room that I had been in alone not a long while since—a different room, looked at with different feelings. I shivered as I thought of it, just as I had shivered a moment since in the hot air without.

The squire came in. He looked as though he had been ailing, but he did not look ill, and his smile was sunshine in its welcoming.

"Why, Miss Margaret, this is an honor for an old bachelor," said he. "It's worth while being ill for—or *saying* one has been ill, for there has been precious little the matter with me. I should have been out long ago if it hadn't been for that tiresome doctor that Mrs. Dalton insisted on calling in."

I smiled. I did not know what to say—how to begin.

"Mother sent you this jelly," I said, hurrying to get over the avowed object of my visit. "It's some we make at home, and she thinks it'll cure anything." I held out the basket, and then placed it on the big table behind me. "And father wants to know if you would like him to come to-night and have a chat," I went on, hurriedly, before he had time to answer.

"Oh, I couldn't let him do that," said the squire. "I heard he wasn't so well again the other day. I'm quite recovered now. I'll come down to the Grange. I should like to have a chat with him about the election. I hope your father isn't disappointed?"

"Oh dear, no; father doesn't mind a bit," said I, impatiently. "But do come. I'm sure mother'll be downright glad to see you at the Grange again. She says you never come near us nowadays."

"What, have I been missed?" said he, with just the very tiniest bit of sarcasm in his good voice.

"Why, of course," I answered, simply. "You know how fond mother is of you—and father too. Excepting Captain Forrester, I don't think he gets on so well with anybody."

His face fell, and I was sorry.

"He's had more practice with me," he laughed.

"Yes," said I. "But he is so fond of Captain Forrester. He's dreadfully cut up about this accident of his. If it hadn't been for that Mr. Hoad coming in and worrying him this afternoon he was coming up to see you about it. But he gave me this letter and told me to ask you to put the address on."

"Oh, Frank's all right," said the squire, a trifle impatiently. "It's nothing but a sprained wrist and ankle. Only he didn't feel like coming down; perhaps he was half glad to get out of it; I'm sure he ought to have been ashamed ever to have promised to come."

It was rather a fall, after all the sympathy I had tried to win for Frank, and the reproaches I had made to Joyce for her coldness! But Joyce's strange conduct was none the less so because he had only sprained his ankle.

"I'm glad he is no worse hurt," said I; and as it came home to me how very glad I was I added, "Oh, I'm very glad."

"The boy's right enough," repeated the squire, in the same manner.

He advanced to the table, against which I had been leaning all this time, and said, in a very grateful sort of way, "So you really made this jelly for me, and came all the way across here on purpose to bring it to me?"

I looked at him, astonished. One would have thought making jelly was dreadfully hard work, and the distance from the Grange to the Manor at least five miles instead of not one.

"Oh dear, no," said I. "I didn't make it. Mother made it; I only helped her strain it. And I didn't come here on purpose to bring it."

It was the squire's turn to look at me, astonished. "No, I came to ask you something," continued I, hurriedly, rushing violently upon my subject. "Do you remember once—in the summer—Mr. Broderick, you told me that if ever I was in any trouble, that if ever I wanted help, I was to come to you?"

"Yes, I remember it very well," answered he. "I meant what I said."

"I knew you did," said I. "That's why I've come." He came close up to me.

"Thank you," he said, and at the time it did not strike me that it was strange he should say "thank you." "I'm glad you have come. So you are in trouble up at the Grange! Ah, I was afraid, I was sorely afraid it was coming! Come and sit down and tell me all about it."

He took hold of my hand and led me towards the oaken settle. We had not sat down before; I don't think either of us had supposed that I was going to remain more than a minute.

"It's about Joyce," I said.

He started, but he did not look distressed, rather more surprised. "I'm dreadfully unhappy about Joyce," I repeated.

"Indeed!" answered he, concernedly. "How's that?"

"I promised mother not to tell anybody," I replied; "but I can't help it—I must tell some one, for I don't know what to do."

"Yes, tell me," he repeated.

"Do you remember that ball you gave here at the Manor last spring?" asked I.

"Ah, yes, I remember," answered he, I thought sadly.

"Well, Joyce was engaged to Captain Forrester that night," said I.

I saw his face grow stern as it had grown when he had warned me about Frank at first.

"Mother didn't like it, she—she wanted something else for Joyce," I went on, evasively, not caring to let the squire think that mother had noticed his liking for my sister—"she said they must wait for a year. Yes, and not meet all the time, and not write to one another. But it's not possible that two people who care for one another can go on like that. Is it, now?" cried I, eagerly.

"Yes, it would be possible if they really cared for one another, Miss Margaret," he said, presently; "but it would be hard."

"Oh yes, yes, too hard," cried I. "They *have* met. I managed it once. But now I want them to meet again."

"That's why you were so anxious that Frank should come down for the elections," he said. "I wondered why you were so anxious."

"Yes, that's why. Don't you see?" I explained. "And now that he has had this accident it's worse than ever. You say it isn't very bad, and I'm glad; but don't you see how bad it must be for Joyce? It can't be good for her, can it? And so I want you to get him down here so that they can meet sometimes. You easily could. It would only be kind of you. He ought to be nursed up and made well again."

He dropped his eyes from my face, where they had been fastened, and got up and walked away towards the window.

"There is no one to do any nursing here," he said. "Frank can go to his mother to be nursed."

"Oh, well, I didn't mean nursing," I hastened to say, correcting myself. "I don't suppose he needs nursing, if it's no worse than you say."

There was a silence.

"You *will* ask him to come, won't you?" repeated I, softly.

The squire turned round. His face was quite hard.

"No, Miss Margaret," he said. "I can't do it. I would do anything to please you, but I can't do that. What you have told me distresses me very much—far more than you can guess. I had feared something of the sort in the spring; but then Frank went away, your sister and he were separated, and when she came back from her holidays, well—especially of late—I made sure that there had been nothing at all in it."

He paused, and I wondered why, especially of late, he had made sure that there was nothing in it.

"If your sister cares for Frank, I am very sorry," he went on, gently; "but I cannot but hope that you are mistaken."

"I am not mistaken," cried I, vehemently, starting to my feet.

He looked at me with a strange pity in his eyes.

"Well, then, I can only hope she will forget him," added he.

"Forget him!" cried I. "Do you think girls so easily forget the men they love?"

"I think it depends partly on the girl," said he, still with an unwonted gravity in his tone, "and partly on the kind of love."

The words stunned me for a moment; they seemed to be an echo of something in my own brain that kept resounding there and deafening me.

"I don't think that Joyce will ever forget Frank," repeated I, doggedly.

"Well, then, I can only say again that I trust you may be mistaken," answered the squire, firmly; "for I'm afraid that he will certainly forget her."

"I don't believe it," cried I.

"You can imagine that I do not willingly say such a thing of my own kith and kin," he answered, with just a touch of his old irritability in his voice, "but I fear that it might be so. Frank's mother is an ambitious woman, the family is poor, and she has set her heart upon his marrying an heiress. In fact, there is a particular heiress to whom she is now urging him to pay his suit. He is a fascinating fellow when he likes. I dare say he will succeed if he tries. And he appreciates the comfort of having his bread buttered without any trouble. I'm afraid he might try."

I was silent—dumfounded.

"No," added the squire; "far from trying to bring your sister and Frank together again, I shall do my uttermost to keep them apart. I shall work upon every sense of honor that Frank has—and, thank God! he may be weak, but he is not wanting in a sense of honor—to induce him never to see her again. Then you will see soon, very soon, she will release him from the fictitious tie that binds them, and will leave herself free to choose again, and to choose more wisely."

"Joyce will never choose again," muttered I.

There was a great lump in my throat that almost prevented me from getting out the words. My tongue was quite dry and would not move, and I was conscious of a cold chill upon my forehead and upon my lips, even though they were parched. I locked my hands together—they, too, were quite cold.

The squire came towards me, he came quite close. The room was very dim now, although the sun had only just set without, for the windows did not look towards the sun-setting. All the irritability called up by my insane obstinacy had melted out of his face; it was very tender. He looked at me again with that strange pity in his eyes.

"Ah, my child," said he, taking one of my hands in his, "why do you try so hard to persuade me that your sister loves Frank? Why do you try so hard to persuade yourself of it?"

Yes, why did I try so hard? I did not answer, but the lump swelled bigger than ever in my throat. I unclasped my hands, and let my arms fall down straight at my sides, and looked up into his face. For a moment a wild impulse seized upon me to tell the squire something of why I tried to persuade myself of that thing. I felt so sure of the deep, loyal friendship that shone out of his eyes as he looked at me. It was as though he were some big, strong, unknown brother come to help me in my trouble; I had never had a brother. But the moment passed.

"You must surely know that it is not really so," he added.

And then I snatched away my hand.

"I know nothing of the kind," I said, fiercely. "You said you would help me whenever I came to you, but you did not mean it. Now that I come to ask you, you will not help me. But I will help myself, I will help Joyce. I will write to Frank, and tell him that he must come back to her. I don't care what he thinks of me—what any one thinks of me. You are cruel, you are all of you cruel; but I do not believe that he will be cruel."

"No, I am not cruel," answered the squire. "I am only doing what is right—what I believe to be best for your sister."

"Yes, you are cruel," cried I, beside myself. "You are all of you cruel and selfish. Mother is cruel too. I know why she is cruel—it is because she wants Joyce to marry you. And I know why you are cruel—it is because you want to marry Joyce."

Oh that the darkness might have come, might have come quickly and at once, to cover the blush of shame that rose to my brow! Oh that the great window would have opened, that I might have rushed forth into the open air—away, away from everybody! How could I have been so unwomanly, so cowardly, so ungrateful?

I stood still—even to my heart—waiting for the squire to speak.

At last he said, in a voice that was not in the least angry, as I had expected it to be, but that sounded to me deep and far away, and quite unlike his own, "What made you say that?"

The voice was so gentle that it gave me courage to look up. If all the regret that was in my heart, and all the sorrow for having hurt him, rose into my eyes, they must have been very big and sorrowful that day.

"Oh, I don't know," I said, lifting up my hands as I used to do when I said my prayers, only that I don't think I had ever hitherto said my prayers with so much feeling—"I don't know. I don't know anything. I think I am losing my wits. Will you forgive me?"

"There is nothing to forgive," answered he. "But tell me what made you think that?"

"Oh no, no; don't make me say any more," I implored.

"Yes, you must tell me that," insisted he.

"Everybody always thought it," murmured I. "Mother used to say you would never think of coming down to the Grange so often as you used to do only to quarrel over things with an old man. Oh, I can't think how I can repeat such things! It's dreadful. But, you see, mother thinks such a deal of Joyce. She has been quite unhappy because you so rarely come now. You must forgive her and me too. *I* thought it just the same. Only Joyce didn't. She's not that sort of girl. And father didn't. If mother ever hinted at it, he told her that you would never think of wedding out of your own class, and that, indeed, he would never have allowed it. Father is very proud."

"Yes," answered the squire, "and he is right. But such pride is a poor thing compared with a deep and honest love. There is a girl, not of what is called my own class, whom I would marry if she would have me, but her name is not Joyce Maliphant."

"Not Joyce!" cried I, genuinely surprised, genuinely disappointed, and for a moment forgetting all my many emotions.

"No," he said, gravely.

He did not try to take my hands again. I dropped them down once more, and stood looking at him. His eyes seemed to travel through mine into my heart. Their look frightened me, it was full of such a wonderful tenderness. I had never thought before that his eyes were beautiful; good, kind, frank blue eyes—nothing more. But as I remember them that night, I think they must have been beautiful.

"What do you mean?" I murmured.

"I mean that I love *you*," answered he.

I don't know what I did. I think I crept backward, away from him, till I stumbled upon a chair, and that then I fell into it. I was stunned.

"How is it that you didn't guess it?" asked he, tremulously.

I did not answer; I could not. I believe I covered my face with my hands.

"I don't want it to distress you," said he. "Whatever you may do about it, please remember that it will not have distressed me. At no time will you have brought me anything but pleasure. I think I understand a little, and I will not trouble you now. I did not mean to have told you. It slipped out because of what you said. Go home and forget it. Only, if at any time you should be lonely and need love, remember that I have always loved you. Yes, ever since you were a little girl, and used to come and have your frock mended in the house-keeper's room. I am not a sentimental sort of fellow, you know. It's not my way. I shall never be that; I shall never fret. But I shall always love you as I do now."

He did not make one step towards me; he remained where I had left him—standing in the middle of the hearth-rug. Still stunned, bewildered, ashamed, I struggled to my feet and walked towards the door.

"Good-bye," said he.

"Good-bye," murmured I, mechanically.

I stood outside in the quiet evening, on the steps of the Manor gate-way. Vaguely I remembered that as I had rung the great echoing bell there had been a craving in my heart for something that I could not reach—for something which the request I was going to make might perhaps help me to secure. Was that something love, and had I secured it?

CHAPTER XXXV

One morning about a week after my visit to the Manor, mother and I chanced to be alone together in the dairy.

I had spent the last days in a trance; I seemed to have lost all count with myself, only, as I look back across the years that intervene, I am certain of one thing—I was glad that the squire loved me.

In the turmoil of surprise, of something akin to fear, of the vague, wretched sense of crookedness throughout, and of a touch of some sort of remorse at what I had unwittingly done, there shone forth one bright, sharp ray of light; it was a sense of pride and satisfaction that this man, whom every day I felt more sure was good and loyal, should have chosen *me* to love. Beyond that I was sure of nothing, and was chiefly thankful that there was no decision to take, and that I need tell no one of what had happened. The squire had been kind, he had asked no question and needed no answer.

The hop-picking was about to begin, and mother was arranging how much milk should be set apart for the hoppers; she never made her usual quantity of butter in hopping-time; she always said that butter was a luxury, and that she wasn't going to have working-folk deprived of their proper quantity of milk so that those who didn't work should have butter.

Things had not been cheerful at home this while past. To be sure, though I went about my duties with a feverish energy, and mother had no more occasion to upbraid me for those "moping silly ways," I was seeing things myself through a dark haze; yet I do not think it was entirely my fancy that matters seemed gloomy.

I had not been able to get hold of that newspaper that Harrod begged me to keep out of father's way; he had seen it before I got home, and had taken it away with him, and I never found it afterwards; all that I could make out about it had been from Harrod, who had answered my questions somewhat curtly, but had led me to understand that it had been some kind of attack on father for having held aloof from the Liberal cause, with covert allusions to certain reasons for his doing so remotely connected with the condition of his finances.

I could not make head or tail of it at the time, though a day came when I learned how a vile man can suspect an honorable one of his own doings, and then I was thankful to Trayton Harrod for having fired up for father as he had done. But at that time I only saw that father was visibly depressed. I could see that he could scarcely even bear Harrod to talk about the farm matters. There was a dreadful kind of irritability upon him which is piteous now to think of, as I remember how it was varied with moods of strange gentleness towards every one, and of an almost child-like humility towards mother whenever he spoke so much as a keen word to her.

Even to Harrod, with whom I don't think he ever had any real sympathy, he showed sorrow for any sharp speaking by a very patient hearing, from time to time, of all the new schemes of that busy practical mind. But he seemed to have lost his love of argument, once such a feature in him; he seemed to be withdrawing himself more and more into himself. Selfish as I was, and absorbed in my own hopes and fears, it made me sad. Even in his dealing with the Rev. Cyril Morland that feature seemed to have vanished. He was as eager about the philanthropic scheme as ever; more eager, as if with a feverish longing that *something* he had undertaken should be brought to a good issue quickly; but though the two sat hours together, wrapt over details and figures, it was hard, silent work now, with none of that brilliant enthusiasm that there had been about it in Frank's day, none of the pleasant dreams, none of the sympathetic affection; and when, one evening, I surprised him in his study, standing almost as though entranced before that portrait sketch of the young Camille Lambert, I hated Frank for a new reason for not coming to Marshlands.

But we none of us spoke of him now. Even I did not—not even to Joyce. I had written him that letter that I had intended to write, and was awaiting the answer to it, but I did not speak of him. Mother was the only one who did; she spoke of him that morning in the dairy.

"Meg," she began, "I can't make out how it is that the squire don't come to see us as he used to do. I've sometimes thought that you might have something to do with it."

I looked round quickly. I was alarmed.

"Why on earth should *I* have anything to do with it?" I cried. But I saw that I was distressing myself needlessly; mother was as far as ever from guessing the truth.

"None so very unlikely, I'm afraid, my dear," she replied. "You're but young, and you might even let a thing slip out without meaning it. And then you're masterful, and you've set your heart upon this affair coming straight between Joyce and the captain, though the Lord alone knows why you should suppose a young butterfly such as that would make a better husband than Squire Broderick. The truth is, Margaret, I'm afraid you have been telling tales."

She had guessed part of the truth, but what a little part of it! I was silent, and she looked at me sharply.

"Of course if you have," said she, severely, "it's just about the worst piece of mischief you could well have set your hands to. That other affair 'll never come to anything, as I guessed pretty well from the first it never would. The dandy young beau has got other fish to fry by this time, and, luckily enough, Joyce is too sensible to fret after a bird that has flown. She never did set that store on him that you fancied, and before the year's out she'd be very sorry to have to keep to her bargain."

"Well, however that may be," answered I, with an inward sense of superiority, "Joyce will never marry the squire, so you needn't bother about that."

"You'll please to keep such remarks to yourself, Margaret," said mother, coldly. "You can't possibly know anything at all about the matter."

Alas! but I was just the one who could and did know everything about the matter. As I think of it now, it is a marvel to me that mother should have guessed nothing at all of what was really going on; but it was too evident that she did not. I suppose her mind was so fixed upon one thing that she thought of nothing else. After all, it is the way with us all.

"Am I to understand that you *have* been talking nonsense to the squire, then, Margaret?" asked she, in her most dignified manner.

It was not in me to tell a lie.

"I told the squire that Joyce and Frank were engaged," said I, "if that's talking nonsense."

I did not say it crossly. I think my fits of fiery temper were becoming less frequent, but I said it without wincing, although I knew what mother's feelings would be. She sat down in a despairing kind of manner, and drew in her breath, rather than let it out, in a long sigh.

"Engaged!" ejaculated she at last, with a withering accent of scorn.

"Well, it's the truth," insisted I, doggedly.

"No, it's not the truth, Margaret," replied mother, emphatically. "*You* may choose to consider them engaged, but *I* don't. And what's more, Joyce don't. I'm thankful to say I've one daughter who always had a grain of good-feeling and respect towards her elders and betters. Your sister *never* considered herself engaged to the captain."

"They were to be engaged if they were of the same mind in a year," said I. "Well, they are of the same mind so far, so it's practically the same thing."

"I don't think so," said mother, in a conclusive sort of voice. "But I don't need to discuss the matter with you. I must acquaint Squire Broderick that he has been misinformed. And meanwhile I'll trouble you to keep yourself to yourself, and not discuss things that don't concern you with people outside the family."

Of course I deserved the rebuke, and I took it silently. But I could not help feeling a little anxious as to how that proposed conversation between mother and the squire would resolve itself. If mother allowed the squire to see—as I feared she would do—what she supposed to be the state of his feeling, would he be able to keep from telling her that she was mistaken?

It was at the first of the hop-picking that she met him. That odd medley of strange folk who go by the name of "foreigners" among the village hop-pickers had already begun to appear upon the scene, and mother always went down at the beginning of the season to see that the poor creatures were as comfortable as possible in their straw huts, and generally to inquire into the condition of life with them. I can see her now scolding careless mothers for unkempt children, and careless maidens for rent skirts and undarned elbows, inquiring into the cause of pale faces, suggesting remedies, procuring relief.

She had gone down to the camp with Joyce, for she had sent me riding over to Craig's farm for some butter, ours had come so badly. Trayton Harrod overtook me as I came home. I had seen him in the neighboring village, but I had spurred Marigold on, for I did not want to speak with him.

"You shouldn't ride that poor beast so hard, Miss Margaret," I remember him saying as he came up with me; "you'll break her wind."

"Oh dear, no," declared I, laughing harshly, for I was in no soft mood towards him; "she's a very different creature to that old black thing you're riding, and she understands me. Mother's at the hopping to-night, and I want to get on to meet her there."

I lashed the horse again as I spoke, and she started forward wildly. We had just come to the place where there is a short-cut across the marsh, and I set her to the gate. She took it like a deer, and flew as though she were borne on wings when she felt the turf beneath her feet. She made me dizzy for a moment, and when I looked back I saw that Harrod was on the ground—his horse had refused to take the fence. But even as I meditated turning back I saw him leap into the saddle again, and in a few minutes he was beside me once more.

"What possessed you to do that?" he cried, out of breath. "You might have had a serious accident. It was folly."

I did not answer. Indeed the pace at which I was going made speech difficult, and he could not expect it.

"You're going too hard, Miss Maliphant," cried he again. "Stop the mare, if you please."

The peremptory tone irritated me, and far from doing as I was bid, I gave Marigold a touch with the whip. Her blood was already up; she reared and tried hard to throw me. Mr. Harrod leaned forward and caught at her bridle.

"Don't, don't," cried I, petulantly. "You only chafe her; leave her alone."

But still he leaned forward towards me and held on to the horse, and still we thundered on over the soft ground across the empty plain. There was no road; we were quite alone; and at any moment I knew we might come upon some unseen dike that would send Marigold upon her knees and me over her neck.

I knew that if ever I were in danger of my life I was in danger of it then; but the sense of peril, and of the strong arm—*that* strong arm—ready to save me if it could, his breath that came hot upon my cheek, his eyes that burned upon me though I could not see them—all lifted me into a strange delirium of excitement, of anger, of delight. Yes; I think that, if I thought at all, I wished that that ride might go on forever. But it came to an end soon enough. Marigold stumbled at nothing, she flew straight as an arrow from a shaft, until at last she knew her master, and was still.

"Now, Miss Maliphant," said he, quietly, after a panting minute or two, "won't you be so kind as to give me that whip?"

I looked at him; my cheek was burning, my bosom rose and fell wildly.

"No," answered I; "why should I?"

He smiled. "Well, I know you won't use it again," he answered, almost vexatiously careless of my discourtesy. "I hope you have had a lesson that Marigold can't be tampered with."

"I wasn't in the least bit frightened," I said, in a low voice.

"Upon my word you're a splendid girl," said he, still looking at me.

I felt my face grow redder than ever, but what I had said was no mere boast.

"But *I* was frightened," added he; and then, in a very gentle voice, "You won't do it again, will you?"

His temper had done me good, his tenderness was almost too much for me.

"No," murmured I; and the sense that he *cared* made my voice tremble so that I dared say no more.

"A girl doesn't know how soon she has played one prank too many. I can tell you that we ran a greater danger just now than we did when the bull was near tossing you. Do you remember it?"

Did I remember it? Ay, and many other things since then. The thought of them kept me silent, and kept my heart beating till I was afraid he would see it. Ah me, what would I have given to be back again under that five-barred gate, with Trayton Harrod standing over me, and all the future before me! But now — what was the future?

"Will you promise me not to be so foolish again?" repeated he, gently. "There's no fun in breaking one's neck, you know."

My heart was big; he was very kind to me, very careful of me — just as he had been always. I waited — waited for him to say something more, for him to lay his hand once again upon mine, though it were to check Marigold's bridle.

But the mare was going quite quietly now, and there was no need for him to lay his hand on her bridle. He did not seem even to notice that I had not answered his question. We were riding up alongside the hop-fields where the camp was set. Along the lanes groups of village hop-pickers were coming home; whole families, who sallied forth every morning with dinners in bag and basket, and babies in blue-shaded perambulators. The conical straw huts made a circle under the maple hedge, and in the middle of the field the folk were filling their pitchers and kettles at two large water-butts on wheels drawn up there for their use. We tied our horses to the fence, and walked up. The women were beginning to light their fires, and father was expostulating with a tall, handsome girl who had begun to lay hers too near the dangerous straw.

She lifted a pair of splendid eyes upon him, insolently, but the words upon her lips were swamped in a smile, for he had stooped to pick up a crying child, and the little one had stopped its whimper at his tender words, and was gazing up at him confidingly. "It ain't often she takes to strangers," said the young mother. "She's proud and masterful—and a good job too. She ain't got no father to fight for her, and she may well learn not to trust the men-folk."

I don't know what father said, I didn't listen. Mother was talking to the squire in a far corner of the field, and, though I was shy of seeing the squire, I wanted to know what he was saying to mother. But it seemed only to be commonplace talk.

Mother took me to task for my disordered appearance, and asked me what I had been doing to get the mare in such a state, and Harrod came up and gave some kind of explanation for me, and then the squire, shaking hands with me, asked me what I thought of the weather.

He was self-possessed. It was I who was shy and who could find no words.

"I'm afraid we shall have a pocketful of wind," said he, looking up anxiously at the sky.

It was a gorgeous sunset. Banks upon banks and piles upon piles of cloud, fortifying the horizon, and flung wildly across the heavens till, overhead, they were airy puffs upon the blue vault; seas and billows and cataracts of cloud, all of them suffused with rosy remembrance of the fiery furnace on the ridge of the purple downs—a gorgeous sunset; but the squire was right—a stormy one.

"'Tis the Lord sends mists and 'eat, rain and gales, and we've got to submit, whether or no," murmured Reuben behind my back.

"I've thought of late Mr. Harrod seemed anxious about the crop," said mother, "but it's *my* belief it's above the common."

I looked quickly round for Harrod, afraid lest he should have heard the remark. I need not have feared: he stood beside my sister, with a strange, dreamy look upon his face which I had never seen there before. There was nothing in their standing together side by side, but there was something in the way they thus stood, an indefinable sense of a companionship in suffering which hardened me to stone.

"I wonder you venture to have an opinion on such things, mother," said I, in a voice loud enough for him to hear. "Men don't like us women to have any opinions. They only like women who care for nothing but house-keeping."

Mother looked at me dumfounded, and the squire turned grieved eyes on me; Joyce bent her head, but Harrod glanced round at me with anger on his heavy mouth. Ah me, how sharply two-edged a sword was that bitter pride of mine!

I turned away and began to untie the mare from the hedge. The squire came to help me. He did not speak, but he held my hand a moment longer than usual in his own, and I felt that *his* trembled. And when he had done at last arranging my habit over the saddle, he looked up at me with that same pity in his blue eyes that had made me feel so strangely a week ago. A disturbed feeling, half pleasure, half pain, stole over me, and as I rode up the steep lane in the dusk, under the arching ash and pine trees, the memory of the squire's face made me feel things less entirely dead and dreary in the midst of those vain and endless self-torturings, those angry struggles, those heart-sickening hopes and fears.

CHAPTER XXXVI

The reply to my letter came on the morrow from Frank Forrester. What a day it was! I recollect it well. All the summer had gone in one terrible storm of wind. Alas! Reuben had been only too just in his sad prophecy: the red sunset upon the citadels of cloud had meant mischief indeed.

The gale had burst that very night. Before midnight the wind was tearing up across the marsh like some live thing, rending the air with its threatening voice, almost rending the earth with its awful tread, as it swept, grieving, muttering, moaning, and rushed at last with a wild shriek upon us—a restless, relentless, revengeful foe. Even to me, strong and hearty girl, whom not even trouble and heartache, that was sore enough in those days, could keep from the constraining sleep of a healthy youth—even to me that night the voice of the wind was appalling.

I lay in bed waiting and listening for its grim footsteps as they sped across the dark waste without, distant at first and almost faint, growing nearer and nearer, louder and louder, till with a yell, as of fierce triumph, the maniac burst against the windows, as though it would rend the house in pieces for its sport. Afar the sullen roar of the sea mingled with the lash of the pitiless gusts breaking, baffled, upon the distant beach, only to renew its unwearied attack with ceaseless, weary persistence.

I got up and looked out of the window. There was a cold moon shining faintly in a gray sky, where the clouds hurried wildly about as though seeking to escape some fierce pursuer; it gave a veiled feeble light, in which the near farm buildings looked like unsubstantial things that the wind might lift in its unseen hands and scatter like dead leaves upon the ground; in the phantom whiteness the black trees waved helpless, beseeching arms, bowing themselves to earth beneath the mighty grasp of that great, invisible strength; one could almost fancy it might pass into shape, so near and terrible seemed its personality as it advanced, sure and strong, across the wide, dim distance that was only marsh-land to me who knew that it was not sea.

Some one stirred in the house. It was father; he was coming up-stairs; he was still dressed; he had been sitting up all this time with those papers of his. I upbraided him for it, and said it was enough to give him his death of cold, but he seemed scarcely to hear me. His face was very pale.

"It's a rough night, a very rough night, Meg," he said, sorrowfully.

"Oh yes, father, it is," answered I, sympathetically, thinking of the hops that this would be the ruin of. But he made no allusion to them, he only said: "Those poor creatures down in the huts will have a bad time of it. And so many children too! They will be frightened, poor lambs."

And then after a pause he added: "Little David Jarrett was very weak when I called this afternoon, Meg. I'm afraid he'll not last out this gale. I think he would like me to go round and see him."

"Not now, father, not to-night?" I cried. But he did not answer, and I remember that it was with the greatest difficulty that I persuaded him to go to bed.

In the morning I was sorry that I had done so. The little lad was dead.

We were all seated at breakfast. The gale still raged outside; the garden was strewn with boughs of fruit-trees and blossoms of roses that the wind had ruthlessly torn from their stems; even from the distance of our hill we could see the white storm-crests upon the bosom of the laboring sea, and the snow of the foam as it dashed against the strong towers upon the coast.

Mother sat silently pouring the tea and looking anxiously across at father, who was eating no breakfast; Joyce alone was much the same as usual, for I—well I don't know what I *looked* like—I felt wretched. The post had brought me the reply to my letter to Frank Forrester, and it was not what I wanted.

I sat moody and miserable. And to us all sitting there—very unlike the bright family that we generally were—came a messenger with the news— little David Jarrett had passed away in the night. I can see father's face now; not sad, no: grave, and with a strange drawn look upon it that I could not understand. His eyes shone out very dark and deep from the white face that almost looked like parchment; the shaggy eyebrows and strong tufts of gray hair a mockery of strength upon it. But this is as it rises up before me now in terrible reality; then I saw nothing, I guessed nothing. Oh, father, father, that the old days might come back once more!

He said nothing, he gave no outward sign of trouble; he got up and went out, and we cleared away the breakfast-things. We were not given to expressing ourselves.

I took Frank's letter out of my pocket and read it over and over again; it was very short—there was scarcely anything in it, and yet I read it over and over again. He thanked me for writing; it was very kind of me to write; he was sorry his friends had been so anxious about him; it had been a needless "scare," there never had been much amiss, and he was all right again now. He was sorry his friend Thorne had lost the election. What did my father think of it? He was afraid it would be a long while before he should get time to come to Marshlands again. That was all.

No wonder I read it over and over again to try and find something more in it than was there! There were only two sentences that meant anything at all, and they made my heart wild with anger.

"What did my father think of it?" And "he was afraid it would be a long while before he should *find time* to come to Marshlands again."

They were insulting, heartless sentences. Yes, even as I look back upon it now, with all the bitterness of the moment passed, I think they were that. As if he—who had been honored by my dear father's intimate friendship, who knew his views as few of his friends knew them—should not have known better than I "what my father thought of it." If he ever *found time* to come to Marshlands again perhaps he would find out. Not a word of Joyce in it—not a stray hint, not a hidden allusion! Was it possible, was it really possible, that a man could seem to love so bravely, and could forget in a few short months? Were the squire's warnings just after all? Forget, forget? I repeated the word to myself, to me it seemed so impossible that one should ever be able to forget. At that time I don't believe I even thought it possible that one should live without the thing that one most craved for.

I sat there on the low window-seat, crushing the letter in my hand, looking out at the wild clouds that hurried across the sky, looking out at the havoc that the gale had made, and thinking perhaps of another havoc than the havoc wrought by the wind. But it was all Joyce's fault, I said to myself; she might have prevented it if she had liked. Why had she not prevented it?

Some one came into the room. I crushed the letter into my pocket and started up.

It was Trayton Harrod. He wore that same harassed, preoccupied look that I had noticed in him before; it maddened me, though I might have known well enough why he was preoccupied—there was anxiety enough on the farm.

"Where's your father?" asked he, quickly.

"He's out," I answered, shortly.

"I wanted him particularly," said Harrod again.

"Well, he's out," repeated I. "He has gone to Mrs. Jarrett's. The little boy died last night."

"Oh, I'm sorry, very sorry," said he. "I know he was very fond of the child." And then, after a minute, he added, "But it's really very important that I should see your father at once, Miss Margaret. Could you not go across and tell him so?"

"No," said I, ungraciously. "I don't think I could; I shouldn't like to disturb him." And then, half penitently, I added, "Can't *I* help you?"

He smiled, but gravely. "No," answered he; "I'm afraid this time your father must decide for himself."

"Is it ruin?" I asked, after a minute. "I suppose so."

He started and looked at me sharply. "What do you mean?" he asked. "No, I sincerely hope it's nothing of the kind."

"Oh," answered I, "I was afraid there wasn't a chance after this gale of anything but ruin to the whole crop."

"You mean the hops," replied he, as if relieved; and it did not strike me at the time to wonder what he could have thought I meant. "I'm afraid it's a bad lookout for them. That's why I want to see your father at once. It *must*, I fear, alter some arrangements I have made. I must telegraph." He paused a moment, thinking; then he added, "Is the squire expected here to-day, do you know?"

I flushed. "Not that I know of," said I; "but how should I know? He never comes to the Grange now."

I jerked out these sentences foolishly, incoherently.

"No, I know he has not been here quite so often of late," said he. "I've noticed it, and I've been sorry. But he'll come back. Never fear, he'll come back," smiled he, looking at me.

The heat in my face grew to fire. "I don't care whether he comes back or not," stammered I.

"No, no, of course not," answered Harrod, quickly, as though he were afraid he had said a foolish thing; "but *I* care very much. I have pinned my faith on the squire."

Something rose, choking, in my throat. How dared he say that he had pinned his faith on the squire! In what way had he done so; what did he mean?

"I want to have a long talk with you one of these days," he added, gravely.

I looked at him. I think my face must have grown white. I could not make my lips form the words, but I suppose my eyes spoke them, for he added, "About many things." And then after a pause again: "There's something I think squire may be able to do that I haven't been able to do. I want you to ask him."

He spoke in his most hard voice; evidently it cost him a pang to have to say that he had not been able to do that something. "Of course it would be in a different way," he said, half to himself, "and the old man is proud; but it's the only chance." And then he added, "And he would do anything for you."

My eyes must have flamed, for he stopped.

"I shouldn't think of asking the squire anything—no, not anything at all," said I, trying to speak plainly. "I don't understand you."

"Well," said he, as if that settled the question, "anyhow, I must get a word with your father this morning. Do you think you can help me?"

"No," repeated I, my voice trembling, "I can't. You had better ask Joyce. She will be able to do any of these things that you want, I dare say."

He did not reply. He just turned his back and went out. I think it was all there was for him to do. And as I stood there, looking after him, with my heart swelling big, and Frank's letter crushed in my hand, Joyce passed across the lawn to the parlor porch.

In a moment, unbidden, unsuspected, like a watercourse broken from its banks, a great anger surged up in my heart towards her. She came gliding into the room with her usual quiet, graceful gait, and went up to the old bureau to get a china bowl that stood there and wanted washing. She fetched it and was going out again, but I stopped her. "Joyce, I want to speak to you," I said.

I suppose there was something in my voice that betrayed my feelings, for as she turned and stood there with the bowl in her hand her face wore just the faintest expression of alarm.

"What is it?" she asked.

"I have had a letter from Frank Forrester," said I. Her face flushed slightly.

"Oh, Meg!" said she.

"Yes," answered I, defiantly; "I wrote to him. There was no reason why, because you were heartless, I should be heartless too. I have no reason for being so prudent. I wrote to him."

Joyce flushed a little deeper, but she did not answer a word to my cruel and unjust accusations; she was always patient and gentle.

"What did he say?" she asked, presently.

"What *could* he say?" I said, scornfully. "He thanks me for writing; but I ask you how much he can have cared for my writing when the person whom he supposed loved him didn't care to know whether he was dead or alive?"

"That's nonsense, Meg," said Joyce, quietly. "He knew very well that I cared; he knew very well why I didn't write. Why should he expect me to break my word?"

"Why?" cried I, vehemently. "Because if you had had a grain of feeling in you, you *must* have broken your word; you couldn't have helped yourself. But you haven't a grain of feeling in you. You are as cold as ice. People might love you till they burned themselves up for loving you, but they would never get a spark to fly out of you in return. I suppose you *think* you loved Frank. Why else should you have said you would marry him? Was it because he was a gentleman, and you were only a farmer's daughter? No; I never imagined that," I added, confidently, seeing that she made a movement of horror. "You're too much of a Maliphant. It *must* have been because you loved him as much as you can love anybody. And you'll be faithful to him—oh yes, you're too proud to be fickle! You'll hold on silently to the end, just as you said you would hold on! But, good gracious me, does it never occur to you to think that perhaps such milk-and-water stuff might put a man out of heart? He may wait and wait for the ice to melt, but, upon my word, I don't think it would be so very astonishing if, at last, the fire went out with the waiting!"

I stopped, panting, and waited for what she would say. She lifted her eyes to my face—her dark-blue limpid eyes; there was no anger in them, only surprise and distress.

"Oh, Meg," she said, sadly, "do you know that I think you sometimes make up things in your own mind as you want them to be, and then you're angry because they're not like that. Can't you be different?"

"No," said I; "of course I can't be different any more than you can be different. We've got to make the best of one another as we are."

"Well, then, let's make the best of one another, Meg," said Joyce, gently. "We have always done it before, let us do it now."

"I can't make the best of you, Joyce," answered I, half appeased, "when I see you so cold towards the man whom you have sworn to love. I can't. I know you can't be different—people never become different—but, oh, you do make me angry."

"I'm sorry," said Joyce, penitently. "Don't be angry. Perhaps you don't quite understand, although you think you understand so well. I *am* proud, and I don't think I am fickle; but I am not cold either."

Why should her words have poured oil upon the flame which her gentleness but two minutes before had allayed? I don't know, but they maddened me.

"You're one or the other," I said. "You are cold, or you are fickle." I went up to her and took hold of her by the wrist—the left wrist, for the right hand still held the blue bowl. "Which is it?" I said, in a low voice; "which is it?"

Her face grew very pale, but she neither winced nor struggled. "Don't, Meg," she said.

"Yes, I will," cried I, fiercely. "Which is it, tell me?"

"It's neither," repeated she.

"I tell you you lie!" cried I. "You are as cold as ice. Frank knows it; Frank feels it. It is killing his love for you. Ah, go away; for pity's sake, go away, or I don't know what I shall say!"

I flung her hand away from me and rushed towards the door; but the sudden movement had jerked the bowl that she held out of her other hand; it fell onto the floor and was smashed into many pieces.

I turned round. Joyce had stooped down and was tenderly picking up the fragments. She had self-control enough to make me no reproach—she was always self-controlled; but the bowl was mother's best blue bowl. The sight of her there, with her concerned face, irritated me beyond endurance. Was there nothing in the world that was worse to break than a blue bowl? I went back to her again and stood over her, watching her with hands that trembled and heart that beat to very pain.

"If you are not heartless," I said, in a low voice; "if you *can* care for anybody's feelings as much as you care when the china is broken, who is it that you can feel for? You didn't seem to care very much when we thought that Frank had broken his back. Whom *do* you care for, then?"

I felt my lips tremble with anger, and for one moment I hated her. Oh that I should have to write it down! My own sister, who had been all the world to me two months ago! But it was true. Even through all the crystallizing, cooling mists of distance, I can recall the horrible feeling yet: I knew that—for one moment—I hated her.

"What do you mean?" said she, below her breath, trying to draw back.

"Ah, I can see very well how it might be," continued I, hurrying my words one on top of the other breathlessly—"how you might persuade yourself that you were true to him, and persuade yourself that you were doing a fine honorable thing keeping so strictly to your bargain with mother, when all the time it was because you never wanted to see him, and didn't care whether he loved you or not, and cared very much more whether somebody else loved you—somebody else who, but for you, might have belonged to another person. I can fancy it all very well," cried I, tearing Frank's letter that I held in my hand into little atoms and scattering them about the floor; "I can see just how it might happen, and nobody be to blame. No, nobody be to blame at all."

"Margaret, Margaret, for God's sake, collect yourself!" cried Joyce, her voice breaking into something like a sob. "You frighten me. What do you mean? What can you mean?"

"No, nobody to blame," repeated I, wildly, without paying any heed to her; "only just what one might have known would happen. One, with every gift that God can give, and the other, with—nothing but a vile temper that makes folk shun her even after they've seemed to be friends with her. What does it matter that you have promised to marry another man? Nobody knows it; and when one is as beautiful as you are, I suppose it isn't in human nature not to like to see one's beauty draw people away from what had been good enough for them before. I ought to have known it. There's nobody to blame, of course."

"Margaret," said my sister—and even in the midst of my fury the firm tone of her voice surprised me and checked me for a moment—"you must explain yourself. I don't understand you; I don't, indeed. Perhaps, if you knew everything, you wouldn't have the heart to speak so. You are cruel, and you are unjust. You say I am cold; but even if I am cold I can suffer, Meg; you must recollect that I can suffer."

"Suffer!" cried I, bitterly. "I wish you could suffer one little tiny bit of what I suffer. Ah, for pity's sake, don't let me say any more; don't let me go on; let me go!"

"I can't let you go," said Joyce, with that unusual firmness that did crop up at times so unexpectedly in her. "You must tell me first what you meant when you said that I took people away from what had been good enough for them before."

"Meant!" cried I. "You know well enough what I meant. I meant that it was easy enough for you to be noble and self-sacrificing, when all the time your thoughts were elsewhere. Yes, very easy for you to be patient, waiting for your own lover, when you were busy robbing me of my lover. Oh, don't speak, don't deny it! It's useless. You have done it, and you know that you have done it."

I think I expected Joyce to be crushed—I expected her to cry. I stood there panting and waiting for it. But she was neither crushed nor did she cry; she was not even angry. She stood there quietly, looking away from me out of the window, and at last she said: "You're mistaken, Meg; I never wanted to rob you of your lover. If you remember, when first I came home I told you that it was my hope such a thing might happen between you. I always thought you were too clever for the folk about here, and I thought he was clever. But you know you told me it never could be. You led me to believe you hated him, and always should hate him, because he had come to the farm to do your work. I believed it. Yes, until quite a little while ago I believed it. Then—"

"Well?" asked I, scornfully. "Then? What then?"

"Then, when I began to suspect that I might be mistaken, I resolved to go back and live with Aunt Naomi until matters were settled between you. That's what I was telling Mr. Harrod the day you came into the parlor last week."

"Oh, that's what you were telling him," cried I. "You don't say what he said to you that made you tell him that. You don't say if you also told him that you were engaged to another man."

"I didn't, because he said nothing to me to warrant it," answered my sister. "If he had I should have told him that I was not free."

"Ah, you do mean to keep your word to Frank, then?" asked I.

"I mean to keep my word to him if he wishes it," answered she, in a low voice.

Her face ought to have shamed me, but it raised the devil in me.

"Well, if you still love Frank there is no need for you to go away," said I, brutally. "Or is it because you are afraid of Mr. Harrod's peace of mind that you want to go?"

"Oh, Meg, how can you?" murmured Joyce.

Yes, how could I? The evil spirit was stronger than myself.

"It doesn't occur to you that this fine generosity of yours comes too late," cried I. "But the mischief is done. I won't have you go away now. I will go away."

"You!" exclaimed Joyce. "Where?"

"Not to Aunt Naomi's," I began, scornfully; and for a moment the temptation rose up in me to show her that I too was loved, was sought—to tell her where I might go if I chose, and be cherished, I knew it, for a lifetime. But the memory of the squire's face, of the little tremble in his voice, came back to me, and I could not speak of his love. "Not to Aunt Naomi," I said. "To be a governess."

"Oh no, Meg, I couldn't let you do that," said Joyce, concernedly. "I thought perhaps you were going to say something quite different. I have had a fancy now and then of late that we were all of us mistaken in that foolish notion of the reason why the squire has been such a faithful visitor to us all these years. Supposing it were as I fancy, don't you think you could grow to love him, Meg? He is worthy of you in every way."

She spoke with a strange pleading; her words heaped fuel on the fire within me; she paused for an answer, but I gave her none. "He is coming here to-night. I heard him promise mother he would come. Oh, how I wish it might be about you! Do you think there is any chance?"

Her voice flew at me like a shaft from a bow. I felt myself grow cold.

"How dare you?" I cried. "How dare you?"

I could say no more—I was paralyzed—I had no words.

Poor transparent Joyce, who had meant to be so generous, and who undid her work so thoroughly! How little I repaid her with my gratitude. She stood there gazing at me with a frightened expression on her lovely face.

"Go away, go away!" I stammered, wildly. "I want you to go away."

She made a movement forward as if to beg my pardon for anything she had said amiss. There was concern, pity, distress in her eyes, but I put her away. She went out of the room slowly, clasping the fragments of the broken bowl in her apron.

I threw myself down on the far window-seat. I did not cry, I never cried; but my whole body was trembling convulsively. I sat there in a trance till the latch of the front door roused me, and I heard some one come slowly, very slowly, across the hall.

Father came into the parlor; he came across to where I was, and laid his hand upon my head. The touch of it seemed to pass into me and soothe my troubled spirit.

"God help us to forget our troubles in those of others, Meg," he said, gravely, after some minutes.

And then I remembered that he had just come from the death-bed of that little lad whom he had loved so well.

I think there were tears in my eyes then.

CHAPTER XXXVII

The squire came that night to visit us, as Joyce had predicted. We were still sitting round the supper-table when he came in—a gloomy party. How unlike the merry, argumentative gatherings of old! Joyce and I did not look at one another, but Trayton Harrod glanced now and then at us both. The traces of tears were on my sister's face.

But father pushed his plate aside untouched, and turned to the bailiff with his business manner.

"Will you see to those poor folk down at the camp having a week's wage before they are discharged, Harrod?" said he. "Those of them who won't be needed, I mean."

"We'll see first how many will be needed, sir," answered Harrod, trying to be cheerful.

"Our own folk will be enough," replied father, quietly. "It's rough weather, and there are children down there. It's useless keeping them about for nothing."

Harrod was silent, and father lit his pipe. We none of us spoke of the little child who we knew was in his thoughts, but mother sighed. I think that little grave was very near to another little grave that she had in the abbey church-yard.

The squire shook hands with me just as usual when he came in, looking full into my eyes, with such a concerned look of kind inquiry as made me feel ashamed of my heavy face; but I made an excuse to get away at once—I could not stay in the room. I went into the kitchen to make cakes.

Not long afterwards I heard the front door close upon Trayton Harrod—I knew his step well enough—and then Joyce came into the kitchen. I know I asked her what she wanted in there at that time of day, for I did not care for the squire to be left alone with my parents, but she said that mother had sent her away. I saw Deb raise her eyebrows and purse her mouth in a way that was, as we knew, a sure forerunner of some sharp, good-natured raillery.

"Oh, what was that for, I wonder? What's the secret now?" said she, wiping her big red arms, and then stirring up the fire with a sharp brisk motion that betokened her most biting mood.

"I don't know," said Joyce, but in a tone that said she knew very well.

"Well, well, we've all expected it this long while past," said Deb. "I'm glad it's come at last."

She plunged her hands into the dish-tub once more, and looked up with a comical expression of triumph on her ugly old face.

"I don't know what you mean," said Joyce, faintly.

"Oh, don't you?" answered she. "Perhaps Meg does. Eh, do you know, Margaret?"

"I think you had better mind your own business, or talk of things you know something about," said I, tartly.

But Deb only laughed good-humoredly.

"I suppose you make no doubt it's your pretty face the squire's after, eh, Joyce?" persisted she, mercilessly.

Joyce flushed painfully.

"Don't, Deb, don't," said she.

"Well, my dear, no shame to you," added the old woman; "we have all thought the same thing. But maybe it isn't. Maybe Meg knows what he has come for, and is thinking over what answer she'd give him now."

"It wouldn't take me long to think what answer I should give *you*," cried I, fairly out of patience. "If the squire wanted an answer from me I could give him one without asking your advice, I dare say. But he's not such a fool."

"No, the squire's no fool," retorted Deb; "but I'm thinking other folk aren't so very far off it. The Lord grant you don't all of you get a lesson stiffer than you reckoned for one of these days, my dears," added she, with a little sigh.

We said no more on the subject. Joyce soon went up-stairs on some household job, and Deb and I went on silently with our work. But before my cakes were ready for the oven mother called me into the parlor. The squire had left. As Joyce had hoped, he had spoken to mother about me.

I knew it the moment I went into the room. I am sure he had not spoken willingly; but that he had said something, I knew the moment I looked at mother. There was a flush upon her cheek and a light in her eye that told of surprise, but of pride and pleasure also. It proved how there was never really any favoritism in her for my sister, for she showed not the slightest disappointment that the squire's proposal was for me and not for Joyce.

"Margaret," said she, sitting down in the big wooden chair opposite to father, who leaned forward in his favorite attitude, as though about to rise—"Margaret, the squire has just been here." She stopped a moment and half smiled. "The squire is very fond of you, Margaret," she added, gravely, going at once, as was her way, to the heart of the matter.

"The squire is fond of us all, I know," I answered, evasively. "He has known us such a long time."

"But he is fond of you in a different way to that," continued mother. "He loves you as a man loves the woman whom he could make his wife."

I did not answer for a bit, and mother, fancying, I suppose, that I must be as surprised as she was at the news, went on: "I had thought once it would be different, but now many things are explained. I think he has loved you ever since you began to grow up. It ought to make any girl feel proud, I'm sure."

"Yes," said I, softly. And I did feel proud, quite as proud as mother could wish, but I was not going to show it in the way that mother expected.

"Of course," she went on, after I had been silent a little while, "I quite understand how such a piece of news must come as a great surprise to you, almost as though it would take your breath away, I dare say. I don't wonder you don't know what to say."

Still I was silent. I stood by the table, twisting the fringe of the table-cover in my hand.

"I don't want to press you now," continued she. "Take your time about it, and tell me your mind in a day or two."

"Did the squire ask you to ask me my mind?" I said then, hurriedly.

It was mother's turn to be silent at that. And I knew that I had guessed aright, and that the squire had probably only had his secret drawn from him against his will by some remark showing the mistake that mother too had made about his love for Joyce. I even felt sure that he had specially begged that I should not be spoken to on the matter.

"Squire Broderick was speaking mostly about your sister," answered mother, evasively. "You know I told you I felt it my duty to set him straight about what you allowed you had made him think mistakenly about. And he was very much relieved when I told him there was no engagement between Joyce and that nephew of his. It's plain to see he thinks no good of him."

"Gently, gently, mother," murmured father, in remonstrating tones.

"But I suppose in that way he came to guess what was in my mind about him and her, and thought it best to put it right," concluded mother.

Of course I saw in a moment that it had all happened exactly as I might have been sure from the squire it would happen. The knowledge gave me courage. "I will give my answer to the squire himself when he asks me," I said, bravely.

Mother looked at me. I fancied there was a half-apologetic look in her eyes.

"The squire will not ask you, Margaret," said she. "I suppose he's timid. I suppose all good men are timid before the woman they love, however much they may really be worthy of her—the worthier perhaps the more so. It seems strange, but the squire'll never ask you to your face. So you'd better make up your mind to it. Your answer'll have to come through your parents in the old-fashioned way."

I went back to my occupation of pulling the fringe of the table-cover.

"But there's no need for you to say anything yet a while, lass," said father, after a few minutes.

It was the first time he had spoken, and I looked at him reassured.

"Oh yes, I think I had just as well say what I have to say now," I answered, with sudden boldness. "What's the good of waiting? I sha'n't change my mind. I can never change my mind. I can't marry Squire Broderick, if that's what you mean he wants."

There was silence. Mother seemed to be actually stupefied.

"But perhaps, after all, it isn't what he wants," added I, cheerfully, after a bit. "He's fond of me, because he has known me ever since I've been a little girl, and—well, because he is fond of me. But perhaps, after all, he doesn't want to marry me. I shouldn't think he would be so silly. I shouldn't be a bit of credit to him. I shouldn't be a bit suited to it. Not because father's a farmer, but because—well, because I'm not that sort of girl, like Joyce."

Mother had found her tongue.

"That's for the squire to decide," said she. "I know well enough it's a rise for any daughter of mine to marry into the Brodericks. Yes, you may say what you like, Laban," insisted she, fearlessly, turning to father, who had looked up with the old fire in his eye. "Our family may be older than his, but as the world goes now he's above us, and marriage with him would be a rise for our child. And I think that it would be a very good thing for one of our girls to be wed with the squire, and that's the truth."

Mother spoke emphatically, as though this were a question that had often arisen between her and father, as indeed I knew that it had, although not on my account. I looked round to see him fire up as I had seen him do before. I waited to hear him say that if the squire thought he was doing us a favor by asking one of us to marry him he was mistaken; but the light had all died out of his eye, and if his lip trembled, it was plain enough that it was not with anger.

"No doubt you're right, Mary," he said, very slowly. "Let class and family and such-like be. There's times when we forget all that. The squire's a good man, a good man."

I was dumb. I had certainly never thought that father would want me to marry the squire. But a retort that had risen to my lips at mother's speech, to the effect that I certainly shouldn't marry the squire, because it would be "a good thing" for me, died away. I was ashamed of it. It was so true that the squire was "a good man," and I was proud of his love.

"I can't marry the squire, mother, because I don't love him," said I, humbly.

Mother rose from her seat in all the height and breadth of her soft gray skirts.

"You and I never were of one mind as to what we meant by love, Margaret," said she. "But you take my advice. You don't say anything about this now, but just go away and think things over in your own mind for a while. Maybe you'll see you're not likely to be loved again as squire loves you. And maybe you'll say to yourself there ain't anything very much better to do than to make yourself worthy of it. Of course I don't know; folk are so different; and there's such a deal talked about love nowadays that most like it's grown to be something better than it was when I was young. But it won't hurt you to consider a while anyway."

"It's no use," said I, doggedly. "I suppose folk *are* different; but I can never marry a man I don't love as he loves me. I can't help it. That's the truth."

Mother had reached the door; she was going out, but she turned round. She was angry. The squire was rich, a gentleman. She had known him all his life, and knew that he was a good and kind man, and would make a good and true husband. Would not any mother have desired him for a son-in-law? She guessed at no reason why I should not wed him, and I think it was natural that she should be angry at mere obstinacy. I think so now, but I did not think so then.

"You can't marry a man you don't love as he loves you," repeated she, with an accent of something very like scorn. "Well, my girl, let me tell you that the very best sort o' love a woman can have for a man is gratitude, and if she can't live happy with that she's no good woman. There's no happiness comes of it when the woman's the first to love, for it's heartache and no mistake when she must needs pass her life with a man she loves more than he do her. There—I'm prating to the wind, I know. There never was a girl yet thought an old woman had once known what love was. You must go your own way, but you may take my word for it that your opinion about love'll be more worth knowing in twenty years' time than it is now. A chit like you, indeed! At least squire knows what he is about."

And with that she went out of the room and left me standing there, frozen into silence. The torrent of her unwonted speech, poured forth from the furnace of an unwonted fire in her, had fallen upon me like a cold stream of icy water. Had she guessed? Had every one guessed? Was I the sport of the community? Had I worn my heart upon my sleeve indeed?

I turned round to find father's gaze fixed upon me anxiously. I couldn't make out just what it meant—it was so full of a keen yet half-puzzled inquiry; but it was tender and sympathetic, and it soothed my ruffled spirit.

"You mustn't let mother's words hurt you, child," he said, kindly. "Mother's tongue is sharp sometimes, because she puts things in plain English; but she's a wise woman, Meg, a wise woman. There are never any clouds and mists round the tract of country mother travels. She sees things straight."

"I don't believe one person can ever see for another," declared I, stoutly. "However poor my opinion may be, it's all the light I have. I can't wait twenty years to decide what to do now."

Father smiled, but sadly. "Yes, we must all fight our own fight," he said, with a sigh.

"Oh, father, I can't believe you want me to marry Squire Broderick," said I, turning from the reflective which father so loved to the practical side of the question. "You always used to say that you wouldn't like us to marry out of our station."

"My dear," he said, "there's many windows that'll let in light if we'll only open them. But sometimes we're a long while before we'll open more than one window. I dare say, if the truth were known, it wasn't all at once the squire made up his mind that he wanted to marry out of *his* station. We mustn't forget that, Meg. It shows he loves you truly, child, and that he's a man above the common. The squire's a good man, a good man and true. And, after all, that's more than theories and such like."

I looked up at father anxiously.

"Would you have liked to see me the squire's wife, father?" asked I.

He held out his hand, beckoning me to him, and I went and knelt down at his side.

"Meg," said he, "you've always been a good girl, a bright, brave, smart girl, with understanding of things beyond your years, though, maybe, sometimes that very thing in you has led you to be less wise than quieter folk. You've often been a help and a comfort to me."

My heart swelled big within me, and I could not speak.

"Now, if I say something to you that I wouldn't trust every girl with, will you promise me to be just as wise as you are brave?"

"Yes, father," whispered I.

"I'm afraid when I'm gone, Meg, that mother won't be so well off as I had hoped to leave her."

"Why, what does that matter?" cried I, with the scorn of a youthful and energetic, and also of an inexperienced spirit for such a thing as poverty. "So long as we live in the old place we needn't mind having to be a little more economical. Mother's very lavish now."

Father only sighed. "Besides," continued I, "you're not an old man yet, father. You've many years before you, and the hops'll be better another time."

I said it hopefully, but something in my heart misgave me. I lifted my face to find those gray eyes, dark in the fire's uncertain light, fixed upon me tenderly.

"Child, I don't believe I'm long for this world," said he, gravely. "I don't want mother to know it. Time enough when the day comes, but the doctor has told me that I carry a disease within me that may kill me at any moment."

I felt all the blood ebb away from my heart. I clasped his hand tightly, but I did not speak.

"That's right. You're a brave girl," said he, with a smile. "But you see, when I'm gone, there'll be nobody but you to take care of mother."

"Doctors are often wrong," murmured I, faintly.

Margaret Maliphant | 333

"Yes, yes, so they are," answered father, "and I may last many a year yet; but if it were possible, I want to be prepared—I want some one else to be prepared. Perhaps I've done wrong to tell you, Meg. Perhaps it's too heavy a burden for a young heart."

"No, no," cried I, eagerly, though in truth I was frozen with a terrible fear. "I like you to trust me—I like to think you lean upon me."

"I do trust you," repeated he, resting his hand upon my head in that way that he sometimes had. And then he added, "And I trust Squire Broderick too."

I was silent. I began to see his drift.

"The squire will always be our friend," I said. "He has told me so."

"I'm sure of that," replied my father; "but don't you see, Meg, that if the squire wants to marry you, it will be difficult for him to be just the same to you as he has always been."

"Will it?" said I, doubtfully.

"I'm afraid it might be so," answered he; "but of course that must make no difference. I can't teach you what to do in this matter. Nobody can teach you. You must do what your heart tells you. But you're a young lass yet, and if ever you come to think differently of the thing, remember what I said to you to-day, dear, and don't let any fancied pride stand in your way. Where hearts are true and honest, there's no such thing as pride; I learn that the older I grow."

"I will remember it, father," answered I, religiously; and something in my heart forbade me to add, as I wanted to, "But I never shall think differently."

How could I tell him that I loved a man who had never spoken to me of love, who I had every reason to suppose loved another woman, and that woman my own sister? No; I had not the courage so to humble myself; I had not the courage so to grieve him. Mother's voice sounded without. "Bring in prayers, Joyce," called she, using the well-known topsy-turvy phrase that I had known ever since I was a child. "It's late enough."

But as I knelt there that night, mingling my voice with the voices of all those I loved, in the familiar words of the Lord's Prayer, I thought God had been very hard to me, and the fear that he might even take away my father from me brought such a storm of terrified and rebellious agony that I felt I could not honestly say the words that had passed so easily over my head these fifteen years, "Thy will be done."

CHAPTER XXXVIII

A week went by—silent, uneventful—the world of action and emotion as leaden as the sky was leaden above our heads.

Father led his usual life, and seemed in no way worse than he had been for some time; so that the sick fear within me was lulled for a while to rest, and, realizing the emptiness of the present, I forgot the possibility of even greater evil in the future.

The summer was gone—the summer that even the oldest people in the village declared to have been more wonderfully bright and long than any they had ever seen; September closed with a whirl of storms and a drenching of bitter rain.

In the deserted hop-gardens—strewn with the unpicked tendrils of the ruined crops, or studded with the conical tents of the stacked ash-poles—only dead ashes recorded the merry flames that had leaped up towards the merry faces; the summer was gone, and everywhere trees and hedges were turning to ruddy tones upon the brooding sky.

Ah me! Harvesting had slipped into winter before, and green leaves had turned to gold, and summer birds had flown to southern homes, but never had storms followed so quickly upon sunshine, nor flowers withered so fast upon their stems, nor hopes fallen so quickly to the ground!

But the uneventful week was to end in events. It was the 1st of October. I remember it because it was mother's birthday, and the esquire, who had never before failed to come and congratulate her personally, only sent his gift of flowers by a servant. I know I felt guilty, and realized something of what father had meant, for I fear mother was hurt.

When I went into the parlor at tea-time, mother and the bailiff were there alone. They were evidently engaged in a deep and earnest conversation.

I thought it was about Mr. Hoad, who had rarely been at the Grange of late, but who was closeted with father that afternoon, somewhat to my own vague anxiety. I had a notion that mother had spoken to Harrod upon the subject before, and thought at first that her sudden silence was only because she did not care for one of us girls to know that she so far confided in the bailiff. But a certain half-confused look, that was very foreign to mother, led me to wonder whether, after all, she had been talking to him about Mr. Hoad that time; and when she sent me to call father in, she bade me shut the door after me, although I was only going across the passage.

If I had not been so very preoccupied I should have been more alarmed than I was at the sound of Mr. Hoad's voice, raised in loud tones, as I approached the library door, and I should have taken more anxious note of father's face, as he only just opened it to bid me tell mother he was busy just now but would come presently.

She looked vexed when I gave her the message, and took her seat before the tea-tray with an aggrieved air. "I don't know why, if Mr. Hoad doesn't care to drink tea with us himself, he should choose this particular moment to keep your father busy and away from his food," she complained.

"I suppose it's something very particular," said Joyce, in her even tones, and without noticing the frown on Harrod's brow. "Mr. Hoad is always so polite; it must be something particular."

"Very particular!" repeated mother, pursing up her lips. "I don't know why it should be so particular it couldn't be said at the table, only that men must always needs fancy they've got very weighty and secret matters on hand. It was only about those unlucky hops, for I heard him mention them as he went in. Why he must needs remind father of his losses, I don't know. It's bad enough without that, and when I wanted him to cheer up a bit. The hops can't matter to Mr. Hoad. But men are so stupid and inconsiderate!"

We finished tea and drew round the fire. It was dark—half-past six o'clock and more—and we had had tea by lamplight. Mother remarked how quickly the evenings were drawing in. Then she suggested sending again for father, but Harrod begged her to be patient.

"Mr. Hoad must be going soon or he will have a dark drive home," he said.

I laughed. "There is a moon," said I, "unless the clouds have swallowed it." And I got up to go out on the terrace and see.

The voices in the library rose and fell as I opened the door. I heard father's deep tones, strong and firm, and Mr. Hoad's, lighter and jarring. Joyce rose too and followed me, and so did Trayton Harrod.

The library window stood ajar as we crossed the lawn.

"You'll pull through all right," came Mr. Hoad's voice; "Squire Broderick's your friend. You were wise not to stick to your colors over that election business. It would have offended him. He's not a poor devil like me who must needs look to the pence. He can afford to be generous about debts and rents. And if rumor says true, there's one of your young ladies can give him all he needs for reward."

I stopped, paralyzed. Had Joyce heard?

But Trayton Harrod strode past me to where she stood a few steps before us. "Miss Maliphant, you must fetch a wrap for your head," he said, hurriedly; "the mist is falling."

She went in obediently. I noticed she always did behave obediently towards him now. If she had heard, she gave no sign of it. Probably she had not understood.

Some one stepped forward inside the room and fastened the window. I heard no more.

"Come down onto the terrace," said Harrod, authoritatively. "We can wait for your sister there."

He led the way and I followed, but I looked at him. Had he also not heard, not understood? Oh yes, he had heard, and he had understood — as I had understood.

"What did that man mean?" cried I, looking at him straight in the eyes.

We had not spoken to one another frankly and freely for some time, but this had roused me.

"The fellow is a low cur," he said.

"Yes; but what did he mean?" insisted I. "I've always known that; but I want to know what he meant by talking as he did of Squire Broderick."

Trayton Harrod was silent.

"Mr. Harrod, if you know, you must, please, tell me," said I, firmly.

He had looked away from me, but now he turned his face to me again.

"Yes, I will tell you," answered he, simply. "I think it is well you should know. The farm is in a bad way; perhaps you have guessed that. I have not been able to do what I hoped to do when I first came to it. I have not been successful."

He spoke in a heavy, dispirited tone; it roused afresh all the sympathy that had been stifled a while by my bitter passion. "Don't say that," I cried. "You have done a great deal. I am sure father thinks so, and I think so," I added, softly. "But you have been hampered."

"Well, anyhow I have failed, and the farm is in a bad way," he repeated, rather shortly. "Your father has been pressed for money, probably not only since I have been here; he has been obliged to get it as best he could to pay the men's wages. He has got some of it from Hoad."

"From Hoad!" repeated I. "Not as a favor?"

"No," continued he, with a laugh; "your father is indebted to Hoad, probably for a large amount. I fear it. But not as a favor. Hoad is the man to know well enough what rate of interest to charge; and he is threatening now to press him for payment. So long as your father could be useful to him, so long as he hoped to get his help towards securing the Radical seat for Thorne, he was forbearing enough—made out that he would wait any length of time for it, I dare say; but now it's a different matter. Thorne lost the seat and Mr. Hoad some advantage he would have had out of the affair. He doesn't mean to be considerate any more. He means to press for his money."

"How could father ever trust such a man, ever have any dealings with him?" cried I, indignantly. "It's horrible to think he could have done it. But now, of course, he must be paid at once, and we must never, never see him again."

Harrod was silent.

"Why does father stop there arguing with him?" cried I, looking back towards the library window. "How can he condescend to do it? Why doesn't he pay him his money and tell him to be off?"

"Perhaps your father hasn't got the money, Miss Margaret," said Harrod, slowly, after a pause.

"Not got it!" cried I. "How much is it?"

"I don't know," he answered, "but I'm afraid it's more than your father has at hand at the moment. He must need all his ready cash to pay the men, and there's the rent due presently."

"The rent!" echoed I, under my breath. "The rent is due to Squire Broderick."

"Yes," agreed Harrod.

"Father has been punctual with his rent all his life," continued I, proudly, "I've often heard him say so. Nothing would persuade him to be a day late with the rent."

"No, of course," said Harrod, quickly.

And then he was silent. I flushed hot in the dim light.

I knew now what Mr. Hoad had meant, and I hated him in my heart worse than I had ever hated him before, for what he had meant.

"But that's what Hoad counts on," continued Harrod, rapidly, as though suddenly making up his mind to speak. "He is a low, vulgar fellow, and he would think such a thing natural enough. He can see no other reason why your father should not have consented to stand by his candidate at the election."

A sudden revelation came to me.

"Was that what the article was about that you tried to keep out of father's way?" I asked.

He nodded. My heart flamed with anger at the treachery of the man who had called himself father's friend, but through it there was a very broad streak of gratitude to the man who had been his friend without calling himself so. But I did not say so; I only repeated aloud what I had told myself inwardly.

"I hate him," I said. "Whatever happens, he will never get his money that way. But, oh, isn't it horrible to think that father should owe money to such a man! Is there no way in which he could be paid off now—at once?"

"Not any that I can see," said Harrod, sadly.

"Won't there be any money coming in for the hops?" I asked again, eagerly.

"Oh, if the season had been good for the hops!" echoed Harrod. And then he stopped short.

I did not ask any more, but I understood a great deal in that short sentence, and when I thought over all that he had said, I understood more still: that perhaps he had guessed long ago, when he first came, in what position father then stood; that perhaps he had even advised the hop speculation as a last chance, having as I knew he had, special facilities for disposing of a good crop. He had worked for us, he had our interests at heart, but the task that he had undertaken had been harder than he had guessed; knowing him as I did, I knew how very, very bitter must be to him the sense of failure. His work: that was the first thing with him, and he had failed in it.

"If it hadn't been for you, things would be much worse than they are," said I at last, full of a really simple and unselfish sympathy. "You have done a great deal for the farm."

"It might have been of some use if the circumstances had been different," said he, half testily. "As it is, I have done no good, no good at all. But that's neither here nor there. The thing is what to do now."

"Must something be done at once?" I asked, anxiously.

"Yes," answered he, briefly, "at once."

I was silent, looking out over the plain. The last of the daylight was dead; the moon fled in and out among the clouds that swept, swift and soft, over the blue of the deep night sky, on whose bosom she lay cradled sometimes as in a silver skiff, but that again would cross her face with ugly scars or hide her quite from sight—a murky veil that even her rich radiance could only inform with brightness as a memory upon the hem of it. The marsh always looked wider and more mysterious than ever under such a sky as that, until no one could have told where the land ended and sea began; it was all one vast, dim ocean—billows of land and billows of water were all one.

I could not but think of the night, three months ago, when I had stood there on that very spot with Trayton Harrod, and when, at my request, he had consented to stay on at the farm and help us. He had stayed on, and he had done what he could. Was it his fault if he had not brought us help and happiness?

I remembered the night well; I remembered that then it had been warm, whereas now it was chilly. The twilight had faded and the night was dark, save for that fitful, fickle moon. A thin gauze of cloud hung now before the white disk, and the light that filtered through it showed another thin gauze of mist floating above the sea of dark marsh-land; the breeze that crept up among the aspens on the cliff had scarcely a memory of summer.

"What can be done?" asked I, in answer to that brief, terse declaration.

"There is only one thing that I can see," said he. "You are right; Hoad must be paid. It is not a matter of choice. The money must be borrowed to pay him with."

"Borrowed!" cried I. "From whom could we borrow it, even if we would? There is nobody who would lend us money."

"Yes, there is one man," said Harrod, quietly.

"You mean Captain Forrester," said I, "because you have seen him here so intimately with father; but I assure you"—I stopped; I had begun disdainfully, but I ended up lamely enough—"he has no money."

"No, I did not mean Captain Forrester," answered Harrod, with what I fancied in the half-light was a smile upon his lips, "I mean Squire Broderick."

I flushed again. I did not look at him.

"Father would never think of asking Squire Broderick to lend him money," I said, quickly.

"No, I dare say not," answered the bailiff. "Your father is a very proud man, and however well he may know the squire is his friend, they have not always exactly hit it off. But you, Miss Margaret, you could ask him, and for your father's sake, you would."

"Oh no, indeed, I wouldn't," said I, almost roughly. "It's the last thing in the world that I would do." And then I turned quickly round. "Joyce hasn't come down," I added. "We had better go back and look for her."

I moved away a couple of steps, but he didn't follow, and I stopped.

"Don't go in just yet," he said. "Your mother does not need you. I want to talk to you a little. We used always to be such good friends; but we haven't had a talk for a long while."

I stood still where I was.

"If it's about borrowing money of the squire that you want to talk to me, I don't think it would be any use for you to trouble," said I, with my back still turned to him. "I shouldn't think of asking him to lend father money—not if I thought ever so that he would do it."

"Of course he would do it to please you," said Harrod, frankly. "He loves you. But I quite understand how that might be more than ever the reason for your not asking him."

I did not answer; the suddenness of the way in which this had come from him had taken away my breath. It had not even struck me that he could have guessed it; and now that he should speak of it—*he* to *me!*

"It would be a reason if you did not mean to accept his love," continued Harrod, ruthlessly. "But since that could not surely be the case, are you not over-delicate; do you not almost do him an injury by not trusting him to that extent?"

"Mr. Harrod, I don't know how you dare to talk to me so," said I, fiercely, but under my breath.

"Dare!" echoed he, with a little laugh that had an awkward ring in it, and yet at the same time a little tone of surprise, "I thought we were friends. Surely one may say as much to a friend?"

"You may not say as much to me," retorted I, in the same tone. "And I don't know why you should think that the squire loves me."

"Is there any insult in that?" smiled he. "I did not suppose so. Surely it is clear to every one that he loves you? I have seen it ever since I have been at the Grange."

"You have seen it!" ejaculated I, dumfounded. "Why, it was Joyce! We all thought it was Joyce!"

"I did not think it was Joyce," said he.

I was silent once more. Ever since he had been at the Grange he had seen that the squire loved me. What, then, had been his attitude towards me? What had ever been his attitude towards me?

"Well, if the squire loves me, he will have to get over it," said I, in a hard, cold voice. I was hurt and sore, and my soreness made me hard for the moment towards the man to whom in my heart I was never anything but reverent. But the very next moment I was sorry; I was ashamed of even a thought that was not all gratitude towards him. "Perhaps," I added, gently, "it is not exactly as you fancy. I am not good enough for the squire."

"Not good enough!" echoed he, and there was a ring of genuine appreciation and loyalty in his voice which set my foolish heart aglow. "I don't see why not. Anyhow, *he* does not seem to be of that opinion, from what your mother tells me."

Mother! That was what they had been discussing so secretly.

"I'm sorry mother could talk about it," said I. "It wasn't fair. It's a pity such things should be talked about when they are never going to come to anything."

"Why is it never going to come to anything?" asked Trayton Harrod.

"That's my own business," said I, defiantly.

"Yes, that's true," answered he; "but I had thought, as I have said, that we were good enough friends for you to let a little of your business be mine also. I beg your pardon."

His tone unaccountably irritated me, but his allusion to our friendship touched me nevertheless.

"You needn't beg my pardon," said I, more quietly; "only I don't want you to talk any more about that. Mother may be mistaken about the squire wanting to marry me. I hope he does not. If he does, I shall find my own way of telling him it couldn't be."

"Well, Miss Margaret, if I'm offending you by speaking of the matter, I must hold my tongue," said Harrod; "but I feel as if I must tell you that I think you are making a great mistake."

I did not answer, and he went on:

"Your father is in a bad way. He would be very much relieved to think that one of you was comfortably settled for life. Apart from anything that you could do for him in this crisis, and which, no doubt, he has not thought of, you must see for yourself how that would be so."

"A girl can't marry to please her father," said I, "and *my* father is the last one to wish it."

"Of course," said he, persistently, "neither your father nor your friends would wish you to marry against your will for *any* advantage that might result. But why should it be against your will? The squire is such a good-fellow."

"Oh, don't ask me to talk about it," cried I. "I know he is good; I know all you say."

"If the truth were known, I expect there's a good bit of pride in it," smiled he. "You are your father's own daughter about that. And there's the squire, no doubt, thinks he's not half good enough for you. A man mostly does if he cares for a woman."

"It isn't that. I can't marry the squire, because I don't love him, and there's an end," cried I, desperately.

I wished he had never spoken to me about it; I could not understand how he *could* do so, even to please mother, at whose instigation I felt sure it was done. It seemed to me to be very unlike him, but since he had forced himself to speak, I must force myself to tell him that much of the truth. But I turned down away from him, and walked to the edge of the terrace.

Harrod, however, again followed me.

"Perhaps you don't know exactly what you mean by that," said he, gently. "Young girls don't always. And they think, because a man is a few years older than themselves, that it can't be a love-match. But sometimes they find out, after all, that it was a love-match, only they didn't know it at the time. Wise folk say that the best sort of love comes of knowledge, and isn't born at first sight, as some think it is."

They were mother's arguments. It was out of friendship for me, no doubt, that he repeated them, but they were mother's words, and they didn't touch me at all. All that I felt was a rage, rising horribly and swiftly within me, against the man who dared to utter them.

I did not reply. I only drew my cloak closer around me, for the marsh wind rose now and then in sudden puffs that found their way to the very heart of one; they sent the clouds flying across the sky, and the moon disappeared deep down into a bed of blackness—so deep that not even the hem of it was fringed as before with the silver rim; upon the marsh was unbroken night. I can see it still, I can feel the chill of it.

Margaret Maliphant | 343

And yet, within, my heart was hot, and it was out of the heat of it that I spoke. Shall I write down what I spoke? I can hardly bear to do it. Even after all these years, when fate, kinder than her wont, has helped me to bury all that spoiled past, and to begin a future upon the grave of it that has its foundations deeper still. Even now I am afraid to look at the stern record of my words in black and white before me. I am ashamed—not of my love, but of my selfishness, though these pages are for no other eyes than mine, I am afraid. But I have set myself the task, and it shall be accomplished to the end.

"Can't you understand," said I, in a low voice, "that perhaps I cannot love the squire because I love somebody else better?"

He was silent—he did not even look at me. He gave no sign of being surprised at my revelation.

"Are you sure of that?" he said, after a pause. "And is he as worthy of you as Squire Broderick?"

"Worthy!" echoed I. For a moment a proud, rebellious answer flashed through my mind. Was he worthy of me—he who gave so much the less, for mine that was so much the more? But I trod the demon out of sight. Was he to blame if I gave the more? "What is worthiness?" asked I.

He did not reply at first, and then it was in a voice that somehow seemed to me different to any I had heard him use before.

"I don't know that there's any such thing," he said, with a sort of grim seriousness. "But a man can give the best he has, and I don't think a woman should put up with less."

Queer, plain words; there was nothing in them to hurt me, and yet they seemed to fly at me. My heart beat wildly; I could feel it, I could hear it, fluttering like a caged bird against the hard-wood of the fence against which I leaned.

"The squire gives you the best he has," said Trayton Harrod. "Does the man you think you love do as much?"

I don't know whether it was my fancy or not, but his voice seemed to tremble. I had never heard his voice tremble before.

"How can I tell?" said I, as well as I could speak the words for shame and heartache.

"A woman can tell fast enough," murmured he. And then he stopped; he came one step nearer to me. "And the fact is," said he, emphatically, "it seems a shame for a fine, clever girl like you to throw away such a man as the squire for the sake of a fellow who she isn't even sure gives her the best he has. I've no right to talk so to you, and I couldn't have done it if your mother hadn't made me promise to. She seemed to think I ought. But, upon my word, I'm of her mind. You think you care for that other fellow now, but if he don't give you what you've a right to expect, you wouldn't be the girl I take you for if you didn't put him out of your mind. There isn't anything in the world can live when it has nothing to feed on."

How every word seemed to fall like a stone into the bottom of a well! They echoed in my head after he had finished speaking. Another gust of wind came sweeping up from the invisible sea of water across the just visible sea of land. The moon made a little light again through a softer gray cloud, and shone with a wan, covered brightness upon us; the aspens on the cliff shivered—and I shivered too. The fire in my blood had burned itself out, I suppose, and the cold from without struck inward, for I felt as though I were frozen into a perfectly feelingless lump of ice.

"I wonder what would have happened if the squire's proposal had been made to Joyce, as we all supposed it would be?" said I, slowly.

I did not look at him, but I felt him start.

"Do you think she would have accepted him?" asked he. His voice did not tremble now; it was hard and metallic; it did not sound like his own. It drove me into a frenzy. All that had happened of late, all that had happened in the last half-hour, had been piling up the fuel, and now the instinctive knowledge of the feelings that had prompted that last speech of his set a light to the fire. I was mad with jealousy.

"I don't know," said I. "If the squire had proposed to Joyce, and she had known that she would help father, as you say, by marrying him, she might have brought herself to it. She is more unselfish than I am. *She* might have brought herself to marry one man while she loved another."

Harrod did not answer at first, but I felt his face turned upon me waiting for me to go on, and I heard him draw in his breath and breathe it out again, as if he were relieved.

"What makes you think she is in love with another man?" asked he, in a low voice.

"Oh, I know it," said I, stung to the utterance by the knowledge that he thought I meant with himself. "She is engaged to him."

My heart almost stopped beating, waiting to see where the shaft would strike.

It struck home. "Engaged!" muttered he.

"Yes," I went on, quickly, perhaps lest I should repent of my wicked purpose. "She is engaged to Captain Forrester. They do not meet, because my parents wished it to be kept secret for a year. But they love one another."

Oh, Joyce, Joyce! how could I have said it? A hundred excuses came swarming into my head, but in every one of them there was a sting, for through the buzz of them all came a strong, clear voice telling me that the man whom Joyce really loved stood at my side. I knew it, I knew it, and yet I let him think that she loved some one else; I let him go away with an aching heart. That was my love for him—that was my love for Joyce, who, until he crossed my world, had been all my world to me.

I remember nothing more. I suppose he said something and I answered it, or else I said something and he answered it; but I remember nothing—nothing until I saw him thread his way down among the aspens on the cliff and disappear onto the desolate marsh-land.

That I remember. I often see it happening. The moon still hung behind that veil of gray cloud; the breeze still crept chill among the trees, piercing to the heart; the faint white light showed a very wide world, wider far than in the brightness of day; there seemed to be a great deal of room for longing and heartache. But was the heartache in it all mine? In a moment the horror of what I had done came home to me. I who suffered had made others suffer.

"Oh, come back! come back!" I cried, in an agony of grief, hurrying down the cliff till I stood over the marsh, waving my arms wildly in the dark night. "Come back! I have something more to say."

But he was gone. The moon was the same moon looking sadly on; the world was the same world as it had been ten minutes ago, but he was gone. And who was to blame?

I came slowly up the cliff again—cold, stunned. What had I done? Where should I go?

"Margaret! Margaret!" came a loud, terrified cry from the porch.

It was the voice of my sister Joyce.

CHAPTER XXXIX

That night father was struck down with the stroke that was to end in his death.

That was what the terror in my sister's voice had meant when she had called down the garden to me through the chill darkness. Her cry had roughly summoned me from the contemplation of my own woes, and the mourning of my own cruelty, to a sterner death-bed than the death-bed of my own selfish hopes, to the darkest experience that can cross any loving human creature's path.

He lay ill three weeks, but from the first we knew that there was no hope, and knew that none could tell when he might finally be taken. We took turns night and day watching beside him, and during the first dreadful night following his seizure I was sitting alone in the dim parlor waiting for my turn, when, towards midnight, there was a knock at the door. I thought it was the doctor, who had promised to come again before morning; but when I opened the door the squire stood outside. The bad news had crept up to the Manor during the evening, and he had come to learn if it was true.

For the first time that evening a little breath of something that was warm crept about my cold heart. I forgot that the squire had wanted to marry me, and that I had practically refused him; I forgot everything but that here was a friend full of real sympathy in our trouble, and thinking at that moment of nothing else—perhaps the only friend whom I instinctively counted upon in a world that seemed to me just then very wide and empty.

He stepped inside at once, and I told him what had happened, there in the hall, in a quick, low whisper.

"There is no hope," I said. "I knew that quite well, although the doctor said that there was just a chance. He knew himself that he might die at any moment. He told me so yesterday, only I didn't really believe him."

My heart swelled at the recollection of that scene, but I did not cry. I wonder if he thought me heartless.

"How did it happen?" asked the squire.

"Mr. Hoad was with him. I heard them talking as I went out into the garden," answered I, sickening with the recollection of what I had gone there for. "Joyce says Mr. Hoad went out suddenly, and then they heard father fall. He has never spoken since."

"Ah, if we could only have kept that man away from him!" murmured the squire.

"Yes; and I feel as if it were my fault," whispered I. "He owed him money, and he came to press for it just now when the hops have failed and the rent is due. He is so mean that he had a grudge against father for not helping on Mr. Thorne. But how was I to get the money? It was cruel, cruel to suggest it!"

I caught the squire's eyes fixed upon me with a strange, pitying, questioning look. I did not understand it at the moment, but in the light of what I afterwards learned I understood its meaning.

I stopped abruptly. I felt as though my senses were leaving me—my head was whirling. I knew I had said something, in this moment of unusual craving for sympathy and support, which I should never have said at any other moment.

But there was no time to go back upon my words, even if that had been possible. I just caught those eyes that shone so blue out of the squire's bronzed face fixed intently upon me in the dim light of the little hall, when Joyce ran quickly down the stairs.

"Father wants to see you, Squire Broderick," said she, eagerly. "He heard your voice and he wants to see you."

"Oh, then he *is* conscious again!" cried I, joyfully.

"Yes," said Joyce; "he is conscious."

She said it with a marked accent on the word.

"But—" asked the squire.

"He can't speak," added she.

I turned my face away from them.

"That means he is dying," said I. "The doctor said it might be before dawn."

All at once a cowardly, horrible longing to run away took possession of me.

"Oh, perhaps not," said Joyce, gently. "We must hope while there is life. We can do nothing; he is beyond us. We must submit ourselves to whatever is God's will."

She was right. Perhaps for the first time in my life I felt all the awful force of it—that we could do nothing, absolutely nothing; that we must submit ourselves.

But why was it God's will? Again it angered me, as it had angered me once before, that Joyce should be able to submit herself apparently so easily to what was God's will. I was unjust. There were tears on her cheeks and mine were dry. We were different, that was all.

"Come," said she, turning again to the squire, "he is impatient."

She turned up the stairs, flitting softly in her blue flannel dressing-gown, with the golden hair slipping a little from its smooth coils.

The squire followed. I sat down on the old oaken bench below to wait.

"You, you too, Meg," said she, turning round. The oak staircase was dark, but a yellow ray from the oil-lamp hung on the wainscoting showed her face surprised. Mother's voice came from above, and she ran on up the stairs.

The squire came back again to me. "Come, dear," said he—and even at that solemn moment I could not help noticing the word of tenderness that had unconsciously slipped from him. "I want you to come, because afterwards you would be sorry you had delayed. When you see him you will not be afraid."

He took my hand and led me up the stairs, so that we entered father's room together.

Yes, he was quite conscious. Those piercing gray eyes of his shone as with a fire from within like coals in his white face; they were terrible in their acute concentration, as though all the strength of that once strong frame, of that once active mind, had retired to this last citadel; but, black under the shadow of the overhanging brows, they were the dear familiar eyes of old to me, and I was not frightened.

As we approached—I in my trouble still letting my hand lie unconsciously in the squire's—I saw one of those gleams that I have said were often as of sunshine on a rugged moor cross the whiteness of his face.

For a moment the effort to speak was very painful, but he took the squire's hand in his—in both of his—and looked at me, and I knew well enough what he meant to say.

Margaret Maliphant | 349

I did not speak. I could not have spoken if I would, for there was a lump in my throat that choked me; but I had nothing to say. How could I have found it in my heart to tell him that what he had seen meant nothing, yet what words would my tongue have made to tell him that I would give my hand to the squire forever? It was not possible. I slipped my hand out of his, but father did not see it. He was looking more at the squire than at me; upon him his eyes were fixed with a strangely mingled expression of pride and entreaty. Thinking of it now, it comes before me as a most pathetic picture of proud self-abandonment and generous appeal. It was almost as though he said: "I have wronged you. Creeds and convictions are nothing. We have always been one, and you are my only friend. Help me in my need." So I have often since read that look in his deep, sorrowful eyes. My dear father! Should I say my poor father? No, surely not. Yet at that moment I thought so; I wanted to do something for him, and the only thing that I might have done I would not do. But the squire came to the rescue.

"I know," he said, tenderly; "be at rest. I will take care of them all."

Not I will take care of *her*. "I will take care of them all."

My heart went out to him in thanks. He had said I should have courage. He had given me courage.

When he was gone, I took my place at the bedside; I was no longer afraid of Death, or if I was afraid, my love was more than my fear; I stayed beside father till the end. I was thankful that the end did not come for those three weeks. He did not suffer, and he grew to depend upon me so, to turn such trustful and loving eyes upon me whenever I came near him, that they took me out of myself as nothing else could have done. Dear eyes that have followed me all through the after-years to still the pangs of remorse, and to warm the coldness of life. Ah me! and yet those were sore days. Knowing that he was taking comfort as he lay there from the thought that I and the squire would one day be one, I longed to make a clean breast of it. I longed to tell him that a very different figure from good Squire Broderick's crossed my mind many times a day, unbidden and horrible to me, who wanted to give every fibre of myself to him who lay a-dying.

I cannot explain it, I can only say that it was so: dearly as I loved my father, the thought of him did not keep out every other thought. All through those weary watching hours, I was watching for other footsteps besides those that were coming—so slow and sure—to take away what I had loved all my life; black upon my heart lay the shadow of a deeper remorse than that of letting a dying man believe in a possibility that set his mind at rest: I wanted to see Trayton Harrod that I might undo what I had done, that I might tell him the truth about Joyce.

Yes, though I knew well enough that I loved him far too well to think of another, it was not of my love that I thought, sitting there through the dark hours with the sense of that awful presence upon me that might at any moment snatch, whither I knew not, the thing that I had known as my dear father. I only wanted to see him that I might rid my conscience of that mean lie, that I might make him happy, and hear him say that he forgave me; and many is the time I started beside the still bed, thinking I heard that light firm step on the gravel without, or the click of the latch in the front door as the bailiff had been wont to lift it.

But Trayton Harrod did not come, and, with the self-consciousness of guilt, I dared not ask for any news of him. It was not until more than a week after father's first seizure that I learned he had gone to London at daybreak on the morning following our parting, and had not yet returned. My heart sank a little at the news, although I knew he had intended going away for a little just about this time, and I guessed, of course, that he could have heard nothing of our trouble before he left.

Deborah said that one of the men had left a note from him the morning of his departure, but in the confusion of father's illness neither she nor I could find it, and I was reduced to sitting down once more to wait face to face with another grim phantom of Death besides that one that was keeping the house so quiet and strange for us all. Once I think mother said Harrod must be sent for, but nobody thought of it again, for everything was really swallowed up in that great anxiety, while we waited around that bedside hoping against hope, watching for that partial return of speech which the doctor had told us might perhaps be given to him once more.

The Rev. Cyril Morland came to see him, and told him all that he had been able to do about that scheme for the protection of little children which lay so near his heart. I well remember, though his poor body was half dead, how pathetic in its keenness was the effort to understand all as he had once understood it—how touching the fire that still burned in his sunken eyes—how touching the smile that still played about his white lips.

Yes, I remember it all; I remember how, after many attempts, he made me understand that I was to fetch that crayon sketch of the young man's head that hung above the writing-desk in his study, and put it opposite his bed. I remember how his eyes were turned to it then, as he listened to the good young parson's explanations of what had already been achieved in that branch of the great question upon which his mind had so long been concentrated.

Margaret Maliphant | 351

The minister had scarcely gone out before Deborah came into the room with a message. She whispered it to mother: Captain Forrester was staying at the Priory, and had sent round to ask how Mr. Maliphant did.

Father's eyes were closed, he did not open them, but I saw a look of suffering, as though a lash had passed over him, cross his features.

Mother sent Deborah hastily out of the room with a whispered reprimand, and father beckoned me to his side. As far as I could make out, he wanted me to send for Frank.

A few weeks ago how gladly would I have done it! But now I knew too well that it was too late; and when I saw the telltale flush of trouble on Joyce's face, and her quick glance of entreaty, I was loath to do father's bidding. I could see that she had it on her lips to tell him something— something that she no longer made a secret of soon afterwards; but how could any of us dare to disturb him, dare to do anything but simply what he wished? Even mother, much as it cost her to let me send that summons, would not interfere. We felt instinctively that the visit could do neither good nor harm. We need not have troubled ourselves. Father died before Frank came. He had seemed a little better; in fact, just for a day we had been quite hopeful. The squire had been sitting with him, and when he left him alone with mother and came down-stairs, I met him in the hall; I had been waiting for him. I led the way into the deserted parlor, and the squire—I fancied, half-unwillingly—followed.

"I hope I haven't kept you away," began he, concernedly. "He's dozing now, and your mother is with him. But he'll be asking for you again presently."

"Yes, I know, I know," answered I, absently. "But, Mr. Broderick, I wanted to ask you whether you don't think Mr. Harrod ought to be sent for?" said I, hastily.

He turned away his head; I could not help noticing that he looked embarrassed.

"I'm sure he can't know of father's illness, and I feel that he ought to be told," said I. "I know very well he would never choose this time for a holiday if he knew how very urgently his presence is needed. Everything must be going at sixes and sevens on the farm."

"I see that things aren't going at sixes and sevens," murmured he.

"You!" cried I, aghast. "Oh, but that isn't fitting."

Still he looked awkward. "Don't you trouble your head about it," said he, kindly. "You have enough to do without that. My bailiff has very little work just now, and he can as easily as not see to things a bit."

Something in his whole manner froze me, but I cried, eagerly, almost angrily, "But he *must* come back; it's his duty to come back. You are too kind—you don't want to spoil his holiday; but that isn't fair, and not real kindness. He would much rather come back, I know. If you won't write to him, I will."

I spoke peremptorily, but something in the way the squire now looked at me—pitifully, and yet reproachfully—made me ashamed, and I lowered my eyes. He came up to me and said, in a low voice, for I had raised mine: "Will you leave it all to me? Do. I promise you that I will do you right; and for you, just now, anything—everything but one thing, must remain in abeyance."

I could not answer, something choked me. He took my hand in his to say good-bye. "I thought he seemed easier, less restless to-night," said he.

I nodded, and he pressed my hand and went out. Not till the last yellowness had died out of the twilight did I go up again to the sick-room.

Mother sat on a low chair by the bed; her hand was in father's, and her head rested on her hand. There was no light, only just the grayness of the twilight. One might have thought it was a young girl's figure that crouched there so tenderly. All through the years of my childhood I had very rarely seen any attitude of affection between my parents; I scarcely ever remember father kissing mother in our presence, although his unfailing chivalry towards her, and the quiet, matter-of-course way in which her opinion was reverenced, had grown to be an understood thing among us. I felt now that I had intruded on a sacred privacy.

Mother turned as I came in, and drew her hand very gently away from father's; he was dozing. She rose and walked away towards the window.

"Shall I bring the lamp, mother?" asked I.

I felt that there were tears in her voice as she answered. It was the first time I had been aware of this in all the time that father had been ill, she had been so very quiet and brave. I went up to her where she stood in the dim light of the window-seat, with her back towards me, and after a moment I kissed her reverently, as I never remember to have done before, save that once when she said that things would have been different on the farm if our little brother had lived. Her tears welled over, but she did not speak, only when I said, "He is better to-night, mother, don't you think so?" she nodded her head, and turned and went out of the room.

That night the wave we had been watching so long broke over our heads.

Mother had sat up the night before, and had gone to rest; Joyce held watch till midnight, and then I took her place. The hours wore away wearily through the darkness. Father was very restless, moaning often, and throwing his arms from side to side.

Once he had held his hand a long while on my head in the old, affectionate way, and had looked with mute, passionate entreaty into my eyes. What did he want to know? If I guessed, I did not satisfy the craving. I only murmured vague words here and there, smoothed his pillow and his brow, putting water to his dry lips, ministering to a physical thirst, and ignoring the bitterer thirst of the mind. I was a coward.

At last he fell into a restless doze. I left the bedside and went to the window. The dawn was breaking; behind a rampart of purple clouds a pale streak of orange light girdled the marsh around; sea there was none, or rather it was all sea—silent waves of desolate land, silent waves of distant water, and over all a sullen surf of mist that hid the truth; out of the surf rose the far-off town, like some dark rock amid the waters, statelier than ever above the ghostly bands of vapor that crossed its base, and made the crown of its square belfry loom like some fortress on a towering Alpine height. Purple was the town, and purple the cloud battlements, but overhead the sky was clear, where one patient yellow star waited the coming of day.

At the foot of the cliff the water was up in the tidal river; it lay blue and cold amid the dank, white mist. I remembered the day, six months ago, when I had stood and watched it, just as blue and cold against the white winter snow; I had thought it looked colder than the snow in its iron depths; I had thought it looked like death. Yes, how I remembered it! It was the first time I had ever thought of death.

I went back to the bed. I fancied father had moved; but he lay there quite still, with his face upturned, and a strange blue grayness on it. I stood over him a long time, till my hands were so cold with fear that I could scarcely feel if his had still the warmth of life. I thought I would call mother, but the breath still came faintly from his lips; so I waited a while, creeping softly back to the window, whence I could see the living world.

The yellow star was no more, for slowly from behind the purple ramparts a glory of silver rays grew up; the purple became amethyst, the sullen cloud-cliffs broke into soft flakes of down; they cradled the rising sun, whose fire flushed their softness; they bore him up until he was full-orbed above the horizon; then suddenly a rent ran across them, and it was day. But the white mist still lay just as thickly on the ground; it was gray with shadows, and the water was cold, and the wide, wide sea of surf-bound marsh was desolate.

A sound came from the bed. My heart stood still. It was so long since we had heard father speak that to hear him now seemed like a voice from the grave.

"Meg," he said, distinctly.

I did not turn. He repeated the word, and it was his own voice, and I went to him. He lay there just as I had left him, excepting that he had turned just a little on his side, so that the portrait of his friend should be the better within his view. The same blue shadow was on his face.

"Meg," said he, slowly, "mother will be very lonely when I'm gone. You will take care of mother."

I sank slowly upon my knees so as to bring my face on a level with his. I wanted to hide it away from him, but by a great effort I kept my gaze upon him.

"Yes," I answered, firmly.

"You've always been a good girl, my right hand," continued he. "Take care of them both."

His voice was getting weak; I could see the drops of perspiration standing on his brow. I tried to get up that I might call mother and Joyce, but he held me fast.

"The squire—trust the squire," he murmured. "He loves you as I loved your mother." And then, with a smile of peace, he added, "The squire said he would take care of you all."

I was too much awed to speak, but I put my lips gently to his hand. It was quite cold, and a shiver ran through me.

His eyes were closed, and I drew my arm as well as I could from his grasp, and flew to the door.

In a moment I was in the room where mother and Joyce lay resting together; my presence was enough to tell them what was the matter.

Margaret Maliphant | 355

When I got back to father, his eyes were open again—fixed on that picture opposite to him.

"Now we see through a veil darkly," he murmured. "Ah, Camille, I have done what I could;" and then, "God has a home of his own for the little ones."

He was wandering.

"Laban!" cried mother, with a low cry.

A smile broke through that gray shadow, as light had burst through the purple clouds when the sun rose.

His lips seemed to move as if in some request.

"'The peace of God, which passeth all understanding,'" began mother, in a broken voice.

There was a long silence in the room, and then a sound: it was a sob from our mother's heavy heart.

His voice was still forever.

CHAPTER XL

On the day of father's funeral the sun shone and all the summer had come back. Against a pale, fair sky, dashed with softest clouds, golden boughs of elms made delicate metallic traceries, and crimson creepers shot like flames across the gray walls of sober cottages. Even passing birds had not all deserted us, and swallows swept again around the ancient ivied aisles of the old cathedral, under whose shadows we laid him away in the earth.

We put him under the yew-trees beside our little brother John, with his face towards the sun's setting behind the pine-trees; every one said it was a beautiful place for him to rest in; and Joyce wept her simple, silent tears over the hopeful words spoken by the Rev. Cyril Morland, whom mother had chosen to read the service. But as for me, my heart was too hot and rebellious to shed any tears or to see any hope or comfort; I hated the sun for shining so brightly, the world for being so fair, and folk for thinking it natural enough that an old man should come to an end of his life.

Yes, they spoke of it sadly, compassionately—all those many folk who followed him to the grave; folk to whom he had told his thoughts, whom he had helped and taught, and with whom he had sympathized in his life; folk who would not have been what they were without him—whose friend he had been, who would never find such another to lead them! But for all their honest tears, they spoke of it as a worthy life brought worthily to an end—they could think of his grave as beautiful, whereas to me God was cruel to have taken him, and no place in the world could be anything but cold earth that hid him from my sight.

Towards mother and Joyce my heart was soft because of the promise I had given him with his darkening eyes looking into mine, but even towards Joyce I was sore when I saw her bend her head towards Mr. Hoad as he held open the gate of the graveyard for her; and it was with a grim feeling of satisfaction, and no sense at all of the unfitness of the occasion, that I turned aside from his out-stretched hand, and said, in a loud voice, that every by-stander could hear: "No, Mr. Hoad, I don't think I shall ever care to shake hands with you again. You don't fight fair. It is through you my father lies there, and I'll never forgive you."

I swept on after mother without even giving one glance at the angry face I left behind, without listening to the suppressed murmur that ran round, without even seeing the vexed, distressed look on the squire's face close beside me. My heart was very sore, and not the less so because I had missed around the grave one face that I had made quite sure would be there.

The squire and I had never spoken again of Trayton Harrod since that day when he had begged me to leave the recalling of him to his discretion. I don't think I had seen him more than once during that time, and then it had been about the arrangements for the funeral, when I should not have liked to speak to him on such an apparently trivial matter, however much I might have wished to do so. But all through the dreadful days when we three had sat silently in the darkened parlor, hearing no news from without save messages of condolence and flower-tokens of humble friendship, brought in by old Deb with her swollen eyelids—all through the time when we were waiting till they should take away from us forever that which was left of what had once been our own, there had come sudden waves of unbidden remembrance mingling with my holy sorrow for the dead, and interwoven with my regrets over the much I might have done for my dear father which it was now too late ever to do, were other genuinely contrite thoughts, which I resolved should not be without fruit.

I wanted to make amends for my wrong-doing, and Trayton Harrod would not give me the chance. Where was he? Surely by this time he must have heard of our trouble. How could he remain away? And as the dull hours wore on from morning to evening and from evening to morning again, I longed to see him with a heart-sick longing that not even my tears could quench; I longed to see him, though his face might be ever so stern, his voice ever so cruel, his hand ever so cold.

But he did not come, and on the fourth day after the funeral, mother, awaking slowly to the knowledge of outer things and people, asked for him. "Meg," she said, "it's very strange that Mr. Harrod hasn't been near us all this time of our trouble. Is he sick, do you know?"

"I haven't heard, mother," said I, faintly; "but I believe he has been away."

"Away!" echoed mother. "Well, then, he might have come back again, I think. I wouldn't have believed he was such a fair-weather friend as that. I thought of him so differently."

My heart swelled with a bitter remorse, for deep down there was a little voice that told me that if Harrod was away I was not without blame for it.

"You and he haven't had a quarrel, have you?" said mother, after a bit.

"A quarrel!" repeated I, faintly. "Oh no!"

"Well, I'm glad of that," answered she. "He's a nice lad, and it's a pity to lose a friend. I fancied he might have been speaking to you about something you didn't choose to be spoken to about. I'm glad it isn't so. I wonder what keeps him away. And not so much as a line. Well, I dare say he'll be back to-morrow."

Her voice dropped wearily; in truth, she cared very little whether he came or not; there was only one whom she longed for, and he could never come again.

But I—sorely as I too longed for that presence that she mourned—I cared whether Trayton Harrod came again, and when he did not come I went to get news of him. Joyce thought it very dreadful of me to go for a walk when our dead had been but so lately laid to rest, but Joyce did not know. She too, perhaps, wondered at his absence, but she did not know, as I did, the reason for it.

I went out of the house, across the garden, down the cliff where I had seen him disappear on that weird, moonlight night a month ago, down onto the marsh. The sun had gone behind the hill, for it was afternoon, but the sky was clear and limpid, the sea blue beyond the mellow marsh-land; along the banks of the dikes thorn-bushes studded the way—rosy-flushed from afar, but close at hand coral-tipped on every slender branch; and the water, shorn of its green rush-mantle, lay still and bare to the sky.

I walked fast till I came to the white gate that divides sheepfold from cattle-pasture, and then I turned round to look back: if I chanced on the squire I should get news; but there was not a living thing to be seen on the land—I was alone with the birds and the water-rats. The cattle had been called off the marsh when the stormy weather set in, and I had forgotten to bring even the dog with me; it was so long since I had been for a walk.

But the dear familiar land soothed me with its sadness. Far away upon dikes where the scythe had not yet mown the rushes, broad streaks of orange color followed the lines of the banks or were dashed across the stream, tongues of flame in the sunlight. In the distance blue smoke soared slow and straight into the pale air from the fires of weed-burners in the ploughed furrows, and a shadow crossed the base of the town, whose pinnacle was still white in the afternoon light. Along the under-cliff of the Manor woods the crimson of beeches made gorgeous patches of painting upon the sombre background of pines, and larches held amber torches up among the paler gold of elm-trees.

Margaret Maliphant | 359

God's earth was very fair, but why had he taken away all that made it glad? Not far from here had we two first met in the rain and mist; here had we started the lapwing in the green spring-time and scared the cuckoo from its nest, usurped; here had we many a time followed the game and learned the ways of birds and beasts; here had we gathered the hay and the harvest, and watched the sheep-shearing; here had we crossed the plain in the thunder and lightning of the storm.

And all these things would happen again—the spring and the summer and the winter would come with their sights and their sounds, their life and their duties; the marsh-land would always be the same, but would it ever be the same again to me? Ah, that day I did not think so!

A shot sounded in the woods. It was the squire's keeper after the pheasants. It awoke me from my dream, but I must have been so still that even the rabbits thought I was not alive, for two of them ran out across my path.

Was I alive after all? I shook myself and went slowly on to where the marsh meets the road, and then I turned up across the ash copse on the hill—bare already of leaves—and took the path towards "The Elms." Yes, I had come out to hear news of Trayton Harrod, and I would not go back without it; somehow and from somebody I would learn where he was, and why he had gone.

I walked fast when once I got in sight of the house; my heart was beating. It stood there—serene and solitary as usual—a bare, lonely, uninviting house, looking out from its quiet height upon the downs and the sheep-pastures, the sun-setting and the sunrising.

There was never anything human about "The Elms." It seemed to be intent just upon its daily work and its daily duties, and as though it might think that anything which interfered with them was not to be considered or countenanced. That day it looked more inhuman, more uninviting than ever; its white walls seemed to grin at me; its straight, tall chimneys, whence no friendly blue smoke sought the sky, seemed to point jeeringly away into the void. My heart sank as I climbed the hill and opened the gate of the farm-yard. I knew why the place looked more uninviting than ever—it was deserted, the shutters were closed, the house door was bolted; it was as if some one had died there, as some one had died at home.

I knocked once, loudly, in desperation, but I knew that nobody would come. Nobody did come; nobody came, though I knocked three times; all was still as the grave. As I walked down the hill again at last, I met Dorcas's niece with her "youngest" in her arms.

"Lor', miss, who would ha' thought to meet you so soon after your poor father died!" said she, reproachfully. "I've just been down to the village to fetch some soap."

"Oh, I see. Is Mr. Harrod expected home?" asked I, lamely.

"Home!" repeated she, gaping. "Why, he's left the place this month past. All his traps went last week."

I suppose my face showed how my heart had sunk down, for she added, half compassionately, "Didn't you know he was going, miss?"

I pulled myself together. Miserable as I was, there was an instinct within me that did not want strangers to guess at my misery.

"Oh yes, I knew he was going," said I, carelessly; "but of course we have had too much to think about at home for me to remember just when it was."

"Why, yes, of course," echoed the woman, in the commiserating tone of her class under such circumstances. "Ah, farmer was a good man, and none can say different! And, to tell the truth, many's the one have thought it queer Mr. Harrod should choose this time to go away. But he always were odd, and I suppose we must all look to our own advantage. There's no more work to be done on poor old Knellestone farm—so folk say—and I suppose he had heard of something as would suit him. Ah, it's very sad after all the years the family have been on the place."

I dared not think what she meant, although I knew well enough; but this other blow had stunned me, and I could not speak, even had I chosen to bandy words, about poor father's affairs with a village gossip.

"I'll go up with you and look round the house," said I.

"It ain't tidied yet, miss," answered she, apologetically. "I was just going to wash and settle it all up."

"Never mind," insisted I. "I want to look for a book," and I led the way up the hill.

"Lor'! you won't find anything there," laughed she, following. "There isn't anything in the place."

I went in, nevertheless. But she was right, he was gone indeed. The homely room was deserted where I had sat in the window-seat that summer evening reading words of Milton that I did not understand, and watching the rising storm and the sheep cropping sleepily over the grassy knolls. There was not a book left of all those books that I had envied, and had thought he would think the better of me for reading; not a pipe on the rack above the mantle-shelf; not a sign to show that he had ever been there. And yet I saw it all before me just as it had been that day; I felt that unseen presence that I had never seen there, just as if he might open the door at any moment and come in.

The woman left me for a moment, and I sat down on that window-seat once more. The sun was setting redly, as it so often set beyond those wide marsh-lands and their boundary line of downs; the valley was full of blue mist—blue as a wild hyacinth—against which the bended, broken, broad-topped pine-trees laid every branch of their dark tracery, abrupt, unsuspected, alert with individuality, strangely full of a reserved irregular grace. I remember the picture, yet I scarcely saw it; it must have fastened itself upon my memory, simply because it fitted so well with my own mood. Oh me! when I had last been there Harrod had not seen Joyce, and now I said from my heart, "Would to God he had not seen me!" Yes, I said it from my heart; so much so that I was not content with mere regrets, I was resolved that Trayton Harrod should not go out into the world with that lie of mine in his heart—not if I could help it.

I started up. I would go to the squire; I felt convinced now that the squire knew all about Harrod's departure. The squire could at least tell me where he was that I might write to him. I walked across the empty room, and at the same moment Mr. Broderick opened the gate of the yard without. Everything was happening just as it had happened that day; but oh, with what a difference!

The squire's face grew pale—I could see that through the tanning on it; he had not expected to see me here, and his hand trembled as he took mine. But he said, gently: "I'm glad to see you out again. I came to look round the place. I hope we have been lucky enough to sublet it till your lease is up."

From a business point of view the words swam over my head, but they were ominous. I felt that they confirmed what the woman had said. "You think we can't afford to keep on 'The Elms?'" I asked, absently, not daring to put the question that was at my heart.

"I think it would be unwise," answered he, evasively. "I think any one who manages your property will have enough to do without it."

"Mr. Broderick," said I, suddenly, looking him full in the face, "has Mr. Harrod left us for good?"

"Yes," he answered, firmly, "for good."

I could not speak for a moment, then trying hard to steady my voice, I said, "Did you know it?"

"Yes," he answered. "I knew it."

He no longer looked at me now, nor did either of us say anything for some time. He spoke first, saying, in quite an ordinary voice: "I don't think he was quite the fellow for the place. An older man with fewer new ideas would have been better."

"Was that the reason that he left?" asked I, in a muffled voice, although indeed I knew well enough that I was talking idly. "Father did not send him away because of his new ideas."

The squire brought his eyes round to my face. "I don't know the reason that he left," said he. And although I said nothing, I suppose there was some sort of an appealing look in my face that made him go on: "I only know that he came to me the night before your father was taken ill, and asked me, as a friend, to see after his work for him until a substitute could be found, because he was obliged to leave immediately. I asked no questions, and he told me nothing. Of course I was glad to do what I could for—you all."

He was silent, but I felt his eyes upon me. I met them, with that tender, pitying gaze in them, when at last I lifted mine.

"Mr. Broderick," said I—and I felt that my voice faltered—"will you give me his address? I must write to him. There is something that I must say to him. I thought I should have seen him again, but—I must write it."

He took out his note-book and wrote it down, handing me the leaf that he tore out.

I don't think I even thanked him; I don't think I said good-bye; I just walked out of the door. The squire followed me for a few, steps. "I want to have a talk with you soon about your father's affairs," said he, trying to reach a cheerful and commonplace tone of voice.

"Yes—some day," said I, in a dull way. And I don't think I even turned round again to look at him.

It was very rough, very ungrateful of me, but I couldn't bear another word. The only thought in my heart was to be at home—to be alone—to write my letter. I tore down the lane under the pine-trees in the gloaming. I ran so fast that I did not even notice two figures that passed me under the shadow of the wall on the opposite side; their heads were close together, and the woman, who was much shorter than the man, clung very close to his tall, slim person. It was not till some days afterwards that it occurred to me who those figures had been.

I had not even a word for poor Taffy, who sprang upon me reproachfully as I opened the gate of the farm-yard. I had forgotten to take him, but I had no thought even for that dumb and faithful companion just then; I only wanted to write my letter.

I wrote it, but it was returned to me from the dead-letter office. Two days afterwards Deborah, taking courage at last to clean up the poor deserted parlor, found another letter in the old Nankin jar on the mantle-piece, which served well enough as an answer to mine although it was sent so long before it; it was the letter which Trayton Harrod had written to father the day before he left.

I had been in the garden, and when I came in mother sat with it in her lap. There was a shade more trouble than before on her worn white face, whence the dainty tints had all fled in these hard weeks. Directly I came into the room I knew what the letter was. I had never had a letter from him—no, not a line. I don't remember that I had even seen his handwriting, but I knew whose the rugged uncompromising capitals were the moment I looked at them. I took the letter up and read it, and when I had read it I found some means of slipping it into my pocket; I wanted to keep it—it was the only letter I could ever have from him, but a strange love-letter truly. It was written in his curtest, most uncompromising style, saying what it had to say and no more. Somehow I was glad that father had never seen it; it did my friend such grave injustice. It made no sort of excuse for quitting the place as he did, it merely said that as he felt he was useless there, he had decided to accept a post in Australia, which would, however, oblige him to leave Knellestone without the usual warning. It enclosed the sum of three months' salary, which he would have been supposed to forfeit for leaving without notice. It gave no address, and left no message; that was all.

"It's very odd," said mother, looking at me as I read it, and slowly opening and shutting her spectacles in a nervous manner. "I don't at all understand it. But I suppose he had something better in view—and the farm is not what it was. It shows how one can be deceived in folk."

And that was my punishment. I was obliged to let people think that they had been deceived in him. It was on my tongue to tell mother what I could. Was it cowardice that kept me back, or was it that I scarcely knew what to tell? There seemed so little that was not bred of my own fancy— only I knew well enough that my fancy was right.

And as the time passed, I knew more surely than ever that my fancy was right. He had said in his letter that there was nothing to keep him in the old country, but if he had seen Joyce as I saw her, surely he would have guessed at my lie—he would have known that there *was* something to keep him!

Two days after the discovery of Trayton Harrod's letter my sister told me that she had broken off her engagement with Frank Forrester.

There had never been quite the same understanding as of yore between us two since that horrible scene of passion, when I had been so cruelly unjust to my poor Joyce. She would have forgiven me, no doubt, but I was too proud to invite it. That day, however, she told me quite simply that she had broken off her engagement.

"I ought never to have made it, Meg," said she. "I did not think it was wicked then; I liked him to love me; but now I think it was wicked. It may be wrong to depart from one's word, but—I can't marry him."

She spoke in a half-apologetic kind of way—as she had, no doubt, written to him. She had not seen those two figures pass along under the wall in the twilight, as I now remembered for the first time that I had seen them. But I said nothing; I was dumb. I think from that time forward I was dumb for a long time—dumb with remorse and the sense of my own utter helplessness—standing alone to see the river run by, which I had once fancied I could set in motion or stem at will.

But her face, though stained with tears, which mine was not, was calm, her blue eyes were serene and trustful as ever. Yet, ah me! how guiltily did I creep about her, how hungrily watch for every piece of news—for her!

But he was gone, and it was through my fault.

CHAPTER XLI

What more is there to say? If I had written all this ten years ago I should have said that there was nothing more to say, I should have said that my life was ended. But now I am not of that mind. Thank God! there is more to say, and though there have been sad hours to live through, the haven has been reached at last.

When father was dead and buried, they told us that we should have to leave the Grange. I can remember how the blow fell on me. Reuben had just buried Luck, the old sheep-dog, under the big apple-tree.

"The Lord'll have to take me now," he had said, with tears in his dim eyes; "but I'd sooner die than see the old place go to the bad. I knowed what it 'd be when the master was called; and now that the dog's gone as well, there's no more luck for us. Ay, if he'd ha' stuck to Early Perlifics we shouldn't ha' seen old Knellestone come to the hammer."

I don't believe I felt the thrust, I don't believe I ever saw the comic incongruity of the situation, when, leaning forward on his spade and gazing tearfully at the grave of his old dumb comrade, he had turned to me saying, confidentially: "There'll be a rare crop of apples this year, miss. There's nothing for an apple-tree like a dead dog."

But Reuben was a philosopher and I was no philosopher; and of the days that followed, the days when Deborah went about with a grim, wise air, as one who had known all along what would happen—the days when mother wandered aimlessly from the chairs and presses to the old writing-table where father had sat so many years, and the eight-day clock that had summoned us as children to breakfast and prayers—of those horrible days I cannot speak. I dare not remember the guilty feeling with which I felt mother's eyes upon me when the squire delayed to come for that "business talk" that he had asked leave for; I might have found spirit once more to scorn Deborah's more openly expressed upbraiding, but mother's silent reproach made my heart sick.

We were wrong, however, to doubt the squire. He came in spite of Deb's cruel, covert taunts, in spite of mother's hopeless eyes. If he had not come earlier, it was only because he was waiting till he had good news to bring.

I can see him now as he walked once more into that parlor where we had had so many eager discussions, so many friendly meetings and half-fancied quarrels, so many affectionate reconciliations! The late autumn sun shone in through the three deep windows upon the worn old Turkey carpet and leather chairs, upon the polished spindle-backed seats that stood on either side of the hearth—one empty now forever; it almost put the fire out, and touched the copper fire-irons into flame. I suppose it was the sun that made the squire's face look so ruddy and so radiant.

Radiant it most certainly was, and yet, at the same time, half shamefaced too as he said that he had just come from a meeting of the creditors, and that he had every reason to hope that father's affairs would be satisfactorily arranged. I don't think I believed him at the time, I think I was almost hurt when he met my trembling question, as to whether we should have to leave Knellestone, with a laugh. But oh, what a relief was that laugh from the visits of condolence we had had!

He did not forget father although he did not speak of him in words: the awe that had surrounded the death-bed was gone, but not the sacred burden that it had left. Yet I did not understand when he said that the creditors had been satisfied. Even when the dreaded day of the sale came, and mother kept her old friends in chairs and tables and presses, and linen within the presses, and Joyce kept her favorite cows in the dairy, and I even the mare that had been the innocent means of first bringing romance within our quiet family—when the farm was not even deprived of a single one of the mowing and threshing machines that had caused so much strife—I, ignorant as I was of business, never even guessed in what way an "arrangement" had been come to!

It was old Reuben again—sitting by the chimney-corner crippled with rheumatism, or, as he himself expressed it, with all his constitution run into his legs—it was poor old Reuben who had told me the truth. Shrewd Deb knew it and was silent, but Reuben—too shrewd or not shrewd enough to be silent, told me the tale: if squire had not bought in all the stock and the furniture before it ever came to the hammer, we shouldn't have been in the Grange now, living practically very much the same life as we had always lived.

Ah me! I knew well enough why the squire had taken such pains to conceal from us all that he had done anything more than effect a compromise with the creditors. But I ought to have guessed. If I had not been so much wrapped up in my own personal pains and feelings I *should* have guessed it, and when I next met him I nerved myself to speak on the subject. How well I recall his explanation! "Folk in the country grow to depend so on one another that I couldn't do with strangers at the Grange while I'm alive," he had said; "so you must forgive me if I played a game to serve my own ends. The place might have stood empty ever so long. Farms do nowadays."

We must have been riding eastward over the downs, for I can remember that the wind blew keen in our faces, and that the sky was leaden overhead, almost as dull as the wide, dull marsh below it: it was winter. I know that, even at the time, I recalled another night when I had ridden with the squire; then the west was raging crimson behind us, and the moon rose yellow out of the sea; it had been summer.

"There is no one else in the world who would have done for us what you have done for us, nor any one else in the world from whom we could take it," I had murmured, in a trembling voice. "It is for father's sake."

"It is not all for your father's sake," the squire had answered, softly, with grave and tender face, his blue eyes shining down on me with a deep, bright light.

By a sudden impulse I recollect holding out my hand to him. "I know you are my friend and I am your friend," I had said. "We shall always be friends till we die."

And all through the dreary days that followed, that friendship, that needed no words to tell and that no parting could weaken, warmed my empty heart at a time when the world seemed to hold no further joy nor even such comparative content as a respite from remorse.

For, alas! Joyce slowly faded and saddened before my eyes, and all my passionate love for her came back, making the thought of her wasted youth, her tarnished loveliness, her happiness uselessly spoiled through my fault, almost heavier than I could bear.

For it was spoiled though she spoke no word. At first the tall, slim figure—more Quakerly neat than ever in its straight black gown—went about the household duties just as serenely as before, and the face, so dazzlingly fair a flower on the dark stem, shone as innocently content as of yore. I could scarcely believe that she could have seen that cruel letter, with its upright, rugged characters, that seemed to have sent away the last drop of blood from my heart. Her hope must have been high or she could never have kept so patient a countenance.

But however high it may have been, it began to fade. I had said to myself that Joyce could not feel, but—ah me, how little can we know how much other people feel! I could see her feeling through the tremulous sensitiveness of the face that once seemed to me so impossible to ruffle—I could hear it through the thin sound of her timid voice, in her rare speech and rarer laughter—and I knew that my loved sister was unhappy. Yes, she was unhappy; life was as dead to her as it was to me, and it was I—I, loving her—who had killed her joy for her, and killed it wilfully. May no one whom I love ever know, what it is to feel remorse!

A whisper ran round the village that Joyce Maliphant was pining away her beauty for love of the gay young captain who had once courted her, and who was now going to wed with Miss Mary Thorne, the heiress. Deb told me of it, she had heard the rumor coming out of church; but I don't believe we, any of us, thought that it mattered much what Frank Forrester did. He could never have made Joyce happy, why should he not make Mary Thorne happy? There had been tears in her eyes when the news of his accident had come, there had been no tears in Joyce's.

No, what really mattered was that my sister's face was growing paler and thinner, and that at last the day came when they told us that unless we could make up our minds to part from Joyce for a while, we might have to part from her forever.

I hope I may never feel again the heart-sick pang that went through me as the doctor said those words. I had thought that no such pang could be worse than that I had felt when father had told me he was going to die; but this was worse, for Joyce was young, and had the right still to a long and happy life, and if she was deprived of it, it was I who had deprived her.

I went to work with an aching spirit to arrange how it should be that Joyce should leave us for warmer lands. Mother had a married brother living at Melbourne, and to him it was decided at last that Joyce should go for a couple of years. We found her an escort in some friends of the squire's, and the only little grain of comfort I had in the whole matter was that if Joyce was to leave us, it was to go to the same country whither Trayton Harrod had fled a year before. But Australia was a large field, and unless they were to meet by the purest accident, Trayton Harrod was not likely ever to seek Joyce out.

Was it some such faint and wild hope, I wonder, or merely the feeling that I could not part from that dear heart without making a clean breast of my sin to it, which made me say what I did when the last moment came? I don't know. I only know that as we stood there in the little waiting-room of the London Docks, while mother stooped from her usual shy dignity to beg the kindness and care of this unknown friend of the squire's for her suffering child, I felt suddenly that I could not let Joyce go from me with that lie weighing on my heart—I felt that I *must* have her forgiveness!

I cannot imagine how I had endured so long without it. I had hungered for *his* forgiveness, whom I had wronged less cruelly, because I owed him less devotion, and had been able to live side by side with her without asking for her pardon whose life I had so wrecked.

Many a time in those past months I had started to find the squire's perplexed eyes upon me, following mine that were fixed upon Joyce, and I had blushed with shame, knowing what it was that put that look in me which puzzled him; and many a time I had vowed that I would abase myself and tell her all, yet never had found the courage. But now, when the last chance was slipping from me, the courage came. It came, I think, because Joyce stood suddenly revealed before me in the grandeur of her simple goodness, her power of silent and loving sacrifice; it came because I had no fear, because I was ashamed of my very shame, because I was sure of her forgiveness.

She stood with her hand in mine, her figure very tall and slim in the straight black gown, her face very fair and fragile in the frame of the neat little close bonnet. She might have been a nun, so quiet and orderly her outward demeanor, so calm her beautiful face, and yet when I looked again I saw that there were tears in the blue eyes that looked away from me to the tangled mass of shipping in the dock, and to the confused net-work of masts and rigging that lay black against the leaden, wintry sky.

"O Joyce, darling," I cried, seizing her hand wildly, "don't cry! I can't bear it."

She did not answer, she was afraid of trusting herself to speak, but, true to her perfect unselfishness, she turned to me and smiled. "You'll get well, you know," I went on, with determined cheerfulness; "you'll get quite well and come back to us very soon."

Still she smiled that heart-breaking smile, nodding her head, however, as though to confirm my cheerful words. Then came my burst of confidence. "If you were *not* to come back quite well," said I, in a low voice, "I think, Joyce, I should die. It's all my fault."

At that she spoke. She did not seem surprised at my words, but only anxious to deny them so as to remove any pain of my self-reproach.

"Oh no, no, Meg," she said, softly. "Not your fault, dear. Things like that are never any one's fault."

She thought I only meant that my love for Harrod had stood in the way of her accepting his, because *she*, brave and unselfish in what I used to call her coldness, would have given him up to me.

But I couldn't let her think that I had meant only that. "Joyce," said I, firmly, "if it hadn't been for me, Trayton Harrod would have married you."

I saw that the name hurt her like the lash of a whip. "Oh, don't, don't!" she murmured, with pain in her eyes.

"I beg your pardon," said I, humbly, "but I must tell you. I can't let you go away without telling you the truth. O Joyce, my poor, dear Joyce, however much it pains you I must tell you. I don't mean only what you think. I don't mean only that I didn't go away, that I didn't behave as generously towards you as you would have done towards me. I mean—O Joyce, how can I tell you? But I was mad with jealousy, and I told him that you loved Frank. I sent him away from you." I had hurried the words out without preparation, I was so afraid of being interrupted—and now I was frightened.

Every drop of the blood that was left in that poor, wan face fled from it. I thought she was going to faint, but she stood firm, only her eyes seemed to turn to stone, to see nothing.

"O Joyce, darling, don't look like that!" cried I, in an agony. "Speak to me. Say something."

She closed her hand over mine, and her lips moved, but I could not hear a word.

"I shall never, never forgive myself so long as I live," murmured I, a sob rising in my throat; "but if *you* do not forgive me, Joyce, I think I shall die, Joyce."

"Poor Meg!" murmured my sister at last, and then the lump that had been rising in my throat broke into a sob, and the tears rushed to my eyes.

For a moment I could not speak. I got rid of my tears as well as I could, and looking at her, I saw, yes, thank God! I saw that her eyes were wet too.

"Can you forgive me, Joyce?" I faltered. "Yes, I think *you* can. You are good enough."

"Forgive you!" echoed she, faintly. And her sweet mouth breaking into the tremulous smile that was its familiar ornament, she added, "Dear, *you* have been unhappy too."

They were few words, but what more perfect expression of tenderest forgiveness could there be? I wanted no more. I knew there was no bitterness, that there never would be any bitterness, in my sister's heart towards me.

There was no one in the waiting-room, mother had gone out onto the wharf with the strange lady; I put my arms round Joyce's neck, and drew her face down to mine. "God bless you!" I said, reverently, and I think for the first time in my life I felt what the words meant.

Margaret Maliphant | 371

"It's all for the best, dear," added she, gently, leaning her cheek against my hair. "You know we never really do alter things that are going to happen by anything we do. It's arranged for us by a wise Providence." It was the simple faith that had always guided her life; it had often annoyed my more impetuous and self-willed spirit, but it did not annoy me now; there was a soothing in it.

But there was no time for further speech; mother came back again, it was time to go on board. I busied myself with the luggage and with talking to Joyce's escort—a kindly, good-natured couple—and left mother and daughter together.

The parting was over all too quickly, and we were left standing on the wharf alone, mother and I, watching the big black mass steer its way slowly among the crowd of shipping, watching the tall black figure on the deck until, even in imagination, it faded from us, and we looked but on the interminable rows of black masts against the lurid sunset of a bleak winter evening.

When we were safe in the cab again, homeward bound, I did what I had done only once in my life before, and that was on the night when the mare threw me and I had first fancied that Trayton Harrod loved my sister—I put my head down on my mother's breast and wept my heart out on hers. It was selfish of me, for I should have thought of her grief, and yet I do not think that it intensified it; I think, somehow, my tears did her good.

She said nothing, but she stroked my hair tenderly, and from that moment there was opened up between us a new vein of sympathy that had never been there before, and that left something sweet in life still, even in the sad and empty home to which we came back.

It was an empty home indeed. The squire could no longer cheer its solitude with his genial presence. He had gone abroad. The Manor was shut up, and there was no sign of life about the dear old place, that held so many happy memories, but the sound of the keeper's gun in the copses above the marsh, and the cawing of the familiar rooks that circled round the old chapel at eventide.

I dared not complain, things might have been so much worse. The farm was still our own. A new bailiff and I managed it together, but though I had reached what, a while ago, would have been the summit of my ambition, it was gone. I no longer cared to have my own way; save for a somewhat vain struggle to keep up father's theories as far as I could, I let the new man do as he liked; he made the farm pay us a moderate income, and I asked no questions. My duty to mother was the plain thing before me, and I threw myself into that now, as I had thrown myself into personal ambition before—the farm must be made to keep her comfortably.

But for all my devotion to her, these were dreary days. With my new passion for self-sacrifice, I refused to leave her for the rambles of old, and the want of fresh air and exercise told on me a bit. The only things that broke the monotony of our life were our letters from Joyce and from the squire. He wrote to me regularly, telling me of all that he was seeing, of all that he was doing—the kind letters of a friend, from whose thoughts, it made me happy to think, I was never long absent. I would scarcely have believed a year ago that it would have made me as low-spirited as it did, when one of the squire's letters was a little delayed. I think I missed them almost more than I should have missed one of Joyce's, for—save for knowing that she was better, and, as I faintly began to hope, a little happier—her letters were so entirely unlike herself that they gave one but scant satisfaction; whereas the squire's, without breathing a word that was out of the common, were full of himself and his own characteristics. In spite, however, of these red-letter days, the hours were long hours, and the days gray days for me. I worked as of old through summer and winter, spring and autumn, flower and fruit, sowing and reaping, but the seasons were not the same to me as they once had been. I loved the sunless days, with their fields and mysteries of cloud, soft promises of a far-off heaven, ever-changing, ever-unknown depths—I loved them as I could not love the sunshine. I was not always unhappy, for I was young, and out of the past upon which I mused, many a note of suffering had had its answering whisper of joy; but upon the marsh there lay a shade which had not been there when I was a merry, thoughtless girl.

Thus far had I written, and I thought my task was finished; but to-night, as I lean out of my window, watching the pale moon sink cradled in gray clouds, and make a misty silver path across the lonely land that is woven into my life, I want to reopen my book that I may set down in it one last word.

It is not half an hour since I stood down there on the cliff waiting for a carriage to come along the white road that crosses the plain. Two were in that carriage—the sister whom I had loved and betrayed, the man whom I had loved, and for whom I had betrayed her. They were returning together from a distant land, where they had met once more. My heart was full of thankfulness, and yet—when I felt the aspens shiver again in the night breeze as they had done that evening ten years ago—I seemed to hear the deep voice in my ear, and to feel the cold strike to my heart as it spoke.

But it was not *his* voice that spoke; another stood at my side, one who had come back to me from a long parting, the friend of my life, the lover of ten years who had never spoken but once of his love, who had never put a kiss upon my lips. I scarcely know what he said—simple words enough, but they told me of his tender pity and untiring sympathy, they opened the floodgates of my burdened heart, and I told him all my tale. I shrank from nothing. I told him of my wild, unreasoned passion that, deep as it had been, was not all that I could imagine love might be; I told him of my selfish sin, of my long and bitter remorse, of my thankfulness that the punishment was removed, and that Joyce was coming back to me happy in spite of my great wrong to her. I did not ask myself what this longing to confess to the squire meant in me, and yet the confession was by no means an easy matter; and when all was told, my heart sank within me at his silence, and I felt as though I could not bear it if *he* should be ashamed of me, if he should take away his friendship from me because I had done an unworthy thing.

But I suppose one does not love people nor cease to love them for what they do or for what they leave undone; for certain it is that when the squire spoke at last there was something in his voice that told me he was not ashamed of me, that same "something" that had been so silent all these years, that I sometimes wondered if it was still alive.

The squire has gone home, and all the house is at rest; but I still look out of my little attic window whence I have seen the sea for so many years. Below me a mist lies upon the dike like a white pall upon some cherished grave. It is just such a night as that night ten years ago—only with a difference: the dim plain is not so cold, the light has a promise of brightness. And in my heart, too, there is a brightness which I am almost afraid to believe can be mine. I am happy because Joyce is happy, because Joyce is beautiful once more as she was beautiful when I first wanted a lover to love her. But it is not only thankfulness for the stain blotted out, peaceful resignation to the inevitable, which makes light in my soul to-night. There is a new picture growing slowly out of the clouds as they part and melt around the moon; there is a new harmony coming to me at last out of the very monotony of the marsh-land.

Above the lonely plain the night is blue and vast.